# SAVING SIMON

By

Tammy Watson

Saving Simon
Copyright © 2009 by Tammy Watson
Cover Design by Jeremy Helm
Cover Photo Copyright © Raisa Kanareva, 2009
Photo used under license from Shutterstock.com

Published by:
Helm Production
215 Laura Wilkes Rd
West Monroe, LA 71292
USA

Library of Congress Control Number:
2009936192

ISBN-13: 978-0-9842287-5-1
ISBN-10: 0-9842287-5-6

www.TammyWatson.com

# SAVING SIMON

# Prologue

*London England*
*1853*

The black coach broke through a wall of fog like a ghost emerging from another world. The horse's hooves clicking upon the cobblestone street were the only sound made on this all but silent night. Even the moon seemed to turn its back on the evil about to be done this 27th night of October 1853. It refused to cast its light on the London streets below choosing instead to cower behind the thick fog in fear.

The clock in the London tower began to announce the midnight hour as the black coach pulled up alongside the curb. It blocked the alleyway from any straying eyes. There must be no witnesses.

The lone occupant inside lit a match. Rather than identifying who or what waited inside, the small flame only brought the coach's occupant into a hazy light that flickered in and out of reality. The match was blown out and a wisp of smoke slowly curled its way up from inside the coach, merging with the heavy fog.

Three men emerged from the shadows; their eyes cutting to the left and right, anxious someone might guess their intentions. The tallest of the three, Jack, caught sight of the coach and nodded, elbowing one of his companions in the side. The short fat one spun around and something shiny glimmered in his hand. Jack grabbed the object and spoke furiously at the man who rubbed his bloated, beard-stubble face before peering out into the night, spotting the coach.

The third man, silent in the background, stepped into the shadowy light. His shoulders were straight and covered with a threadbare coat obviously not his. It failed to hide the silk cream shirt underneath or the dark expensive pants and polished leather boots. He lowered the large felt hat down over his eyes, and gestured to the other culprits. They shot one more look in the direction of the coach before reluctantly stepping back into the shadows.

As if on cue, a well-dressed couple and small girl of about ten emerged from around the corner heading straight for the waiting coach unaware of the dangerous men lurking in the alleyway. The occupant of the coach purposely lowered the shade. This was the signal the men had waited for.

Two of the men, the one called Jack and the short one Tom, approached the laughing couple. Only the man seemed instinctively aware of the danger approaching as he deftly pushed his wife and child behind him, just moments before the men struck. Taken by surprise and distracted by the presence of his wife and child, it took very little time before the other two men overpowered him. Knocking him to the ground despite the blows he inflicted on them, they pinned his struggling body to the dirty street.

"Charles!" the beautiful woman half screamed, half sobbed his name.

The young girl watched in wide-eyed terror as her father valiantly fought for his life. She felt nauseous and so terribly frightened that she could not even move despite the hands urging her to do so. "Hurry Sarah, run to the coach", her mother ordered, shoving her daughter in that direction in an effort to save her life.

"Ann get out of here now", demanded her husband lifting his sandy blond head to shout at her when he realized she was still standing there in plain sight.

Tom smirked at his victim's carelessness; one should never take one's eyes off his opponent unless he wanted to forfeit his life. His own father had taught him that little lesson. His short, stubby fingers clutched the knife tighter before ramming it into the man's side.

Ann frantically looked around the ground for something, and then spotted it, her husband's gun. It was not more than two feet away from her now cocked and ready. The tall angular man over her husband's body noticed it as well, and threw the now dead Charles off him, before scrambling for the gun. Just when it looked as if she might reach it first, a well-manicured hand snatched it from her fingertips.

Ann stumbled to her feet, looking up into the most beautiful and coldest green eyes she had ever seen. Instinctively she took a step back. The man looked her straight in the eyes, then without a moment's hesitation, pulled the trigger. She clutched at her stomach, the red stain widening ever further on her gown, her midnight colored eyes filling with shock as she sank in a heap of shimmering blue silk at his feet.

"The child you fools, she's escaping", came a harsh warning from inside the coach.

Sarah yanked once more on the handle, but the person inside refused to let her in. So she began to run. She could not have stopped running even if she had wanted to. Crying so hard now it was becoming difficult to breathe, she paused to frantically search the dark streets for a safe place to hide. Tears ran down her cheeks, as visions of her mother and father's deaths caused such intense pain she thought she would die with the weight of it.

Gulping down air and tears, she spotted the pier and raced for the safety of the immense boxes and crates that possibly might save her life. She dove into an opening between two huge pillars of wooden crates, unable to ignore the overwhelming pain in her lungs any longer.

"Mummy, Daddy", she whispered to the cold unfeeling night, seeking comfort from the empty words. Then ducking her honey colored head onto her knees, she began sobbing with heart wrenching fear and loss.

Her reprieve was short lived. All too soon Sarah felt a strong tug on her ankle as she was pulled out into the nightmare once again. Her blood-curdling scream filled the night. With a single forceful slap that threw her sideways into a crate, her mother's handsome murderer silenced her. He ran a shaky hand through freshly cut hair and approached her unconscious form in order to finish the whole distasteful business.

A small elderly China man, who seemed to come from nowhere, stepped between them effectively blocking the villain's path. Although he looked entirely harmless, his small brown eyes bore an intimidating light in their depths. He crossed his arms serenely in front of him.

The handsome man studied the insignificant China man with his funny looking clothes and long reddish pigtail. Then with a voice devoid of any warmth, he ordered, "Out of my way, China man."

"Tell me, insignificant pig, what evil lurks in your black soul that you would harm this girl child?"

Tired of games, the man smiled and drew a solid silver knife; it glinted dangerously in the light from the torches overhead.

The China man remained expressionless as he slowly unfolded his arms and bowed. "It appears you are rude as well as stupid. It is bad conduct to not introduce yourself to your enemy. I am Lee O'Shay, the man who will take your life."

The other man scoffed at the wizen old man who was beginning to wave his arms around in front of him like a fool, "Now China man, I suggest you move out of my way, or else I just might cut off your pigtail after I kill you. Then you won't make it to heaven."

With a puzzled frown the small man ceased his movements and seemed to consider the threat, then slowly he smiled, "I am only half Chinese, my father was an Irish missionary, and he went to heaven without a pigtail you worm of the earth."

The larger man growled in rage and ran at him with the knife ready to plunge into his interfering heart. Quick as lightening, the China man kicked it from his hands, before spinning around with a back kick to the face that sent his opponent flying backwards into a stack of heavy boxes. Boxes and man fell in a noisy scattered heap. When the man stubbornly refused to give up but instead came up swiping furiously at a now bloody and broken nose, the China man shrugged and prepared himself.

"I'll kill you for that, China man."

The Chinese man raised an eyebrow, "I quake much in my boots, most loud one."

"It's shiver, and well you should. Say your prayers, China."

Not bothering to answer, the elderly man landed two double punches to the man's already sore nose, and then threw a fist sideways into his temple, managing to knock his opponent to the ground. Hesitating only a fraction of a second, he lifted his heel and slammed it downward into the man's chest knocking the wind out of him. The man groaned once in agony before passing out cold.

The China man straightened his small round hat, and bowed once, "You are a man without honor but unfortunately, I am forced to let you live." He shook his head regretfully, "Yes, sometimes it is indeed a great inconvenience to carry my father's words in my heart."

Seeing the child start to awake beside him, he turned to assist her. Her tousled light-streaked hair fell back over a velvet clothed shoulder. Slowly, she turned golden brown eyes to his, her fear and suspicion evident in their depths. Instinctively she scooted back against the wooden crates. A red whelp was rising along her right cheekbone, showing up strong against her golden skin. The child was beautiful even for a foreigner.

He saw her eyes widen in confusion, moments before snapping her head around at the unfamiliar setting. The China man recognized the look. It was the look of the lost, as his village called them. Through some tragedy, they had forgotten their place in destiny. It then became others' place to care for them till a new destiny was given them.

Trying not to frighten her, he placed a comforting hand to her shoulder, "Child, are you unharmed?"

Dazed, Sarah barely managed a nod.

"Can you remember to what English family you belong, Little One?"

Sarah shook her head, wincing from the pain such a simple movement caused, "I can't seem to..." frightened she huddled her knees up to her chest, her bottom lip trembling in fear.

The China man nodded. The God of all things must have given her destiny to him for a time till a new destiny could be found.

"Well, no matter Little One", he bent down on one knee and smoothed her troubled brow, "I will help you search for them when you are ready."

In wonder, the little girl studied the strange old man speaking at her through the thick fog that covered her mind. His voice was soft and steady, sending waves of comfort over her soul. Uncertain why she felt compelled to stay rather than run, she scooted back a little more even though there was nowhere else to go. The whelp on her cheek began to throb painfully, reaching up she gingerly touched it.

"My cheek hurts sir" she said softly as uncertain tears gathered in her golden brown eyes.

The China man placed his hand softly over her hurt cheek and smiled in sympathy, "You may call me Grandfather, Little One."

She began to tremble from shock. Suddenly all she wanted in the world was to sleep. The strange looking man now called "grandfather" gently wrapped her in his jacket and gathered her up against him. Too tired to fight, she rested peacefully in his arms. Warm at last, her trembling lessened. The large man in the shadows began to stir. A moan escaped his lips. Deftly, the China man blocked her view of the pig.

"Are you, Sir?" Came the child's weak voice from his arms.

He gathered her closer to his heart and began walking, "Am I what Little One?"

She clutched at his shirtfront anxiously, with the last of her strength she tried to focus on his face, desperate for an answer, "Are you my grandfather, Sir?"

For a long moment they looked into each other's eyes. He too knew what it was to be alone, which is why he answered her honestly from the depth of his soul, with an oath he fully intended to keep. "From this moment on, Little One, I shall truly be your grandfather. As much as it is in my power, I will keep you safe."

For the first time since the assault Sarah let out a contented sigh and loosened her death grip on his shirt. Resting her head against his tunic, she closed her eyes and drifted off to sleep, one small hand curled trustingly over his heart.

Determined to keep his word to the child, he boarded the huge ship, the one he had just exited a scant few minutes ago in search of fresh air. He would take the Little One with him to America. Whoever meant her harm would not find her there. When and if her memory returned, then he would find a way to deliver her safely to her family.

He shifted her weight. She moaned quietly in response, her tiny fingers automatically reaching up to feel his face. Whatever she found there must have soothed her for she drifted off to sleep once more. The old man smiled protectively down on his gift from God. She had a brave heart and gentle spirit this one. She would give him much joy and peace in these last remaining years of his life.

# Chapter 1
*August 14, 1861*

Would he ever know peace again?

Lee sighed as his granddaughter pleaded with eyes turned golden by the hot New York sun. "There is no use my most stubborn granddaughter. Your dreams have decided the matter."

"But Grandfather, I do not wish to go back to England."

The ancient man had heard enough. Without saying another word, he left her standing in the middle of the road, neither speeding nor slowing his pace, a stern look on his weathered face.

Sarah raced to catch up, trying to explain as best she could.

"Please Grandfather, my heart tells me something terrible will happen if I go to this place."

"You must face this fear Sarah or it will become the victor in your life", with pig tail swinging, his displeasure was obvious from his brisk walk to the way he shoved knotted hands deeper into the sleeves of his silk top. How easily he accepted fate and the degrees of the God of all things. Why did this girl child doubt not only her destiny but also his superior wisdom? He began mumbling in Chinese to himself. Something about the English and their belief in only what they saw.

Embarrassed by the stares sent their way, the young girl hurried to keep up, mimicking his stance out of respect, "Won't you please listen to me? My destiny lies here with you Grandfather, not with strangers in another country. I have nothing that bonds me to these Englishmen except this locket bearing my name and even it seems as if it belongs to someone else."

She fingered the small gold locket around her neck. It felt cold and hard to the touch sending a shiver of impending doom.

The small wiry man stopped suddenly and looked at her from over the top of his spectacles, "I also believe in destiny Sarah. That is why I know the time has come to return you to your people."

With an unusual show of defiance she shook her head, insisting strongly, "You are my people, Grandfather."

"Would you shame me by arguing in front of strangers", he reprimanded her.

The light of defiance faded from her eyes. Before her, stood the dearest person on this earth to her, the man who had raised and taught her about such things as honor, love and a sense of duty. And yet here she was actually shouting at him on a busy street corner in the middle of China Town over nothing more than this terrible feeling crowding into her innermost being. Instantly contrite, she bowed respectfully.

"Forgive me Grandfather, I forgot the respect due your wisdom, which comes only from living many long and full years", she bowed her tawny head lower, as she succumbed her will to his judgment.

Hearing the heartfelt sincerity of her words, his tone softened in affection, "Little One you must trust me in this matter. When I found you many years ago I knew in time you would be given a new destiny, or your old one would be restored. That time has come. For many nights now your soul cries into the night for your English family. It is time I returned you to them."

Sarah's hands trembled as she gripped her arms tightly inside the sleeves of her light green cotton jacket. Even her voice trembled slightly, "Please Grandfather, these dreams only bring cries of pain in their coming, do you truly believe that returning to darkness is better than light?"

He grew quiet, lost in thought. Slowly he closed his eyes, speaking softly, "Listen Sarah, what do you hear?"

Used to her grandfather's sudden changes of topics and odd requests, Sarah obediently closed her long sable-colored eyelashes. No one paid any attention to the old Chinese man and willowy young girl standing in the middle of the boardwalk with their eyes shut. Years of seeing even stranger occurrences made them callous to such an oddity.

Focusing inward as she had been taught, she tried to eliminate everything from her mind but the sounds around her, reaching out and drawing them into her being. With a practiced ear she heard the sounds of street vendors selling their wares and children's voices raised in a singsong chant.

"What do you hear?"

Sarah cocked her head and raised it slightly before answering, "I hear children and vendors, horses, and the insects that swarm them."

"Do these things frighten you? Perhaps, you can cause the children to cease their singing just by wishing it were so."

Sarah's eyes flew open, "Of course not Grandfather, but..."

His eyes still closed in meditation, he nodded, "And neither can you silence the voices inside of you by wishing they not exist. For they too dwell in the realms of darkness and are just as real. It is only by opening our eyes that the fear leaves us", he opened his own eyes and looked off waiting for her understanding.

The golden highlights in her soft brown eyes held sadness as well as love, "As usual your wisdom is greater than my fear. Of course I must go back," she leaned over and placed a soft kiss to his brow, "besides, you will be with me and you are braver than ten warriors", she winked," or so you constantly remind me."

"Hah", he frowned, "It takes ten warriors to keep such a one as you out of trouble."

Laughing and tossing off the overwhelming feeling of gloom their conversation brought, she said a little too brightly, "Now Grandfather, I assure you even I can manage to stay out of trouble today. After all, what could possibly go wrong at Chan's Laundry?" Bending over, she kissed the top of his graying head, all evidence of misgivings carefully hidden behind her sunny smile.

A disbelieving eyebrow cocked up towards his hairline. "And, what of the street urchins last week?"

She blushed guiltily. "Oh, that."

"Not only did you give them the wrong clothes..."

"How was I to know that pile was Major Nelson's? Besides he could certainly stand to delve out a little charity once in awhile. Heaven knows he could use a good deed or too in his favor when he stands at heaven's gate. Which won't be too much longer, given the man's temper.

He must start a fight with every southerner in pants who crosses his path," she hurriedly explained.

Scowling and mumbling to himself he glared her into silence, "But, my granddaughter, wise beyond her years, that does not explain why Chan and I must pay penance for your error. Nor why you chose fit to leave the cash box open within easy reach of the two small thieves you delved out this very same charity to. This was most foolish, especially since it has taken many weeks of living off cabbage and weak tea to pay your employer back."

Sarah bit at a full bottom lip, till it became rosy against her dusky skin. "I suppose I should be thankful Chan has such an understanding heart", she admitted, her voice tinged with sadness, "But if you could have seen how hungry those children were."

Her attempt at submissiveness made him shake his head in defeat. How could one scold a child such as his dear one? Heaving a deep sigh, he sent up a prayer to heaven for patience. If only his granddaughter did not possess such a tender heart for those less fortunate, or perhaps if she possessed a bit more wisdom in her dealings with them they would all be better off. "Oh, I am certain they were most convincing. Now off to work unrepentant one. For it will take at least a week more of delivering laundry to pay for your last good deed."

He stopped just short of entering the laundry, a worried look in his old eyes, "Remember child to think more deeply before rescuing anymore hapless victims."

"Yes, Grandfather", she answered, truly sorry to cause him even a moment's worry, "I promise. From now on I will try harder to use my head and not my heart when helping others."

He knew she truly meant the words she spoke. Yet...a worried look crossed his brow, as he watched her hurry inside the laundry, her thick rope of tawny hair, swinging happily behind her. He also knew that if someone needed her, her heart drowned out any common sense that might try to surface. And for some reason this worried him even more today. There was trouble in the air. He could feel it. But as with most of life, worrying would not help battle it. Shaking off the dreary premonition he scurried off towards the tenement house they shared with several more immigrants. After all, he still had many more loose ends to tie before leaving America.

He stopped suddenly, a puzzled frown crossing his weathered brow. Although he was a scholar by nature and had studied many years the Americans and their beliefs through the Farmer's Almanac, he still could not understand their logic. Loose ends...such strange sayings. Shrugging over the puzzlement, he started off once more, before snapping his fingers in remembrance. Ah, he must remember to go by the booksellers and obtain a copy of their Mark Twain. He had read a short story by the young author in a newsletter last night over supper and liked it very much. Wisdom seasoned with humor was much easier to swallow.

"Sarah."

Chan's gentle rebuke startled her out of her daydreams. Hurrying over to the forgotten pile of starched white shirts, she began putting them quickly into a woven basket. Placing the last one on top, she rubbed the residue of starch from her hands and turned innocent eyes his direction, "There you go, all finished."

The middle aged man bowed, but there was a noticeable twinkle in his black eyes when he raised his head, "Ah, Sarah. I must admit a terrible fear overtakes me", he nearly laughed at the perplexed way her pert nose wrinkled up at him, "Yes, it is for those shirts left in your too soft hearted hands. The very ones my dear Lucy has spent many hours over. I wonder if they will find their way to this Lexington Hotel where they belong, or whether their end lies at the bottom of our bay as you dream of showering the orphan children with baskets of money."

She blushed guiltily. His guess had not been far from wrong; only it was imaginary blankets she packed for the many cold and homeless ones she met every night on her way home. Yesterday, it was the orphan children. She ran a long slender hand across one shirt's silky mass. Oh, how she loved the feel of silk sliding through her fingers. She could well imagine how pleased Crazy Kate, the filthy flower vendor, would be to possess such a treasure. Instead the poor woman would be forced to spend the rest of her deprived life wearing thin, threadbare rags, while the rich filled their closets with more of the same. It was not right.

"Sarah, you have been blessed with a kind heart. However, you must guard it more carefully. There will always be the poor and less fortunate, you cannot save them all."

Sarah responded by giving him a heart stopping smile, naive love shining back at him, "I know my most honored employer, but perhaps if I could save just one of them. That would be something. Would it not?"

Chan threw up hands in mock surrender, "So it would, but please don't do it with my customers clothes. After all you are still paying me back for last time I was a party to charity."

Then shooing her towards the door, he placed the laundry basket into her capable, if somewhat misguided hands.

"Okay, okay, I am leaving", she groaned good naturedly, bumping the door open with her backside and placing the basket on her head to keep it from being knocked out of her hands on the way over. "So, what is this rich gentleman's name anyway?"

"Sir Simon Conway"

"Sounds very stuffy"

Chan pushed her the rest of the way out the door, "Most earls are".

"An Earl" She nearly dropped the basket asking in stunned disbelief, "What on earth is an Earl doing in New York City?"

"Waiting on his shirts no doubt" Chan answered before closing the door with a final thud.

It looked as if the elusive earl was never going to get his shirts after all. After one more pass up and down the hallway, looking for Sir Simon Conway's room number, she decided to give up the search and admit defeat. Disgusted with herself, she placed the heavy basket at her sandaled feet, and pushed a strand of honey colored hair out of her eyes. Drat and double drat, now she would have to climb down three flights of stairs to ask for the number again. It would not have been quite so embarrassing had she been listening in the first place, instead of daydreaming about all the elegant people flowing in and out of the lobby.

A loud gunshot interrupted her thoughts, filling the small corridor with its deafening roar. Sarah automatically flinched, covering her ears and hitting the ground.

"What in the world", she whispered to herself, uncertain exactly what action to take next. As if an answer to her question, coming from the very same room as the shot, she heard a man's shout and then the sound of a struggle going on. Fear continued to hammer inside her chest, although Sarah did manage to take a couple of deep soothing breaths in order to try and think more clearly as her grandfather had taught her. He was right, she must think first before acting. Remain logical although all her being wanted to go and help. After all it was no small thing to interfere in another's destiny. Who knows, perhaps she wouldn't even have to get involved. For one thing, there was the fact that apparently the evildoer was not a very good shot. This was a good thing. She wished they would be a little quieter; the sounds coming from inside the room were distracting to say the least. She just needed a few more moments to pause and consider her actions before – a crashing sound of glass hitting the floor jerked her out of her good intentions.

Pushing her grandfather's warning aside, her instincts now taking over, she pointedly ignored the logic warning her to go and get help instead of running straight for the door. She really no longer had a choice. Why else would she be here at this particular point and time if not to save the poor soul inside the room.

"To get help perhaps?" Was the sarcastic reply that instantly came to her mind. Still all the logic in the world would not stop her now; it was as if she were drawn towards the fight. Yes, the time for logic had passed. Someone needed her. She couldn't just stand there and wait until someone was killed. It was against her very nature. So, without further debate, she instinctively raced down the hall towards the sounds coming from behind the heavy Maple door with the number 319 above the knocker. She barely glanced up at the broken number nine dangling upside down, before shoving the door aside and entering the elegant room.

It was in a shambles. The square patterned carpet beneath her feet was cluttered with broken vases, and stained with split brandy. Chairs were laid on their sides, pictures hanging precariously by one corner. And all three men in the room were locked in a life and death struggle by the window, amidst all the chaos.

Noticing her standing there, they all stopped in various poises of stunned disbelief as she entered the room. A beautiful dusky skinned angel, dressed in light green cotton and sandals. It was so out of place in the dark deeds apparently taking place. And it didn't take a genius to see exactly what was happening. The only question was why. For apparently two of the men, both dressed in hotel clothing, were trying to force a third, much larger man, out the hotel window and were failing miserably by the looks of things.

Both evildoers had various purpling blotches on their faces and split lips. Relieved to see their victim only sported a look of unconcealed fury and twice the muscle, she smiled. It was nothing to worry about; she need not get involved after all. Thank goodness. Grandfather would not be pleased if she took on this giant of a man's destiny. Apparently he drew danger to him, like markets drew flies. No, he would not have been pleased at all.

Simon's eyes met the young woman's standing so quietly at the door. Who was she? Her expression was one of shyness, and then oddly…turned encouraging of all things. As if he were attempting sailing rather than fighting for his life. Simon could not believe when she simply looked straight at him, flanked on both sides by knife welding villains and simply nodded for him to continue, as if a spectator at the games. Stunned that she simply meant to sit there and watch he was taken totally off guard when a hard fist slammed him back into the fight at hand.

Sarah decided to stay and watch. Why exactly, she could not say, except that something drew her to the large handsome giant. Maybe it was the way he fought so valiantly like her grandfather, or maybe because...well to be honest...she liked looking at him. If Grandfather knew her thoughts, he would surely scold her and he would be right. It was a very serious thing to interrupt another's fate. Especially if the only reason was that she found the man attractive. But, it was.

Realizing the girl actually meant to do nothing but watch him get beat to a pulp; Simon's frustration caused a strong wave of adrenalin to surge through his body. Throwing the pock-faced man holding his right arm up against the wall, he demanded, "Quick girl, throw me that gun at your feet."

A slight frown of uncertainty crossed her delicate features. Then she looked down at the gun and frowned as if in indecision. Unbelievably, he realized, the woman was actually thinking it over first. He let out a woof of air as the other man assaulting him rammed a hard head into his midriff. Simon went flying backwards over the bed and landed in heap at her feet, sending the gun sliding even further under the bed and out of reach. And what did the tawny haired angel with freckles sprinkling her pert nose do? She flattened up against the wall, and tried to move out of the way.

Simon groaned. So much for hoping she might change her mind and actually help him here. He gave her a disgruntled look, shoved a hand through tousled hair a moment and kicked the lumbering idiot coming at him in the face.

"Who are you", he managed to ask in an agitated growl.

"Oh, pardon me for my rudeness warrior. I had not meant to distract you. I am Sarah." She bowed in an obviously Oriental way; only she was as white as he. Her bow was cut short by the pock marked man finding his feet beside her, she quickly jumped out of the way and up on a side table.

Simon's body reacted instantly to the softness in her voice. Never had a woman caught his attention so quickly, but then again never had he met a woman quite like her before, or exactly in these conditions either. Barely managing to roll out of the way before a chair was slammed down on top of him, he demanded sarcastically, "Well, Sarah, now that we have been properly 'introduced'," he paused to slam his fist into the just recovered bearded guy, "Do you think it might be convenient to throw me that gun NOW?"

Sarah stiffened at the insinuation that she refused to help him because of some silly manner thing. Unfortunately for them both, the problem went much deeper than that, and without Grandfather here she was not sure if throwing a gun to him would be considered saving his life. She shrugged apologetically, "I don't think I can, I do apologize though."

The redheaded bearded man covered with freckles ran straight for Simon who deftly moved over to one side. Momentum caused him to run head long into the wall beside Sarah. Grabbing his throbbing head, he sank slowly to the floor.

"Would you mind telling me why not?" Simon demanded, lunging for the gun under the bed. The fat one, still rubbing a bruised jaw went over and stomped down on Simon's outstretched hand. His shout was more anger than pain.

"Because", Sarah continued as if nothing had happened. Then stopped a moment as the handsome man who had been about to shout at her again, received an awful blow to the nose, obviously breaking it.

Shaking off the pain, he got to his feet fully intending to beat the man senseless who was responsible for the injury.

Sarah thought perhaps this was a good time to explain, "Grandfather says I must not interfere with your fate. It would be most unwise. Besides we must leave for..."

Simon drew back a well-muscled arm, ramming his fist into the other man's face breaking his nose as well.

"Do I, perchance, know this grandfather of yours", Simon asked breathing heavily as he picked up a large book and whacked the moaning man to the side of his head, knocking him out.

One down.

"Oh, no. It is nothing personal. I just cannot be responsible for anyone's fate right now. We are soon to leave this place and Grandfather says..."

"Please spare me anymore of your grandfather's insights."

Sarah smiled at his irritation. She took no offense at his words. After all, he was fairly busy at the moment. And besides, not many people understood her grandfather's strange mix of Irish Christianity and Chinese superstition, even when she did try and explain it.

The last ill-mannered lout, his freckled face bruised and bloody, picked up a chair leg and was coming straight for Simon. He figured he had approximately three minutes to take the weapon away from him and get out of there before the police arrived, which should not be a problem provided, of course, that the girl was not one of them. If so, that would take an additional thirty seconds. She was a tiny thing.

Simon's eyes grew darker as the man came in closer, swinging the weapon in a large arch above his head. He was fully prepared to kill the man if he had to. But, being as his ship sailed in less than three hours he hoped he would not be forced to. It was vital he was on it. And hours answering the law's questions would make him late.

Sarah heard a sound behind her and turned towards it. Her amused smile faded. Slowly she slid down off the table, her eyes never leaving the doorway, as her hand groped underneath the bed in search of the gun. She had no choice.

The man approaching was the most frightening thing Sarah had ever seen. He had to be nearly seven feet tall and weighed at least three hundred pounds. If that were not bad enough he carried a gun that matched his size, or at least she thought it was a gun. It looked more like a small cannon.

As he neared the doorway he cocked the sawed off shotgun in one hand.

She had to find that gun or the handsome warrior would die. Closing her eyes, she focused harder until she felt the cold metal underneath her fingertips. She nearly shouted in triumph, had her throat not been closed in terror.

Watching in fascinated horror, Sarah saw the man raise the cannon to a greasy heavily muscled shoulder, fully intending to shoot the young earl in the back. A scream stuck in her throat. She had to do something. The man named Simon had not even noticed his presence.

The monstrous man slid a fat finger onto the lever and sneered in pleasure at what he was about to do, reveling yellowed and decaying teeth.

Something primal snapped inside Sarah. All she could think was, please not again! She would not stand by and watch another soul die in front of her. Her spirit could not take being responsible for this man's death. A silent scream seemed to burst through her mind and travel throughout her whole body until it exploded out through the weapon in her hands.

The echo of a loud gunshot rang out into the now silent room. Simon instinctively spun away from the threat. His body was tense and ready.

It was then he saw her face.

She stood pale and trembling in the middle of the room, the still smoking revolver clutched tightly in one white knuckled hand. And she was standing over some massive thing…no, one massive man lying in a pool of his own blood on the polished wood floor of the entranceway. The deadly cannon lay resting unused just outside his meaty fingertips.

Pushing himself to his feet and hurrying over to the obviously in shock young woman, he gently pried his gun from her hand. His heart instantly went out to her. He owed her his life, this strange young girl who had walked into his life uninvited.

Worried she might faint; he slowly reached out and touched her cold hand. "Sarah", her glazed eyes turned to the sound of his voice. He pulled her trembling cold body into his arms speaking soothingly to her. "Sarah it's all right, he's dead."

She buried her face in his chest, shaking her head in denial.

"Shhh. It wasn't your fault. You had no choice. Without your courage Sarah, I would be dead right now. You saved my life."

Her head shot up at his words, her expressive eyes wide with fright. He laid a chaste kiss on her brow. "I don't want you to worry. I'll handle the authorities. Why don't you go home, and I'll..."

"What have I done," she moaned.

Simon who had been resting his chin on the top of her silky head reluctantly released her. She smelled of newly starched shirts and fresh air. Oddly enough, the smell stirred his blood. He frowned at that ridiculous notion. Next, he would find the smell of beeswax enticing. What was wrong with him? Here he was thinking about how good she smelled and she sat here obviously distraught over what she had been forced to do. It was never easy to kill a man.

Trying to remain calm so she would not dissolve into tears, he pulled her with him over to the bed and lowered them both onto it.

"What you have done Sarah is save my life."

She still refused to raise her head, looking down at her hands as if they were some strangers'. He raised one of them to his lips and kissed it reverently. Then, tilting her chin back with a steady hand, he looked deep into her eyes.

He expected to find horror, tears, anything but what he did find. Instead he found acceptance and an outpouring of love. Not the passionate kind of love a woman feels for a man but rather the kind a small child feels for a newly adopted puppy. He dropped his hand away, suddenly wary.

Sarah, on the other hand was awed at the depth of protectiveness she felt towards this handsome stranger. Grandfather was right. Even if she had not believed before, she did now. Through one act of will, this man's destiny and hers were now forever entwined, merged by a twist of fate. With wonder, she lifted a hand to his rough unshaven face, touching it lovingly. His green eyes clouded with confusion at her odd action.
None of this swayed what she now knew. With firm conviction filling her voice she stated simply.

"No, Warrior, what I have done goes beyond mere debt. Your life belongs to me now."

# Chapter 2

There she was again.

Simon shook off the impossible hallucination, closing his eyes then reopening them to find...absolutely nothing. The beautiful woman who had saved him in America must have left some impression. He could have sworn he spotted her on the ship several times throughout his journey back home to England. But of course that was impossible. Besides the last time he had laid eyes on her, she was surrounded by smiling Chinese in a China Town laundry thanking him humbly for the generous gift of Two hundred dollars. It was the least he could do. Apparently she was living with some eccentric China man in the slums of New York. And from her sweet disposition and trusting demeanor had absolutely no idea how miserable she really was.

He had tried to give her more money when he had taken her home, but was refused politely before she graciously refilled his chipped cup with the faded roses encircling the upper rim. The tea so weak it was nothing more than colored water. Not to mention it tasted of being seeped too many times in one week. No doubt, since they both refrained from joining him, it was also the dregs from the bottom of a blue and white oriental tea canister that rested on the cabinet along the far wall.

After only a few moments of taking in his surroundings, he decided to send her more money later through his solicitor. That she wouldn't take it now was utterly ridiculous. They obviously could use it, and she had saved his life after all. No, it was nothing more than foolish pride that stopped her. He saw it in the stubborn jutting out of a small chin. Taunt jaw. And eyes that flashed golden as they looked directly into his. Yes, if not for the poor decrypted older gentleman she took care of, he doubted she would have taken the two hundred.

At the sound of a ship whistle hurrying the passengers along, Simon threw the heavy leather bag containing important documents and a few changes of clothes over one shoulder and exited the ship. The vision of the small wiry man with reddish gray hair, yet all the mannerisms of an

Oriental still amused him. And then there was the girl; so beautiful and innocent he could have sworn she had been born yesterday. That is, if not for his reaction to her, which was knee-buckling desire.

The memory of dusky skin kissed by the outdoors and eyes so full of light that – his pulse quickened at the thought of those golden eyes looking so deeply into his own. Yes, they were definitely a strange pair as they sat cross-legged on the floor across from him while he occupied the only piece of real furniture in the entire room, one chair. What kind of person had only one chair?

He supposed the very kind that owned only one scarred up dresser teetering on three legs and a pile of books. In the far corner of the room he had observed two mats that must have sufficed for beds and besides the one low table that came barely to his knees when he sat down…there was nothing else. But somehow, despite their lack of funds and odd appearance, the two had a closeness he envied. For although they were obviously not flesh and blood, there was no denying the adoration on the young woman's face when the older man spoke; or for that matter, the China man's protective watchfulness as she waited on him. Strange or not, there was a bond there. And if he had had more time, he might have found out what exactly it was.

He pulled at his collar remembering the tiny room. Except for the window thrown wide, there wouldn't have been a breath of air in the entire room. Luckily they graciously moved his chair over by the window, a hot summer breeze cooling the sweat gathering on his brow. But nothing could have helped his freshly washed shirt from sticking to his skin or strengthen the patience worn thin from too many setbacks on this trip. Yes, it was good manners alone that had forced him to remain and accept the second cup of watered down sugarless tea. And those very same manners that further forced him to choke down the single piece of dry toast offered on a platter in lieu of biscuits.

Coming suddenly to a stop, and causing one overdressed fop of a gentleman to run into his back, Simon's brow furrowed. It was that feeling again. He couldn't seem to stop himself from peering over a shoulder and up at the docked boat, one last time. Was that a glimpse of a honey colored head ducking down behind the ship's railings or his imagination again?

Rolling his eyes at his own paranoia, he readjusted the heavy bag and began whistling softly to himself. He gave a false impression of casual indifference, while in reality his body was taunt and ready for an attack. For something definitely had not been right since first boarding the ship in America. His instincts were sending a warning of danger. And they had never been wrong. But why on the earth would a young woman and her odd grandfather be following him? It made absolutely no sense. This is precisely, why he knew it had to be something else.

Or, he supposed it could be simply that the young woman's words still bothered him. Actually, haunting him was more like it. Never had anyone affected him so deeply. What was it she had said to him anyway? It was something about destiny and being his protector, whatever that meant. As if the small tawny haired angel barely out of the schoolroom could protect anyone. Why, he easily made two of her. No, it was that unsettling look of adoration and maternal love she bestowed on him as she took the small amount of money he pressed into her hand that worried him. Still.

He had expected her to refuse the money again, but she only smiled before turning to her grandfather and whispering that word again… "Destiny". And something about the way she said it, so full of ominous meaning, sent chills down his spine. As if his whole life would forever be changed from that one moment.

He shook off the ridiculous notion. Now who was being irrational? This whole trip had turned out strangely. First, his contact was murdered. Then, his bank account depleted and his ticket home was stolen. All of which, forced him to stay on an extra day. The meaning of which, became only too clear the next morning, when two ruffians posing as room service showed up at his door. Any idiot could have seen through their disguise. They were obviously sent to kill him. But the question was why?

And now, this hallucination about some American girl he barely knew. She seemed to be everywhere he looked. It wasn't like him. He

23

was known for his calm and rational manner; his ability to function under extreme stress.

Picking up the nearest bag off the pile of luggage on the dock, he placed it in his left hand. He tried to shake off the feeling in his gut telling him, crazy or not, people like his beautiful savior and her Chinese grandfather didn't take destines lightly. He just hoped they were the only ones from America dogging his footsteps. Whoever was responsible for sending those men to kill him would not give up so easily. And he certainly held no illusions that being home would make him any safer. Especially given the enemy and how much was at stake.

"Hey, old boy, you look like you've seen a ghost."

Simon's look of puzzlement changed to genuine pleasure at his cousin's greeting. John looked as carefree and rumbled as usual. His dark hair was badly in need of a comb. From the looks of his wrinkled clothing and loose white scarf, his cousin had spent most of the night somewhere other than his townhouse.

"I am beginning to believe I have", he answered honestly before slapping John on the shoulder, "So, I see you were nominated to welcome the prodigal home. Although from the looks of things, you're the one in need of saving."

John gave him a charming lopsided grin; "Actually, there was a certain young lady who needed my services last night. And being the gentleman I am, I could hardly refuse. Besides I am not here to bring the prodigal home, my good man, more like lead the sheep to slaughter."

Simon rolled his eyes, "Who is she this time and precisely how much time do I have to plan my escape?"

Reaching down to help with Simon's luggage, John promised, "We'll talk on the way over old boy. But, I have to warn you; your mother is the least of your worries right now. The prime minister has been sending messengers over practically every hour the last two days."

Simon nodded. "I was…shall we say…delayed by a couple of acquaintances."

Both men knew this was not the place to go into details. Picking up the rest of his luggage, Simon strode towards the waiting hansom cab, wondering what would come of his news. Unfortunately, the Prime minister would be even less pleased when he gave him the information from America. For if he was right, and he prayed he wasn't, this could mean war.

He felt the hairs on his neck rise. He stopped suddenly, all senses alert. This time there was no mistake. Someone was following him.

His own hackles raised by his friends' strange behavior, John peered into the crowd around them. "What's wrong?"

Though Simon's trained eyes searched the crowd, he could find nothing amiss. Yet, something was not right here, he could feel it. "I'm not sure. I could swear someone has been following me."

Without questioning him further, John eased his free hand up under his dark brown jacket and slid his derringer out into the palm of his hand. He had known Simon most of his life. In fact, a number of times been saved by his instincts. If he said someone was following him then they were.

"I gather the information you bring back is not entirely to someone's liking."

One more glance told him whoever was following him must have disappeared in the crowd. "Hardly." Simon casually replaced his own gun.

Understanding the danger had passed, if only temporarily, John replaced his derringer back into the shoulder holster. His watchful eyes were belaying the too easy smile. "You really should get in another line of work. No wonder your mother is always trying to marry you off and get an heir."

Simon grimaced at the reminder of his mother's matchmaking attempts. "My mother knows nothing about my line of work. She simply wants grandchildren. That definitely puts me in more danger than fighting for my country."

Both men strode in watchful silence to the waiting coach. John did not even look up before throwing his bag up to the driver. This was fairly impressive, since the object practically unseated the poor man sleeping contentedly in an alcoholic haze above them.

Harrison came awake fighting, knocking the bag to the ground and doubling up his bony fists as if fully prepared to waylay the Dickens out of his next opponent.

John hid his grin behind a forced cough.

Leaning one hand against the side of the cab, Simon remarked dryly, "Harrison, I'm glad to see some things never change."

Harrison rubbed bleary eyes. Realizing the master was back; he grinned down and saluted as if still in the army. "Might I be permitted to say, sir, how very good it is to see you back home?"

"And you Harrison", Simon one handed a heavy leather bag up to him, "How are you and mother getting along."

Frowning slightly, the old codger struggled with the bag a moment, banging it around and falling backwards, before finally shoving it off him. Realizing he would have to move the thing over to make room for the others, or either sit on top of them, he frowned in indecision. Then with a shrug, he gathered up the other two lighter bags, bent over, and to the surprise of both men, threw them into the side window. They slammed into the opposite wall inside the coach, before landing with a thump onto the floorboard.

Satisfied with himself he wiped his forehead with the pair of white gloves in his pocket. The same ones he repeatedly refused to wear because no real man would, and remarked, "Her ladyship fired me three times last week."

John and Simon exchanged grins. "Then I would say you must be improving."

"Yes sir", Harrison replied with a wink.

Both men climbed in around the bags and were thrown into opposing seats as their oblivious driver whipped the horses at a pace that could only be labeled, suicidal.

"You know, your mother should do something about that man."

"Ah, but then she would have to get rid of Maggie who spills every dish she ever touches and then there is Albert who does well to remember his name much less what you sent him to do."

John's laughter rocked the coach. "You have a valid point cousin."

"Besides, you know what a soft spot Mother has for servants. I think she forgets they are hired for actual labor." Taking his hat off and laying it beside him on the expensive leather seat, Simon turned more serious, "How is she by the way?"

"As well as can be expected. The doctors worry about her heart. Even your father has started refusing her trips to the orphanage. Your sister goes for her."

Nodding his approval, Simon continued, "So tell me old chum. Who am I suppose to fall madly in love with this time?"

His cousin crossed one leg over the other, "Caroline Bishop."

"Caroline Bishop! The girl can't be more than sixteen."

"Simon, not only is she out of the school room, but beautiful enough that she's received three offers without even being presented yet. As a matter of fact, I just might fall in love with her myself."

Just the mention of marriage and grandchildren made Simon feel as if the walls of the carriage were closing in on him. He decided to change the subject.

"When does he want to meet?"

They both knew who he meant.

"He said tonight after supper around ten."

"Are you going to be there?"

John leaned forward, his laid back persona abandoned now that they were alone. "I don't think it's wise. The less I know the better."

"I agree. But I still believe you should be the one dealing with the prime minister. Let me deal with Banister. You might just get yourself killed, and then who would marry Elizabeth for me?"

This time John ignored his attempt at humor. "Seriously Simon, we both know that of the two of us, I'm expendable. Our country needs you. Besides you my friend would end up killing the man. And last time I checked it is hard to get a confession, or anything else pertinent, from a dead man."

"Oh, I would get the information the first. Then I would kill him."

The familiar two-storied townhouse appeared outside their window ending all talk of enemies and war. Still, John could not help the concern in his voice, "Simon be careful around that man. I know him probably better than anyone else, especially after the last couple of months. He would kill you if he got the chance."

Simon's dark green eyes turned the color of a summer storm, "He can try."

An hour later Simon knew Banister was the least of his worries. His mother would be the death of him. Very much more of this and he would die of boredom. He yawned lazily and motioned a servant over to refill his glass. Hoping they could at least hurry this supper along and retire to the parlor. He needed a smoke.

"So, Simon", his mother's hopeful voice broke through his boredom, "Isn't Caroline's gown lovely?"

All eyes turned expectantly his direction. His sister looked as idiotically hopeful as his mother. You would think he were proposing marriage to the dark haired beauty sitting across from him instead of simply commenting on her attire.

He took in creamy well-rounded shoulders peeking demurely from a deep purple satin gown and violet colored eyes daring him to deny the truth. Taking his time about answering, only because he couldn't abide vain females, he answered coolly, "Yes, it's lovely."

Caroline flipped her fan flirtatiously before asking demurely; "So Simon, do you have a date for the Harrington picnic this weekend? If not I might be persuaded to..."

Turning to the fumbling lanky man serving them, Simon barked impatiently, "Albert, I would appreciate some additional gravy on my beef Wellington. Only this time I would like the actual gravy instead of the custard you dribbled on it earlier."

His mother blushed, "Now, dear, you know Albert suffers from an old war wound and can't help becoming confused at times."

"Mother he was shot in the foot, not the head. Although from the looks of things, his head might have been a better target."

Kate snickered into her napkin.

"Simon, do tell us about America", Kate entreated, coming up and squeezing her brother's arm. "Are there really Indians in America? What are they like?"

Never able to resist his little sister's charm, Simon wrapped his hand around hers, "Yes, Briar. They are real enough. However a majority of them have been pushed further West and South. I personally only met one."

His sister sighed in disappointment, then, her eyes lit up with excitement, "But the Americans themselves. Are they terribly frightening? I hear they shoot pistols at each other and now the papers are saying the South actually declared war on the North. Can you imagine anything as ridiculous as that?"

"Kate stop bothering your brother", their mother admonished. Then noticing John sitting peacefully beside Caroline, she ordered, "John do give Simon your seat. He must be exhausted after his long trip."

Before Simon could stop her, and surprisingly energetic for a woman on her sick bed; she managed in one fluid motion, to tug him loose from Kate, motion John up, and push him back down beside Caroline.

Caroline cocked her head at him and pretended to rearrange her skirts till she was practically sitting on top of him. Simon chose to ignore her. She touched the woven leather band holding his unfashionably long hair in place, "Did your Indian give you this? It is very primitive looking."

It was the way she said 'primitive' that caused him to pry her hand off his arm and answer shortly, "He wasn't my Indian and no…he didn't."

Growing braver she touched his wavy brown hair, "And do all the American men wear their hair so long?"

Simon had had enough.

"Miss Bishop, as much as I enjoy your company, I am afraid I have to be going."

He rose and called out for Albert to fetch his overcoat.

"But son you just got home. Where could you be going at this hour?"

"Mother I have to meet John at the club."

"But John is sitting right here."

Now what? He looked over at John for help. He simply lifted his glass in a toast as if to say; let's see you get out of this one cousin. So help him, if Simon every lived through this evening he would swear off females of any kind.

"What I meant to say was John and I both have to go. Isn't that right John?" It wasn't a question.

Willing to finally let him off the hook, John walked over and kissed the back of his aunt's hand. "I'm afraid so Aunt Stella. There are some friends of ours who are most anxious to win back the money they lost to your son before he left."

Impatient to be gone, Simon strode towards the parlor door, "Father I will probably be getting back late tonight, maybe we could meet in the morning and look over those account books for the warehouse."

"Well, all right son...but I think your mother..."

Albert hurried over and draped Mrs. Bishops red cloak over Simon's shoulders. John burst out laughing, but Simon did not find it the least amusing. "Albert, does this look like my coat to you?"

Albert looked genuinely hurt. "No, Sir." He stiffened his spine, making him only slightly taller than his hunched over height of five foot seven, "Perhaps I should find other employment if you are not satisfied with my work."

"Perhaps, you should." ground out an exasperated Simon.

"Simon!"

"Sorry mother. Never mind about the coat Albert, I'm late enough as it is." He inclined his head towards his guests, "It was nice seeing you again Mr. and Mrs. Bishop, now if you will excuse me I must be going." If he could make it outside before his mother gained her senses, maybe the night might not be a total waste.

"But, Simon dear, aren't you forgetting about Caroline?"

Simon tried to look contrite, "Oh, quite right mother."

Caroline batted her big blue eyes at him as he bent politely over her hand. "Goodbye to you too Miss Bishop. And may I say it has been an unexpected pleasure. Now I must go."

Caroline's face fell. "Certainly. And I look forward to our picnic."

He chose to ignore that last remark.

"Simon, you can't mean to just leave like this in the middle of your party." his mother pleaded once again as she rushed over to his side.

As a matter of fact, that is precisely what he proposed.

But before he could answer that question, Maggie burst through the double doors, her white cap sliding sideways on her Red head. "Sir, if you be leaving, well, I am quite sure your young Miss would like to…" She chewed on her bottom lip in indecision before blurting out in a supposedly hushed voice of secrecy. Only to save his life, he swore the entire room turned their direction, "to have a word with you. If you know what I mean."

He had absolutely no idea what she meant, or who she was referring to. Simon looked behind him to see if perhaps she were speaking to John. The maid took the opportunity to rush over and commence weeping on his shoulder. It was then he realized the poor misguided fool was actually addressing him.

"Oh, sir, you have to come quick. The China man said he'd place a curse on me if I dinna fetch you right away. I already have an Irish curse on me head and I dinna think I could put one foot in front of the other with a China man's curse too. But, thens I said to myself, what if the master fires poor Maggie then I…"

"Would you stop that blubbering and tell me what you are talking about."

Maggie wiped at her eyes with the only unsoiled portion of her apron. "Why, your China lady, sir. I dinna know what to do with her. I mean, we don't have rooms set up for…you know… lady friends." she began to blush a fiery red.

Mrs. Bishop gasped.

"So then I thought to myself maybe we could open up the attic room for her. But, thens I said to myself that the master'd not be likin' to go traipsing up to that old drafty attic every night…"

Shocked, Simon grabbed her arms and forced her to look at him, "Are you daft woman!"

Mrs. Bishop gasped again. Her daughter now sank onto the couch sobbing.

"Now look here Simon I won't stand for this sort of thing. This is a civilized English household. And I think you owe Caroline here an apology." roared his father.

"Oh, my. Oh, dear", whimpered his mother, reaching behind for her husband, "did she say a China lady? What if he marries her? I imagine she isn't even Church of England."

Kate's eyes danced with merriment, "He must have gotten her in America. They have all manner of people there."

"Don't be ridiculous Kate", Simon ground out.

Maggie now began blowing her nose so loudly into her apron that it made it impossible to hear much else. Albert hurried into the room, and regally laid Mr. Bishops Coat over Simon's shoulders.

He shrugged out of it, turning a furious face on poor Albert, "Would you stop bringing me coats." Then exasperated, he turned on Maggie and tried to shake some sense into the hysterical girl. "Get a hold of yourself and explain what you are talking about."

Mrs. Bishop began fanning herself furiously, "The very idea. Imagine flirting with my poor Caroline while the whole time you had that awful American waiting in the kitchen."

"I say old chap, you shouldn't have left her in the kitchen," intoned her husband, "we would have pulled up another chair." To which he received another whack across his balding head.

In the midst of all the commotion Sarah and her grandfather entered the room and stood just inside the doorway. The sight was enough to have frightened many a seasoned soldier. Yet Sarah took it all in stride. From the hysterical women weeping, to the butler trying to dress Simon in ill-fitting coats, all the way to the unfamiliar young man laughing so hard he was clutching his sides.

"Grandfather, whatever are they doing?"

There was a slight twinkle to his black eyes. "I am uncertain child. Perhaps it is an English ritual of great joy and welcome."

Mrs. Bishop continued to pound her husband over the head with her fan.

"Perhaps, but I do not think so."

Caroline Bishop was the only one who noticed the beautiful girl dressed in a pale green silk shirt and matching silk pants standing quietly at the door. Slightly behind her, a China man stood with arms crossed inside his sleeves and a serene expression on his face. She stopped her mother's raised arm, "Mother, I think that must be Simon's..."

Mrs. Bishop snatched her arm away and shook a finger at her husband, "You imbecile. Do something. Can't you see he has sullied our daughter's reputation?"

"Mother."

"Not now, Caroline. Can't you see I am talking to your father?"

Weeping, she struck him again.

"Annabelle, listen to me", Mr. Bishop pleaded as his wife shoved past him to get her cloak. "I am sure if we give the young man a chance to explain."

Simon's father was trying to comfort his distraught wife, pressing a glass of sherry at her.

Shoving the glass away, she moaned, "Henry, how could our son do something like this. What if they have children? How will I ever talk to them? I never even learned to speak French much less something so uncivilized as Chinese."

Albert picked that precise moment to bring Mrs. Bishop...Simon's coat. It hung off the ends of her hands and off her shoulders, swallowing her in its over sized black embrace. She hardly noticed. "Are you coming Caroline?"

"But, mother..."she answered, motioning Sarah's direction.

Thinking Caroline was being friendly, Sarah waved back.

Caroline huffed indignantly, turning her back on the vile creature that had destroyed all her plans.

Simon's mother let herself be lead over to the couch, "Oh, Henry", she moaned, reaching for her husband's hand, "I believe I just might faint."

"Simon look what you are doing to your mother", boomed his father, drawing his attention.

Simon fought off another coat and hurried over to his mother, helping her onto the couch. "Mother, I can explain, or at least I think I can. I assure you Maggie must be delusional. If there is a woman in our kitchen I can say with complete confidence, I have absolutely no idea who she is."

The two new visitors gave each other a perplexed frown. These people were very confusing...and loud.

"Granddaughter."

"Yes, Grandfather?"

"I believe you are only a whisper in a huge canyon."

"Yes, Grandfather", Sarah answered meekly.

"It is time to gain their attention."

That said, he motioned her over in front of him before placing two fingers inside his mouth and letting out a shrill whistle. The result was deafening.

The sound ricocheted through the room as if a shot had been fired. Each person in the room turned slowly Sarah's direction. Then, once seeing her standing there so serene, they waited in stunned disbelief. Embarrassed Sarah searched the room for the familiar face she had traveled across an ocean to find. It didn't take long.

And when she saw him? All the other people in the room faded when her eyes met his. Her breath caught at the sheer beauty of the man. How could it be that he touched something deep within her, every single time she laid eyes on him? And to think he was her destiny. Maybe this was how all people felt when they protected another's life. For ever since meeting him, she didn't know whether to fall on her knees in humble thanks, or run as fast and hard as she could.

One look at her grandfather's encouraging expression, made the decision for her. She chose to stay. So, with a sweet and open expression she smiled at Simon and it was as if the sun itself had come out. It basked them both in a glow that filled the whole room.

Simon was speechless. He sat transfixed; drinking in the dusky colored vision before him. Shocked, he slowly rose to his feet, whispering one word, "Sarah?"

His poor mother gasped, a hand going to her heart. There was no mistaking the look of deep affection on her son's face. Or that he knew her. And well.

The sound of his strong masculine voice stirred something within Sarah, something warm and inviting. A tender smile greeted his look of disbelief. Then before he could stop her, she sealed their fate so completely that even he could not save them.

"Warrior, I could not stay hidden. Now that our destinies are one, it is difficult for me to continue this way. Please forgive me if I have interrupted your family ritual of welcome and much joy."

Simon moaned. Now how was he going to explain that statement? He hurried over, hoping to stop her before she said anything else damning.

Unfortunately Kate beat him to it. His naive sister had stars in her eyes as she helped the beautiful stranger forward.

"Oh, Simon", she chided, "you should have told us."

Sarah's hesitant smile brought a reassuring hug from the kind girl now embracing her. It seemed the petite brunette was the only one who truly welcomed her. But it still did not explain the odd manner in which she was doing it. For even true hospitality would hardly cause the young girl's eyes to water with extreme emotion.

"Told you what?" an exasperated Simon bellowed. He was feeling more trapped by the moment. And from the way Kate kept giving his 'lady' understanding pats on the arm, there didn't seem any way out of it. Not without revealing the whole truth, which he couldn't.

"Oh, for heaven's sake, it's obvious."

Simon's mother sat up, truly interested now and gripped her husband's arm, "What's obvious dear?"

Kate smiled secretively first at her frowning brother, then at a totally confused Sarah, "Just look at the two of them, anyone can see the truth."

37

Simon let out a sigh of relief. Who would have thought his little sister would be the only voice of reason in the entire room.

Kate savored the moment before announcing, "Don't you see?" She placed Sarah's hand on top of her brothers, giving them a reassuring squeeze. "They are obviously deeply in love and couldn't find a way to tell us. Personally I think it's terribly romantic."

Simon would have objected had he not been choking at the time.

"And you." She scolded her father, "Doubting him. Imagining he was up to no good and sowing his wild oats. When in truth this whole time, she was the reason for all those secretive trips to America."

Sarah was already shaking her head as Kate announced proudly, "Don't you all see? He hasn't brought back a mistress. No, what he brought back to us…is a wife."

# Chapter 3

"Wife!" Simon and Sarah shouted simultaneously.

Sarah's golden brown eyes widened in shock. Instinctively, she turned to her grandfather for help but only received a slight shrug. But, before she could react and deny the crazy assumption, the young woman holding her arm, started pulling her towards a well-dressed older woman lying on the chintz sofa.

Once reaching her, the pale woman held out a trembling hand towards Sarah, while the other clutched loosely at her heart. Sarah automatically went to her knees. He knew instinctively, from the kindness residing in the ancient one's eyes, that this woman only wished to comfort her. Although why she felt the need to do so, Sarah could not understand. This was all a simple misunderstanding. Once the old one knew the truth, the woman's heart would ease. For it was oblivious that the news of Simon having a wife pained her.

Sarah's own heart turned over in sadness however as she took in how weak and frail the mother of Simon looked. No doubt her time on this earth must be very near the end. Looking back at Simon for wisdom on how to precede, Sarah felt a little lost. But his drawn features relayed only pain. When he did speak it was with gentle words meant to soothe the old one.

"Mother I can explain."

She waved away his words giving them both a brave smile, her voice full of understanding and love for her wayward son. "There is no need. Your father and I were young and in love once. Although, back then, it was fairly unheard of for one to marry for love. Especially being as I was a simple victor's daughter from the country…and he the youngest son of an impoverished Lord. No, I can hardly cast stones about someone being unsuitable. Therefore, I wish to apologize dear." Then giving Sarah's hand a pat, continued, "And don't you worry about a thing. We will simply give the town something to gossip about. It certainly won't be the first time our family has filled that position."

"Welcome to the family dear", the woman whispered, her faded blue eyes filling with what Sarah could only describe as relief, "I cannot tell you how pleased I am to know the two of you are married. At first it seemed as if…well, never mind. Why, how truly lovely you are child and I must say for a Chinese you look remarkably like one of us. I think with a little imagination we may be able to make up a fairly believable tale…not too far from the truth of course…well, I will just have to think on it a bit."

Simon groaned and tried to interrupt. His mother smiled while placing his hand over Sarah's.

"I am so ashamed of my reaction. It is just this came as such a shock. You understand, don't you dear?"

"But there seems to be some mistake, we aren't... "Sarah began.

Simon took one look at the shock on his mother's face and reacted from the gut. Without thinking, he grabbed Sarah's face and placed a kiss so passionate, it stunned her into silence.

When he at last raised his head from their mind-altering kiss, he looked straight into Sarah's eyes and lied, "What my wife meant to say mother is that we aren't certain how it happened either. And knowing how important it was to you that we be married in the church, I couldn't decide exactly how to tell you."

Jerking out of the deranged man's arms, Sarah practically hissed at him, "Why are you doing this? You know perfectly well your words are... "

He forced a smile and pulled her towards the door. "Now if you will all excuse us a minute, I need a moment alone with my wife. Isn't that right sweetheart?"

"But, I don't choose to go with you. You must explain."

"Later, China." His words were meant to intimidate. Instead she glared back at him in defiance. Grabbing back up the arm she had jerked away from him, he started pulling her towards the French doors leading into the back gardens.

Sarah clenched her fist to stop from hitting him. Her cool voice belayed the real struggle of his will against hers. "Let go of me,

Englishman. It is little wonder that in China you are called foreign devils. For you have no honor at all."

"That is enough Sarah." He ground out as they reached the double doors.

His mother fluttered her hands in agitation, "Dear, maybe you should go with him, after all it isn't polite to argue in front of guests." Then worriedly asked of her son, "Simon, are you quite sure she is your wife? I would hate to think anything improper has occurred between the two of you."

His mother's venerability struck at Simon's heart, he stopped dragging Sarah long enough to give his mother a reassuring smile, "Of course she's my wife. It is just a little overwhelming for her right now. Meeting the family and..."

Sarah stomped down hard on the top of his foot. His exclamation of pain drew looks of horror from the others in the room and laughter from John. His cousin had a morbid sense of humor as far as Simon could tell. Except for the moment of worry about his mother, he hadn't stopped laughing yet.

Needless to say, Sarah found nothing humorous about their situation. She was furious. So much so, that by the time Simon managed to pull her through the double doors, her years of schooling in the art of meditation and control weren't enough to still her shaking hands. She couldn't believe he would actually dishonor her by lying to his mother and then include her in his deceit.

Simon seemed shaken as well. She watched him pace back and forth along the stone balustrade deep in thought, her presence completely forgotten. After several more minutes of thought, he picked up her hand and practically jerked her down the massive steps and out into the darkened garden.

Sarah did not fight him this time. She also wished for privacy. For his mother was right. It was impolite to shout at him in front of his guests. And she was determined not to forget herself again. Shivering in the thin clothing more suitable to the Americas rather than England's moist cool nights, she said nothing.

Once reaching the iron bench by the small cluster of remaining irises, Simon released her with a sigh. Arms crossed stubbornly in front of her, Sarah waited. For truth to tell she was still too angry for words.

After several more seconds of silence, he looked over one shoulder at her and frowned, as if noticing her for the first time. "I guess you're wondering why I did that."

"Not particularly. We must go back and tell the truth."

She still couldn't believe he would tell such an untruth to his family. Wondering why he told it was not as important to her as fixing the wrong done to an honored elder. But most of all, she wanted no part of it. Grandfather said a lie was like a heavy stone tied around your neck. Eventually you would have to cross a river and the weight of it would drown you.

When she stood there in accusing silence, he turned around and sat on the rock edge of the pond, one leg propped up alongside him. He rested his head back against the cool stone of the cupid statue behind him and tried to explain. "Look, none of this would have happened if you hadn't followed me."

She opened her mouth to argue, but he continued on with his accusations.

"And by the way, why in heaven's name would you announce to the entire room that 'we are one'? What could I possibly say to that pray tell?"

She refused to take the blame for his untruths. "I expected you to honor your family with the truth."

He gave a snort of disbelief, "And... tell them what? That while spying in America, this Chinese girl, who isn't really Chinese saved my life. And now she thinks I belong to her?" He waved off her interruption, "I don't even believe that story myself. Believe me if it wasn't for the fact you saved my life back in America I would have gladly thrown both you and your grandfather out on the street two minutes ago."

She spun around on him, "Are you actually saying this is my fault!"

He sighed and glared sideways at her through one hand, "Well, I certainly wasn't the one who followed a complete stranger all the way to England and then decided to make a grand entrance right when the most renown gossip in London was visiting, now was I?"

"You must go back and tell the truth."

He closed his eyes at the urgency in her voice. What was she doing here anyway? None of this would have happened if she had just stayed in America where she belonged. Knowing they both were trapped, he rubbed at his aching head before answering. Then, looking straight at her said simply, "I can't."

His words knocked her anger out of the way, and a strange shock took its place, "You can't?"

Running a hand through his hair, leaving it disheveled and boyish looking, he tried to explain, "Do you have any idea what the gossips will do to your reputation and my mother's if I do?"

"I don't care what the English say about me."

"But my mother does. Did you fail to notice she is not a well woman? She has a bad heart and any kind of prolonged stress could kill her. And believe me gossips talking about her son traveling with an unmarried woman who admits to being one with him would definitely be described as prolonged stress."

"Oh." Sarah slumped down on the rock wall beside him, "I did not think about your customs here in this country. Still, if I explain about saving your life and our belief that I am now guardian of your days, then..."

"You might as well throw my mother from that balcony, it would be quicker," he grabbed up her left hand and turned her towards him, "Sarah, I am about to tell you something that must not, under any circumstances be repeated, understood?"

She should not be listening to this English reasoning. What he proposed was morally wrong and would be written in the angel's black book in heaven. Surely this sin was much worse than the cutting of a China man's queue. Yet, somehow his touch and the husky lowering of a voice too beautiful for a mere mortal held her immobile. She looked searchingly into his intense sea green eyes and nodded.

"Go on."

"I work for the British government as a spy, but my family knows nothing about it. They think I went to America to discuss my companies' interest in some pottery and linen exports. I doubt finding out I work undercover for the government and that three men tried to kill me would be any better than finding out your son is a philanderer with a Chinese mistress."

He was confusing her and causing havoc to her insides. She pulled away, "But none of that changes the fact that we are not married. As a matter of fact, I am not even sure I like you very much. Perhaps Grandfather is right and I shouldn't have mingled our destinies, but it is sand under the bridge now."

"Water."

"What?" She looked taken aback a second.

"You said sand, but it's water under the bridge."

She blushed angrily, mostly at herself. The man rattled her brain when he was near. She couldn't think properly. "You know what I mean."

A shrug was his only response before continuing, "What I propose is a pretend marriage. Just for a few months, then you can die from…I don't know…some sickness when you go back to America to visit relatives. Just like that, I become a widower. You have your old life back, and neither one of us is hurt by the inconvenience."

Aghast by the sheer absence of a conscious, Sarah's voice came out in a hoarse shout of indignation. "Unfortunately, man-of-many deceits, I do not lie. Especially, for an Englishman."

She was making him crazy.

"All right. Then, we will get married. A few months down the road, I am sure it can be annulled in private. Provided we don't consummate the marriage, it shouldn't be a problem. Does that satisfy you ridiculous antiquated sense of morals?"

Her hands balled up into fists, as she slid calmly to her feet, eyes ablaze. "I would not marry you even if you weren't a foreign devil. For you are worse than the evil ones you chase, you are a warrior without honor. And one who gives up his soul surely has nothing left to believe in. So, why should I lose my soul as well?"

Her words hit so close to home that he physically flinched. Angry denial forced his pain outwards to the one forcing him to see what he had become. Rising so quickly that the young woman challenging him took a cautious step back, he refrained from throttling her and restated firmly, "What you think of me hardly matters. It is beside the point. As I said earlier, I don't wish to marry either, but it seems neither one of us has a choice. So either we will do as I first proposed and simply pretend marital bliss until I finish this assignment. Or I will marry you. The choice is yours. Afterwards you can leave for America, with say a few thousand pounds, and I become a widower. My mother will live, and my country avoids a war. Surely even your morals can find nothing wrong with such a small sacrifice in order to save lives."

Crossing her arms, she answered in frustration, "You have the smooth tongue of a cobra and just as deadly. But I believe when one does right, evil does not win."

"Are you willing to take that chance?" A slight smile touched his lips.

From the way she was grinding her teeth to maintain control, she very likely would have killed him right then and there if she could have gotten away with it. And the truly insane part was he had never been so attracted to a woman in his life. Her shapely chest rose and fell with barely restrained fury, golden brown eyes sparkling with intensity challenged and excited him at the same time. And her shapely mouth with that sexy slightly fuller lower lip? He couldn't seem to take his eyes off the way she held it between white teeth making it swollen and rose tinted. He shook off the impossible notion of kissing her into submission and tried to reason with her instead.

"Sarah, someone wants England involved with the South's succession. He has promised them a trade deal on England's behalf. I

45

plan on finding out whom, and stopping them.  But, if it gets out that a girl saved my life in America.  Well, some very dangerous people will start to ask questions and my chances of catching this traitor is slim.  Besides, having a wife might prove beneficial.  It would protect me from the Caroline Bishops of the world so I can get some work done."

Never had she met a man with so little honor.  "I should have let that man shoot you."

He ignored her insult.  "My mother has a heart condition, Sarah.  Surely you noticed how pale she was in there.  What possible explanation could I give her in front of a house full of guests on why a beautiful young American girl would follow me across an entire ocean?  Especially after that line about our destinies becoming one.  There just isn't one."

Comprehension dawned across her beautiful features.  Her light brown brows lifted slightly.  "But, I only meant that I am your life protector now.  See, when I saved you, I became your guardian.  For your end time had come and I interfered in the God of my ancestors plans.  In China, this blending of destinies means in a Spiritual way."

"Well, here it means in the physical way."

Her nose wrinkled in confusion, and then soft full lips rounded in shock. At last understanding, she lowered her eyes in shy embarrassment.  "I see.  I have shamed your family with my words."

Blushing profusely she began picking at a stray thread on her third button, "I seem to have a bad habit of that."

She looked adorable.

"A bad habit of what?"

Her anger gone, she shrugged.  Then with a heartfelt sigh, she plopped down beside him once again, "Of saying the wrong thing.  Grandfather says it is because I am English instead of Chinese."

She sounded so forlorn; he tried to ask seriously, "What has being English have to do with anything."

He noticed every time she quoted her grandfather, a soft smile touched her lips and a warm glow lit her eyes.  "Grandfather says the English think little and talk much, but the Chinese think much and talk little."

Simon wondered at the unexplainable urge to laugh whenever she was near, "Do you know what I think?"

Earnest brown eyes met his, "No, what?"

"I think your grandfather, dear girl, is prejudice."

Her unrestrained laughter lifted his spirits. It had been such a long time since he had heard real laughter. The kind that pours out of someone's heart and fills up all the empty places within. He grinned in response and getting up offered a hand in friendship. "Shall we go back in, wife?"

At the word 'wife' she withdrew her hand from his and stepped back, her words full of quiet determination. "I will not lie. My grandfather's father was a missionary and regardless of what you think, he raised me to know God's laws. And telling lies, even for good, is wrong."

He gave a tired sigh. "All right. I'll lie. You just stand there."

"I will fix this thing," she looked at him pointedly before turning toward the doors, "without lies."

He slowly followed her in. He wasn't sure what she was muttering under her breath, but he did recognize immoral Englishman in the tirade.


For a sick woman Simon's mother moved surprisingly fast, thought Sarah.

They had barely crossed the threshold, before being engulfed in the supposedly deathly ill woman's iron clad grasp. Crying softly as she embraced them enthusiastically she explained, "Oh, can you ever forgive a sentimental old woman, dear? You are the answer to an old woman's prayers. Of course I had never entertained the idea of my son marrying an American; however I can see how happy you make him."

"Mother, I am sure Sarah understands. Isn't that right, sweetheart?"

Trying to ignore Simon's false endearment, Sarah focused instead on the dear kind soul trying to accept what Sarah knew was an untruth. Her heart went out to the woman. Not wishing to cause her further pain, but needing to clear up the misunderstanding, Sarah squeezed the cool hand holding hers and gave a wan smile. "It is most kind of you to welcome me into your family, however, my grandfather and me... "

"Are probably exhausted Mother. It's been a long night." Simon finished for her.

If looks could kill, Simon would be picking out headstones.

Sarah cleared her throat and tried again, "What I meant to say most honored mother of Simon is that sadly we... "

"Mother", Simon's deep voice interrupted softly, "there has been some sort of misunderstanding concerning Sarah."

Would the man never let her finish a sentence? And her grandfather was no better, standing there along the farthest wall with an amused twinkle to his eye. Why he chose this particular moment in her life to remain silent and let her handle things was confusing to say the least. Usually he invoked some calm reassurance. Some words of reason. But tonight he sat in quiet reflection, as if watching a scene play out whose conclusion he knew all too well.

Simon's mother tightened her grip on Sarah's hand, her mouth drawn in a thin line, "What sort of misunderstanding?"

Sarah felt awful. The older woman's face fell and she could have sworn she became even paler.

"She's not Church of England is she? Well, we will just have to keep an open mind of course. Or, perhaps she might convert. I believe the missionaries do that sort of thing all the time in those foreign countries. Don't they dear?" She asked hopefully of her stunned husband on the sofa.

"Actually Stella, I believe we should let that be Sarah's decision."

"Oh, yes. You're quite right dear. Simon? Was there something else? You have the exact same expression on your face you had when you pruned all my best rose bushes to the ground, when you were six. O'Malley still hides the pruning shears every time you come home."

"Mother, if you would just let me get a word in edge ways I could..." his mind sought for some explanation. There was none. Besides, his mother looked as white as a sheet. Whatever explanation he came up with would have to wait until she was stronger. Resigned to his fate, and praying Sarah would cooperate, he laid an arm comfortably around the beautiful young woman's waist at his side, "As a matter of fact she isn't our religion…in fact her great grandfather was a Christian missionary in China. Which, for that and other reasons that are equally hard to explain, Sarah and I…"

Sarah held her breath waiting for Simon to deal the poor misguided woman the blow that was inevitable.

"Wish…to be married again? With the church's blessing, of course. Here at home maybe in a month or two, after you are feeling a little more yourself."

Sarah gasped. She would have sunk onto the sofa his mother had just vacated except Simon's steel grip was holding her hostage. Simon pulled her in closer to his side nearly squeezing the breath from her, silently asking, no, demanding she back up the ridiculous statement.

Sarah shook her head in denial, strands of tawny hair escaping from the thick braid that reached all the way to her tiny waist. The shock made her words unguarded, "Warrior I cannot…"

"Of course, she should not be forced to wait an entire month dear", his beaming mother interrupted, "No woman should. Imagine the damage to her reputation. It would be unsalvageable. Just to make sure all is legal, we shall fetch Father Mullen from down the street and the two of you can be remarried in the eyes of the church tonight by special license."

Mrs. Bishop who decided to stay when she recognized a juicy piece of gossip huffed indignantly, "I've never heard of such a thing, whatever could you be thinking Stella."

This news even shocked Simon who dropped his arm and took a step back away from her, "Tonight?"

"By George, what a splendid idea", Mr. Bishop chimed in deftly ducking his wife's fan.

Caroline began crying softly into a monogrammed handkerchief, as if Simon were breaking off her own engagement.

Kate grabbed John by the hands and danced a few steps in excitement, "Oh, how wonderful. Imagine a wedding."

She stopped dancing long enough to whisper earnestly to John ten years her senior, "When I am quite grown up, I would like you to take me to America. It must be a very romantic place to affect my sober brother this way."

"Does this mean you won't need your coat, sir?" Alfred asked, rolling his eyes at his betters. He never had understood how the upper class could possess all that money and not a lick of common sense to go along with it.

"I'll go fetch the good Father right away", bobbed Maggie on her way out the door.

Sarah was panicking. "Warrior, do something."

He turned a scowl on her fierce enough to melt the ice caps off the Swiss Alps, "Apparently I am doing something."

Then, kissing the back of her hand in a resigned fashion with only his eyes betraying how thoroughly trapped he really felt, he added wryly, "It appears sweetheart…what I'm doing is getting married."


Two hours later, sipping sherry from the finest cut crystal, Sarah stared down at the large emerald ring sliding around on her left hand. She was married. Hesitantly, she peeked up at the stranger who was now her husband as he secretly slipped a note into John's hand whispering intense instructions.

So many secrets between the two of them and yet here they were tied together by one twist of fate. Watching Simon replace his glass and head her direction, she wondered why someone in England would want to be involved in America's war badly enough to kill for it. Behind her handsome husband's easy smile hid a man obsessed with finding out who. Yet although she tried to deny it, she read loyalty there as well and she accepted the fact that by taking vows both his secrets and his loyalties were now hers to protect.

Reaching her, he yawned and gently took the empty glass from her shaking hand. "Have you ever had a drink before?"

Feeling suddenly shy, she rubbed her sweaty palms along her silk jacket. The man unnerved her. "No. I do not think it agrees with me. I dislike the taste."

"Yet you drank an entire glass."

His knowing grin spoke volumes. How she wished she were not so open with her feelings. Grandfather said it made one vulnerable. It certainly was proving true as far as her new husband was concerned. Rather than make up a more dignified response, she chose the simple truth instead. Her chin raised a notch, daring him to mock her, "It seems to possess a calming effect."

Looking down at her through dancing green eyes, he lifted her chin with one finger and placed a light kiss to her moist lips. "There are times when I admire your refreshing honesty. I think you may make an honest man out of me yet, love."

Trying not to think how his casual touch affected her senses, she looked awkwardly around the room. Her eyes slid automatically to the pistol just inside his coat. She cocked an eyebrow. No doubt she would miss more sleep this week. Did the man have a death wish?

"Grandfather says a leopard never changes his stripes, no matter the cage."

"It has spots, not stripes. Am I bothering you again sweetheart?"

Momentarily confused, she dismissed his correction with a wave of her hand. "You cause much confusion for me. The point is you lied...again...only this time to the holy man. I fear for your soul Englishman."

She couldn't believe he actually winked at her, before nodding a farewell John's direction, "Hate to point it out wife, but it looks like I have corrupted you as well."

He really made her angry sometimes. "For your information, husband," she too stressed the word that bound them together, "I did not lie."

His smile instantly vanished and for once his usually steady nerves failed him, very deliberately he sat down his glass on the serving cart, "What do you mean by that little statement?"

The look in his eyes frightened her, so she raised her chin in defiance, "I said I meant every word. Grandfather says to lie to a holy man would be to take up an entire page of wrongs in the angel's black book."

"I don't care what 'Grandfather' says, in a few months, after everything dies down, we go our separate ways. I, to mourn my lovely young bride's early demise, and you, back to America a few thousand pounds richer. We have an agreement."

"You have an agreement, Englishman," She muttered under her breath.

"What did you say?"

He didn't look in the mood to listen to her explanation about honor and losing face. Besides, he would never understand her truth. For regardless if she left or not, they would always be married in the only place it counted...her heart. All she knew was truth, loyalty and faithfulness; how to keep one's word. Apparently in England, those things did not exist. But in her world they did.

"Sarah I asked you question."

Thankfully she was not forced into a public display of anger with him for Simon's father came up and swallowed her up in a bear hug at that precise moment. If she hadn't known better, she would have sworn it was his intention to rescue her. "I just wanted to congratulate you for capturing Simon's heart. To be honest I didn't think it was possible," he winked, "that he had one that is."

Sarah laughed. She believed she liked this man much better than Simon. She bowed to honor him and warmed instantly when he bowed back. "At times I too have wondered the very same thing."

The large handsome man let out a loud bark of laughter.

"Simon, I like her."

She felt Simon's eyes on her and saw something in them that resembled a grudging respect. "As a matter of fact father, I like her too."

She must still be in shock because her hand trembled and her insides rolled over in reaction to the deep timber of his voice. She believed she liked his dishonorable side better, this warm charming side made her extremely nervous.

Giving Simon a sound whack across broad shoulders and wiping tears of laughter from his eyes he added affectionately, "Why don't the two of you slip upstairs? You have to need a little privacy by now. After all, it wasn't too long ago your mother and I were first married you know."

Sarah could have kissed him. She was so weary. Still, as weary as she was her grandfather had to be more so. "I sincerely thank you sir, but of course Grandfather must have his hot green tea first and a warm place to sleep. Perhaps if it would not be too much trouble, we could sleep in the small house out back tonight. Tomorrow we can begin our new duties and not be such a burden on you."

Bushy gray eyebrows rose in amusement, "Are you talking about the carriage house?"

Simon groaned. If he didn't get her out of here fast, she would next be offering to rub down the horses. "Very amusing Sarah, but your grandfather is probably already asleep in the room across from ours. We'll send Maggie up with some hot tea if you like. What do you say we call it a night sweetheart?"

Her knees grew weak when in a horrified voice she croaked, "Ours? You mean the two of us? Share a room?"

Simon's father cleared his throat uncomfortably, "Well, I'll see you two in the morning. Sarah, it has been a pleasure."

She barely nodded. No, she was much more preoccupied with this new development. She slowly sank down on the sofa. How could she have forgotten? This was her wedding night. Not that she had a clue what that meant exactly. And she very much doubted she wanted to know.

She grabbed a full glass of sherry off a passing maid's tray and downed it in one huge gulp. Her body, unused to such abuse rejected the idea by refusing its entrance, closing her throat. Sputtering and coughing loudly as the burning liquid slid down her clenched throat, Sarah reached out an arm as if for help. She had never drunk anything in her life and this glass was the second and likely to be the last time she did.

"Sarah, I think that is enough sherry for tonight." Even though Simon patted her back until her coughing subsided, it was not in sympathy.

Wishing to not be alone with her now even more irritated husband, Sarah suggested frantically, "Are you certain Grandfather is all right? Perhaps it would be best if I shared a room with him tonight. By tomorrow I could help clear out an extra bedroom for me to use since one is not prepared."

"Sarah, shut up."

It was then she noticed most of the room was staring their direction.

No doubt trying to save face, Simon gave a forced laugh before commenting dryly, "If you will all excuse us, I think I'll take my wife upstairs."

"Do you have to?"

She looked scared to death. Simon's shoulders relaxed. He had nearly forgotten she was an innocent. Or that they barely knew each other. Still, he couldn't help the enjoyment he got from making her nervous for a change. Oh, he fully intended for nothing to happen between them tonight, but apparently she didn't understand how thoroughly trapped he would be if it did. So regardless the temptation she was, he valued his freedom more. She was in no danger from him. But she didn't know that.

Placing a hip on the arm of the sofa, he leaned down to whisper in her ear, "Do you know that when you blush, the freckles on your nose stand out?"

The English air must be suffocating, because she was finding it hard to breathe at the moment. She quickly scooted away and struggled to rise from the sofa holding her captive in its cushioned softness.

Pleased with himself, Simon stood with a suspicious grin on his face and offered her a hand up, "Ready, sweetheart?"

Flustered, Sarah gave up her struggle with the sofa and nervously started drawing rings around the top of her empty glass. She totally ignored his hand, while trying to think of a way out of going somewhere else, anywhere but upstairs with Simon.

Simon was once more floored by her unpretentious beauty and innocence. Until now he wouldn't have believed any women capable of bravery or honesty, much less both those traits. For even now, her emotions were open and readable. She was scared to death. It was refreshing to say the least.

But she was right about one thing. Sharing a room tonight was a bad idea. After all, how in the world was he supposed to stay away from her during the few months of their sham marriage, if he had to sleep not two feet away from her innocent beauty?

He shook his head at himself. To hear him talk, you would think he had never been tempted by a beautiful woman before. Golden brown eyes looked imploringly up at him, taking his breath away. He reached down and pulled her to her feet. If he didn't start showing some self-restraint, their fate would be sealed. And he wasn't quite ready to settle down yet, even with his China bride.

Avoiding his intense and curious gaze, she stammered, "I feel most tired Warrior, perhaps we might do this another time."

He tried to keep a straight face at her slip of the tongue, "Funny, you don't look tired."

"Well, I am," There was a stubborn look of panic and determination, "Please let the other English know I require rest now."

"You know, I feel a little tired myself. I think I'll join you."

"No!" She realized she had shouted the word when Mrs. Bishop gave a worried look their direction.

Lowering her voice, she hissed at him, "You have no honor whatsoever do you."

It was a statement not a question.

He reached down and removed the glass from her clutched hand and placed it on the table, his fingers lingering a moment longer than necessary on hers. He was so close she could feel his breath on her cheek. It smelt slightly of expensive smoke and brandy. A shiver went down her spine when he whispered, "It's time to go, China."

Unbidden thoughts of the night ahead and days ahead as this man's wife nearly sent Sarah running from the room. However, all she said was, "I suppose I have no other choice."

His unbridled laughter rang out at his much too honest wife. "Afraid not. It being an English custom and all."

She nodded, and as if going to her execution followed Simon upstairs.

If only her grandfather had not insisted on leaving soon after the wedding to retrieve their luggage from the Irish priest, who had befriended them on the trip over. And now, he was sound asleep when she needed him the most. How she missed his wisdom and gentleness. Amid everything crazy in her life, he had always been her stabilizing factor.

Soon the warrior would lay claim to her body and soul, as was his right. Still, it frightened her beyond words. Her husband was little more than a stranger. If only she would have spoken up and told the truth or, at the very least, not repeated the vows binding her to him.

"Sarah?"

Her frightened eyes jumped to her husband's worried expression, "Is something the matter?"

She took a deep breath, shaking her head in hesitant denial.

Feeling slightly guilty for teasing her, when he spoke next it was with a sad sort of sympathy. "I have found a strange way to reward you for saving my life, haven't I? Let this be a lesson to you. The next man God puts in your way, don't' ask questions, shoot him."

Even though his voice was filled with sarcasm and regret, Sarah found it as soothing as the ocean on a clear day. No longer did she feel so frightened, so alone. She tried to ease his feelings of regret. After all, none of this was either one of their faults really. One could not always control the powerful adversary 'Fate'.

She gave him one of her warm smiles and his shoulders relaxed. Clasping her cold clammy hand in his he grasped the door handle of their room, preparing to go in. Comrade souls in the trick destiny had played on them.

They never made it inside.

Kate and his mother chose that precise moment to emerge from their rooms before heading back downstairs to the others. Kate, the blood hound, zeroed in on them, "My heavens but you're going to bed early it isn't even eleven o'clock. Why, we were going to play a little backgammon. You two couldn't possibly be tired yet, why don't you come back down with us and..."

"Katherine Ann leaves your brother alone. If he says he's tired then he's tired," her mother announced.

Perplexed why Sarah had gone from gray to a flaming rose color she argued, "But Mother I hardly think Sarah should have to leave the party."

Simon was crushing Sarah's hand. "Kate sometimes I think you must be as dense as a post. This is my wedding night. I don't have to be tired to go to bed." Although he said the words in a harsh whisper, Sarah could have sworn everyone in the parlor downstairs heard him.

"Ohhh." Understanding exploded in that one drawn out word, then her face flamed a bright red to match Sarah's.

"Now if you will excuse us, it has been a long day."

"Of course, son."

Simon could have sworn his mother was grinning and counting months till a grandchild as she exited down the hallway, a noticeable jaunt to her step.

There was no help for it now. Sarah would be mortified. Whatever short truce they had reached was gone. Both grew extremely quiet once inside the ominous bedroom. The bed loomed threateningly at them from the middle of the room. Simon meanwhile had mixed emotions as he set about lighting candles and turning down bed covers. He barely restrained himself from walking over and kissing her trembling bottom lip. Just to ease her mind of course. On the other hand, it might have the opposite effect. Still, he barely knew her and if he didn't do something to change her mind about those silly vows downstairs she would not help him keep his distance.

Simon bolted the door.

She jumped. It was then he knew how to solve the problem of her page in the angel's black book. It seemed there was something she was more afraid of than not keeping her vows…him. She just needed to be reminded of what being married really entailed, an insight on the more intimate aspects of the deed.

Sarah tried to concentrate on her surroundings, anything but the strong virile man only two steps behind her. But the room was as magnificent as its owner. The wood floors polished so brightly they could have been used for a mirror. The furniture was heavy and dark. Well made. The whole room spoke of brooding masculinity. Even the deep blues and browns added to the strong feel of the room. Much like the man himself, the room made her feel protected and safe.

Her eyes stopped on the massive object taking up most of the room.

It was all safe except for the bed, of course. It made her feel anything but safe.

It loomed in the center of the room, a threat or a promise she couldn't decide which. She only knew that at all costs she must avoid its clutches. She turned a forced smile on Simon.

"Where do I sleep?"

He removed his jacket. "In the bed."

"Oh", she breathed, watching him throw the expensive jacket carelessly across the foot of the bed. She didn't care one bit for that gleam in his eye. "Then, where do you sleep?"

"With you." He had to turn away, so she wouldn't catch his grin.

Her heart was pounding so hard, it hurt. Surely he didn't expect her to just…this was taking things too far. "Simon, I do not think it is wise to share a bed until we know each other better. After all, one should never enter a river unless he expects to swim."

He unbuttoned his top button. "Oh, but I plan on…what is that you call it? Oh, yes, swim."

Sarah gulped and took a step back, tripping over the heavy floor rug and falling backwards onto the bed. He advanced like an army.

"Well, I don't!"

"You don't what sweetheart?"

By now he was leaning over her, their lips nearly touching. Without even thinking, Sarah automatically bunched up a right fist and landed a backhand to the side of his head that knocked him instantly to the ground at her feet.

He was not happy. Now he looked even more determined than ever.

"Warrior, wait. I can explain."

She realized her mistake right away when he looked up at her, still rubbing his sore jaw. He was furious. She looked around for an escape route. She hurriedly swung off the other side, while trying to explain. "You were going to kiss me."

"I wasn't aware it was a crime. Besides...I thought you wanted to be married...wanted to keep your vows. Well, sweetheart, kissing comes with the territory."

He was coming around the bed for her now and she knew if he got much closer he would have the advantage. "Stay away from me, I warn you."

"Sarah, you're being hysterical. If you would just calm down for a minute, I could talk some sense into you."

When he rushed her, she moved deftly to one side, grabbed his arm and flipped him into a wall. She wasn't sure who was more shocked by her actions, him or her. He looked at her from dazed pain filled eyes as he slowly slid down the length of the wall...and passed out. Oh, heavens, this did not look good.

"I warned him," she whimpered at the accusing room.

In dismay, she bit her bottom lip at his prostrate form on the beautiful blue vine rug at her feet. She had tried to be careful but what if she killed him? She collapsed to her knees and searched frantically for a pulse. Finding one, she expelled a rush of relieved air that lifted feathery bangs off her forehead.

Thank goodness she hadn't killed him.

Now that he was no longer a threat to her, she absentmindedly brushed a strand of brown hair from his quickly swelling left eye. She didn't quite understand why she felt this maternal love for him. She supposed it was like that tiny kitten she had rescued from an alley one day. Perhaps, when you took care of things, it made you protective of them.

"I am deeply sorry Warrior for throwing you into the wall."

Then it hit her how ridiculous that sounded. The truth was she wasn't sorry in the least.

He deserved much worse.

Still, when she looked down at the features she was beginning to know so well after days of following and protecting him on the ship, she regretted having to hit him. And shameful as it was, the truth was...she had wanted him to kiss her. Maybe that was why she hit him so hard.

She shivered. All the time growing up on the streets of New York she had never been attracted to a man. Many had asked her grandfather for her hand in marriage, but he always refused. Yet, tonight, for some perplexing reason he not only agreed to her marriage, but left her to Simon.

Her eyes strayed to his split upper lip. Her finger glided lightly over the puffy cut.

Standing, she walked over and gathered a pillow off the rumpled bed and laid it underneath his head. Then dragging off a thick brown covering, she placed it over his fully clothed body. That would have to do. After all, she couldn't very well call someone. What would she say? That he had tried to kiss her? And she had knocked him out? She groaned in embarrassment.

As little as she knew of such things, she was fairly certain no one knocked out their husbands on their wedding night.

Walking a little unsteadily to the window, she pressed her forehead against its open shutter. "Oh, Grandfather what am I to do now?"

Suddenly the cold green eyes from her dream seemed to materialize in the reflection of the glass. Reminding her why she had come here in the first place. She stepped back frightened. Strange how much stronger the dreams had become on the ship. Lately, it was as if they were not dreams at all but memories.

How was she to find herself and her past when this man lying at her feet confused her so? She wasn't even sure who was more dangerous to her right now, the phantom from her dreams or him.

The pieces of her night terrors resurfaced trying to form a picture she had long ago rejected. Unbidden, she could picture the ship that night. How clearly her mind's eye saw its huge swollen side weather-beaten and massive. She even felt the same paralyzing fear again.

Looking out over the dark manicured gardens, she whispered in agony, "I wish I would have never come back to this place."

For deep inside, although she knew that once before she had fought the demon and won…this time she might not be so lucky.

# Chapter 4

Sometime before dawn, the dream awoke her.

Sitting straight up, heart racing and sweat clinging to her body, Sarah tried to focus on her breathing in order to calm herself. This time the nightmare was even more vivid and real. The echo of a woman's anguished scream still rang in her ears. The smell of blood filled her nostrils. In every fiber of her being she felt the horror of the dream.

The sound of Simon stirring into wakefulness beside her, forced Sarah to quiet the sobs racking through her being. Wiping at the salty tears streaming down her face, she rose from the bed and stepped over the man snoring softly on the floor.

Grandfather would know what to make of this latest dream.

She padded across the hall in bare feet, the cool floor helping to rouse her further from her dream state. Knocking softly, she eased the door open whispering, "Grandfather?"

His voice sounded calm and awake. No doubt, it was because he had risen more than an hour ago, as was his habit. He said that every day was heaven's gift to us, a chance to begin again, and he never wanted to waste one moment of its glorious welcoming. "Yes, Little One?"

Relief washed over her as she sailed across the dimly lit room, the soft colors of dawn beginning to wash over its interior, and into his waiting arms. He held her quietly while she wept, not bothering to say anything, instinctively knowing her need. Finally, her weeping ceased and she smiled tenderly up at him.

The familiar heart warmth touched his spirit. He would never stop feeling amazed at the gift she was to him. She was a beautiful English child and not just because she belonged to him. Perhaps it was because the God of all things had given her such a good and loving heart. For his people did not ordinarily see beauty in the foreign devils. Supposedly only the children of heaven were beautiful.

However, two cultures wrestled within his breast; those of his Irish ancestors and those of his Chinese mother. And throughout his travels he had found that true beauty came from inside a person. That was why the essence of this young woman's spirit before him, being one of kindness and generosity, made her a beauty in any culture. Both were a rarity.

He patted her hand and waited.

"The dream woke me and this time I realized it was no dream at all, but rather a memory."

"What was different this time Little One?"

"My mother. I know now why I have forgotten my past life." Sarah gulped in air to force the tears back down, "Oh, Grandfather, the man with green eyes killed her. I watched her life blood flow from her body."

Realizing her grandfather was not surprised by this new revelation, she sat back on the bed and stated calmly, "You knew."

Slowly pouring her a glass of water from the pitcher by the bed, he answered, "I felt this to be true but, no, I did not know for sure."

"Then how did you..."

He sighed. "I think it is time to tell you about that night eight years ago when the God of all things entwined your destiny with mine."

She wasn't sure if she wanted to know. Something inside her churned and she felt nauseous. "I am afraid, Grandfather."

"You are afraid only of the unknown, child."

Knowing he was right, but feeling still the evil of her dream, she nodded with uncertainty. For she trusted his wisdom...relied on it...yet what he proposed frightened her.

Knowing no other way to calm her fears, he began. His voice was low and soothing as he took her back in time to that night long ago. Back to a man he had fought and the loss of her destiny. When he was done the sky was full of glorious golden light, the moon giving way to the sun's superior strength. "So you see Little One, I feared the worse for those you loved. The man I fought embraced evil and his own desires. And I felt you were the final obstacle in his way. I could only pray my instincts were wrong."

"But, they weren't."

"No."

It seemed ironic that just when the sun filled the sky with red's and oranges, she should feel such a loss. "Now that I know my parents are dead, there is nothing to keep me here. I think we should leave this place. If what you say is true, he will not rest until I am no longer a threat. Without any memory of him, I have no way to protect myself."

Rather than agreeing with her, he led her over to the door and kissed her forehead. "Perhaps, or it could be the very time to face your enemy. There is much we still do not know. However we will speak of this another time. For now you should go back to your husband before he awakens.

Her husband... She had nearly forgotten. With a groan, she sagged against the door and admitted sheepishly, "I have to confess something Grandfather."

"Yes?"

"I believe my husband will not be pleased with me when he awakens."

"And why is that granddaughter?"

"I became nervous last night and...well...I might have overreacted."

A twinkle entered the old man's eyes. "In what way, Little One?"

"I threw him into a wall."

In the shadowy light she could have sworn she saw his lips twitch.

"This is not a good thing."

"No. And one other thing..."

"There is more?" The old man was grinning now.

She heaved a huge sigh. "After I knocked him out, I noticed his eye looked swollen. I am afraid I gave him a black eye."

"This too is not good. You have caused your husband to lose face."

The irony was not lost on her. "I know. Anyway, I think maybe we should get ready to leave this place. I doubt my husband will want such a wife. If we leave now before he awakes..." Simon's dazed, angry expression rose up in her memory and she grimaced.

Unperturbed, the China man opened his door and gently shoved her through it, "Oh, I think you are wrong Little One. I have seen the way this man looks at you. It is not the look of a man who wishes you to go."

"But, Grandfather, you did not see the anger in his eyes."

"Run along child, and remember that a humble spirit can cover many a wrong."

She very much doubted anything would erase the fury she glimpsed on her husband's face last night. Still she had learned long ago not to argue with her grandfather. He always won.

"Good day child."

"Good day Grandfather."

She passed his door three times, trying her best to build up courage to face the warrior. The bedroom loomed threateningly before her. If only she had some sort of gift, a peace offering.

Not wanting to return without one, she decided to go down to the kitchens and find...something. Then after her warrior calmed down, she would explain about her views on marriage and kissing. How she needed time to adjust. She shivered. Surely even an undisciplined Englishman would have to understand so simple a request. At least she hoped so. Otherwise the nights would become very long indeed for the both of them.

In much better humor once making a decision, she whistled softly to herself as she skipped barefoot down the massive staircase. Then, stopping half way down and looking around to make sure no one was watching, she did something she had wanted to do ever since first entering the beautiful townhouse. She placed a shapely backside onto the thick walnut railing that curved gracefully to the floor and sailed the rest of the way down in youthful exuberance. The grin never left her face. Even when landing in a heap at Albert's dignified feet.

She simply brushed herself off, with a cheerful, "Good morning Albert." Then, she continued onward to the kitchens.

She never even saw the butler's most undignified twitch of a mustache or heard the soft humming of a Welsh tune from his boyhood as he went to wake the rest of the household. His own restraint sorely tested by her cheerful optimism.

Unfortunately, the warrior seemed impervious to the very same cheerfulness when she entered their room an hour later, placing a steaming plate of scrambled eggs and kippers before his bloodshot eyes.

"For heaven's sake, what are you trying to do, kill me? Get that awful stuff away from me. What time is it anyway?" He bellowed, before wincing with pain and grabbing at his aching head.

It was then he slowly opened one bloodshot eye to peer out at her, "Do I know you?"

"Rather well I'm afraid."

Then recognizing it was not some servant, but his new 'wife' standing there smiling down on him, he glowered back at her sunny smile. Lowering his voice to a whisper, he groaned, "Then maybe wife, you can tell me why I feel like I've just been in a fist fight with the reigning champion."

Sarah gave a sheepish shrug, holding out the peace offering once more. "Are you sure you wouldn't care for some breakfast Warrior?"

She saw the fog lift from his expression, as dawning irritation made him scowl darkly her direction. No, doubt the memory of their wedding night was slowly but surely crashing in on him.

"Before you say anything, I wanted to apologize for…" her eyes skidded away from his swollen right eye. His other eye was no better. It flashed a warning that promised bodily injury if she continued.

"What I mean to say is that when you tried to kiss me…well, I panicked."

If possible his look darkened even more.

"There is no point in scowling at me like that. None of this would have happened had you not tried to frighten me." She pointed out accusingly.

He glared thunderously back at her. Then suddenly, as the smell of cooked eggs came wafting through his nostrils, his stomach churned threateningly. Throwing off the covers suffocating him, he decided to ignore her apology if you could call it that, and began searching the room for his boots.

"Frightened you? I must say you do have a way with words, China. But believe me, normally when I kiss a woman she actually seems to like it. Now get those eggs out of here, and tell Albert I need my horse saddled and ready in ten minutes," then lifting articles of clothing off the dresser he finally found the object he was searching for, his pocket watch. Nine o'clock. He had told John he would meet him at the Prime Ministers an hour ago.

"Wonderful," he growled, shoving the watch into his front vest pocket.

In aggravation he noticed she was still standing there watching him. Well, at least she had placed the eggs well out of smelling distance.

"Is there some problem with delivering a simple message for me?" He ground out between tugging on his boots and looking for the rest of his clothing. His stuff was everywhere. And his new wife stood there in her dressing gown like he owed her an explanation of some sort. He groaned.

Sudden realization causing him to drop helplessly on the bed and blow hot air straight upwards causing the stray locks of rumbled hair to billow outward. Who was he kidding? He owed her more than that. His memories of their hasty marriage and wedding night came flooding back into his pounding head. He winced. He couldn't believe he actually married the girl. What had come over him? Had he completely lost his mind last night?

He looked up just in time to catch her grin. His own answering smile was contrite.

"I glad you find this all so amusing."

She smiled openly now and handed the black jacket with one dusty shoe print stamped on the back to him. He stuffed an arm inside a sleeve, and then cocked an eyebrow at the sound of her snicker. "Now what is so funny?"

Her snicker burst into full fledge laughter when his blood shot eyes met hers, "Actually, I was thinking how you are just the sort of warrior I probably deserve. A grouchy rumbled one."

His intense storm colored eyes looked her over, from borrowed pink dressing gown to bare feet peeking beguilingly out at him. "And tell me, Sarah; are you just the sort of wife I deserve?"

She blushed and looked off, her pretty hands trying to find something to do in order to overcome her embarrassment. They finally settled on clasping themselves together in front of her gown.

He looked down in order to hide his grin. She was a pretty little thing and so down to earth. It was refreshing to say the least, a woman who actually spoke her mind.

"Perhaps I am. After all, I did warn you. You should have told your people the truth." She jutted her small chin proudly in the air, and added, "Last night would never have happened if you would have just listened to me."

"Listen to you?" His head was pounding so hard, his teeth hurt. No doubt all of England was involved in a war by now and she was lecturing him. "I did listen to you. Not to mention the biggest gossip in all London listened to you. Believe me, when you announced we were 'one' in front of a houseful of company I had little choice but to marry you. It was either that, or damages to both our reputations."

"So you spoke lies in order to appear more honorable?"

Her crossed arms and tapping foot forced him to say irritatingly, "You don't understand how it is here. There are certain expectations –"

Her look of disappointment made him blush. He tried again. "Certain people –"

Why did he feel so guilty? He shook his head in wonder at himself. Perhaps it was because she had a point. He despised the hypocritical ton. And now he had forced her to defend a principle he didn't even believe in.

She opened her mouth to argue. His raised a hand to stop her. "I really don't have time for this right now. I missed a very important meeting last night because of you. And now I am late to another."

That did it. Her English temper overrode her Chinese philosophy. All her good intentions of trying to make peace with her husband flew out the window. "Because of me? Was it my fault you dragged me out of the room before I could explain about our customs? Was it my fault that you lied not only to your entire family, but to a holy man, as well? Now, thanks to you, I will never get into heaven. You have caused me to lose much face in front of your people and all you can worry about is what other English pretenders will think?"

She was so beautiful standing there shouting at him, which he justly deserved, that she stole the very breath from his body. He stopped trying to excuse his behavior and just answered honestly, "You're right. And the truth is I don't know what came over me last night."

When he approached her, she took a step back, her eyes wary. Yet her entire being seemed to visibly relax at his admission. As if all it took was an apology to make up for forcing her into a marriage she wanted even less than he did. It amazed him how easily she forgave, the innocent trust still resided in her brown eyes.

Slowly, to avoid another panic on her part and a black eye on his, he reached out and pried loose the hand clutched so tightly at her left side. Gently he opened each finger, seductively placing a kiss to her palm when he was finished. He knew he was affecting her, because wonderment made her cock her head sideways, sending long loose hair spilling over one shoulder. He refrained from pulling her in closer, choosing instead to slip her hand into his.

The too big emerald ring slid sideways on her second finger, reminding him of the serious step they had been forced to take because of his work. If anyone were to ask him, he would have to admit he didn't even know this small, furious girl wearing his grandmother's emerald. He had never even met anyone quite like her and certainly never met her equal in a fistfight. He reached up to rub his right eye and winced.

She flushed guiltily. The strange new feeling he invoked, made her feel vulnerable somehow and uncertain. "I do apologize for hitting you. It was instinctive."

"Well, that kind of instinctive was not what I was shooting for. Tell me, do you plan on throwing me into a wall every time I try to kiss you?"

This charming side of him was worse than the warrior. She had no walls of protection against such onslaught. She tugged at her hand, willing him to release it. He didn't.

"I don't know. It just happened. I might as well tell you I have a tendency to do a lot of things without thinking them through."

"So I noticed."

Her calm amazed him. Even in the throes of a heated argument, she had not once raised her voice. Oh, there was no doubt she was angry. Her dusty complexion was flushed; her hand trembling as she tried once more to tug it free gave plenty of evidence to the fact. But she remained calm, her voice fairly even.

And she was getting to him again.

He ran a hand through his hair, expelling a pent up breath. "Look, I admit I tried to make you see how ridiculous you were being last night."

"Ridiculous?"

He didn't like the sound of her voice, it had the quality of a badger strangling to death. So she did possess a temper after all.

"Yes, ridiculous. We hardly know each other and agreeing to go our separate ways after a few months is the sensible thing to do. We both know those vows meant nothing to either one of us. Anyone with the least bit of common sense could see we're not really married, not in the real sense anyway."

"I see."

Reassured she sounded more reasonable, he continued, "Let's not complicate things anymore than is necessary by getting emotionally involved agreed?"

"Does this mean you won't try to kiss me again?"

He wished she hadn't sounded quite so pleased, "If you don't want me to."

"I don't."

"Fine. I have to admit being slammed up against a wall when I attempt the act is a bit unpleasant anyway," she tugged harder on her hand.

He responded by drawing her up against him. Whether it was male ego, or simply that she looked furious and beautiful, he really had no idea.

Her cheeks were now flushed; her golden brown eyes the color of warm caramel.

"Besides," his mouth moved in dangerously close to hers, his breath hot against her ear and a shiver went down her neck. "Like I said, I wouldn't want to complicate things."

"Complicate things?" she whispered back, the sound of his warm deep voice drowning out all coherent thought.

"I'm not that much of a cad. I hardly think ruining your life is fair repayment for saving mine do you?"

Sarah felt an odd tenderness. She supposed in a demented sort of way, he was apologizing. Feeling her relax against him, he stepped a safer distance away. Then, giving her a tired grin, he twirled the ring on her finger absentmindedly. They both turned serious, mesmerized by the object as his thumb pushed it back into place.

"Warrior...I must tell you something."

"My name is Simon, Sarah."

His voice sent a shiver of anticipation down her spine.

"All right, Warr...I mean...Simon," the name caressed her tongue before rolling out in a soft embarrassed whisper.

He was equally off balance.

Was her hair always that adorable and rumbled looking in the morning?

"China."

"It's Sarah."

He smiled and her heart stopped. Did he have to be so...so...charming?

The sound of a clanging tray broke the spell. Soon servant's voices rose up along with Albert's thundering tirade. When Maggie's blubbering apology tumbled on top of the butler's furious words, it became obvious that Maggie's aim off the balcony had hit its mark.

As the shouting intensified, it brought a questioning glint to Sarah's eye.

Simon sighed. "My mother has a soft spot when it comes to hiring servants. Apparently, she means to take on all the infirm ones. It's one of her most endearing attributes."

Sarah had finally managed to pull her hand from his and took a small step back, "I like your mother. Did you know she would like four grandchildren?"

He ran a finger along the inside of his suddenly too tight collar, "Let me guess, at breakfast."

She nodded. "Yes, right after she asked how well we slept."

He groaned. "I better have a talk with her."

Sarah handed him a comb. "Soon, I hope. I spewed orange juice across her nice lace tablecloth."

He laughed, one hand holding open the door, while the other ran the comb through his thick brown hair. "Good. Maybe that will teach her a lesson. Just do me a favor and at least for now, don't say anything to upset her. Meanwhile, I'll try and come up with some way out of this mess without killing her."

"You must love her very much."

He opened the door, waiting for her to exit ahead of him and answered honestly, "Yes, I do. I married you didn't I."

So as Simon hurried down the stairway and shouted for Albert, his words echoed around inside his wife. Because for some unexplainable reason, the same kind that causes you to jump a hedge when you can't see what's on the other side, she now found herself in a situation that frightened her more than any murderer.

She found she actually liked her husband.


"So dear, I thought that perhaps you and Kate might like to accompany me to the orphanage today."

"Mother, your know Dr. Hargrove said you weren't to go there."

Sarah noticed Stella's look of stubborn determination and wondered why Kate kept arguing. It must be an English custom to argue with their elders. Still, it was very disrespectful and Sarah shifted in her seat.

"I assure you that old fuddy duddy knows nothing at all about heart conditions."

"But, mother he said..."

She snapped her fan shut; her faded blue eyes full of pride and frustration. "Albert, please fetch the carriage."

When Albert's head rose in disapproval, Sarah could not sit still a moment longer. She quickly crossed over to her new mother in law, bowing in honor, before turning on the poor servant.

"In China a servant obeys orders without question, or loses his head. Perhaps here in England it is different?"

Albert's look of initial shock was quickly replaced by one of discomfort at being criticized yet he still didn't make a move to obey the order.

Sarah's eyes grew moist as she pleaded for understanding from the old servant. "I cannot understand why someone's life joy would be denied. Without purpose a person's spirit dies. Is it your wish to do such a thing to your mistress?"

The old servant stood stiffly. His war riddled body jerked as if she had struck him, the words striking a cord deep within him. If not for Lady Conway he would be at his daughter's house right now more dead than alive, wilting away in a broken down rocker. Instead, he had a job he loved.

His eyes shifted to Sarah's.

"I'll be right back my lady," he responded proudly throwing the doors wide, "Maggie, fetch our lady's porridge."

Sarah stifled a broad grin.

A warm hand reached over and squeezed her own, gratefully. "Thank you dear."

Surprised and touched Sarah smiled warmly in return, "I only spoke the truth."

"And I shall ever be grateful for a drop of common sense around here. Kate, go and make sure Maggie does no such thing as bring me porridge," she winked at Sarah, "I abhor porridge. And do point Albert in the direction of the stable."

The older woman's eyes, once full of tears, were now shining with excitement, "Come ladies, is it not a glorious day for an outing."

Even Kate was not strong enough to resist her mother's happiness, "So it is mother."

Riding in the open carriage a short time later with the warm August breeze pulling at their bonnets the three women sat in companionable silence. The orphanage was on the outskirts of London and Sarah was awed at the beautiful field of flowers on both sides of the road.

"I had no idea England could be so beautiful."

Kate who had been daydreaming about balls and handsome suitors waved away her compliment, "This is nothing. Wait until my brother takes you to Hilary's ball next week. Oh, you can't even imagine how glorious a ball can be. Why, the orchestra plays while men and women, looking like swirling bolts of satin and silk dance gracefully in each other's arms. Upon my word, their jewelry sparkles so brightly under the lights that it looks like the stars fell right out of the sky." She sighed heavenly and rested a chin on a gloved hand.

"Then, of course, a gentleman tries to steal a kiss on the balcony. But a lady must resist. Or sometimes, a lost love will suddenly appear and declare satisfaction for your honor. It's all terribly romantic."

Sarah didn't think it sounded very romantic to her. "I do not think I should like to be kissed. How far up is this balcony?"

Simon's mother answered automatically, "Oh, they are usually on the second floor overlooking the garden, why dear?"

"Well, if I am forced to throw men off of them I should hate to kill one."

Kate gasped in shock.

However, Simon's mother hid a smile and patted her hand consolingly, "Oh, don't worry dear. I am sure after you throw the first one over, amorous suitors won't be a problem. Besides, knowing my Simon, he'll probably shoot anyone who dares."

"Mother, I hardly think you should joke about such a shocking thing," Kate croaked. Then eyes wide with shock asked, "You wouldn't really throw a man off the balcony?"

Realizing she must have made a blunder and uncertain how to answer, she looked down in embarrassment and shrugged.

Simon's mother smiled warmly before saying matter of fact, "Why, of course she would dear. Any woman worth her weight knows how to handle a man...one way or another."

Sarah looked up in time to catch her wink.

The orphanage's large iron gate brought an end to discussions of balls and balconies. Its rusty unlocked gate shut tight. So, after waiting several minutes and no one coming to open it, a mumbling Harrison finally jumped down from the driver's seat. Swinging the massive thing back, Harrison eyed it a minute as if making a decision. Then instead of securing it, he ambled back at an awkward gait and swung himself up in the driver's seat, grabbing the reins in one fluid movement.

The gate was closing fast.

"Harrison, the gate!"

All three women watched in horrified silence as the massive gate began closing in on them. However, instead of jumping down and catching it, Harrison readjusted his top hat and shouted over one shoulder. "Hang on to your hats ladies."

Kate's screaming drowned out anything further he might have said.

With shoulders bent forward and whip cracking overhead, the groom shot the carriage forward as if they were in a starting gate at the races. Skirts billowed, hats flopped and lacy petticoats shot in the air as the three women were flung about like rag dolls.

"Harrison, stop this instant," Stella shouted angrily after just before being bounced down into the floorboard.

But, Harrison, who was well past the gate, now, seemed a man possessed. He raced forward over jarring bumps and thick limbs; even his top hat flying off didn't slow him down.

Sarah held on for dear life, one hand gripping the edge of the carriage, and the other searching for anything tied down. Apparently, the insane man fully intended to kill them. She only hoped Simon would remember his duty and take care of Grandfather. She squeezed her eyes shut as they brushed past a massive oak on two wheels. On second thought maybe she didn't want Simon anywhere near her grandfather. The English were crazy.

Opening one eye, she saw the old mansion looming ahead, and it definitely was not getting out of the way. Kate's screams were getting louder which Sarah wouldn't have believed could have been possible.

"We're going to die! We're going to die!"

Simon's mother, now on the seat, bounced around with one hand on her hat, "Katherine. Stop that shouting this minute."

Unbelievably, Harrison swung them around just in time to miss the massive structure and came to an earth-shattering stop perfectly aligned with the door.

Sarah looked at her mother in law's furious face...Kate sobbing softly across from her...and decided she just wanted out.

Harrison climbed slowly down and opened the door for them, proudly holding out a gloveless hand to assist them. Seeing him standing there so dignified with his thin flyaway hair the only evidence of their mad flight, Sarah wondered if she had only imagined the whole terrifying thing.

Lady Conway, her hat slightly askew, with dust covering her nice copper colored traveling dress took the hand offered her and exited the carriage.

The only evidence of her anger was the thin, tight way she held her mouth. Kate, on the other hand, hit at the man with her purse on the way past him. Sarah decided to get out on the other side without Harrison's help. Oh she had nothing against Harrison, she just didn't trust him.

Grandfather said some people were just born living in a world of their own making. And frankly, she didn't care for Harrison's. However, what really amazed her was how cool and collected Simon's mother seemed to be. After all, her groom had nearly killed them. Yet, looking at her calm exterior, Simon's worries about her fragile health seemed grossly exaggerated. Obviously, if she could survive her servants the woman was invincible.

Stella, pulling out a dainty white handkerchief, wiped at the dust covering her slightly wrinkled complexion.

"Harrison."

"Yes, ma'am?"

"You're fired."

"Yes ma'am."

With that out of the way, Lady Conway regally climbed the steps leading to the group of wide-eyed children and horrified nuns.

Harrison on the other hand seemed not worried in the least about being fired. He handed the young girl waiting by the carriage, the two baskets of fresh baked bread and sweet creamy butter. Then, mumbling to himself went in search of his hat.

Sarah forgot all about runaway carriages when she entered the orphanage's walls. And fell instantly in love. She loved every inch of it, from its drafty windows to its peeling wallpaper. The stairs creaked and the doorknob fell off in her hand, but she fell in love anyway. How could anyone not love a place full of children? She just knew that once Simon saw this place he would understand why it was so important to his mother to be here.

After hearing of his new wife's outing, he did understand…he understood he was going to throttle her.

When he arrived home to find they had all went for a drive, he felt a little aggravated. However, when Maggie blurted out the truth, that they were at the orphanage and Harrison drove them there?

He was furious.

He at once shouted for Albert whose only defense was some story about killing people's heart joy, whatever that meant. He didn't stop to find out, he simply ran out the door, grabbed Chancellor and raced through the woods, hoping to cut them off before they ever reached their destination. He cringed when he thought of Harrison's driving and wild dirty urchins clambering about his sick mother's skirts. What was she trying to do, kill herself?

In record time, he rounded a corner and entered the main road leading to the orphanage, where he found Harrison, walking the horses sedately towards him. He kicked his horse into a run.

The carriage was empty.

"Where are they?"

"Can't say as it's any of my business anymore, one way or another."

Simon gripped the saddle horn till his knuckles turned white. "I asked you a question man."

Harrison bristled and stared right back at him, "And I answered it."

"Harrison, so help me..."

The threat lay between them for a moment before Harrison shrugged and threw a thumb back behind him. "The orphanage, not that it's any of my concern anymore. No siree."

Simon wheeled his horse away from the carriage and ordered, "Turn this thing back around. I can't imagine what she's thinking sending you off like that."

"Can't do that, sir."

Perplexed and aggravated, he shouted, "And why, pray tell, is that?"

"She fired me sir."

"Again?"

"Yes sir."

"Well, I'm hiring you back. Now get moving."

Harrison began mumbling under his breath something about the gentry never making up their minds, as Simon raced forward envisioning his mother suffering one of her attacks as wild orphans circled around her.

What he found was a far different picture.

He saw Sarah first. She sat calmly on the sofa with clean quiet children at her feet totally enthralled. His mother, far from being disheveled drank tea and absentmindedly played with the bouncy curls of a two year old boy in her lap. The serene nuns were bringing out account books and more cookies for everyone. Even Kate, while playing hide and seek with twin boys, laughed gaily as they jumped out at her from behind a sofa.

A small girl with two front teeth missing caught his eye. She shyly stepped forward to present his wife a wilted and somewhat worse for wear yellow flower. It was the poorest excuse for the word flower he had ever seen. But, oddly enough, Sarah acted differently. She admired its delicate petals, all three of them. Then, she placed it carefully behind one ear. She looked like a vision from his dreams in her borrowed light green dress. Her hair hung down the middle of her back in soft light brown waves with the sun highlighting the blond streaks in its lush mass.

"Why are your eyebrows all wrinkled up like that?" asked the sweet little gift giver.

"Because she hates us," answered a nine-year-old boy who sulked in the corner.

"Oh," sighed the little girl sadly, "but, I was so hoping she'd like us."

Sarah gave the little boy one of her best frowns, before contradicting, "But, I do like you...very much."

He watched as Sarah tenderly gathered the sweet cherub and touched the few sprinkles of freckles across the child's nose, "Did you know that freckles are really angel kisses?"

The child's eyes widened, "Honest?"

"Well, that's what my mother use to say..."

Sarah's heart constricted with a longing deep inside. For until this moment that sweet memory had been buried beneath a wall of pain. It was overwhelming how many memories were surfacing since reaching England. That is, all but the one that mattered most. Which was who had destroyed her family?

She stroked soft freshly brushed hair. "Don't ever let people convince you your not loved. It simply isn't so."

The little girl pulled at her patched skirt, blue eyes filling with tears, "But no one really loves orphans."

She was breaking Sarah's heart. "That's not true at all. God loves every child, especially orphans. I shudder to think what would happen if I

79

got to heaven and then Saint Peter found out I actually frowned at one of His Little Ones."

The red haired boy, Donovan snorted in disgust, "God don't care what happens to us orphans. No one does."

The little boy's words touched a chord in Simon's heart. Apparently his young wife was just as affected. She quickly left the chair and bent down before the sullen child. Her heart in her eyes, Simon watched as Sarah looked down at her wrist. And after only a moment's hesitation untied some rough twine from around her wrist and held it out to him.

Funny, he had never noticed it before, but then again when would he have? The first time they met he was about to be killed and the second married.

Donavon looked at her like she had lost her mind.

All the occupants in the room watched in fascination as the beautiful woman in the elegant gown knelt before the skinny freckled faced boy, scowling down on her.

"A long time ago, I was an orphan too. I remember how very scary it was to be all alone. And even when the God of all things sent my grandfather to me, I felt in my heart of hearts, he too would leave me."

The little boy's gray eyes shone with unshed tears.

Simon, fascinated now, watched as she captured his attention with the sincerity and openness of her words. The elegant lady, who he had trouble recognizing as his wife, ran her delicate fingers back and forth along the rough twine at her wrist.

"To make me feel better, my grandfather gave me this."

She once more held up the small-corded twine.

With arms crossed the boy backed up a step. "But, that's just a stupid piece of string."

She cocked an eyebrow at him and whispered almost reverently, "I guess you could say that. But to me, this is a special sort of string."

And somehow Simon believed it, and from the looks around the room everyone else did too. Maybe it was the tender way she stroked it, or the pride in her voice that convinced them.

"See, a long time ago, my great grandfather left his family to travel to China. In China, he met a beautiful Chinese girl and they fell in love. However, her father hated the foreign devils, which is what he called all white men, and refused to let them marry. Still, so great was his daughter's love he knew she would run away. So, he decided to prevent that from happening. Each and every night he would tie her to the bed."

Kate, who had inched up closer dropped to the sofa with a horrified whisper, "How awful."

Sarah looked over with such sweet compassion and acceptance on her face it took Simon's breath away. "It was his way to try and hold on to something that did not belong to him, as we all do."

"Then what happened?"

"My great grandfather offered to work for her hand, but that too was refused. Instead of his heart softening towards the young man, her father's great hate grew greater. Sadly, hate has a way of destroying not only its enemy but the person who possesses it, as well. Finally, her father relented, but only on one condition. If my great grandfather would allow himself to be caned and if he survived, he could marry his true love."

Kate sobbed softly in the background.

"That night the girl begged her young man to run away, but he refused. You see love is very brave. And it never ever deserts us. So, when the sun rose the next morning, he was caned."

"Did he die?" came the boy's reverent response.

"No, he lived. But, he was very sick for a long time and when they left, he had to be tied on to a stretcher with the very same rope used to tie her to the bed."

The little boy's eyes went to the twine in her hand. "Is that it?"

"Yes, it is a very small piece of a much larger rope. You see this twine represents commitment and love. In a sense, it is the reminder of its existence. My grandfather tied it in his hair, and when I doubted his love, he gave it easily. I keep it tied to my wrist always, but today..." she gently tugged one of his arms free and solemnly tied it around his thin wrist, "you need it. To remember that great love does exist. And, by the way, you're wrong. God must love you very much, or I would never feel compelled to give this up. I guess in a way that makes us family."

Simon's knees went weak. He had already experienced firsthand the power of such a statement. He just hoped she only possessed one piece of string. If not, he would have to build a bigger house. The lady did not make those types of promises lightly. Their marriage was evidence of the fact.

Donovan looked down at the rough twine as if it were made of pure gold, then back at her with happiness shining from his once disillusioned eyes. "I won't take it off ever."

She hugged him close and whispered in his ear, "Oh, someday I hope you will…when the time is right."

Simon slipped out undetected. His anger had long since abated and in its place was a sense of wonder. Where did this girl come from? She was bright, confident, and yet so terribly innocent. To top it off she was the most honorable and noble person he had ever come across. He walked past Harrison and called up his black stallion, a fierce scowl on his face.

The scowl because he now knew, that no matter how hard he fought against it, his life would never be the same again.

# Chapter 5

Simon sighed deeply once reaching the townhouse. Sarah's grandfather, lost in thought, sat on the top steps writing away. Never mind that he had a perfectly fine library inside or that half of London must be wondering at the strange sight of the old Chinese man writing in ancient script on parched white paper outside his house. No doubt there would be quite a bit to explain once he found his way to his club: his hasty marriage, to name one. And, exactly how he proposed to do it was beyond him.

Simon paused just short of the man and cleared his throat.

The old man looked right past him deep in thought, a thick book balanced on his knees, while holding between sturdy teeth a quill that dripped ink onto his sleeve seemingly unnoticed.

"How are you sir?"

The older man held up the back of a gnarled hand, finished putting his thought on paper, then after several more guttural mutterings looked up as if in surprise to see Simon standing there. His alert eyes took in Simon's disheveled form and swollen right eye.

"Ah, my granddaughter's husband. I see you have not fared well your first day of marriage."

Out of reflex, Simon touched his tender eye, and then shrugged. Apparently the old man didn't believe in small talk. "We still have a few things to sort out."

Lee pushed the heavy book aside and motioned down beside him as he pulled out a small skinny pipe, "So it would seem. It is a rare English morning is it not?"

Simon grinned, knowing that it was indeed rare when the sun shone so warmly, especially the end of August. It had been raining on and off for the last three days. Realizing the old man was right about it being too lovely a day to go inside, he flipped his coattail out of the way and sat down beside him. Besides, whether he sat down or not he would never really belong to the ton, or care to.

"What are you working on?"

Heaving an aggravated sigh, the China man slowly blew on the paper to dry the ink. Then pulling out a small pouch filled his pipe with dried tobacco. "It is a book of my life's journey. Lessons learned. However, it seems one can do very little work in this place called London. It was the same many years ago. Your people choose to rush about, do they not? Strange how little of life they experience, and how much time is wasted in the pursuit of pleasure. It makes a soul most unhappy."

"Perhaps. But I have found New Yorkers just as aimless."

"Yes, I noticed this is true of many westerners. Most of your people do much and accomplish little."

"Is that in your book? If so, I assume you plan on selling it only in your own country. After all, we Englishmen prefer not to be lumped together with other westerners, especially Americans. Another flaw we have."

Lee chuckled, and carefully laid the page down with the others, before replacing the huge volume of History on top to keep the wind from blowing its pages.

"I think my granddaughter is wrong about you."

"Oh? In what way?"

Lee studied the young man over the top of his pipe. His hand steady as he put a lit match to the top and begin drawing air down into the cavity. After a few more seconds the pipe caught and he drew a contented sigh before continuing. "She thinks she has wounded your ego, and has forced herself upon you. She thinks that you would not want such a wife."

"And what do you think?"

Lee folded his fingers together and thoughtfully placed his chin on top, "I believe you are a man full of secrets. One who has seen much evil. A warrior, like myself. Therefore, one would think you were also a man who would recognize a rare treasure when he saw it. After all, only a foolish man throws away a gift like that. I do not believe you are such a man."

A carriage rolled past, as a well-dressed young woman with a feathered purple hat hung out the window, "Hello Simon, so nice to see your back."

A knowing look came to Lee's face, as he prepared to push himself up, "A friend of yours?"

Simon shrugged and offered a hand up, "A casual one."

"So I see. No doubt your marriage will break many a woman's heart. And cause Sarah much sadness as well. Your 'friends' will not be hers."

"I will protect her." But they both knew he couldn't protect her from feeling left out. She would never fit in with the artificial world of the ton. No, his wife was innocent in the ways of deception and pretense. And his peers will consider her lack of guile as a weakness.

Simon unclenched his fists. Somehow he would try and protect her from being hurt too badly by their pointed indifference. Besides in a few months both her and her grandfather could return to America where they belonged.

Another well-dressed couple strolled past, staring in fascination at the funny looking man rising to his feet. For some reason it riled Simon that his own kind would judge a man simply by the clothes on his back and odd habits, never mind that a few minutes ago he had been guilty of doing exactly the same thing. Suddenly feeling protective of the strange older man Simon offered his arm and started to steer him towards the door.

"You might find it easier to write in the study or garden. I usually do."

Lee stooped down to pick up his writing tools and Simon easily lifted the huge volume of history into his left arm. "I'll get that."

"I am most grateful my granddaughter's husband. However I must decline the offer of your library, since my writing goal is to see people as they truly are. To do so, I must sit among them. It is my way."

Simon's offered arm to the seemingly frail old man was waved aside as Lee took one last puff off his small pipe. Oddly enough Simon found himself becoming nearly as fascinated by the China man as his wife. The man seemed to possess an uncanny sense of being able to read a man's thoughts. And being a man of many secrets, Simon had learned long ago to steer clear of men like him.

"Did you get a chance to talk to Sarah this morning?  She seemed worried about you last night."

Lee raised a bushy eyebrow, "Really?  I find this odd.  For when I was younger and newly married thoughts of my family were drowned out by more pressing matters."

Throwing back his head in laughter Simon agreed.

"Well, I admit I did try to sidetrack her a bit."

"And?"

"And she threw me against a wall.  Did you teach her that little trick?"

"That and many others," he remarked calmly.  "She will take much patience.  But will bring much joy."

Once reaching the entranceway Simon waved the butler away and opened the door to the library.  Books lined the mahogany shelves, reaching all the way to the ceiling.  Several rung ladders were attached to rollers along brass railings providing access to precious cargo overhead.  The old man sighed contentedly.

"Perhaps I will consider your offer after all.  It is a rich man indeed who owns so great a source of wisdom."

Simon studied the little man standing in awe at the room of bound leather.  His graying hair held a tint of fading red, yet his eyes were slightly slanted in contrast.  And although his clothes spoke of a Chinese heritage his mannerisms were anything but humble.

Snapping open a cigar box intricately carved with a hunting scene of wild boars, Simon offered the man one but was refused.  He pulled one out himself and bit off the end.

"My wife says your father was a missionary."

"Yes."

"Did you meet my wife in China?"

Lee pulled out an edition on poetry.  "No.  Our paths crossed in an English ship yard."

Apparently he was a man of few words.  Simon tried again.

"I suppose you have been together for awhile."

"Eight years."

Lee laid down the thin black book, in order to pull out three more. Tired of games, Simon picked out two titles on history and piled them onto the other three in Lee's hands, forcing the man to acknowledge him. Their eyes met and held. They were two warriors, deciding if they could trust or not. After several seconds Lee nodded in approval. "You wish to understand my granddaughter, the way of her heart. Why?"

"I'm her husband."

"Perhaps, and perhaps not."

"What is that suppose to mean."

Lee liked the possessiveness in the man's voice. It was not the sound of a man who cared little for the treasure God had given him. The books were heavy. He placed them on the desk beside his own. "Now I will ask you a question. Why did you marry my granddaughter?"

"I think it's obvious."

"Not to me."

Simon could no longer hold that penetrating stare with his own. He carelessly dropped the unlit cigar down onto the ashtray resting on the massive desk and turned to look out the window. His mother's carriage was coming up the lane at breakneck speed. He really should do something about Harrison. When he turned back around the old man stood perfectly still waiting. "To be honest with you, I wasn't thinking properly. It all happened so fast."

Lee raised an eyebrow at the obvious lie.

Simon felt uncomfortable under that knowing look. With a sigh he answered truthfully. "For some insane reason, I am drawn to her. When I looked up and saw her standing there last night, I don't know if it was gratitude, or some misplaced sense of honor that drew me to protect her."

A slight smile graced the man's lips for just an instant before he added, "Or destiny perhaps. When you see the one chosen for you it touches you in a way not familiar to the mind. Love is seldom what we imagine."

Simon's head whipped around in surprise at his choice of words. Studying the man who seemed to see into his very soul, he reluctantly conceded, "Since I don't believe in Destiny, or love at first sight, I am leaning more toward insanity. But be that as it may, whatever occurred here last night apparently trapped the two of us, at least for now."

"For now?" Lee seemed to make up his mind about something. "I have much to think about and from the sounds I hear outside, this is not a time for speeches. However, tomorrow I should be greatly honored if you would show me this magnificent garden of yours. Perhaps I could give you some advice as well. After all, we too have many beautiful gardens in my country. Yes, there is much to teach you. Our ways do not usually cross paths. Yet the God of all things has deemed it to be so."

He cocked his head, studying Simon as if he were a science experiment. "Perhaps your heart is strong and it lies hidden under many years of broken dreams. Or, perhaps…my God has a sense of humor. Whatever the reason, I will teach you. Things such as what the bonding of a true person entails. For instance, when a true person makes a vow – to break it would be to lose one's place in heaven."

They both knew they were talking about Sarah.

Simon took a step back. When he did speak, it was with cool disdain. "That is ridiculous."

"Your church laws are so different then?"

The old man knew they were not. Feeling unfamiliar guilt, and the blind panic of a fox caught in a snare, Simon pointed out rationally, "No. But any sane person knows that there are exceptions to every rule. Loopholes."

"Ahh. This is how we differ. You see our marriages are made within ourselves. Not outside. Our own self respect guides our commitments."

What could Simon possibly say to that, without looking as dishonorable as he was beginning to feel? Giving a short nod, Simon responded with a cool English dismissal, "About two tomorrow then?"
Lee gathered up the heavy load of books and headed for the door. "Two will be fine. Tell Sarah I have need of quiet and will see her at dinner. Good afternoon, my granddaughter's husband."
"Good afternoon sir."

In amazement Simon watched the small man effortlessly carry his load up the stairs. He was reminded of the old saying that looks can be deceiving, he for one would never want to tangle with the man. He had the eyes of a seasoned soldier. One who had fought many a battle and won.

The sounds of his mother entering the hallway drew him away from his thoughts and back to the problem at hand, his wife.

"Oh, Simon dear, what are you doing home?" His mother's overly bright voice sounded extremely guilty.

"I live here, remember mother. Where have you been?"

Sarah rushed forward to sidetrack him. "Warrior, how was your meeting this morning? Was that Grandfather you were talking to?"

He might have thought she was really interested, had she not been motioning Kate forward to take his mother away. He tried to step around her. She quickly blocked his path looking like the innocent she wasn't. Still all he could think about were her grandfather's words and how she had looked comforting a little red-headed boy.

Did her eyes always contain those golden specks of light when she was up to something? "Sarah, you have to call me Simon in public, not Warrior."

Distracted by the tender way he was looking at her, she stammered, "Oh, yes. I will try to remember."

"So did you have a nice drive?"

The man never gave up.

"Yes."

"Where did you go?"

Seeing his mother was safely upstairs, Sarah bestowed on him one of the most bewitching smiles he had ever seen. It literally took his breath away.

"Well. I better go check on Grandfather."

"Sarah, I asked you a question."

She was now rubbing the back of her neck. As if he was giving her a headache, and not the other way around.

"Never mind. I am sure Harrison can answer my questions."

She closed her eyes as if in pain. She swore to herself she would explain about the orphanage later when he didn't look so...so very ominous towering over her. "I'm sorry Warrior but I really must change my clothes before trying to eat your English supper. It is a ritual after all."

His lip twitched at her insult to the rich food the hired chief cooked each and every night. Then before he could block her flight, she was gone. However, once she reached the second floor landing, she stopped. Spinning around, she called down to him. "By the way, I have decided that if I die, you do not get to keep Grandfather."

Then in an instant she was gone.

Simon shook his head in puzzlement. He believed it was going to take more than one walk around the garden to understand that wife's heart. And he probably never would her head.


Sarah didn't see Simon again until dinner. Kate came sneaking into her room shortly before going downstairs herself. She said she wanted to discuss how to keep their clandestine trip to the orphanage a secret. She made Sarah promise on a stack of bibles, that no matter how the two men probed she would not weaken. Sarah thought this a bit melodramatic. But since it seemed to pacify her new sister in law somewhat, she did it.

It seemed her sister in law's fears were valid after all, but not about Sarah. It turned out Kate was the weak one.

For a short time after they were seated at the dinner table, Sarah looked over at Kate and smiled. Unfortunately, when the young girl tried to smile back it came out as grimace instead. With eyes wide and guilty, she fumbled silverware and tipped over her brother's wine glass. The only thing she didn't do is stand up and confess her sins.

"Kate, have you taken leave of your senses?"

She jumped as if she had been shot. "I beg your pardon?"

"Whatever is the matter with you girl?"

Noticing Kate start to tear up, confession on her tongue, Sarah tried to save her from herself.

"We had a most interesting drive today, my husband's father."

"Really? How nice. Although, I hardly see what that has to do with Kate's …"

Simon sat back and took a sip of his wine, saying rather a little too causally, "What my wife means father is that Harrison very near killed them today."

"He what?!" Henry thundered.

"Now dear it was hardly that desperate."

"Stella, I will hear this out. What exactly did the man do?"

The question was directed at Sarah who looked over to Simon for help. She had thought this a safer subject. Perhaps it was not.

"I believe we were racing."

"For…who were you racing?"

"I believe the gate dear. Would you care for some more salt; this soup is rather plain, is it not?"

"No, I don't want any salt. The man was racing the gate? What is that suppose to mean? Stella, if you won't fire the man, I absolutely forbid you riding in another carriage with him. And that's final."

"Yes, dear. Simon you have hardly even touched your soup."

"I don't care for it. Sarah?"

"Yes, Warrior?"

Was he ever going to get use to looking at her? She was too beautiful for both their goods. He pushed back his soup. "Is there anything else you would like to add?"

Innocent golden eyes blinked once at him, before settling on her cold squash soup. "I don't believe so, but thank you for asking."

He nearly laughed she was so unnerved.

Once the entre' was served, it took exactly two seemingly innocent questions from Simon's father to 'weaken' Kate.

The duck was just being placed on the table in front of Henry when he looked up, asking casually, "So Stella where did you go today?"

"Why, nowhere really, we..."

"I assure you father we didn't do a thing wrong. Absolutely, not a thing."

Simon hid his smile by taking another sip of white wine.

Sarah rolled her eyes heavenward, so much for weakening. Sending her daughter a stern look to keep quiet, Stella patted her husband's hand to quell his suspicions.

"And how was your day dear? I noticed you and Simon spent the afternoon closed up in your study."

"Yes," he glanced over at his daughter who was shoveling food into her face, "Kate, you're going to be..."

"All right father, just stop hounding me. I admit it. We went to the orphanage today. Are you satisfied now? But, it certainly wasn't my fault; I tried to tell Sarah you would be displeased. That the doctor said..."

"Katherine Ann!"

"I know mother, but I just couldn't keep quiet a moment longer. You saw how he forced it from me."

Lee who had been silent until now spoke up, "It is difficult to hold a secret, in an open heart."

"See, mother. It wasn't my fault."

Henry leaned forward, looking for signs of stress on his wife. The only thing he read was exasperation. Satisfied she suffered no ill effects from her outing, he resumed cutting the meat. "Stella, you know what the doctor said."

If anything his wife's look became even more mutinous. "Now Henry, how could the orphanage possibly be bad for my heart?"

Sarah pressed her spine against the extremely straight-backed chair and waited for the ax to fall.

Simon watched her out of the corner of his eye.

"We have already discussed the matter. Under no conditions are you to go back there."

"But Henry..."

"I mean it Stella. I won't be swayed."

The duck looked less inviting after observing the stricken look on her mother in law's face. And that was even before Albert spooned a thick floury paste onto her plate. It took a moment to realize he must have picked up the bowl of cleaning paste by mistake. She pushed her plate away.

"If you will excuse me..."

Simon rose with her. "Sarah, I have to stop over at John's tonight. Would you like to go with me?"

Surprised and delighted by the unexpected offer, she was unable to conceal her true joy. Thankfully now she would be able to escape the reprimand no doubt headed her way. And be able to control her horrible habit of saying exactly the wrong thing.

It wasn't until Simon's hand encircled her own hand; that she realized maybe it wouldn't be such a reprieve, after all. They would be alone. And since she wasn't very good at deception...who was she kidding...she was terrible at it. She would be forced to talk to her husband. About all manner of things she had been avoiding. Not to mention that he might actually try to kiss her again which filled her with apprehension. So far the kissing idea had not gone well at all.

Feeling a bit nervous, she met her grandfather's eyes across the table in indecision. When he gave her an encouraging nod, she relaxed. If Grandfather approved of Simon surely he couldn't be as fierce and unbending as he seemed. Surely. Then throwing her shoulders back, she made up her mind to tackle her problems head on. It was not in her nature to avoid things after all.

Then as if on cue, Simon gave her hand a gentle squeeze. In that instant her usual optimism came flooding back. With newfound courage she decided a serious talk with the warrior might not be a bad thing after all. In fact, it was long overdue, especially if she wished to make this into a real marriage.

Unwelcome, Simon's words, 'for now', echoed in her thoughts, dampening her spirits. Her hopes that Simon would listen to her beliefs seemed as far fetched as her ever fitting into this way of life.

"Albert, why don't you stop trying to poison everyone and fetch the phaeton for us. I'll save time and get our coats."

Stiffening indignantly, Albert slammed the spoon back into the white paste, "As you wish sir."

Then Sarah watched in disbelief as the insulted servant turned right around and fetched a spittoon, holding it regally out to her husband.

Simon glared at him. "Do I look as if I need –"

He seemed to catch himself and mumbled something about wasting his breath, before pulling Sarah forward and walking in the opposite direction toward the back of the house. "Never mind. I'll do it myself. This makes me wonder mother, why we even have servants."

That said, he pushed Sarah through the door, and slammed it shut.

# Chapter 6

He hardly spoke to her as he harnessed the horses. Sarah started to ask him where the groom was, but was afraid of the answer. If he was anything like their other servants, he was more likely betting on a horse than taking care of one.

In a manner of moments they were headed down the dark street, with him at the reins. She watched the way he handled the black stallions and wondered what it felt like to have such power in your hands. An aching desire filled her so suddenly that it took her by surprise. How she wished someone had taught her to ride. Or, then again, maybe someone had and she simply couldn't remember. The feeling of wind pulling at her hair felt freeing. She closed her eyes and tried to imagine being lifted up on a horse by a faceless stranger before taking off across a daffodil covered meadow. The scent of leather and horse mingled with imagination so that it almost seemed real.

Except that it wasn't.

Tears clouded her vision for a moment before she forced the sense of melancholy such thoughts provoked from her mind. Grandfather said to worry about one's past only robbed one's present. Still, how could she have a future without a past?

"Simon."

"Yes."

"It was my fault your mother went to the orphanage today. I know I shouldn't have interfered but…"

She waited for his angry outburst. His lecture about how sick his mother was. Even for him to tell her none of this was any of her business. But to her amazement, he simply raised an eyebrow and commented matter of fact, "No you shouldn't have."

Clasping her arms for warmth, she stared over at the handsome man sitting so calmly beside her and couldn't think of anything else to say except maybe to try and explain. "If you could have seen how she looked when we got to the orphanage. She was actually beaming."

"I'm not angry with you Sarah. The truth of the matter is I haven't seen my mother this happy in months. Besides ever since the good Doctor diagnosed my excess of green peaches as the flu when I was eight, I have had very serious doubts about him. Tomorrow I'll talk to father and try and reason with him."

Was he actually teasing her? Sarah did not know quite what to think about this new Simon. Then when he turned those dancing green eyes her direction and winked...her own stomach churned as if she had eaten the peaches.

He was such a handsome man, her husband. It was odd, but at times she missed following him around unseen. For then she could stare at him as much as she wanted. And daydream. In her daydreams, she had imagined what it would be like to be kissed by him. Little did she know that her reaction would differ so greatly from her daydreams? And it didn't help that she had that incident on board ship to compare it to. No, he was right; most women like the beautiful passenger with auburn hair who had kissed him on deck of the ship one night had a very different reaction.

That night Sarah had pretended it was her he held in his arms. Her he spoke softly to with the deep timbre of his voice radiating all the way down to her toes.

Seeing her shiver and mistaking the cause, Simon removed his gray satin jacket and placed it around her shoulders, "Cold? I should have controlled my temper in there and fetched our coats. Sometimes I swear what Albert won a metal for in the army – was leaving it."

Sarah snuggled in his jacket with a smile. "He does seem to enjoy baiting you."

He whipped around in comradeship, "Exactly. And the sad part of that is, I half enjoy it myself. I suppose it is a stress release of sorts. If I had any sense at all I would dismiss the man."

"Your mother would just hire someone worse to replace him."

He grinned down on her, the cool wind blowing his dark hair partly free of its leather strap. "Which is precisely, why I don't. As the saying goes, 'better the devil you know, than the one you don't'. I'll tell you what, tomorrow why don't you and Kate go shopping for a few things. You can't very well traipse around in my sister's things for the next few months. And make sure you get a warm coat. It's cooler here than it is in America. The English winters are known for their bone chilling cold."

Right now, his voice alone was enough to heat her insides. It's deep timbre echoed right through her. She shook herself out of it. Was she totally insane? Here she was mooning over him and last night she wouldn't even let him kiss her. She had to get a hold of herself.

"Is everything okay?"

"What?"

"Well, you seemed lost in thought. Is something on your mind?"

She blushed guiltily as if he could read her thoughts, "No. I was just…well…thank you for your offer, but I cannot accept such a gift from a stranger. It would not be right."

"I'm not a stranger, China. I'm your husband."

The words stunned her. And the easy charm in which he said them was unsettling. She wasn't sure how to take this side of him. It was making her feel shy and ill at ease. So rather than argue or have those dark green eyes staring into hers again, she chose to pretend interest in her changing surroundings.

The gaslights of London were fast disappearing and soon the only light consisted of a half moon and a scattering of stars. They soon turned off onto a small country lane that ended at an old wooden bridge guarding a velvet looking brook. Both banks were covered in soft green grass, with daisies reflecting back a portion of the moon's gentle light. Sarah sighed contentedly. The fresh scent of flowers and clean water was a welcome relief from the stench of London.

There were no houses in sight so she was surprised when Simon pulled off the road, "Is something wrong?"

He took his time answering.

As he silently set the brake, she couldn't help watching in fascination as strong square hands wrapped the leather reins around the brake. "I thought we might spend a little time together. As you said, we are practically strangers. And if we are going to pull off this illusion of being madly in love, I think it would be a little more convincing if I knew more than your first name. To be honest with you, the last couple of days have been two of the strangest I've ever experienced. And frankly, between my family and your grandfather I really haven't had a chance to get you alone. So Lady Conway are you up for a walk?"

"We're not going to John's?"

"Afraid not."

"You lied again?"

"Yes, I did. But seeing as I am not a true person, as your grandfather says, it shouldn't shock you overly much, now should it?"

Her eyes were sparkling, "I suppose it shouldn't. You will never reach heaven at this rate, you know."

His easy laughter washed over her.

Simon felt himself instantly relax. "Oh, I gave up on that idea long ago. So, tell me Sarah…shall we start over?"

She blushed prettily as he bowed regally over her hand, softly placing a kiss to the back of her hand, "I would like to introduce myself. I am Sir Simon Conway recently returned from America. And unfortunately, you've already met the rest of my family."

No doubt about it. The man was extremely charming when he wanted to be. Looking down at his outstretched hand, Sarah hesitated only a moment before giving his an answering squeeze. Then as if it were the most natural thing in the world for her to do, she performed a convincing regal nod his direction. "It is a pleasure sir. And I promise I won't hold your family against you."

When he continued holding her left hand, she looked up to study his serious expression. "What are you thinking?"

About you, the thought came instantly to his mind. He loved the way she made him feel. How slowly but surely she was making him believe again. In such things as fairy tale love and the good that resides in people. And the knowledge that she affected him that way? Well, it scared the life out of him.

Which is why he was feeling trapped at the moment. But instead of telling her any of that, he pushed back the feeling of connection he felt when their hands touched and shrugged.

"Nothing...it's just that for a moment," he shook off the strange notion and quickly released her before climbing out of the phaeton and offering her a hand down. "Never mind. How about that walk?"

Simon swore her smile rivaled the moonlight.

"It sounds wonderful Sir Simon Conway."

The late summer night was full of crickets chirping, frogs calling their mates and lightening bugs. When they reached the middle of the bridge, Sarah stopped suddenly and pointed down at the water. "Oh look, isn't the moon the most fascinating thing you've ever seen."

No, you are. His treacherous mind shouted watching as she took the rest of the pins out of her windblown hair, letting it fall forward in a curtain of light when she leaned over the rough railing. He wasn't sure if he had ever seen anyone so content with life's simplest gifts. The moon's reflection shimmered in the ripples of the small brook, but it was her reflection he stared at on its watery surface.

"It always seems so close in the water, as if you could reach out and pick it up. When I was little I use to imagine that if I ever did it would melt between my fingers and splash out like shiny liquid silver all about me."

"And then what?" Simon grinned, leaning back on the railing on two elbows.

"Why, then I would roll around in it until I was covered in silvery light, just like the angels."

In fascination he watched as the moonlight transformed her into something that very closely resembled an angel. She began twisting her hair back up into a loose roll, with feathery curls escaping around her dusky face and down her slender neck. His sister's slightly short gown of pale pink muslin hugged her figure too tightly. She was enchanting and much too beautiful for both their sakes.

"Did I say something wrong again?"

"Of course not."

"Then why are you scowling at me like that?"

"I'm not scowling."

His voice demanded she agree with that absurd statement. Instead, she shrugged, "I guess living your kind of life doesn't allow much time for fanciful rolls in the moonlight."

When he didn't answer or follow her off the bridge, she turned to ask, "Now that I've met your family, I can't understand how you came to work for the government. It must disillusion your soul greatly to hold so many secrets."

He cocked his head sideways at her, "If I didn't know any better I would swear you were a philosopher."

She smiled and sat down on the bank. Her full skirt lay in soft piles around her. "I guess living with Grandfather makes me see things others miss." Taking off her shoes and stockings without a thought as to how this simple action affected him, she repeated, "Why did you choose this lonely path for yourself?"

He decided to stay put. She seemed to read him too easily, and never before had he felt quite so vulnerable. Pulling out a cheroot, he lit it slowly, drawing in the relaxing smoke before answering. "My father's partner was murdered when I was eighteen."

"How terrible for him, but I don't see..."

"My father was accused of killing him. Even his lawyer seemed to think he was guilty. Father was so distraught over it all he simply sat in his cell and drank. I think a part of him wanted to die."

"But, why?"

"I suppose because he felt responsible in some way."

She heard the hurt in his voice and her heart ached for him.

"What happened?"

Her soft whisper encouraged him to talk as he looked out over the water. "No one knows for sure. Apparently, my father was supposed to pick his partner up after a play on the way home from the office. There was some problem with the books and then his carriage threw an axle."

With a flick of a wrist, he flung the cheroot out into the water and leaned forward over the railing. He recounted yet again the events of that horrible night.

"Regardless, my father was late. By the time he got there, both his partner and his wife were dead. The next day it was discovered someone had stolen money from the business and tried to cover it up. It looked very much like my father had killed his partner to keep him quiet. At least that was the story in the papers."

A sense of foreboding was growing inside her.

"But if they owned the business that makes no sense."

"Actually, my father and his partner started exporting fine English china with the help of several investors. Needless to say, when it was discovered that there was not even enough money left over to cover wages for the crews on board ship, the investors were furious and demanded justice."

"It sounds more of revenge."

He looked away from the sympathy in her eyes.

"Yes, it was a witch hunt of sorts. And unfortunately, my father was too demoralized to fight back."

"So you fought for him," it was a statement, not a question.

"You could say I sold my soul to the devil. I agreed to work for the government in exchange for help in clearing my father's name. In a manner of weeks it was discovered that my father's partner was deep in debt to some heavy duty gaming halls. That he, not my father had stolen the money. My father was released from his bondage, but mine had only begun."

She drank in his defiant stance, the dark brown shirt molding against muscled shoulders and knew what his father's honor had cost him.

"And how much more do you owe the devil?"

He reacted with surprise at the fierce protectiveness in her voice.

"This is my last assignment."

"I am glad. It is wrong to use blackmail when another is in need."

"Too bad others don't share your philosophy. Anyway, it's all in the past now. My father went back to practicing law. And I am in the business of stopping a war. But," he strode over to where she sat. She in turn concentrated on trying to ignore the way his presence was making her heart race and her palms sweat, "the main reason for this kidnapping was to find out more about you, remember? So tell me, how did a beautiful American girl wind up with a Half Irish Chinese grandfather?"

If asked that question earlier, her answer would have been easy. However, the story of murder he told created havoc in her mind. There were way too many similarities to her own story. Too many details left unexplained. Before she could stop herself, she blurted out, "Did they have children?"

There was real fear in her question and instinctively he went down on one knee, "Sarah you look like you've just seen a ghost. What's wrong?"

Realizing her mistake at once, she averted her gaze and tried to sound less intense. "I'm sorry, it's just..." she searched for the right words to express her feelings without divulging too much, "I too lost my parents. When you asked about Grandfather, well, I couldn't help but remember how it felt to be alone in the world."

If he hadn't gone to the orphanage today, perhaps he wouldn't have understood. But he did. Visions of her compassion and sympathy for the Little Ones there was the reason he answered gently, "The couple that died had only one child, a little girl. Unfortunately, the men responsible weren't satisfied until they wiped out the entire family. The little girl washed up on shore the next week."

Her quick intake of air caused him to cup her face in his hands and gently turn her towards him. The tears in her eyes tore at his heart.

"I'm sorry. I should have shielded you from that."

He wanted desperately to ease her pain, to place his lips on the one she was biting this very moment.

She on the other hand, found something endearing about the way he was trying to comfort her. She felt not only protectiveness but also something else she didn't quite understand.

Her eyes searched his, and then wandered down to his mouth just a breath away. When she looked back up, there was no mistaking the passion unleashed between them. Slowly his mouth dipped down to meet hers as his hands cradled her face.

She melted. Passion ignited in her very soul and the feeling overwhelmed her so much that for a moment she wondered if she was even breathing.

He must have been similarly affected by the kiss for he jerked away as if she had burnt him.

"Sarah, I…"

Then, as if mere words could not express what he wanted to say, he slowly drew her towards him yet again. This time when he approached her, the initial confusion was gone and only earth shattering fear left in its place. She ceased to think. She reacted.

A loud splash of water woke her from the daze she was in, as a man's furious voice bellowed up at her from the middle of the stream, "Have you lost your mind woman!"

Realizing what she had done, a horrified giggle crept up her throat and threatened to escape. She had done it again, flipped him right into the stream. From the furious expression on his face, she knew the warrior would never believe it was an accident.

Water molded his shirt to his body as dripping shoulder length hair half covered his face. She quickly clasped a hand over her mouth, her eyes widening in repressed nervous laughter.

"Don't even think about laughing right now."

That did it.

One look at Simon's drenched and furious face was her undoing. In response to her nervous laughter, the wet warrior roared indignantly which sent her in a fresh fit of mind washing hysteria. She couldn't seem to stop laughing. That is until she noticed the fat drops of waters that were landing on her lap. When she looked up, her smile instantly disappeared. For the warrior was no longer standing in the stream, but towering over her. She gulped, swearing he had somehow managed to transform into something dangerous and unpredictable.

"Warrior, let me explain."

"No, let me explain."

She was not fooled in the least by his deadly calm. She let out a scream when he jerked her up in his arms and carried her kicking into the middle of the shallow stream, then reaching the middle of it, let go.

Sarah came up sputtering to a sitting position, pushing wet hair out of her eyes and glaring up at him. "My grandfather will make you die a thousand deaths for that."

"Not this time sweetheart. He'll be on my side, believe me."

She opened her mouth to disagree and bring down a curse on his head, but promptly shut it. He wouldn't have heard it anyway, he was half way to the carriage by the time she thought of what she wanted to say. She hit the water in frustration. "Well, that certainly went well Sarah. The only thing you could have possibly done to make matters worse was to blacken his other eye."

# Chapter 7

No one commented on the drenched pair. It was obvious they hadn't gone to see John. The biggest clue was John himself who had appeared fifteen minutes earlier. The second indication was Sarah who stormed in and tried to slam the door on Simon's foot. His loud roar drew attention from the rest of the household.

In fact, they had barely entered the room before Simon, without any semblance of an excuse, snapped at John that he was leaving for the club if he wanted to go to be ready in five minutes. Just as quickly Sarah bowed to her grandfather, begged to be excused and disappeared as well. The only outward evidence of her anger; two red splotches on her cheeks and a refusal to acknowledge her husband's presence.

Kate as usual spoke what everyone else was thinking.

"Perhaps Harrison drove them into the Thames."

To which everyone burst out laughing.


"It seems you and your new wife enjoyed a bit of a swim."

"John, mind your own business."

Taking a look at the white knuckled grip his friend had on the handle inside the hack, he prodded further, "You know, I still haven't quite figured out why you married her. Oh, she's beautiful that much is obvious, but marriage? Don't you have enough complications in your life right now?"

Sighing heavily, Simon readjusted his coat, the glimmer of steel reflecting the coach's lamp. "The girl saved my life, I owe her."

"Well, you've saved my life a few times too and I assure you I don't feel the least compelled to marry you."

"Where are we headed?"

Apparently the conversation was at an end.

"Banister is hosting another game tonight. The minister suggested I join in and cause a diversion, while my partner in crime finds some way into the study upstairs. All preferably without getting shot of course."

"So, after reading my report he thinks Banister is behind the conspiracy?"

Shifting uncomfortably in the seat John's usual good humor faded, "He said...perhaps. Simon you know I will back you all the way but you have to admit this theory of yours is a little hard to swallow. England teamed up with the South. What would be the point?"

"For the idealists, a chance to regain territory lost. For ruthless men like Banister? Profit, of course, what else."

With a curt nod, his handsome friend whacked an arm, "Then let's see if we can obtain enough evidence to stop a war."

"All right old friend, only I have a better idea at how to go about it."

"What's that?"

"Let me join the game instead."

John raised a blond eyebrow, "I don't believe you're invited."

The grin on Simon's face did little to warm the iciness of his voice. "What better diversion than that?"

The later it got, the more worried she became.

She had changed into her soft yellow cotton top and pants. As she paced in front of the small fire, her hands rubbing the sleeves up and down in agitation, she tried to think what to do. It must be nearing midnight. This job of keeping Simon safe was becoming a full time occupation.

And where was Grandfather? She had slipped a note under his door earlier, not wanting to go downstairs and endure more embarrassing questions. If he did not show up soon, she would have to go find Simon on her own. And she didn't have a clue where to start. Not to mention it was a little difficult to work up any enthusiasm for a rescue after her swimming lesson.

A soft thump against her window drew her attention. Trading the warm rug for the cold wood floor caused her toes to curl. More anxious than afraid she leaned out the window, searching the shadows. A man stepped out quietly, the half moon's faint light outlining his form. She relaxed instantly.

"Grandfather, where have you been?"

"To do your errand, Little One. Does the man never sleep?"

"Only when I knock him out," she mumbled, grabbing her slippers and dropping them out the window. "I'll be right down."

One hand balanced against the tree limb and one foot on the windowsill, she groaned in frustration as a polite knock preceded the uninvited entrance of Kate. Her bubbly chatter was instantly cut short when she noticed Sarah perched in the window like one of the stone gargoyles along the widow's walk.

"Whatever are you doing?"

Heaving a huge sigh, Sarah climbed back down, "I was climbing out the window."

"Oh."

Totally perplexed, Kate kept glancing around in confusion, "Why would you want to do a thing like that?"

This was getting more complicated by the minute. There would be no helping it; she would have to include Kate in a deception. It was the only way to keep her quiet.

"I guess this seems a little odd to you."

Kate's raised eyebrows were her only response.

"Simon is late and I was worried."

"So you intend to search the London streets for him? Alone?"

Sarah shrugged.

"Oh, I don't think that is a good idea at all," Kate plopped down on the chocolate colored bed covering, and burrowed down for a nice long sisterly chat. "I mean there are criminals that roam the streets at night. A woman alone, dressed in." her voice dwindled in embarrassment, "anyway, it is not the thing. You might be murdered or worse. Besides, Simon hates people to fuss over him. He'll be home eventually."

She really didn't have time for this.

Reaching down she pulled Kate to her feet and towards the door. "Can you keep a secret, my husband's sister?"

Kate's face lit up in excitement, her voice hushed with intensity, "Of course, what is it?"

"I believe Simon has gone somewhere other than the club."

A blank stare was her only response. Guilt colored Elizabeth's face. She just couldn't lie. It would be dishonorable. To enter heaven gates with such a load would be unspeakable. She would just have to tell the truth.

Kate's eyes suddenly widened with horror, "Hilary, he must have heard she was back in town. How awful for you." She started pacing, "Why this will never do. I just can't understand what has come over him; Simon has always been so honorable, even during the war."

She was not helping.

"Kate, you misunderstand."

Then the dawning of understanding made her mouth shape in a large 'O'.

"Do you actually think they are still in love?"

A tight hug made speech impossible.

"I don't..."

"Of course you don't know what to do. I'll confront him tomorrow; it's the only thing to do."

Surely lightening would strike her dead.

"Really, my husband's sister that won't be necessary."

The clock on the dresser showed fifteen after twelve. If only Kate would just let her finish a sentence.

"And to think I thought Simon over her."

Then just as Sarah drew in a breath to speak, Kate shoved past her and out the door, smiling brightly, "Don't you worry about a thing, I'll take care of everything in the morning."

"But... "Sarah raised a hand, only to have the door slammed shut in her face.

She groaned.

What a mess, hopefully Simon had a sense of humor.

It took only a manner of minutes to climb down the tree and head down the gas lit streets.

"Is Simon safe, Grandfather? I should have followed him at once but my temper was much too great. Of course he was the cause of my temper. Do you know what he did Grandfather, he actually threw me in a stream. My husband has very poor manners, even for an Englishman."

They soon crossed the main road and past a gaily lit house.

"I like this Simon Conway."

"I can't imagine why. Do you realize he has caused me to sin more in one week than I have in my whole entire life? Surely the Pearly Gate will be locked shut against me because of him. He is most arrogant and extremely stubborn."

"Is that so?"

"And dishonorable."

Oblivious to his slight grin, she worried her bottom lip, as they slid through an iron gate and circled around to the back of a two-story house.

"Because of him, I let his sister believe an untruth tonight."

The old man stopped in his tracks, slowly crossing his arms before him. "You must right this wrong Little One. The God of all things will be displeased."

Shame bowed her tawny head. "I know, Grandfather. I shall correct it."

He shook his head sadly at her. "Words are like feathers on the wind, some can never be retrieved."

"I know."

Her sadness tore at his heart. She was a noble child, still so full of innocence and youth. He chucked her under the chin. "This man Simon, your heart recognizes him?"

The muffled sounds of the party distracted her. Not that she wanted to answer his question; in fact, she wasn't sure what the answer would be. "Is Simon in this place?"

Lee was not fooled by her act of indifference.

"Yes, according to the Stable hand."

Her grandfather was wise past his sixty odd years. With him she felt safe from the demons in the recesses of her mind and the ones with disarming smiles.

"Thank you for coming, Grandfather."

"We will always be together Little One.  Even when I am gone to the heavens, we will be together where it counts the most", her eyes misted when he placed her hand over his heart.

"I love you."

"And I you, Little One.  Now let us search for your husband."

The inside of the place was lit with gas lamps that gave a romantic glow, that is except for the smoke fogging the windows and the crowded room full of gambling men and a few women.  The whole atmosphere boded ill for her husband sitting at a round table towards the stairs.  Every eye in the place seemed to be watching him, especially a red haired man with deep black eyes.  He was speaking to a huge man trimming his fingernails with a knife.

Sarah watched as the pock-scarred dealer went to answer the door.

Her gasp drew Lee's attention.

"Is something wrong?"

"It's Kate."

A huge sigh escaped the small man to her right.  He grabbed her arm and hurried across the kitchen.  There was no more time to observe.  "This family needs ten guardians.  It is a wonder their line is still in existence."

Her grandfather stopped her at the dining room door.  His index finger silenced her.  Kate was causing quite a commotion.  From where she stood, Sarah could hear the young girl crying and shouting hysterically at Simon.  Curiosity made her crack the dining room door a bit, to see what was going on.

Sarah stifled a small smile.  Kate was now wiping her nose on his scarf.  While her brother, on the other hand, had a look of pure exasperation on his face as he tried to make sense out of what was upsetting her.  One man at the table racked up the pot and slid it into his coat pocket.  Then without being noticed slipped out of his chair and slowly slid along the back wall towards the kitchen.

He barely got past the door they were hiding behind when Grandfather shot out a protruding knuckle to the man's temple.

"A dishonest man can never escape justice, oh stupid one." The man's answer was a grunt before crumpling at Sarah's feet. "Empty his pockets Little One and place the coins on the kitchen table."

Simon was trying to reason with his sister, "Kate, this is no place for you."

The red haired man blew cigar smoke Simon's direction. "No women allowed Conway, you know that. Now you will both have to leave."

Snatching the offending cigar out of his hand, Simon growled, "Blow smoke in my face again, and you'll be eating this cigar."

The rotund man stuck out his chest in fake bravo. "Get out. And take that whimpering imbecile with you."

Insulted, the whimpering imbecile grabbed a glass of wine from the sideboard. "Why you pompous, overblown ingrate."

"Kate put that down this minute."

"Young lady, I'm warning you."

Simon stepped up, being drenched in the process. He was not a happy man.

"Little One, is that not your husband's friend?"

Tearing her eyes away from the comical scene at the door, Sarah searched for John in the crowd. Only he wasn't one of those watching, but instead was heading up the broad oak staircase to the second floor. Unbeknownst to him, the burly doorman had spotted him as well.

"There are servant stairs at the back of the kitchen. I must warn him, Grandfather."

Those black eyes of his studied her in worried silence. "Be careful. Something is not as it seems."

It seemed as if every step creaked in protest against her slight one hundred and five pounds. That and her pounding heart were sure to give her away. As quietly as possible, she slipped into the hallway, the polished oak floor silencing her footsteps. Her plan was simply to intercept John, warn him and get out. It was nice and simple, right? Then, why was she so apprehensive?

She sighed softly, possibly because ever since meeting Simon her whole life had been turned upside down. And she had no wish to complicate it any further.

John was coming out a doorway to her left. She would have to hurry. She stepped out in warning just as the big dark bodyguard joined John in the hallway. The handsome blond man, instead of anxious looked a little bored. Using sleight of hand, he simply slipped the paper he was holding under the plant on the side table and grinned...her breath caught...straight at her.

She sank back in the shadow of the door. It had to have been her imagination. Surely he hadn't seen her.

"Is there a problem Edward?"

Quietly Sarah leaned back against the shadowy wall. Her mind was racing.

"What are you doing in Mr. Banister's room?"

"Oh, my mistake I was looking for the water closet. These modern houses are quite the thing, don't you think? Your boss must make quite a killing to afford all the conveniences. Too bad he doesn't have taste to go with it."

The man's frown only deepened as he went straight for John. "Maybe someone ought to teach you some manners."

Within an instant John's knife was in his hand, his voice cool and matter of fact. "Too bad it won't be you. Now get in the bedroom."

The dark man only glared at him.

"Now..." His eyes turned cold, as he clutched the knife in the palm of his hand, "I would hate to make a mess."

There must have been something in John's eyes that the man took seriously, for he didn't balk again. After only a slight hesitation, John followed him in. Then as Sarah slipped back into the hallway, John came out and locked the door behind him.

Not exactly sure why, she changed her mind about confronting him, and then pressed herself up against the wall to wait.

He must not have seen her earlier for he never called out to her. Instead, looking both ways John quickly descended the stairs two at a time, the sound of the escalating commotion downstairs reaching up and filling the once silent hallway.

A disquiet feeling settled over Sarah.

Something was wrong. The plant caught her eye. John forgot the hidden paper. She inched out into the light. Surely it must be important in order for him to take such a risk. What could be worth getting killed over? But then again, why would he in the next instant, promptly just leave it here? She picked up her pace. There would be no answers without retrieving that paper.

Swallowing her fear, she snatched up the paper, stuffing it into the waistband of her silk pants. She would read it later at home. But first she had to get out of there before getting caught.

Strange, but getting out was much easier than getting in.

Grandfather was waiting for her by the back door. Neither one spoke as they quickly exited the building and practically flew down the back steps and into an ally. The streets were dark, the fog thickening. Like that night long ago. The same fear was upon her. She stopped suddenly in her tracks, her stomach lurching with sickening fear.

"What is it Little One?"

"It was like this that night."

He didn't have to ask what night she meant.

A warm hand clasped her shoulder. "Only this night you are safe. Let the memory come. It is time to remember. For your parent's love is hidden in the memories as well as your pain."

Her head was throbbing. She placed a shaky hand to her forehead and one to her stomach. "No. I don't want to remember."

Tears flowed down her cheeks unchecked.

A hand on the outskirts of consciousness squeezed her shoulder. "When you are ready, I will help you slay this dragon. But, you are right. Not tonight. For tonight you must climb a tree and greet a husband. That is enough dragons for one night."

With a trembling smile, Sarah nodded. "Thank you, Grandfather. I am sorry to be such a coward."

Pulling her hand into the crook of his arm, he continued walking. "No, Little One, you are not a coward. Believe me; I have known many supposedly brave men who would have spent their life being ruled by what happened to them. Many choose bitterness or fear. You have chosen to embrace the goodness in life. That takes courage."

Too soon they were standing under her open window. The time had come to face one of her dragons. The one named Simon, her husband.

# Chapter 8

She barely beat him home.

Hearing the commotion downstairs of his mother pulling him into the drawing room she was glad she took the time to climb the tree, it was faster.

She paced back and forth wondering how to break the news to Simon. One: that she had spied on him. Two: that she had misled Kate. Picking up one of the diamond studded combs and plopping down on the bottom of the perfectly made bed, Sarah kicked off her sandals as she absentmindedly ran a thumb over the teeth of a comb.

Perhaps he would take it well. She stopped in mid stroke. Remembering how well he 'took' most things, her stomach tightened in a knot. Or, then again maybe she should just keep throwing him against walls the rest of their married life.

"That is a fairly expensive comb you just flipped onto the floor."

The sound of his tired gravelly voice caused her to jump guiltily off the bed, "Warrior, you're back."

He loosened his scarf and draped it over the back of an overstuffed chair, before dropping into it and unbuttoning the top two buttons of his shirt.

"Are you still pretending to be upset with me?"

"No. I mean, not exactly. That is... "

Why did the sight of him relaxed and unkempt cause her to lose the ability to speak a coherent sentence? She quickly looked away, thoroughly disgusted with herself, "What I mean to say is that I realize that I am partly to blame. I can't seem to stop throwing you into the nearest object."

His laugh was rich and inviting, breaking the tension between them. Crossing one booted foot over a knee, he noted, "Well, I think for my own good, I'll just pass on those tempting lips of yours from now on."

She blushed in response.

"Speaking of embarrassing moments, my mother informed me we are invited to Hilary's ball Thursday, only now it is to be thrown in our honor. I hope you don't mind."

"Oh." Sarah brushed honey colored hair out of her eyes and noticed him staring at her feet. She subconsciously placed one set of toes over the other.

"What exactly do we do at this ball? I don't understand this custom."

He continued studying her toes. "Why are your feet dirty?"

She ignored the question and sat down, smoothly crossing her legs and hiding her feet in the process, "I do not wish for a ball in my honor. There is something I must say to you Warrior."

"Simon." He grinned at her obvious attempt to sidetrack him. "I asked about your feet, remember?"

She put her hands together in a steeple and tried to appear serious, "How was your friend John?"

"Fine. You are avoiding my question."

With a deep sigh she finally answered, "I went for a walk without my proper English shoes. I know this is not acceptable, but sometimes I feel my feet cannot breathe when they are bound up all the time."

"It's a little late for walks don't you think?"

He was making her nervous. "You went out."

"I'm a man. Where did you go?"

He was acting downright suspicious now. She glared at him before answering coolly. "I will answer your questions if you answer mine. It is only polite. Where did you, go my most honorable of husbands?"

Leaning back in the chair, he studied her a long moment before flashing a quick smile at her. "Point taken, China. All right we will leave off talking about our little outings for now. But seeing as you waited up, there must be something you wanted to talk about."

She took a deep fortifying breath before answering, "I think we should share many words about our marriage and this mission of yours."

The candle wavered behind her, placing shadowy highlights across her smooth complexion and earnest expression. She looked too beautiful

116

to be real, sitting there cross-legged in a pale yellow jacket with her golden brown hair falling seductively out of a loose braid. He shook off the urge to reach out and touch its soft mass. Instead, he sat up and leaned forward, looking deep into her light brown eyes.

"Do you realize I don't know anything about you? So, why is it that you seem to know everything about me? Why do you think tonight was about my mission as you call it?"

Her delicately rounded shoulders gave a slight shrug. "It's not that difficult to figure out. First there was how fast you took off this morning. Then you and John were off again. Besides, your nose is bleeding."

Simon gingerly touched his sore nose and winched. Then in defeat sighed and ran a hand through his dark straight hair. "Yes, and I meant to ask you about that. Did you tell Kate I was going to see Hilary?"

She looked shocked, "Of course not, that would be dishonorable."

"Like following me would be when I distinctly told you not to?"

Her "what", came out more like a croak.

"You heard me Sarah."

He put both feet on the floor and looked her straight in the eye, "Sending my sister in after me could have ruined everything. Not to mention it's dangerous."

"I didn't send her."

"Really? Then perhaps you can explain why Kate insisted on saving my marriage tonight? In fact said she caught you sneaking out of our bedroom window intending to do just that."

"Did she?"

"Stop playing the innocent."

She refused to look away, "It is my destiny to guard you."

His eyes narrowed. "I don't want my family involved in any of this understand?"

"I would never bring them – "

"That means you as well. You're my wife, or did you forget?"

The note rubbed against her stomach, a reminder that something was not as it seemed. She should tell him of John's odd reaction.

"Simon, about tonight. Did you go after something? Was John supposed to help you retrieve it? If so then – "

His sigh could have awakened the dead. "Sarah, I am through speaking about this with you."

"I know, but there is something –"

"But what I will talk to you about is my relationship with Hilary."

She paused, momentarily taken aback. "You have a relationship with someone? But I am you wife, it is a very great sin."

Simon had trouble keeping a straight face she looked so shocked. But, it had changed the subject, which had been his intention. Reaching over he took her hands and leaned in closer. "Let's just say, Hilary had hopes that I would come around."

"Come around where?"

The dimple in his left cheek made a rare appearance. "She thought I intended to marry her."

"Oh." Sarah seemed to think this over a long moment before asking, "And did you wish to marry her?"

He let go of her hands, leaning back against the chair, "I thought about it."

Her face seemed to fall. Not wishing to lie to her anymore than he had to, he added, "But I couldn't imagine spending a life time with her. She is prone to selfishness and can be a bit shallow at times. In other words, she bored me."

Was that relief he saw on her face? And why did it please him that she cared? But instead of asking him how he felt about her, she studied her hands. Then, giving him a lopsided grin, which was much more devastating to his heart, she added.

"Grandfather said something odd tonight. He said he liked you. I didn't even know the two of you talked."

Her openness took him aback, and made him shift in the chair uncomfortably. He chose to change the subject again. "Your grandfather seems to know an awful lot about what goes on around here, doesn't he?"

"Oh, he is very wise," Sarah answered honestly, ignoring his wariness, "he is the reason I came back to find my family. Well, at least he was before God put you in my path."

Now she had his interest. "Your family? Your grandfather mentioned something about rescuing you from England. However, I was under the impression...what are their names? Perhaps I can help."

She looked down, "I'm not sure." Hugging knees up against her chest, and resting her chin on top, she confessed softly, "All I know is that Grandfather found me in an English shipyard. It happened so long ago and," his green eyes softened as he leaned over and gently touched her hand. She felt an uncanny bond between them that seemed to draw out what really lay in her heart, "the truth is, I don't really want to remember."

She slid her hand out from under his and fingered the locket hanging from her neck, "Except lately I've been having these nightmares." She looked up with true conviction in her voice, "Grandfather thinks they are not dreams at all, but memories. He believes it is time I face the monster of my dreams. But...I am not sure anymore, maybe some things are better left to the past. All I know is that if it wasn't for Grandfather, I would be dead right now."

He believed her. In fact, he doubted she even knew how to lie. How was it possible for one woman to touch him in so many ways? She was courageous and vulnerable at the same time. His feelings for her confused him. If only he weren't so tired maybe he could figure out what to do with her. But, right now he needed a good night's sleep. He laid a comforting hand over hers, noticing her slim fingers slipping shyly between his own, "Then I guess I owe him my life too. Let's face it, if you wouldn't have picked up that gun, I would be dead as well."

She liked the feel of his hand enveloping hers, warm and pulsing with strength. "I am not sorry that you are my destiny either."

He cleared his throat and removed his hand, "I am hardly anyone's destiny."

"But, you are. See, when I saved your life, your life became my responsibility. It is the Chinese way."

He got up and moved away from her. "You are not Chinese. Besides, the only one who holds anyone's destiny is God."

She followed him over to the screen in the corner of the room.

"Grandfather said his missionary father believed that too, but his mother's customs hold him in bronze arms. He said sometimes it is hard to live between two worlds, because you belong to neither. I think Simon that you also understand this. You pretend to be a bored rich son. All the while fighting villains and chasing your own monsters in dark alleyways and foreign hotel rooms."

After removing his clothes, Simon pulled on a burgundy robe and stepped out from behind the screen. "Why is it that when I'm with you I feel like your all-knowing grandfather is in the room with us? Besides, we weren't talking about me. The fact of the matter is that you, China, have to decide for yourself which world you will choose, because in England people do not belong to each other."

With those words, he blew out the candle leaving them both in semi-darkness. Slowly her eyes adjusted and she saw him walk over and turn the covers down. She swallowed. "Except, in marriage."

"What did you say?"

"In marriage the English belong to each other."

He stopped what he was doing, his intense stare making it hard to know what he was thinking. When he did speak his voice sounded full of disillusionment. "Not even then sweetheart."

The bed creaked in protest as he climbed in and sat back against the carved headboard. She couldn't make herself move from the spot. His satisfied grin reached her through the darkness. A dangerous shutter crossed her body. She automatically crossed her arms and glared.

"Don't worry China, I promise to keep my hands to myself. Believe me; I am still stiff from my last encounter with you. Tomorrow, I promise we'll go into town and talk to a lawyer friend of mine about an annulment. You'll be safe after that. Believe me I won't want to do anything to jeopardize my freedom. Then after my assignment is over, we'll end this farce, find your family, and both of our destinies will be back on track again."

120

With a lazy yawn and huge stretch, he patted the bed beside him. "Come on China, we're stuck with each other for at least a couple of months, so might as well make the best of things."

When she refused to budge, his broad shoulders lifted in a shrug, "Suit yourself, I'm exhausted and don't intend to sleep on the floor again."

Rolling over he went instantly to sleep. The sound of his light snoring filled the darkened room. After watching him and making sure he was really asleep, she started to relax, giving an unladylike yawn. Well, truth be told, she was tired and it did seem ridiculous to be acting like a scared rabbit around him. After all, the past had shown she was not defenseless, at least in some ways.

Feeling more in control of the situation, she tiptoed over and quietly slid in beside him. She didn't bother to change; it would hardly matter to her English husband anyway. Soon, her own eyelids grew heavy. Just as she was drifting off she remembered something important. She never did mention her Chinese beliefs on marriage, or the mysterious paper left behind by John. She peeked out at his sleeping form and gave an exhausted sigh. It would wait. Besides, if he kept running into villain's fists, she supposed she would have nothing to discuss anyway. He would not live long enough for it to matter.

The next morning Sarah awoke to find Maggie putting away clothing, or stuffing it into drawers was a more accurate description. The windows were open and a warm breeze fluttered the lace curtains inside. Pushing her tangled braid out of the way, she smiled sleepily at Maggie who smiled back.

In response the ill kept maid quickly gathered a tray with a slice of buttered toast and tea from the marble top dresser. "Good morning Miss Sarah. Tis a glorious day isn't it?"

Ducking to avoid being side cocked by Maggie's flailing arm, Sarah removed the tray from her hands and swung slender legs over the side of the bed.

"Have you seen my husband?"

The maid's cap bobbed enthusiastically, blue eyes wide with excitement, "Aye, Miss. As a matter of fact, your husband sent me to fetch you. Isn't it lovely to be going to town and all? Of course, not that I'd be one to ease drop mind ye, a body can hardly ease drop when people take to shouting their words."

She plumped up the pillow and straightened the sheets as Sarah exited the bed, rambling on the entire time, "Of course, cook claimed I had been listening outside the door...but I ask you...just because a body is kneeling down to pick up an empty glass off the floor does not make a body actually ease dropping now does it?"

Finishing the piece of toast and a swallow of tea, Sarah began washing her face with the water from the pitcher. Knowing the maid didn't really expect an answer to her question.

Stepping behind the decorated screen to change, Sarah glared at the pretty green dress, petticoats and stays. After only a moment's hesitation, she picked up the green dress and nothing else.

Maggie was sitting on the bed weeping now.

"And I'm askin' you if it was my fault that the master walked out and I happened to fall into the room? I ask you miss, isn't it natural for a body to be leaning against a door when rising?"

Sarah opened her mouth to answer, but Maggie plunged on, "Then before I know what is happening, the master snaps, "Quit blubbering and go fetch my wife."

"Blubbering he says, ha, any soul as tender in feelings as myself would have quit right on the spot." She blubbered.

"Maggie," Sarah interrupted gently, "I hate to interrupt your moment of mourning, but have you seen my grandfather? I must speak to him before leaving."

The maid jumped up and laughed, slapping a hand to her forehead, "Sorry miss, I do get carried away. I believe he is in the kitchen. He insisted on helping out, so her ladyship said he could help in the kitchen this morning until we hire a new assistant cook, seeing how Mary Francis is marrying the stable boy tomorrow and leaving for Dorshire," Her head snapped up, "Not that I was listening Miss..."

Sarah laughed and out of habit slipped on her sandals. "Thank you Maggie. And would you please return of all those undergarments to Kate? Tell her I am humbled by so generous a gift."

"Why, yes Miss," Maggie's white hat went to bobbing, "right away. I'll just..." Her shocked face lifted up and stared at Sarah's retreating and suspiciously relaxed back. "Well, I don't think she'd be a mindin' if you wore the whole of it miss."

Her words ignored, Sarah continued walking.

Fully rested Sarah felt ready to face anything. Anything, that is, except Kate on a Mission to save her marriage.

Suddenly snatched up and dragged through the library door, Sarah barely had time to think enough to stop herself from overreacting. She was learning to curtail her reactions a bit since meeting her husband's family. The door was slammed shut behind her, as a very intense Kate blocked her escape with her petite form, a finger to lips in warning. "Don't worry its safe here."

She was unaware she was not safe, except maybe from Kate.

"We are free to talk here about...you know."

Rolling her eyes heavenward, Sarah began shaking her head, "For the last time my husband's sister, I am not jealous of Hanna."

"Hah," her young sister-in-law spat out, "Then why did you pretend to forget her name was Hilary."

"I did not forget, only it is unimportant."

"And why would my brother disappear in the middle of the night and you go after him if it were not a worry?"

Sarah opened her mouth to answer.

"And another thing," Kate continued, pacing now in agitation. "Just who is that China man really? A well-known assassin? Your bodyguard? You can tell me; after all, I have seen how he uses that knife of his." She was really wired up now.

"I assure you little sister, he is only my grandfather, nothing quite so glamorous as all that. And, I could care less about other women whatever there names may be. Now excuse me, I have to go. Your brother is waiting."

"Ah hah!"

Sarah jumped back a step, placing a hand over her racing heart, "Ah hah, what?"

"There you go chasing my brother across town again." She crossed her arms smugly, asking knowingly, "I suppose you only want to see his offices and have lunch is that it?"

It sounded good to her. "As a matter of fact..."

"Hah."

"Would you stop 'hahing' at me? It is most unnerving."

Someone knocked on the door. Kate seemed frozen in indecision.

Calmly reaching behind her, Sarah opened the door.

Maggie came tumbling in at her feet, a suspicious glass in her hand.

The guilty maid climbed to her feet, then noticing the glass in her hand jerked it back behind her back before speaking. "Umm...your husband miss. He asked if'n you'd be joining him now. He is waiting by the carriage."

Kate cleared her throat and motioned with her head wildly at Sarah. "Go on now, we don't want him to become suspicious about...you know what."

Giving the two insane women a weak smile, Sarah tried to ease around them and make it into the hallway. Kate shot out an arm barring her way.

"Well?"

Sarah ducked under her arm, "Well, what?"

"Aren't you going to ask me about the plan?"

The girl was past talking to.

"No, I'm not. Now goodbye."

Then, as she hurried out the door and down the stone steps, Sarah shook off her sense of foreboding. Praying her new sister was more talk than action.

Unfortunately she wasn't.

Watching as the beautiful woman climbed into the carriage ahead of Simon, Maggie laid a comforting hand on her fellow conspirator's

124

shoulder, "Don't you worry Miss, we'll get to the bottom of this or my name is not Margaret O'Flannery."

Kate patted her hand, "Fetch my wrap Maggie. Sarah is not the only one who is good at following people."

# Chapter 9

The solicitor's office smelled of beeswax and expensive leather. The dark gold of the hand-woven rug was covered in brown birds of prey in various stages of flight. The odd looking man sitting across the desk from her wore small round glasses that did nothing to improve his dull colorless eyes. Sarah shifted in her seat. Why was it that she suddenly felt like a cornered fox with the hounds about to move in for the kill?

She twisted her hands in nervous agitation.

The man's intense disapproving stare caused her to slip her sandaled feet back under the hem of Kate's light green dress. The action was not lost on the all seeing barrister. He lifted his nose a notch in the air at her obvious lack of breeding. In fact, he hadn't even given her the curtsy of speaking directly to her, but addressed all his remarks toward Simon. She felt so ill at ease that twice Simon had to draw her attention back to the question at hand. Unfortunately, all she could think of was the reason he brought her here in the first place, to end their marriage.

"Sarah, do you understand the agreement before you?"

She looked down and swallowed. This felt so very wrong. She had given her word before the God of all things and their families. It hardly mattered that the warrior, so lacking in honor, took it lightly. The legal paper spread out before her required yet another lie and if she did this thing she would be empty inside. She would lose face. And as Grandfather said, even a poor man knew not to sell his integrity. The paper blurred through the tears threatening to surface. She took another deep breath.

"I can't."

"I beg your pardon madam?"

Simon sank back into the deep brown leather and sighed. "Sarah, I thought we agreed that this was for the best. If you need more of a settlement..."

She shoved the distasteful paper away and rose to her feet.

"You dishonor me Warrior. I wish for no money at all. It is your paper full of lies. I can't sign it. Excuse me man of law, but I feel most...unwell."

"Sarah!"

Simon's shout followed the firm closing of the oak door on her way out. The solicitor cleared his throat in embarrassment. "Perhaps, sir, if you take the papers with you. She could sign them at another time, when she is feeling more herself."

"I'd have better luck if she weren't feeling herself. Thank you James, but I can't have those papers lying around the house. This annulment must be kept confidential for at least a few more weeks."

The older man shuffled the papers thoughtfully, before stating bluntly, "Are you quite sure Sir about this? The young lady seemed very distraught. I was under the impression she had been the one forced into marriage."

"She was."

"Can I offer you a word of advice? One gentleman to another."

Simon got up and paced over to peer out the heavy drapes. She was halfway down the street. It would very likely take him the rest of the morning to chase her down and cool her temper, as if he were not already behind in his paperwork at the warehouse.

"Sir?"

Brought back to the question at hand, he nodded. "Why, not? Everyone else has offered theirs."

"If you are simply doing the honorable thing by saying she, and not you, was forced into this marriage. Then I would suggest that you correct the story. I could draw up new papers that make you the one duped into marriage, as no doubt you were. I am sure Judge Hawthorne, or any man would take your side. Although tempting, the girl obviously is not, how can I put it delicately...from your own social class."

Simon's grip tightened on the curtain, turning his knuckles white. "I certainly hope you are not referring to my wife in such a manner, man."

Brushing at his sleeves, the confused man tried to defend himself, "But, Sir, I thought you wanted to be rid of the girl."

He felt as if someone had kicked him in the gut. He remembered how the proud young woman looked up at him with tears in her eyes after reading the document. Was this how he paid back a debt, to humiliate her? The anger he felt at himself, turned outward on the flustered solicitor.

"You are right. She isn't of our class. For which I am eternally grateful. She is something better and nobler than any of our breed. She actually tells the truth, even when it is to her determent. She is loyal to little children and a rather strange China man. Would you believe she actually believes that such a thing as honor still exists? To tell the truth James, I am humbled each and every time I am in her presence. And the next time you are fortunate enough to be in the same room with my madam wife, I expect you to pay her the courtesy due her. If not, I will be forced to refresh your manners, is that perfectly clear?"

The man in question nodded stiffly.

"Good. Then, I shall see you in a few weeks."

"Very good Sir."

Sarah swiped at angry tears, determined not to let one legal document take away her self-respect. She breathed in the summer day, trying to calm herself. At least it was warm. She grew tired of English rain and fog. How she longed for busy hot New York streets instead. For the first time in many months, her sunny optimism deserted her. Grandfather was wrong to insist she come back. She might have been born here, but America was her true home. She wanted so badly to abandon her responsibilities, to sign that stupid paper and be free to leave. But, something more binding was keeping her a prisoner here. It was the mystery surrounding her parent's death and her word.

A rag covered woman stuck out a grimy hand, halting her in mid step. Before Sarah could ask why, a bunch of purple violets were thrust under her nose.

"Flowers miss? Only two pence."

Pushing the flowers aside, Sarah gave a weak smile. "No, thank you."

The woman stepped around her, once again halting her retreat.

"These here, they're special flowers from Stone Hedge. Said to have magical powers, they are. Have even been known to cause one's true love to come calling? Surely a pretty miss like you needs true love. Only two pence."

The woman was persistent. Not to mention imaginative. Years of want and hard living showed on the tired lined face. Yet, still there was something touching about the way she spoke of magic flowers and true love. Besides, Sarah could use a little magic today. Removing the small pearl drop earrings from her ears, she gently opened the woman's hand and placed them inside. "I don't have two pence. Will these do?"

The hard face softened and she shook her head. "No, miss. I can't be taking your things."

"I think a pair of earrings is a fair trade for true love don't you."

The woman gave a toothless grin, "So, it is. It's a kind heart you have, love. God bless." And without another moment's hesitation, she deposited the flowers and hurried off cackling at her good fortune.

"I suppose, according to that half baked woman, this makes me your true love."

Sarah gasped and whipped around to stare up into her husband's amused sea green eyes, "What are you doing here?"

"According to you, it's destiny. According to her, it's flowers." His strong jaw clenched in distaste. "You know of course, she probably stole those flowers from someone's backyard and is selling every last bloom to love struck women like yourself, who believe in fairy tales."

A blush crossed her dusty complexion. "She seemed nice."

He took her arm, shaking his head at her, "Sarah, everyone seems nice to you. It's one of your most endearing traits. But, the truth is, she will no doubt trade you precious gems in for cheap ale and spend all night talking with her cronies about what an easy mark you were."

"I think your wrong, Warrior. I believe you scoff at the very things you wish were true."

He shrugged at the conviction in her soft voice.

She tried to tug loose an arm as he headed back the way she had come. "Would you please release me? I don't wish to go with you. I want a moment alone."

"Too late. It's those magic flowers of yours. Now we are stuck with each other."

One corner of her mouth twitched, "Don't be ridiculous. You are much too tainted a soul to believe in true love."

"Do I not? Well, then it must be the way the violets bring out the blue of your eyes."

"My eyes are brown."

He feigned shock, "Really? I'm surprised. Brown is hardly how I would describe them. More like the color of strong English tea on a chilly morning. But, then again, when they are flashing at me, like right now, they turn a deep topaz. And even though I know better, I can't quite decide if I want to continue our argument or kiss you senseless."

His words made her blush.

It hardly seemed fair. His smile alone melted her insides, much less his strong and handsome body touching hers, like now. Yes, he was much too charming and much too passionate...he made her feel things, confusing things. She felt when he touched her, as if her very soul could be lost to him. This is probably why she never allowed it.

So, she dug her heels in and jerked her arm free.

"I very much dislike you kissing me," she flung out a little breathlessly as he began striding purposely towards a small dress shop tucked away down a less busy side street.

He seemed unperturbed by her unflattering statement, "How would you know? If I remember right, I haven't had the pleasure of doing it properly."

Struggling to keep up and flustered by his reference to the two previous attempts at kissing, she opened her mouth to reply, and then quickly shut it again. What could she say? He was right.

He finally slowed down and pointed up at the front of a shop. It was in a quaint brick building with dark brown trim, its one window boasting "Madame Marie's. Fashions straight from Paris."

"I think it's time we got you some new clothes."

For some reason the idea of new clothes made her feel as if she were staying in this life permanently. And she panicked. The whole day had been full of unwelcome incidents that forced her to acknowledge that, at least for now, this was her life. And she hated it. So, she balked at the idea of giving up the one last thing she still controlled, her clothes. "I already possess clothes, Englishman."

"In case you haven't noticed," he looked pointedly down at her straining bodice and too short hem, "that dress doesn't fit you in the least."

She felt like a trapped animal being led to the slaughter and took a step back only to be hindered by his solid six foot frame.

Laughter, rich and deep filled her ears. "It's only a dress shop, China. Not a torture chamber."

"That is a matter of opinion." She replied mutinously.

"Look, China, you can't go around in sandals and silk pajamas forever, you're English for Pity sakes."

Her eyes were flashing orbs of gold. She clutched her hands together and said with false politeness, "Although I am honored by your concern, I must refuse. I am not English in my heart and these clothes will bind my soul. Besides, as you say, I am not staying."

He was tired of arguing with her stubborn pride. He shoved fisted hands down into smooth tan pants and leaned down until his face was close enough to her ear, she shivered. When he spoke, his whisper was harsh and relentless, "As I recall you also refused to sign those annulment papers, full of lies you called it, right?"

She barely nodded.

"Then I assume you mean to honor your vows. And although I admit to being a little upset at the time, I believe one of those vows was that of obedience."

Her face shot up, horror written all over it.

"I thought so. As usual you are only just now realizing the full ramifications of stubbornly refusing to release both of us from this ridiculous marriage. You wanted this. So, if you insist on being my wife you will dress in English clothes, learn English ways and suffer arrogant English husbands. Understood?"

She bit her bottom lip in indecision, pride demanding she refuse. But, unfortunately, her grandfather's teaching and own personal honor won out. "I will wear the clothes of your people," she forced out between stiff lips.

"They are your people, too."

She frowned.

He winked.

Furious, she turned around to enter the shop. Simon watched the gentle sway of hips and bare sandaled feet as she entered the shop. He cocked an eyebrow and grinned. Those papers were as good as signed. He'd give her two weeks tops. Then his precious bride would beg to be released from this marriage, honor or no honor. Whistling, he followed her in and shut the door.


A torturous hour later she knew one thing for sure...she hated the English and their clothes. Even now the whale bone corset was digging into her side and polished leather boots where suffocating her feet and pinching her toes. So as they sat at the table awaiting their food she reached down to loosen the laces, releasing the top two buttons on her shoes. Her ankles were rubbed raw.

"You'll get use to them."

"I am deeply appreciative of your concern, my most arrogant English husband...especially since I am the one who will have to...as you said, get use to them. But, because of the vows of obedience you tricked me into taking, and because I am an honorable person..."

"That statement is beginning to get on my nerves, China."

She cocked a tawny head his direction and buttered her roll, "Really? And I meant only to appear the most humble of wives."

"This is for your own good, you know. The ball is in six days and those society matrons will be ruthless if you do not fit the part of a Peer's wife."

The waiter laid herb-encrusted fish before her.

"Receiving approval from fools only makes you twice one."

He savagely cut into his prime rib, "Sarah, this is important. I need your help to pull this farce off. Several men will be there who are funding support for the South. I don't need you casting doubt as to what I was doing in America. That is, besides fetching the woman I love."

"You just tore a hole in the tablecloth."

Sighing, he purposely laid down his eating utensils. "Are you going to cooperate or not."

"What is it you wish for me to do?"

The setting sun coming through the beveled glass windows highlighted the gold in her freshly styled hair. She looked like an angel. Her sun kissed skin, her full lips set in a determined straight line. All put a slant on words that he was pretty sure she had no intention of conveying. Instead he cleared his throat. He was getting as fanciful as she...angel? More like temptress.

"Tomorrow we start with dance lessons and etiquette."

"And tonight?"

"Tonight you start acting like a woman in love instead of a sparing partner."

She reached over and gently touched his arm.

He jumped and the knife in his hand went sailing over to the next table.

Grinning she continued eating, "Perhaps you'd better start acting the part as well, Warrior. It seems I am not the only one who finds it difficult to live a lie."

The next few days were torturous for Simon. Now being forced into her company day and night the attraction he tried so hard to ignore consumed him. Acting the lady seemed to come easily to his temporary wife. She was gentle, beautiful, and interesting; a dangerous combination. And one he had taken great pains to avoid these past twenty odd years. Then there was the fact that she actually trusted him to act the gentleman and keep his distance when they were alone. She had no idea what it was costing him. No idea, how many nights he stayed up till all hours, pacing with a glass of bourbon, till exhaustion overtook him, and he fell asleep on the library sofa.

Yes, very much more of this sweet torture and he would demonstrate what a real husband does when he enters the bedroom. The only thing stopping him was the certainty that once he did there would be no going back, for either one of them. Even now, standing propped up against the cold fireplace, he could not keep his eyes off her. He took another long swallow of his drink.

"Simon!"

"Yes, mother."

"How many drinks have you consumed since lunch?"

He hungrily took in his wife's low cut light green silk and growled, "Unfortunately, not enough."

Sarah studied him, worry creasing her perfectly arched eyebrows. "Is something troubling you Warrior?"

"My name is Simon. How many times must I remind you Sarah?"

"Now look dear, you've gone and spilled your father's favorite brandy all over the rose carpet."

"Sorry mother. Look it's been a long six days and I think I'll get a nap before the party."

Kate jumped up, clapping her hands in excitement. "Not yet Simon, you still haven't taught Sarah the waltz. I know it is quite scandalous, but I overheard Hilary say she planned on surprising you with one. Isn't it exciting? The whole room will be watching as the two of you swirl gracefully in each other's arms. I think it is terribly romantic."

The image made Sarah want to throw up.

"And whose brilliant idea was this?"

Kate shoved Simon towards his wife. He gave her a suspicious look. She had been acting strange for days now.

"Oh, don't be such a grouch Simon. I will play the piano and Mother will sing. It will be great fun. It is the perfect thing to end with before the ball tonight."

Simon groaned and mumbled something under his breath that Sarah could not quite make out. Then, even though she willed him not to, he bowed and extended a hand in gentlemanly fashion.

"Let's get this little chore over with, shall we."

Oh, yes, there he was being 'romantic' again. She looked around for an escape.

"Believe me, I find this just as unpleasant as you do, but it is a necessary evil right now."

Rolling her eyes, she looked off to the side, once again refusing his hand.

Suddenly she found herself jerked up against him so tightly she could barely breathe.

"I dislike you holding me."

The tone of her voice caused him to smile for the first time in days.

"Are you threatening me, China?"

Looking up at that cocky grin, she answered truthfully. "I assure you, it was not a threat."

He gentled his hold, but whispered for her ears only, "You know, knocking men out who ask you to dance? Well, let's just say, it is hardly the way to fill one's dance card."

She unconsciously swayed against him, feeling the music, "Oh, I disagree. From past experience I have found the English to be an arrogant lot and doing so would no doubt only have them lined up for hours."

He slowed down his movements and lifted her chin with one hand, till their eyes met. Humorous green clashed with golden orbs of brown. "Is that so? Then perhaps I have been neglecting my duties to you for far too long if you think I am like any other man you have met, English or otherwise."

Something happened between them, a current of attraction so intense that it knocked the very breath from her, making it hard to breathe, much less answer.

"Warrior, I warn you..."

But, her words sounded weak even to her own ears.

The music had stopped, but neither one noticed.

Her eyes widening slightly in fear, she watched in breathless fascination as his head dipped lower to gently touch his lips with her own.

His lips barely brushed hers, but a jolt of very real passion shot through her body. Pulling back in confusion she slowly searched his handsome face wondering what could have caused such a reaction. The shock in his eyes told her he had felt it too.

But, unlike his naive wife, Simon recognized something she did not. This feeling between them was rare. Before now he would not have believed such intense desire could exist for one woman. If he hadn't known better he would have sworn she had purposely seduced him. However when he looked deeply into her curious face, all he saw was an innocent. A study in untried passion, so trusting it would humble a good man, and it scared one like him to death.

Quickly dropping his arms, he took a step back, breathing as if he had run a marathon. "I think that is about all the dance lessons I can stand for one day. Now if you will excuse me Ladies, I believe I am in need of some fresh air."

"Well, that had to have been the most romantic kiss I've ever seen," Kate sighed as her brother exited the room, "See Mother, I told you, Sarah has nothing to worry about. After tonight Simon will forget all about Hilary."

"Hilary? Whatever are you talking about dear?"

The panic in Stella's faded blue eyes caused Sarah to wake from her daze. Giving the nervous woman a reassuring hug, she said lightly, "It's nothing, my husband's mother. As you can see, the feelings we share bond us stronger than chains." Sarah gave a too bright smile. Actually what they shared was the feeling of being trapped in a loveless marriage. But this kind woman should not be made to suffer because of her son's lack of honor. Sarah patted her hand reassuringly, "I can honestly say, this woman of Simon's past is of no importance to me."

Grateful to Sarah for covering up her blunder and wishing to erase the worry from her mother's face, Kate announced out of the blue.

"Mother, I've been thinking, I simply must go to America."

Sidetracked, as her daughter planned, Stella fairly shouted, "Don't be absurd, you will do nothing of the sort. Don't you know there is a civil war going on there? I declare Katherine Louise I will never understand how your mind works. One minute you indicate that Hilary and Simon...and the next you're off to America...I swear that imagination of yours will get you into trouble one day child. You must learn to curb it and your tongue. Now kindly take over where your brother left off. Sarah, let's begin again shall we? No more talk of America, or scandalous affairs, there will be plenty of that at the party."

An hour later when she went up to her room, Sarah noticed Simon's clothes had magically disappeared from the bottom of the bed. She had no idea where he finished dressing. In a small way she felt relieved. Her feelings for him were becoming more and more complicated.

A knock at the door allowed steaming pails of hot water in for her bath. This was the one luxury she did appreciate since becoming Simon's wife, warm fragrant baths. It was quite a change from the daily lukewarm bowl of water and frayed stiff wash cloth. She wondered what Grandfather thought about all this luxury. No doubt as strange as she did, how much things had changed for the two of them since leaving America.

Her thoughts turned to Grandfather. How she wished to speak to him right now, but lately he had withdrawn to the world of writing. He was seemingly content to be left with philosophers and world travelers. She was use to him disappearing for days when he was engrossed in writing. Still, she missed him badly.

A polite knock at the French doors from outside on the balcony interrupted her wishful thinking. Grandfather? It had to be him; he always did seem to know when she needed him. Running over, she pulled open the drapes and pushed open the French doors before throwing herself into his embrace. He felt solid and warm. She felt safe.

"Grandfather, you came."

"I have missed you too Little One. So, tell me, are you enjoying this ritual of celebration and your new husband?"

Her smile instantly disappeared. "I know it displeases you to hear it Grandfather, but more than ever it is plain to see that I will never be English."

His voice, although firm, tried to gentle her heart. "Your parents were English, Sarah."

Not put off by the use of her formal name, fire turned her eyes golden. "And it was an Englishman who killed them."

A disapproving nod was his only response.

"I am sorry, Grandfather; I guess I am just a little nervous. I know little of balls and understand less of English husbands. "

Unperturbed by her outburst, he gathered her cold hands in his and gave them a squeeze. "Perhaps I should share minds with your husband Little One. I have been neglecting my duty to you. To be honest, I too wonder if this was for the best. You are the most precious of treasures and you are laid at the feet of a man both blind and foolish."

Sitting on a stone bench along the balcony, she pushed back loosened hair and gave a weak smile. "He wishes I sign a paper making the words we spoke to the holy man a lie. I can't do it grandfather and I can't stay here either. What will I do?"

A comforting gnarled hand brushed back a strand of her hair as they both looked out into the darkening sky.

"You will do what all wise women do, you will stand strong on what you believe and you will fight for those you love. After all, one's only true possessions are our words, love and loyalty. And once given, they can never be taken back, especially by insignificant pieces of paper and ink."

The steady voice of her mentor soothed her troubled heart. She drew in a deep cleansing breath of cool twilight air. "I wonder why I even came back here. This place is full of evil men and vain women. I don't belong here. I never will."

The air was tinged with coolness, but it was not the cause of the shiver that snaked its way down her spine. Nor was the cause of the overwhelming sense of uncertainty and sadness. She felt so alone.

Simon's voice drew both their attention from the doorway, "Don't worry China, you belong here all right. Most importantly, because you are my wife. That alone will be enough for most of the shallow crowd at the party tonight."

Sarah felt awkward at being overheard, her heart pounding at the sight of her husband. Was it the darkening sky that made him appear so dangerous and just as alone as she? Or did she simply imagine the fierce protectiveness in his voice and odd sense of intimacy here in the semi darkness? Both made her want to cry out and be held by the very man who tormented her.

Perhaps she was just as vain and shallow as the rest of the English. Why else would she love simply looking at the shear rugged beauty of him? Love even the way his dark hair matched the dark brown silk of his jacket and how his snowy white cotton shirt clung to broad strong shoulders. Or, for that matter, notice that the green of his eyes reminded her of a New York harbor on a hot summer's day. No, she was in danger of losing her heart to this man. Every instinct warned her of the fact.

The soft touch of her grandfather's hand brought her back to reality.

Simon walked out to the edge of the balcony and nodded at the proud China man who refused to leave Sarah's side. Was it his imagination or did she look more vulnerable tonight. A part of him felt a twinge of guilt. Which failed to make sense seeing as this had been his plan, to push her away. He had no choice. The feelings she aroused in him made him feel out of control. And he had a job to do.

"It is good to see you again Sir."

"Is it? I wonder. You missed our walk and I had much to talk with you about. However, now that you are here, perhaps you can help with something that has been plaguing my mind, Englishman."

Simon raised a dark brow at the tone of insult attached to that one simple word.

"If you are now my granddaughter's protector, who will protect her from you?"

It was the first time Sarah had ever seen Simon blush. "She needs no protection. I would never intentionally hurt her."

The two men in her life locked eyes. "You have hurt her already. What kind of man gives his word one minute, and the next thinks a piece of paper changes anything? Only one who is both foolish and weak. From now on I want no more talk of shameful annulments or divorce. I forbid it."

"Grandfather." Sarah spoke in a tortured whisper, "If Simon doesn't…"

He squeezed her hand in silent protest. "I ask for your word arrogant Englishman. Or, do I break your mother's heart with the truth of your lies."

Simon's mouth tightened into a thin straight line. Restrained anger caused a slight tick along his strong jaw line. Sarah didn't realize she had been holding her breath until she quietly gasped in air to speak. "Grandfather did not mean to threaten you, Warrior, he just…"

"Oh, I think he meant exactly what he said."

Her grandfather looked up at the young man half his age and twice his size before challenging, "Yes, I did. Only a man without honor would treat you so shamefully. He has lied and plans on sending you away when you are no longer of use to him. In China, we treat our poor on the streets better. They are at least allowed their dignity. This man owes you his life and he repays his debt by taking yours."

Sarah watched Simon flinch as if struck. His usually clear eyes clouded over and appeared stormy and hard. He was angry and she was fairly certain that had anyone else spoken those words to him, Simon would have called them out. In amazement she watched him slowly gain control of his temper, and then finally give a stiff bow their direction. "You are right Sir. I have behaved badly. Truth be told, I have been looking for a way out of my obligations to Sarah. But, I swear to you, that is, if you can take the word of an Englishman. From now on, I will protect her with my life, as she has protected mine. She will be my wife in every way. And although I imagine she will live to regret it…there will be no annulment."

The hand holding hers relaxed, letting blood flow through it once more. Whatever had occurred between the two men was over. Yet all Sarah could think about was how Simon had been forced to give his word. Now he would never be free of her. Her grandfather had seen to it. She felt shaky with pent up anger. Anger that a man would have to be forced to stay with her and shaky because for a moment, a part of her feared he might refuse.

Now all she wanted was to be left alone.

She would have risen but her legs felt too weak to hold her up.

"I will leave you with your wife. You both have much to discuss. Good-bye Little One. Come by my room later tonight and I will brew you a cup of green tea from my homeland to ease your sleep."

Then, turning toward Simon, the proud old man bowed. Simon, who hesitated only a moment, returned it. After rising, Simon did something unexpected...he put out a steady hand, an unspoken pledge. Lee gave a satisfied nod and placed his own hand in her husbands. She wished things were that simple between a man and a woman. Unfortunately, what lay between her husband and her could not be solved with one simple handshake.

Once Lee left, it seemed to Sarah as if it got even cooler. She shivered.

"Here, take this."

Placing his expensive jacket around her shoulders, he gave her a grim smile. "It seems I owe you an apology."
Sarah burrowed into the coat's soft warmth, the whole time watching him in silence as he took out a cheroot and lit it. One hip propped up along the banister. He looked the handsome king with a world of troubles on his shoulders. How young he must have been when he first became responsible for his entire family. And now he had one more soul to add to his burden. If only she had never entered that hotel room...she shook her head...no, things happened for a reason. It was wrong to second-guess even a moment of one's destiny.

"I am sure my grandfather did not mean what he said about your honor, he spoke in anger."

"And I am sure he did. Besides, he was right. I have been running from my responsibility to you."

What was it about being referred to as a responsibility that made her bristle with hurt pride?

"I assure you I can take care of myself. I just wasn't willing to lie. If you reworded the document, then perhaps we could... I could...sign it."

"You can't even say the words, how are you going to live with them. You, my love, are everything I am not: honorable, loving, and trustworthy. And I have been fooling myself into believing this marriage was a sham to you as well as to me. But, it's real all right, painfully so."

His free hand traced a tear down her cheek. "Don't be so glum, China. I take my obligations seriously. No more talk of dissolving our marriage or having you disappear out of my life. Besides, it is about time I settled down. The debt to my country is almost repaid...now why are you crying? I thought this is what you wanted."

"No, it isn't what I wanted. What I wanted was to one day join my heart to another and to be more than some obligation to an English husband."

He looked off into the now dark night. His partly undone white shirt was catching the light summer breeze, revealing glimpses of a well-developed chest. She quickly averted her eyes. How she wished things could have been different between them. Perhaps someday.

When he spoke, his voice was low and serious. "You wish for me to love you, is that it?"

She wondered how those few words answered some call within her. Yes. Unbelievably, she did want him to be everything he wasn't...a friend, a lover and yes, even a confidant. Someone she could count on. Tell her dreams to...believe in. Even someone who would help her uncover the man of her nightmares.

"Look at me Sarah."

She slowly turned her face to his, unable any longer to hide the hope and disappointment written there.

He apparently couldn't face either one. He turned out once more and spoke with conviction.

"I can't give you what you ask for. In fact, I don't even know if I have it within me to love anyone," after a weary sigh, he turned back to face her, brushing a stray golden brown strand from her face, "But, I can promise that whatever I have is yours. Who knows, maybe God sent a strange China girl into my life to teach me how to love."

"But if you can never feel love for me," she stammered with embarrassment, but forced herself to continue, "I don't know if I can allow you to touch me as a man touches a wife. I seem to keep..." She blushed shyly, "stopping you."

He laughed out loud, "I do admire your honesty. But the absence of love is not why you throw me into things."

She eyed him suspiciously, "It isn't?"

"No, it isn't. I think you're afraid."

"I don't fear you." But, even as she said the words, she could hear the sound of her own heart beating in her ears.

He bent his dark head and whispered against her lips, "It's not me you fear. It's the way I make you feel, China. This scares you."

When his warm lips touched hers, she drew in a breath of shock. His kiss went deeper and stronger than anything she had ever felt before. Part of her drew in closer to his warmth, the whole while her right arm snaked out to end this sweet torture. But, this time he was ready for her. He jerked her up against his hard body and said savagely, "Not this time, China. Heaven help us both, but not this time."

A strange peace came over her. If he could give his word, then she could honor hers. A heady delicious feeling washed over her senses. For once she didn't fight it. His mouth covered hers in a possessive and all-consuming kiss. She could barely think, didn't even want to. From somewhere outside herself, she was vaguely aware of his hand sliding seductively along the curve of her back. It felt wonderful and yet, there was a yearning growing deep within her. She wanted more, needed it. Unconsciously she leaned in closer, molding her body to his.

Then, ironically, she felt him try to withdraw. Instinctively, she reached up and pulled him back down to her.

143

She felt a chuckle from deep inside his throat. Still, she refused to let him go, that is until his words penetrated passion's fog.

"I believe Maggie's a little shocked sweetheart."

Horrified, Sarah jerked back, eying the closed French doors. Two beaming faces waved back at her. It was Maggie and Kate. Wonderful, she thought. Simon's groan vibrated against her embarrassed face, as the tapping on the French doors continued until, unable to ignore the two intruders, she stepped away from Simon's warmth and glared at them.

Unperturbed, Maggie mouthed something as Kate jumped around, resembling an Indian at a powwow. Sighing, Simon yanked open the door and growled, "Would you two stop that ridiculous jumping about and just tell us what you want."

Maggie curtsied, not in the least upset by her master's roar.

"The mistress sent me up to say Elizabeth and her family have arrived. But can I say Master Simon how happy I am to see you and Miss Sarah getting along so well. The cook and I bet two shillings against Albert that you would patch things up come Friday. And here it is Thursday...not that I'd normally do the devil's gambling, but any newly married man who sleeps on the library sofa – well – it just isn't the way the Good Lord intended for a... "

"That is quite enough Maggie."

Kate saddled up to her big brother, pushing an arm through his and dragging him towards the door. "Oh, don't roar at the servants Simon. Why don't you go and finish dressing. We'll get Sarah dressed and send her down to you. Now hurry or we will be unfashionably late and I will have to tell poor Hilary exactly why."

Simon looked ready to throttle her.

Sarah on the other hand wondered why Kate winked at Maggie behind his back. No doubt about it, her dear sweet sister in law was up to something.

# Chapter 10

Matchmaking.

Apparently, that is what the two women were up to, for when Sarah looked into the full-length gilded mirror, she took a step back in surprise and wonder.

Kate gently pushed her back towards the mirror, "So, what do you think?"

"I think I look like an English woman."

"A beautiful English woman." Maggie sighed.

All three women looked in wonder at the vision Sarah had become. Her apricot ball dress accented all the right curves, the brown velvet trim outlining the modestly low cut top brought out the warm brown of her eyes. The gold combs with topaz stones, seemed to turn her natural blond highlights to honey. And her smooth tanned skin glowed in the candlelight.

Kate could barely contain her excitement. "Can't you see old Hilary's face or Elizabeth's for that matter. Just picture it. You walk in and then Simon, spell bond, takes your hand and leads you out for a waltz onto a moonlit balcony."

Leave it to Kate to make everything into a romance. Sarah wondered what Simon's sister would think, if she were to discover that her so-called, spellbound brother had only this morning drug her to a lawyer's office demanding an annulment. But rather than ruin the moment, she smiled warmly back at Kate in the mirror. "You are a most wonderful friend and I am indeed grateful that I will no longer cause Simon to lose face in front of his people."

"Honestly, Sarah!" Kate moaned, "Aren't you the least excited?"

Sarah swallowed down the lump gathering in her throat, "One is hardly excited when facing a tiger unarmed. All one can do is pray he's already eaten."

"You do say the strangest things."

Maggie clucked her tongue. "It's them China ways Miss Kate. Them China ways."


He reached down to check his pocket watch for the third time. Nine fifteen. Where was she? Simon snapped it shut and walked purposely to the door.

"Simon, don't. You'll ruin everything."

Simon gave his sister an exasperated look, but dropped his hand away from the glass knob and returned to his place by the fire.

But from the look of things he wasn't the only one wondering about his wife. Despite her protest, Kate kept looking towards the door with a worried expression on her face. Only his parents seemed content to sit by the fire all night. At least Elizabeth's family had stopped giving him sympathetic looks twenty minutes ago. When they gave up and left.

He pushed away from the mantle. Enough was enough.

"You all go ahead to the party. I'll see what's keeping Sarah."

Kate jumped instantly to her feet. "But, that's not how it's supposed to be."

Her father helped his wife up and stretched, "Come along Kate. Let your brother manage his own affairs."

For once Stella balked, "But dear perhaps we should wait a little longer. I mean the ball is in their honor after all. And what if the poor dear is hurt and needs assistance."

Placing a shawl around her frail shoulders, he winked at his son, "I hardly think a woman who gives my son a black eye needs our assistance dear."

"Oh, Henry," she swatted at him with her fan, "must you joke about everything."

"But, Father," Kate, protested weakly, as she was pulled toward the door, "Sarah hasn't made her entrance yet."

Henry opened the door, while placing his silk top hat firmly on his head. "She doesn't seem like the entrance type to me daughter. Now come along and let your brother handle his own wife."

Simon could still hear Kate protesting all the way to the carriage about the lack of romance in the family. He sighed. They were already an hour late and that left even less time for him to manage an invitation to that meeting the day after tomorrow of the Southern sympathizers.

Placing one foot on the bottom step, he suddenly stopped. The familiar scent of vanilla and fresh soap embraced him. He shut his eyes a brief moment, breathing her in, before catching a hold of himself and looking up at the face causing havoc to his heartbeat. But, nothing could have prepared him for the sight of her. His knees buckled slightly and his grip around the stairwell tightened. When he managed to speak, his voice sounded gravely and rough.

"You look beautiful."

Embarrassed, the vision before him smoothed out imaginary wrinkles in her dress, but gave a shy smile. "You are most kind husband."

"Kindness has nothing to do with it. What kept you?"

"I had some things to think over."

"And?"

"And, well, I've decided... ", she pulled back her shoulders as if readying herself for battle, "I've decided not to go this time. I am not yet ready for so great an undertaking."

"Sorry, but you're going. I'll get your cape."

A mutinous frown marred her delicate features as she took a step towards him. "I am most honored to be asked, my husband, but am afraid I must again decline."

A reluctant grin tugged at a corner of his mouth.

"Do you know that every time you get angry with me, you become extremely polite and call me 'husband'?"

"Do I?"

"Yes, you do. Sarah, look, I understand you're nervous, but you don't have anything to worry about because I won't leave your side. Besides, I really need your help tonight."

Of all the things he could have said this one thing weakened her resolve. "How could I possibly help?"

He reached out to touch her, but stopped himself. He would be lost if he did. "There are several Southern sympathizers going to this party and there is a rumor circulating that they are planning a meeting in a couple of days. I need to go that meeting. If you could mention how poorly New York is prepared for war and how unfairly the South is treated. I could take over from there."

"They won't invite you."

"You let me worry about that."

Unconcerned about wrinkling her dress, she plopped down on the stairs and pointed out matter-of-fact, "You said those men in that hotel room were sent by a jackal to kill you. The one you are looking for, right?"

He propped his foot up beside her and leaned down, "Yes."

"It is because of this man that you want into the meeting?"

Impatiently, he nodded.

"Then, he knows who you are and who you work for. You won't get invited."

He was amazed by her perception.

"Maybe you haven't noticed, but I can be very persuasive."

She blushed at the memory of how true his statement was, but in a determined voice continued on, "Perhaps, but they will not trust you. It could take weeks to win them over. I, on the other hand, am an unknown American and a woman."

Shaking his head, he quickly stood back up, "Absolutely not. It's too dangerous."

"But, as you said, you will protect me."

"This is not up for discussion."

Yet, even though he bellowed at her like an angry bull, they both knew she was right.

"You are being most stubborn. I can kill a man with a single blow. And am trained in the Arts by my grandfather, yet thanks to Kate I look like one of your helpless English women. It will work. I will be your ears and eyes. It is decided husband, or I won't go."

She watched him pace a minute before stopping with his back to her and heaving a gigantic sigh. "I've never met anyone quite like you Sarah Conway." He turned around and grinned. "All right, we'll try it, but on my terms understand? No going off on your own, or saying anything other than what I tell you to."

Trying her best to appear most humble she nodded.

"And quit playing me for a fool. I mean it Sarah. These are dangerous men."

"I understand dangerous men." She answered quietly, reaching up and touching the small oval necklace at her throat.

The action was not lost on him. Slowly, he sat down besides her, reaching out for the necklace. It was warm from her touch. Flashes of gold danced out from its surface, sparked by the lighted hall scone. "After this is all over, I will find out what happened to your parents. I give you my word."

A tightening in her chest caused the words to come out more harshly than she intended, "How can you make such a promise? I am an English orphan. I don't even know who I really am, much less who my parents were."

Looking down, he noticed her eyes spilling over with drops of liquid light. He cradled her cheek with a steady hand. "I know all I need to know. I know you are brave, kind and so heart wretchedly beautiful that it's hard not to touch you. And I know you are my wife. I protect what is mine, Sarah. I will find a way, I promise."

The fierce protectiveness in his voice made her believe him. For once she actually wished he would kiss her, totally and fiercely without restraint or warning. But, just as suddenly he was gone and pacing once more.

"All right we will try it your way. But, for this to work you will have to appear angry with me." He shrugged, giving a slight smile, when she raised an eyebrow. "Okay, maybe that part won't require a lot of acting on your part. However, you know, there are people who consider me quite charming."

"I am sure Hilda would agree."

His green eyes lit up with laughter. "It's Hilary and you sound rather like a jealous wife already."

"Maybe I will be one – at least for tonight."

Their eyes met and he nodded thoughtfully. Pride was evident in his voice, as he raised her hand to his lips and winked. "Good idea. It just might be the ticket we need, China."

The sound of horse hooves sliding to a stop on a graveled road, slowly cut through the tension building inside the velvet interior of the coach.

"I will not lie."

Exasperated, Simon slapped his gloves onto the leather seat beside him. "Sarah, this is your life we are talking about."

The coach lurched to a stop, but the two beautiful people inside hardly noticed.

"I will find some other way without untruths."

"There is no other way. You have to tell them you're from the South otherwise they will never believe you hold their views. That is unless you can think of another reason why a white wealthy girl from the north would care anything about Southern cotton, or slavery for that matter?"

Refusing to answer, she spun her head off to the side, long curled hair swishing over a shoulder. Frustrated, he rubbed his right temple. She was giving him a headache, "You're going to get yourself killed if you don't stop being so stubborn and listen to me."

Harrison threw open the door.

Simon jerked it out of his hands, slamming it closed again.

"Promise me."

Her gloves suddenly became very interesting.

"I am humbled by such devotion, husband, but must..."

"Don't start." Raking a hand through his hair, he tried to cool his temper. "All right, no lies."

Her head jerked up and she gave him such a brilliant smile that it was nearly his undoing. How on earth was he to keep her safe? This whole thing was a mistake. Just the thought of those men laying a hand on her set his blood to boiling. Yet in order for them to live through this thing he had to be able to maintain a clear head and a certain amount of emotional distance. This meant he had to treat her like any other operative. "We will do it your way. Somehow I will find a way to make your interest believable."

Her smile instantly disappeared. "Last time you said that, we ended up married."

He reached across her and threw open the door. Harrison let out an awful curse as the door bounced off his nose and back again. Sarah gave Simon a terrible glare and started outside to check on the poor man. Simon threw out an arm, stopping her at the door.
"He's fine."

"How can you possibly say he's fine? You just slammed the door on his face."

Harrison, his nose bleeding profusely through one hand reopened the door and slammed the steps down for them. He was cursing under his breath the whole time. Finally, looking up through watering eyes, he ordered, "I don't have all day you two, are you going to this fool party or not?"

"Promise me that you will at least not say anything to contradict me."

"I don't see how allowing others to believe an untruth, is any different than saying an untruth."

"Promise me", he ground out.

"Oh, for the love of Pete, miss, promise the man. I haven't got all night you know. Me nose is swelling up bigger than a dead man three days at sea."

Simon glared at his coachman, "I swear, Harrison, mind your own business or one of these days I will fire you."

The old man threw up his one free hand and walked off, "No such luck. I'm stuck with the whole crazy lot of you. Gentry!"

"Well?"

"Oh, all right." With those last words flung his direction, she began mumbling to herself while exiting the coach, "It certainly won't be your sin to be recorded in heaven's black book, now will it? Why your name is probably not even in the book."

Simon couldn't seem to stop the smile that crossed his face at her mumbling as she pushed past his arm and down the coach steps. No doubt about it, this was going to be an interesting night. In fact, ever since Sarah had been dropped into his lap by fate, his whole life had been turned upside down. And he wasn't sure exactly what he felt about it either.

Sarah looked up at the house and gasped.

For only when she had slowed down and looked up...did she notice the house was no house at all, but a majestic palace. It was massive. Reaching three stories into the dark night, the hundred year old brick interwoven with English ivy seemed more fortress than wall and with windows so polished they reflected the many lights from inside the house, she felt overwhelmed. Even the stairs, all twenty of them, leading up to an intricately carved double door spoke more of exclusion rather than welcome. And despite the openness of the smooth white washed oak and stone railing that ran the length of the front porch, deep inside she sensed that once stepping on its oak surface she would be trapped.

Suddenly it felt as if her nightmare had somehow managed to intermingle with reality, and now she couldn't tell which one was which. Pulling her dark brown wrap more closely around her body, she tried to calm her nerves. But even the soft fox fur that warmed her body failed to reach her soul.

What was she doing here? How did she end up married to a man from another country, another station in life, yet wind up exactly where she had left off ten years ago? It was impossible. Wasn't it? Yet...here she was. At a place that made her heart quicken in memory and her palms sweat in fear.

Oh, the mansion looked innocent enough, all awash in soft lantern light and beautiful gardens with two cherub fountains along the walkway. Yes, what should have appeared romantic induced a different sort of reaction in Sarah. She instantly slowed and took in the massive structure and richly dressed people entering its' depths.

Feeling Simon's warm reassuring hand against her back, she started to breathe again.

"I have a bad feeling Warrior. This house is like a monstrous dragon swallowing up tiny birds in flight. There is evil here."

Her husband's arms drew her in closer until her back rested securely against his warm chest. Then, with eyes closed, she tried to draw strength from his body. The words he spoke into her ear did little to ease the feeling of impending doom. "It's just a house, China. If you are that frightened, it's not too late to change your mind about helping me."

How could she explain that this feeling went deeper than his mission? She felt a coldness enter her bones. This made no sense at all. Instead she pushed down her irrational fear and attempted to sound brave, "I guess it's only my imagination playing tricks. It is just-", she paused trying to find the words, "Well, that so much has changed since finding you. And to tell you the truth, it scares me sometimes. This place England is familiar yet strange. You are my husband but a stranger still in so many ways. And I am not a brave warrior, only a small insignificant person. So I wonder why the God of all things keeps forcing me to take on things that require such great courage."

He turned her around and looked seriously into her face, "I disagree. I think your one of the bravest souls I know, China. And I will always be grateful God sent you to deliver my laundry that day. But regardless of all that, you don't have to do this if you're afraid. Heaven knows I have put you into enough danger already. Besides", He touched one cheek while giving her one those disarming lopsided grins of his that curled her toes, "I am an old hand at this sort of thing and my stomach still turns when I think about what I must face. Only a fool would go in without hesitation."

She nodded. "I know, but I want to help." With that said, she lifted her head bravely, adding; "Now all I need are words of power."

"Words of power? I don't think I understand."

"It is much like the time when I was eleven. I remember how badly I wanted to climb this huge oak in Central park. See, I'd spied a nest of redbirds in its' thick branches. The only problem was an iron fence encircling it, the points sharp as an arrow. But Grandfather, discovering me approaching the tree, stilled me with a hand to my shoulder."

"He was right to do so, it was too dangerous."

"That wasn't why he stopped me." A mischievous smile tugged at her lips. It helped to talk and Simon seemed to sense her need of it. "He wanted to warn me how the pointed fence could pierce a lung or a leg and leave me crippled or dead. Then, he stepped back – his mere presence encouraging me to begin my climb."

Floored Simon could only ask, "Why ever would he do something like that? You could have been killed."

A genuine look of pure trust entered her eyes. "You do not understand. Your ways are different. He loved me deeply. I have always known I am his treasure. And before stepping away to let me make my own decision, he said pretty much what you did just now. That courage without understanding the danger is no courage at all, only stupidity. I climbed the tree, but respected the danger. I can face this danger too, as long as you tell me honestly of what evil awaits me. The knowledge will give me power over my enemy, fear."

A slow smile crossed his features and a real respect for the slight girl looking so intently up at him entered his heart. "Point taken, China. All right. I guess first off, understand that the women inside are going to do everything they can to make you feel unattractive and unworthy of me. Not because you are, but because you are much too beautiful and I chose you over them. This is only aggravated by the fact that you are neither rich, nor deeply lineaged. And then there are the men. They will no doubt tell you all manner of sweet things and try to get you alone. Don't go. A man's words are not to be trusted when he is around a beautiful woman." She nodded, still listening.

"Hilary's father and brother are two of the biggest Southern sympathizers around. But, they are cowards and have a dislike for my

154

politics and me, in particular. Foremost, they dislike me for not marrying Hilary. Although they are richer, my family name is an old and titled one. Their family name is not. They would have dearly loved using my name as a way to secure certain influences. The second reason and perhaps the most important one, is that I am one of the deciding votes in Parliament, and as far as they know, am leaning against importing cheap Southern Cotton. This puts quite a damper on most of their profit. They create fine English lace, which consists mostly of cotton. The cheaper the product, the more they profit. Never mind the fact that all England knows it would be like choosing sides in America's war if we did legally import. But Hawthorne's investors care little about another war. In fact most would welcome the chance to become involved. A large percentage of our people are still smarting from the fact that a bunch of no name rift raft beat them in the first place."

"I see."

"There are many others that are not what they seem, and I promise to catch you up tonight after the party. Just know that if I insist you stay with me it is for a reason. And if I leave you alone with someone, it is a connection. More importantly, remember that the English say one thing, but very likely mean something entirely different."

With sweet tenderness she touched his handsome face. "Thank you Warrior. I will remember. But you needn't have warned me about the English. I already know English people wear many masks. I find myself married to one."

All previous seriousness left his face as he tweaked her small freckled nose. "On second thought, maybe you have a little too much power as it is."

Once entering the great hall all playfulness left Simon. He was once more aloof. A man with a mission and behind his easy smile there was a sense of restrained danger. It seemed to Sarah as if the small group of well dressed people greeting them were completely unaware that he was acting the refined gentleman, while the warrior saw through their false stiff smiles and into their darkest places.

Nervousness made her shy. Not to mention how the unabashed stares were affecting her. If she had thought their manner cool before, on hearing she was married to Simon, most of those she was introduced to raised painted eyebrows and became even more distant, as if that were possible.

The young woman named Hilary was the only exception. She was worse. This was especially hard for Sarah to understand seeing as the ball had been her idea. The open hostility shooting out of Hilary's eyes made her take a step back in reflex.

Of course if she had thought about it logically, she would have been more prepared. After all, it was hardly likely a woman would celebrate her rival. If Sarah had not been so preoccupied with Simon she would have used her common sense and refused the offer.

However it was too late now. Hilary ignored Sarah's hand and swatted at Simon's arm playfully with her silk fan, "You are a scoundrel. Imagine marrying the first American you come across."

Sarah frowned. Did the woman not follow any English rules of etiquette? Heat radiating off her cheeks, Sarah withdrew her hand. So much for hoping to be treated as a welcomed guest. At least Simon would set the pale one straight. After all, it was a husband's duty to defend his wife's honor."

"What choice did I have seeing as the prettiest girl in all of England turned me down cold?"

If she could have found her voice, Sarah would have shouted at him. Instead she smoothly moved up next to him and…stomped on his foot. To his credit, he barely grunted. Giving her a warning look, he moved in closer to his former love.

"Hilary I don't believe you have met my wife. Sarah, this is Hilary, I am sure you remember me speaking of her."

"I am sure I do not."

The gasp beside her, and Simon's hand clenching tightly on her arm as if he wished it were her throat, prevented her from saying more. But if he expected her to guard her tongue, he might try guarding his own a little.

The pale beauty gained a little color, as anger colored her cheeks. "I beg your pardon."

Sarah bowed and repeated calmly, "I said…I am honored to meet one of my husband's former… "

"We are both honored and by the looks of things holding up the line."

He fairly jerked her off her feet and out of line, whispering fiercely, "Are you completely insane? You will apologies this instant."

If he had thought his reprimand would intimidate her, he was very much mistaken. She simply dismissed it. Thinking instead that perhaps English women, even immoral ones, were suppose to be protected by a society she was finding it hard to like. She tried to give her husband the benefit of the doubt, "Was I wrong about the pale one's character then?"

"You live in a make believe world, China. There are some things that are improper to bring out into the open."

Apparently she wasn't.

"One should not apologize for speaking the truth, only for not living it."

Simon groaned in frustration. "I really don't need your words of censure right now. Just an apology will do."

People were beginning to stare. Even worse than that, they had taken to whispering behind shocked hands. Sarah sighed. All she wanted in the world was to disappear for a while. If she gave in, perhaps this horrible night would be sooner on its way to being over. She looked down at the hand leaving imprints on her flesh, and then back up into his dark green eyes. "I will apologize for breaking one of your society's rules. Now let go of my arm Warrior or I will break another rule, the one about being a humble wife in public."

She had thought her words would anger him further; instead he surprised her…there was laughter lurking in his eyes. He turned loose of her however and indicated she lead the way back to the woman waiting impatiently for an apology.

Walking the three steps back, Sarah wondered why it felt as if she were out of body and floating overhead. Noticing the silver haired woman give a smug smile, Sarah knew why – she was furious.

Finding her voice, Sarah remarked coolly, "It is not to my honor to behave unkindly to one who has welcomed me into their home. I apologize if I have offended you by speaking the tru–"

Simon gave her a quick peck on the lips, smoothly interrupting the rest of her sentence, before adding, "My wife's family is from China. Which should explain any further offense; she is not used to our customs. We had better go; the orchestra is beginning to warm up."

Hilary laid a restraining hand on Simon's arm. Then leaning over, she kissed the air beside Sarah's cheek, saying a little too sweetly, "But I had thought Simon told us that you were originally from England. However, that might explain why I don't recall ever meeting any of your family. What did you say your family name was dear?"

Lifting her head a notch, Sarah didn't hesitate, "Conway. Simon is my family now. My parents were killed when I was a child."

Hilary's sky blue eyes turned icy as she flipped open her fan to cool her flushed face. "How awful for you. However, I am sure you possessed a name before Simon came along."

"None that mattered."

Simon barely concealed his shock at this new revelation. Placing a stilling hand on Hilary's clenched fist that was pressed up against her stomach, he bent over, and gave a brotherly kiss to the cheek, "I see George has joined her majesty's service, I better try and talk some sense into him." Then, as if Sarah were not standing right beside him, he looked deeply into his past love's eyes adding in a sultry voice, "It's been a long time Hilary. Perhaps there will be a chance to catch up on old times later tonight."

Once she started breathing again, Sarah fully intended to do her own catching up with him.

Turning intimately in towards Simon's hard muscled form and apparently not caring if she offended his wife or not, the fair skinned woman practically purred, "Yes, that would be nice. I have missed you terribly. Perhaps then you could explain why you chose to marry so quickly. It seemed when we were together you greatly embraced the bachelor's life. What changed?"

Sarah wished they could move on. She did not care for the woman. And people were starting to notice the two flirting shamelessly with each other. Her face went hot with embarrassment. She was losing much face.

When next she heard his whispered words to the beautiful woman throwing herself at him, Sarah barely restrained herself from yanking the fan from the pale woman's hands and breaking it over his head.
"Did I? Perhaps I miss it still, since it requires the loss of refined beauties, such as yourself."

Sending a glare Hilary's direction, Sarah practically yanked Simon off his feet. "I fear we are being rude my husband. Let us continue down this most...interesting line of Englishmen."

His low chuckle was the only response to his wife's obvious jealousy. Still, he managed to keep the rest of his remarks impersonal to the other women in line. Apparently he was not a total philander. That, or either Sarah racing through the line with barely a nod their direction discouraged further flirtations. Whichever was the case, at long last they were gathered in the ballroom, waiting for the dancing to begin.

The sound of the orchestra's lively tune in the background was beginning to irritate Sarah's already taunt nerves. Then there was the presence of her tall handsome husband, pretending cool indifference while she on the other hand was barely able to refrain from bursting into angry tears. Both were equally aggravating. Especially since she was suppose to be immune to her husband. She attempted a smile, but failing that, remarked as casually as possible, "I thought you no longer cared for the woman Hilary as a prospective wife."

"I don't. Besides, last I heard Bigamy is against the law."

What kind of answer was that? And was the man actually grinning at her?

Eyes straight ahead, she said through clenched teeth, "Then, you realize, my most devoted of husbands, she will likely think you mean to charm her for less than honorable reasons."

He winked and pulled her knotted fist through his arm, gently releasing her fingers one by one and forcing her to relax. "I am sure you're wrong."

"I am sure I am not."

The solo violinist began a waltz and Simon led her to the dance floor, his strong arm wrapped around her tiny waist. "Oh, I meant wrong about there being a chance she thinks my intentions the least bit honorable."

She stopped dead in her tracks, pulling at her left hand to free it of his ironclad grasp.

"Have you no shame? To admit such an act is –"
"You're making a scene Sweetheart."

"Not yet...husband."

He didn't like the look in her eye. Being knocked unconscious in front of the town, was not what he had in mind when he set out to make it look as if the two of them had a falling out. Besides, it would be downright hard on his male ego. No, having his five foot two, tiny little thing of a wife get the better of him in front of his peers was not an option. He'd be fighting duels to defend his masculinity for the rest of his life if he did. And hurting her to prevent it was even more out of the question.

So, to be on the safe side, he gathered her up closer instead. What was that old saying? Keep your friends close and your enemies closer? He shook his head at himself. Now he was starting to spout off quotes like his wife.

When he finally spoke, his voice was full of warning and she could nearly swear humor of all things.

"Remember you are supposed to act the part of a woman in love. I hardly think knocking me unconscious in public conveys that message do you? Besides this fight was your idea remember?"

His nearness was making it hard to concentrate. She pushed herself away. He jerked her back, slightly knocking the breath out of her body. "I mean it, China. Cut it out."

Unchecked tears of frustration were coursing down her cheeks. "I hate you to hold me so close."

His touch gentled instantly when he saw her tears, "Am I hurting you sweetheart?"

"Please let me go," her words were barely a whisper, "you are causing me to lose face in front of your people."

He stopped dancing and worriedly looked around for some place private to talk. But, before he could, she was gone. He barely managed to catch a glimpse of apricot satin as it disappeared through the balcony doors leading outside. And even though it was the reaction he had hoped for, his heart constricted to cause her pain.

Stunned by the thought, he rubbed a hand along his chin in sudden realization. He cared about her deeply. When exactly that had occurred, he had no idea. But if he were honest with himself, he would admit almost from the beginning. Looking back, it seemed as if a part of him had recognized her the moment she barged into that hotel room. He blinked at the sudden blinding reality and what the confession meant for the rest of his life. For one thing it meant he could not go through with putting her in harms way. Duty or no duty, He had to find her before someone else did.

A feathery light cool touch caused him to look away from the balcony door and down at the silvery blond smiling smugly up at him.

"Trouble in paradise, Darling?"

Now that he had seen real beauty, he wondered how he had ever been even remotely attracted to this pale vision in light blue with threads of silver bringing out the coldness of her eyes. And the coldness is what reminded him. The surest way to protect Sarah and his family was to catch the man responsible for trying to kill him and destroy England. He had known men like him before and they rarely stop just because you have had a change of heart. No, the only way to keep his family safe was to find him. Since Hilary was known for her involvement with smugglers, she was the quickest route to his enemy. She had a reputation for being drawn to dangerous men. This is what attracted her to him in the first place.

He took a glass of brandy from a passing tray. He needed something to help push down the distaste for what he intended to do. Then he looked unflinchingly at the woman beside him, waiting. Yes, she was weak and vindictive. But, right now he needed her.

"I suppose it goes with the territory when your hand is forced."

Taking a sip of champagne, the blond looked at him from over the glistening crystal. "So, the rumors are true. It was a forced marriage?"

"I suppose you could call it that." He hated this job with its lies.

"Poor, darling. Why don't we find some place to talk? The gardens are lovely in the moonlight. Especially, the gazebo."

Hilary's brother Peter was heading toward the balcony and his distraught wife. It took every last ounce of strength he possessed not to follow him, "Aren't you afraid of a scandal? Being alone with a married man?"

Hilary shrugged glancing seductively up at him, "Oh, I don't mind. Besides, when has what other people thought ever stopped me before?"

She moved in closer, slipping her hand under his jacket and sliding it across his broad chest. Her touch felt as unwelcome as her presence, but both were necessary.

Looking back over his shoulder, he caught Kate's condemning stare from in front of the elaborate punch bowl decorated with hothouse violets. Violets… He instantly thought of Sarah and the old woman's sign of true love. He took a step back and shook his head in confusion; his wife was having an affect on him and not necessarily a good one. He had to keep a cool head.

Destiny and true love did not exist. This was just a job. He had nothing to feel guilty about. Still, unbidden thoughts of light golden brown eyes brimming with tears made his stomach churn in disgust at himself. He swallowed a mouthful of brandy and raised his glass in a mock salute. "That's the thing I admire most about you Hilary, your lack of morals."

Her laughter followed him down the hall and out into the moonlit gardens.

She didn't know what had come over her. She felt raw and all manner of terrible. Swiping at the last of her tears, she took in great gulps of air to calm herself. This place, something was wrong here. Grandfather would say a house only represents the karma of those living inside its walls. It seemed the only sensible reason for her overwhelming emotional response was the terror of facing all the evil she had tried to escape years ago. Since coming here, she had been dropped into her old way of life and even her husband's work with the government. She had the constant feeling of being on her guard. It was so confusing.

She shook her head at herself. Who was she kidding? Her feelings about her husband were causing the most upheaval to her senses. She wasn't sure what effected her more, her loveless marriage, or caring about a man who for all obvious reasons would end up dead, or worse. After all it wasn't as if she truly felt threatened by Heidi, or whatever her name was. One had to own something to feel it could be taken away. Which made it harder for her understand her feelings concerning the warrior.

Why, she didn't even like him half the time.

"You know Robert the gardener is rather fond of those roses you're tearing to shreds right now."

A gasp escaped her lips as she glanced down to notice a hand full of torn petals and leaves from the small potted primrose resting on top of the balcony ledge beside her elbow.

"Oh, I most humbly beg your pardon sir, I was upset and..." her voice trailed off in confusion, looking down numbly at the small drop of blood gathering on her index finger from one of the thorns.

The blond haired man shrugged his shoulders and came to her aid.

"Here let me see."

She jerked her hand back behind her, eyes big a saucers, "I do not believe it is proper for you to attend me Sir. Why, I don't even know your name."

"My name is Peter, and I assure you it is perfectly all right for me to assist a lady in distress." When she failed to warm, he added, "I find your reaction puzzling."

Tears still glistened in her curious eyes. Taken aback by her beauty, he motioned with his head toward the ballroom he had just left, "You know your husband seems to hold no such qualms about morality where it concerns my dear sister. But never you mind my dear lady, I assure you that the shrew can't hold a candle to a real beauty like you. Even your husband could not be that much a fool."

She couldn't stop the trembling smile that tugged at the corner of her mouth. "That doesn't sound very brotherly of you."

He shrugged, "One can't choose one's relatives, and all that. However, one can choose ones friends. And I believe, dear Sarah, after the way you stood up to my usually intimidating older sister, I would like to be yours. Now, why don't you give me your hand, so I can do my good deed for the day."

Her heart pounded in response. This man was flirting with her. What did Simon say? It was something about not being alone with strange men. Unless, of course, he left her alone, then that man became a connection. She closed her eyes in conflict of emotion. His hand was warm to the touch as he ran a thumb over her wound checking for any embedded thorn. Her unwanted thoughts and feelings were running rampart inside her body. She couldn't think properly.

"Grandfather says one should never make a commitment while walking a tightrope."

His eyes were a deep chocolate brown. "All right, I'll bite. Who is this 'Grandfather' and exactly why are we talking about tightropes? I'm not making you nervous, am I?"

"Oh, heavens no. I just meant that I shouldn't make a decision...like friendship for instance, when I feel..."

"Like your about to plunge to your death?"

"Yes. I mean, no." She cringed, biting at her lower lip. "I have insulted you."

A flash of straight white teeth was her only response.

Blushing, she shyly pulled back her hand, "I am most grateful for your assistance, Peter. And as for being your friend? Well, you may call me Sarah."

"The pleasure is all mine, I assure you."

Gently retrieving her hand, he raised her wounded finger to his lips. His eyes searched her own intently.

She could only watch in fascinated shock before getting a hold of herself and taking a step away. Subconsciously she looked down over the side of the balcony to the grass below a good ten feet. If she threw him off she might seriously injure him. Better to simply leave instead. If only he were not blocking her path.

She grew nervous. Even her own husband had not pursued her so openly. "I'd better get back to your English party. The warrior might be wondering where I am by now."

"You do say the strangest things. But, if you're referring to your husband, I last saw him deep in conversation with the shrew."

"Oh." Sarah turned away, so he would not notice the hurt in her eyes.

Rather than leave, he moved in closer beside her. Leaning on the railing, he looked off into the garden. "I know it is not my business, but there is a rumor going around that yours was a forced arrangement."

She gave up pretending, which she wasn't any good at anyhow, and let one tear escape as she wiped at her nose with one delicately embroidered glove.

"Here, this might help."

She took the offered handkerchief and blew her nose. The tall lanky man laughed in response.

"So, tell me, Sarah how did you and old sober sides get together. He is hardly your type."

"How did you...? No, he isn't. But it was America and things are different there."

The moonlight made the man's hair shine like an angel. Except Simon said he was the enemy. Funny, he seemed nice, except for being a little too forward. No, he wasn't as handsome as Simon, but he was very charming. He certainly didn't seem like a jackal.

"Ah, America. That's the accent I couldn't quite place. My family does trade with that country you know. Although there would be those that would say, it is really no country at all, but a Hodge podge of uneducated ruffians."

"And what would you say?"

He studied her intently before answering. "I think, if you are an example, that the elusive 'they' are very much mistaken. However, I do wonder what a lady like you feels about your south starting a war."

Trying to appear vaguely interested, she studied the garden below. Two people were walking in the moonlight, barely touching. She frowned. There was something vaguely familiar about them. "Since it was Lincoln who refused to let the South choose its own laws, I hardly think they started it. But none of that matters now. Grandfather says wars are the conquerors of rational men. I fear everyone will lose, especially the South."

"And what if the South won?"

"Some would say it would be a victory for the States to have the ability to choose their own laws. Lincoln says, it would mean defeat. A divided country is easily conquered. Either way it sounds as if we lose something."

"You know, there are several here who support the South's cause."

Rather than answer, she concentrated harder on the people below. "I believe that is my husband and your sister walking in the garden."

He leaned forward on his elbows and peered over the edge. "He is a bigger fool then I thought then."

His words comforted her somewhat. But the truth was they looked beautiful together. Two ethereal souls floating through an enchanted garden: him dark, and her, a beam of fairy light. She purposely stepped away from the railing and the sadness. "Well, I truly must go inside now. It would be breaking one of your English rules, staying out here so long, alone with you. It seems only husbands are allowed to break vows. However, it has been an honor meeting such a promising friend."

"Wait," he reached out and stopped her from leaving, "I've been thinking. You have a lot to offer in way of information to a small group I meet with every week. In fact, our next meeting is two days from now here in the library. Will you come?"

This was the offer she had been waiting for, so why did she hesitate? It was this house. She didn't want to come back here, even in the daylight. And then there was the fact this man offered her something she had never had before from a stranger: friendship. And now, she was supposed to use this man to help a husband's cause who made it evident he cared nothing for her. No, regardless of her feelings, her word to her husband bound her. There was no choice, at least not tonight. She forced a smile and nodded. "All right."

He stood straighter, a good two inches above Simon's six feet. He was a tall man, this Peter Hawthorne.

"Good. The meeting starts at eleven."

She turned to go inside once more.

"And one other thing..."

"Yes?"

"Don't tell your husband. He wouldn't understand or approve."

Looking past his shoulder to the shadowy images down in the garden below, heads bent slightly together, her tone was melancholy. "I fear there is much I don't approve of, or understand about him either."

The night seemed to stretch out forever. Between Kate's nervous chatter and the sea of faces she was introduced to, Sarah felt exhausted. Not to mention that the fear she felt when she first entered the house had increased sevenfold. Then there was the way Simon totally ignored her and doted on his ex lover. Not, that she cared. No, not in the least.

She snatched a champagne glass from the polished silver tray sailing past her head and swallowed a huge gulp of the liquid fire.

Coughing uncontrollably, she looked up in time to meet Simon's disapproving frown from across the room. Defiantly, and out of horrible sadness, she glared boldly back at him, while forcing the rest of it down. It tasted terrible. Yet amazingly she began to feel a little better as slow warmth seeped into her body, a surprising clearness to her thinking.

Another waltz started in their honor. Sarah narrowed her eyes and snatched another glass of bubbly gold from a servant passing by. The waltz too was a joke. For this was the fourth one tonight, and two of those, Simon had danced with their hostess. She was so lost in feeling sorry for herself, that she hardly noticed as Simon walked right past her and into Hilary's arms. Peter did however, and came to her pride's rescue by asking her to dance.

This time her dancing improved quite a bit. In fact after finishing her glass of champagne, she even ventured to say she was getting quite good at it. At least that was the impression she got from her many dance partners. Although she was beginning to notice that the room seemed to spin around a bit.

So, by the time Kate came up and dragged her over to Simon, saying something about not letting Hilary get away with it. She was in a rather good mood, and working on her third glass.

However, what once seemed painfully clear, was now looking rather fuzzy and off balance. She tried to focus on the two people Simon was introducing her to, but since they looked more than the two he claimed, she smiled lamely and took another sip. Besides, who they were hardly mattered. She couldn't seem to take her eyes off the way Hilary clung to Simon's arm and the way he patted her hand affectionately. Her good mood was evaporating quickly. She glared and took a good long swallow of her half empty drink.

"I believe your little wife has had too much to drink, Darling."

Did the woman actually call him 'Darling'? Sarah leaned in to give her a piece of her mind and nearly lost her balance. Simon caught her just in time. The blue haired woman in the beaded pearl dress looked down her long regal nose and sniffed in disgust. Sarah raised her eyebrows and wrinkled her nose back. A nudge from Simon nearly sent her reeling into the pudgy powdered wigged man beside her.

"Sarah, how many of those have you had?"

How dare he lecture her, when he was off in the moonlight for over an hour with good old Hildee? She tried to shrug him off, but his hand gripped her arm even tighter. When a wave of dizziness hit her, she was suddenly glad for her husband's tight hold. Suddenly all too aware of the stares her direction, she whispered, or at least she hoped it was a whisper, up at her husband. "I feel most unwell Warrior."

"Did the girl actually refer to you as Warrior?" The blurry old men with the funny looking wig asked in surprise.

Sarah, tapping on the bottom of her glass, added in a nasty slur, "At least I didn't call him 'Darling' like old Hildee here."

"Okay, Sarah. I think it is time to say our good-byes."

She handed the shocked older woman with blue hair, her glass. "And I was so enjoying the English party. Did you know, Warrior, that Lord Ashwell's mistress is here tonight at the party? Only his wife is pretending that she isn't. Only everyone knows she is. It is quite the scandal."

A shocked gasp sounded from the crowd.

"Sarah." Simon warned, tugging her towards the door, not even pretending he wasn't dragging her. "Oh, wait, Warrior, we didn't say good-bye to the shrew."

She was waving wildly Hilary's direction, when Simon swept her off her feet and carried her through the door and out to the carriage. She didn't even fight back, but blessedly laid her swimming head against his broad warm chest. He smelt so very good, her warrior.

Once reaching the carriage, Simon laid her gently inside, which surprised her. A lot of things surprised her.

For one thing, she expected him to begin shouting at her the minute they were alone. He didn't.

In fact, after nearly fifteen minutes of silence she even started to relax.

Apparently, they weren't speaking. Which was just fine with Sarah, the carriage was making her sicker by the minute anyway. She could swear Harrison was deliberately heading for each and every pothole. She groaned and clutched at her stomach.

"Does Harrison have to bounce around so much?"

"It's what you deserve for drinking too much. One would think that was the first champagne you've ever had."

Indignant, she attempted to sit up and look down her nose at him like the blue lady, but barely managed to slide back down into the corner clutching the seat in hopes her stomach would stop it's churning, "What I deserve? You're the one who...who...of all the most arrogant...well, Hah!"

He looked at her in disgust. "I can't believe you have a problem with my behavior Sarah, after the way you practically drank yourself into oblivion"

"If I haf a problem, my most devoted huzbund, it's with your behavior. You practically threw yourself at old Hill...Hid...whoever she is."

"I believe shrew was the word you used."

She blushed angrily. "Only because...because I couldn't think of a word horrible enough for you."

His tone was cool indifference. "Oh, but I know a few, China. Shall I quote some of them for you?"

Shocked, she crossed her arms. Which was a mistake, for her iron clasp grip was the only thing keeping her on the seat. She hit the floor with a loud thud, and instantly began rubbing her sore backside. Her stomach rolled in obvious rebellion. She was definitely going to be sick.

His masculine laughter filled the carriage as he reached down to help her. Glaring at him, she slapped his hand away and crawled back onto the seat.

"You are a very rude English heath...health...he...I don't remember, but your one all right."

"And you, my love can't hold your liquor."

"Don't call me your love, and for your information I don't usually drink. After all, Grandfather says it is the robber of one's senses", she argued with a slur.

"This is precisely the reason two and a half drinks got the better of you. Did you get invited to the meeting by Peter or not?"

For some reason his cool indifference and reference to Peter caused her throat to close up in renewed self-loathing. "Unlike you, hez an most considerate and kind man."

Was that a trace of anger in his smoldering green depths? "Not last time I checked he wasn't. Exactly what went on out there?"

"Hah!"

"Would you stop hahing at me and just answer the fool question."

"Nothing worse than what was going on in the garden with old Hildee, that's for sure."

Harrison started banging on the top of the carriage. "You two stop that infernal shouting, my head is aching something fierce".

Before Simon could put him in his place, they both slid sideways as Harrison must have rounded a corner. Simon's head banged so hard against the side, the sound of it echoed throughout the carriage. Furious, he fairly shouted at her.

"Hilary. The woman's name is Hilary. I wish to heaven you would get it right just once. And for your information I had to make you jealous tonight and I had to make it believable. You can't lie remember? So, I made it real for you. Otherwise, you were going to get yourself killed playing spy."

Stunned sober, Sarah's voice was barely controlled as she asked, "You mean you actually planned for me to lose face in front of your English friends? To make a fool of myself?"

He hated the sound of shocked hurt in her voice, "No. I meant to push one of the sympathizers your direction. And it worked."

For some reason, the coldness of that statement washed over her like a dip in a winter sea. She felt more sober than she had all evening. Her chin came up a notch, as her brown eyes darkened; the gold light in them was completely gone as they met his. "It's so easy for you, isn't it? Make Hilary think you're in love with her. Trick a really nice man into giving up his friends. You even went as far as using me and my feelings to further your little masquerade. Why you are really no better than the villains you chase, are you?"

He flinched as if she had struck him. Yet he still refused to defend himself.

"Grandfather says when you walk with evil, your shadows will always cross paths, until at last they merge and one can no longer tell where one begins and the other ends."

The carriage rolled to a stop. The quiet inside was deafening.

"Are you quite finished?"

She barely managed a nod. She felt so utterly miserable.

"Good. And you're right, I am no better than people like Peter. I tried to tell you that from the beginning so don't act so hurt and shocked by the fact. Regardless I intend to keep you alive, even if that means you think less of me in the process."

Ashamed of herself, even if he did deserve it, she tried to apologize, "I am sorry Warrior. I shouldn't have lost my temper. It is just that I'm not use to drinking, or feeling things or...what I mean to say is that you have been nothing but honest with me from the beginning. It is just I had not expected to feel things for you. Especially since I know our marriage is an unwanted burden to you, just as I am an unwanted wife. I even understand that the woman Hilary is none of my business. That it was I who suggested you flirt with her. And I realize I understand nothing about the burden this government has placed on your shoulders. It's just..." she noticed in a numb way how the tears dropping off her chin darkened the apricot color of her gown. She had never allowed herself to cry in front of others before Simon. Now it seemed as if she were constantly fighting off tears.

The door opened and Harrison threw down the steps.

"Notice I'm standing in 'front' of the door this time."

"Close the door Harrison."

Rolling his eyes heavenward, Harrison slammed it shut with a final thud. "That's it. I'm done for the night. Open the door Harrison. Shut the door Harrison. It's enough to drive a body to drink."

Sarah's eyes and heart felt heavy. As if nothing would ever be right again. She had hurt him somehow with her words. They were unkind and not like her. She didn't like much about herself lately. Maybe she should just sign the paper saying her word meant nothing and leave this land. For this place held little but heartache for her.

Simon rubbed the side of his head, tiredness written on every line in his face. Some part of her wanted to soothe away the disenchantment she saw written there. For in spite of everything, he still was the handsomest man she had ever known. And regardless of what she pretended to him or herself, she held a deep respect for his dedication to everything he believed in, including his family. May the God of heaven protect her; she knew something else as well. That she loved him. The thought alone scared her to death. There were a million reasons why loving him was impossible. It was too soon for one. How could love come so quickly? Yet there was no denying, her racing heart every time she looked at him.

But the biggest reason of all for her tears was that she could lose him, as she had lost her parents. She wasn't sure she could go through that kind of heartache again. She might lose more than her memory if she did.

"I am also most sorry my husband for calling your lady friend a shrew. It was unkind."

He gave one of those adoring cocky grins that made her stomach flutter. "There you go being polite again. Which I take it, means you are not in the least sorry, are you China?"

She tried not to smile back, her heart was so heavy, but he affected her in odd ways. She answered him with a tentative smile, the forgotten tears making her eyes shine, "No, I am not. However, I am sorry for accusing you of being dishonorable. It is not true, at least not about the things that matter, like family and country. You are a strong warrior. One who defends everyone else, but himself. I suppose what I really felt angry with you about tonight, was how being with you, changes who I am. I no longer even understand my own feelings."

"You are also right that I am most terrible at deception. And I truly hate seeing you touch another woman. I want to say unkind things and shove her into the punch bowl. Even breathing deeply and thinking on the sounds of a peaceful New York ocean, changes into a daydream about drowning one of you. I know it makes little sense. But I hated showing the world that you cared so little for me. It hurt my pride. My woman's heart."

"Sarah."

Once more those dratted tears blurred her vision. She brushed them angrily away and cleared her voice. Yet it still sounded clogged with tears.

"As to business, I did get invited to the meeting. Only that too confused me. See, I hadn't counted on liking Peter. So I suppose that makes me worse than you, because the whole time he spoke of being my friend, I was debating the pros and cons of using him."

"China, don't."

"And I feel things when I am with you, horrible things. It is rather like riding a wild stallion through a summer storm. One minute I am hoping you'll try to kiss me, and the next, scared to death you will."

"That doesn't sound so horrible to me."

His voice was warm and inviting, sexy.

"But, it is. I have to help you and then leave for my home, no matter what Grandfather says. I can't fall in love with an Englishman. I can't stay here."

"Sweetheart, come here and stop crying."

She shook her head wildly. "No, I can't because you see, every time you touch me I feel like either hitting or kissing you. It's all very confusing and I am never quite sure which one will win out."

Suddenly she felt the heat of his body beside her, as his practiced fingers ran seductively along her lower lip. Soon soft kisses raining along her jaw line and up by her ear were creating havoc to her insides. She forgot to breathe; much less think.

"Let me love you, China. Let me take you into my arms and end this deep ache I have for you."

She closed her eyes as if in sweet torture. How she ached for him too. In a way she didn't fully understand. Yet if she gave in there would be no turning back. No leaving him.

She turned to explain why she couldn't. Deep green eyes, filled with passion bore into hers and she was lost. All it took was one look into those mesmerizing eyes of his and it sucked the words of denial from her parted lips. All that surfaced were simple words of honesty, "I don't know what to do."

He drew her in closer until she felt the warmth of his breath on her lips. "Do you trust me, China?"

Did she? Or did she even care when her heart pounded so wildly every time he touched her. The sound of his voice soothed and excited her at the same time. Truth be told, even in her innocence, she wanted him, needed him.

But all she seemed to be able to manage was a slight nod. Afraid words would make this moment disappear.

"Then I'll show you."

Those few words shut out all thought processes. Sensations of unbelievable warmth and excitement took over every place he touched. His mouth was everywhere. Inviting and blending her body with his. She never wanted it to end. But if it didn't, life would never be the same for him again. For tonight she had seen the truth. They didn't belong together. He was from one world and she another. She was a nobody, an orphan, without a name, or a past. Simply because she had saved his life, he felt obligated to share the rest of his with her. But she knew deep down, he could never truly be hers. Only borrowed, until someone like Hilary took back what rightfully belonged to them anyhow.

Gently she pushed him away. Sadness and regret in her voice.

"This can't be Simon Conway. You belong with a rich, English wife, someone who has more to offer you, than a dark unknown past. If I give myself to you, our destinies will change forever."

He kissed the corner of her mouth silencing her protests, and when he answered he forced her to meet his hard determined glare, "When are you going to realize, sweetheart? You are my destiny. Have been ever since God sent a funny little China angel to rescue me in that New York hotel room. Now would you please shut up and kiss your husband. I have a lot of catching up to do."

And, what could a girl, even a misfit orphan one like her do, but...oblige her husband?

# Chapter 11

The next morning Sarah Conway woke up with a warrior in her bed.

Her head hurt something fierce, but her heart was full. She ran a hand in wonder down along the muscles of his tanned arm and then reverently placed a light kiss to his beautiful strong jaw line. The memories of last night flooded her senses and she sighed contentedly. She was a wife.

Sometime during the night, it had no longer mattered who she use to be, but only who she had become. Even the nightmare did not come to her in the dark of her mind last night. It was the first time since arriving here that she had sleep peacefully through the night. She looked down in wonder at the sleeping man who was now her husband, his unkempt hair making him look more adorable than usual. Could it be that he defended her even in the dream world? Some things were beyond her understanding. She only knew how grateful she was to the God of all things, for bringing such a good man into her life.

She slipped out of bed and into a silk robe hanging on the back of a chair. Simon moaned and turned onto his stomach, snoring softly.

She hesitated only a moment, allowing him time to drift off again before tip toeing out of the room and into the dressing room. Within minutes she had washed off and dressed. The sounds of the awakening morning urged her to finish her toilet quickly. Grandfather would already be out in the garden.

Braiding her long hair on the way back through the bedroom and out the door she hurried down the stairs. She had to speak to Grandfather before breakfast. It was important.

She found him in the gardens. Right where she had known he would be. His eyes closed in meditation, his gnarled bare feet crossed at the ankles, dressed in traditional Chinese garb. She wasn't sure exactly why the sight of him practicing the ancient arts of his ancestors gave her such peace. It simply did.

Automatically, she removed her own sandals and moved alongside him. Closing her eyes, she let herself breathe in the cool morning air, let herself feel the moisture-ridden breeze touching her warm skin, forcing her to relax.

Before long, they were up and moving in sequence. Her own silk pants, loose and cool, sliding softly against her skin. She had missed their morning stretches and spars this past week. The time of meditation. Both were acts of unspoken bonding that she shared with the wisest man she had ever known.

The older man moved with the grace of a twenty year old. His movements were quick and sure. The swan and crouching tiger stance, through it all neither one said a word. They were each in tune with their own breathing, their bodies like fine thoroughbreds; every muscle was sleek and controlled. The sun was now setting the earth aglow, and Sarah felt the excitement of the approach of a new day. She always believed this to be the best time of day. It was the gift of a new beginning. It was the promise of one more chance to fulfill one's destiny before leaving this life. She drew in a deep breath of dew filled air and smiled.

"Grandfather. Do we spar today?"

He stretched a leg up near his head and nodded solemnly. "It is good to do the familiar. It brings order to chaos. Ready yourself Little One."

Sarah tied the corded black belt around her waist and bowed once. Then suddenly, giving a fierce shout, she jumped into the air before landing in a solid horse stance, automatically throwing up her hands in defense.

Lee walked around her, hands clasped behind his back, shaking his head. "You are growing sloppy granddaughter. I think this husband of yours captures your mind as well as your body."

Appearing unaffected, Sarah spun around and narrowly missed Lee's head with a well-executed roundhouse.

Immediately, she crouched down in ready position once more.

"Strange. For I find you are growing ancient and slow like our friend the sea turtle." She replied almost casually.

With one fatal swoop of his leg, she found herself on the ground and looking up at the sky.

"Perhaps you are right my young pupil, I will meditate on it and get back to you."

Her musical laughter was her only response, before quickly rising to her feet and producing a fierce warrior expression. "I was only testing you old one. For my mind is sharp as a raven's beak and my body strong as an ox."

She did a feather light double punch to his middle, before deftly stepping aside and around the back, catching him into a most impressive choke hold.

The two sparring partners did not even notice they were being watched from the window above.

Simon shook his head in wonder at the magnificent spectacle below. Apparently his wife was not only beautiful, but graceful as well. He watched as the old man was thrown to the ground. He automatically flinched in remembered pain. It seems his wife was well versed in the art of catching a man off balance. Not to mention being extremely dangerous. She knew some moves even he did not recognize. Strange, he had always considered the martial arts no match for the pistol or a well-placed fist. Yet, watching the two of them, he found himself gaining respect for the Chinese way of fighting. To watch Lee and Sarah fight was rather like watching a ballet. It was beautiful in a deadly sort of way.

Before meeting Sarah he would have scoffed at the notion that his small frame, one hundred and five pound wife could have thrown anyone. That is, had he not been on the receiving end of her wrath not once, but twice already.

Who knows, perhaps he would take lessons himself from his sexy marriage partner. He grinned, as thoughts of her wrapped around him assaulted his senses. Unfortunately, it was thoughts like those that would definitely put him at a disadvantage. Suddenly, he wanted to be near her. To soak up her beauty once more before beginning the endless stacks of paperwork awaiting him at the shipping office.

Quickly throwing on a pair of soft wool pants and shoving his arms into the billowing white silk shirt from last night, he fairly raced down the staircase. Determined not to interrupt, but only enjoy the show, he made sure to exit by the servant's stairs, which came out directly behind the pair locked in combat.

Once reaching the garden he noticed the two people were no longer speaking. Each one concentrating so hard that sweat trickled down the side of his luxurious bride's head. Lee on the other hand barely moved, or so it seemed. Yet, when he did, he rarely missed.

All thoughts of Simon's surroundings were swept from his mind as he watched in fascination. This was no child's play. He recognized true skill when he saw it and the two before him were masters at their craft. His eyes narrowed at a dawning of understanding. He really could have been killed if his wife would have willed it. His frown deepened. Not to mention how senseless it had been to worry about her. Apparently feeling as if he had to protect her was as unwarranted as protecting a seasoned solider. And if looks right now meant anything, heaven help anyone who crossed her path. Leaning one hand against the cupid statue covered in ivy, he didn't know quite what to make of this newest discovery about his wife.

Undoubtedly she was the same gorgeous, warm female he had made love to last night. But yet, it was as if she had morphed into some magnificent ancient warrior from a legend in a book. He would have never believed a female could ever be his equal in combat if he hadn't seen it for himself. And he felt? Well...proud. After all, this magnificent creature belonged to him in every sense of the word. And right now he wanted nothing more than to prove his point by gathering her into his arms and carrying her right back upstairs to their bed. Instead, he placed one booted foot on the chubby cupid's foot and waited for them to end their battle of wills.

Albert cleared his throat.

Simon jumped as if shot, "Albert, must you go around sneaking up on people."

A loud sniff issued out of his over sized bulbous nose, "There is no need to shout Sir."

"I was not shouting. And you can be grateful to my wife for that, I don't wish to interrupt her and Lee. Now what is it?"

"Oh, quite, I say. Are they fighting Sir?"

"Obviously."

The servant wrinkled his forehead and straightened his vest as if in uniform. "Odd I hadn't noticed. I am very observant." He took out his monocle and peered out over at them, "Why I haven't seen that kind of fighting since the Boxer Wars. Not quite the thing for a young lady though. But, that is neither here nor there. What was it you wanted Sir?"

Trying his best not to lose his temper, Simon ground out his words through clenched teeth. "You came out here to me. I certainly did not call you."

Unruffled by his employer's frustration, he looked down his nose, checked his pocket watch and informed him, "Now, why would I come out into the damp garden with my war injury making my knee so stiff I can barely walk unless you called me, Sir?"

Intending to get the butler away before he disturbed the fight, Simon started walking back towards the house, hoping he would follow. "You shot yourself in the foot, not the knee."

"If you say so, Sir."

"You said so when we hired you."

Sighing, the servant gave him the look of an idiot. "Well, if that is all Sir, may I be excused?"

"Gladly seeing as I did not call you out here in the first place."

"Perhaps the reason slipped your mind while spying on your young lady."

"I was not... "Simon patted his shirt for a cheroot, forgetting he didn't have on his jacket. "Never mind. That will be all Albert."

"Yes, Sir."

Simon stepped into the dining room and glared at Albert's retreating back. He could nearly swear sometimes that Albert was saner than he was letting on and deliberately goading him. His mother entered the dining room and smiled sweetly at Albert before coming over and laying a kiss on her son's cheek.

"Mother, about these so called servants of yours..."

She placed a finger to his lips and motioned towards Albert. "You wouldn't want to hurt the poor dear's feelings. He can't help his shortcomings, being injured in the war and all. The least we can do is be understanding."

He counted to ten. Then, knowing it was useless to argue; he filled his plate from the buffet and sat down at the table. She joined him a minute later. His plate contained kidneys, an omelet, and sweet pastries. Her plate contained a single scone with orange marmalade.

"So, how is Sarah this morning dear?"

He took a mouthful of food and swallowed, "Fine."

Kate sailed through the door about that time, saw her brother and threw her chin up into the air. This caused her to nearly trip on the pale pink chiffon day dress. When he continued to eat his eggs and ignore her ire, she filled her own plate and slammed it down next to his. He frowned at her and continued eating.

"I suppose you're just going to sit there and eat those eggs like nothing happened."

Sighing, Simon slowly lowered his fork, "Is there some reason your upset with me Kate?"

"Of course not. What could possibly be wrong?"

"Good." With that he took another mouthful of pastry.

"Unless of course, you count openly flirting with Hilary at the ball. I bet poor Sarah can hardly drag herself out of bed and face the day. She probably cried herself to sleep last night."

"She seemed fine this morning to me."

Stella gave her son a stern look. "Now son, you know I try not to interfere in my children's lives." Simon looked at her incredulously, "However, I must point out that you are married now and to an extremely sweet girl. Therefore, I can't imagine why you were chasing after...well, that other immoral woman. I never did like the looks of that girl and her conduct proves I was right. "

"You seemed to like her looks fine when you wanted me to marry her last year, or had you forgotten. And by the way, her name is Hilary. Why no one can seem to remember that little fact is beyond me."

His food was becoming more and more unappetizing. Still, he was starving. So, sawing off a bite of kidney, he tried to ignore both his mother's lecture and Kate's glare.

"It's her coloring. I never really did care for it. Did you ever notice she glows? Never trusted a woman who glowed. There is something innately evil about glowing."

"Mother would you listen to yourself. You sound ridiculous."

Kate pointed an empty fork at her brother accusingly. "Only if you beg on bended knee will Sarah ever forgive you. And, maybe not even then. Which will be just what you deserve too, you philanderer."

"Don't call your brother names, Katherine."

"Thank you, Mother."

"If anyone is going to call him a philanderer it should be his own mother."

Simon shoved his plate away and picked up the empty coffee cup by his plate and held it out to Albert, who purposely walked right past it, carrying the silver pot full of coffee with him. Simon slammed the delicate china to the table. "If you two are through lecturing me on what a cad I was last night, I wish to be excused. It's getting late and I have to get down to the office. I have two appointments with investors this morning. Tell Sarah, I'll see her at dinner."

"Not if she got any pride you won't," mumbled his little sister.

His glare silenced Kate instantly. Then exiting, he left in his wake a room full of contemplative silence.

His mother was first to break the mood. She daintily bit off the tip of a scone. "I have been thinking Kate that perhaps some matchmaking is in order. Do you remember that quaint little cabin in Dover?"

"I thought Father said it was hardly practical for a vacation. Why there is only the one room and it is stuck miles from anywhere. Why it takes a full days ride just from the main road in order to reach it."

"That's right dear. It sounds perfect. I'll just have to arrange a few little details."

Puzzlement made Kate tilt her head at her mother, "But, it is so isolated. One couldn't even manage to bring with them one solitary servant."

"Exactly."

"Oh. Right." Slowly understanding made Kate's eyes light up with excitement. "So when do we tell Sarah and Simon?"

Wiping her lips with the snowy white napkin, Stella winked. "We don't."

"But..." Kate raised an eyebrow in suspicious awe, "You mean for them to be stuck out there for days all alone, cut off from everyone, including Hilary?"

"Precisely. What do you think?"

"I think, dear mother, that you are a genius."

Sarah knew something was up when she grabbed an apple as she passed through the dining room on her way up to bathe and change clothes.

Both women were blushing guiltily.

When she asked them bluntly what was going on, Stella changed the subject. Instead, asking her to go with them to the orphanage and help with plans for the fall bazaar. The harsh English winter was fast approaching and the orphanage was always in need of extra cut wood, kerosene oil, candles, boots, warm socks and clothing. It would take the better part of a month in order to accomplish the charitable event before the first frost.

Glad to think of something else besides the meeting tomorrow with Peter and the Sympathizers, Sarah readily agreed.

However, now that she was up in her room, she could avoid the subject of the dreaded meeting no longer. His note reminding her of the time lay on her dresser. It pretended of a tea she was invited to attend. Her heart sank when she thought of betraying Peter. How she dreaded the whole thing: spies, wars, lies, and deception. Perhaps, if she understood a little better what Simon was hoping to accomplish, but of course he wouldn't tell her anymore than he already had. That would make her a liability.

In other words, he didn't trust her. They may have shared their bodies, but he still kept a part of himself closed off from her. He would continue to do so until he felt he could trust her.

Even Grandfather had been vague this morning when she had asked for his advice concerning Simon. In fact, he had been worse than vague; he had been absolutely no help whatsoever.

She had waited for the perfect moment to approach him. This was after their workout. As he sat down beside her on the iron bench drinking a glass of cool water, she took considerable time building up courage. The sweet fragrance of honeysuckle and the soothing hum of bees seemed the perfect setting to bring up her problem. It was all so peaceful. Yet, it still it took awhile. And even longer to get over her shameful feelings about at how she had acted at the ball. Why between the champagne and calling Hilary a shrew she had thrown out every principle he had ever taught her.

Oddly enough when she did unload on him, he grew strangely quiet. His only response was a slight smile when she described the look of horror on the blue lady's face. After she had finished, he had slowly wiped off the sweat from his brow and nodded. Not really commenting one way or another.

Frustrated, Sarah had finally blurted out, "Grandfather, what do you think I should do? I hate having Hilary flirt with my husband and I hate deceiving the man Peter. Simon says it's because I don't know him, but I really don't know my husband either. Even after..." she looked down in embarrassment,"...last night. I still feel like there is much he is not telling me."

His hand covered hers.

"So this is the reason your tea grows cold on my night stand every night. Your mind seeks quietness but your heart finds only turmoil."

She barely smiled. She felt tense and uneasy, even after their strenuous workout.

"Little One, it sounds to me as if you have already made your decision. Last night you set in motion things that have their own

184

consequences as well as rewards. By making your husband a part of your destiny, you have accepted being apart of his. You have taken a great risk. Yet you want a guarantee. But there is none. For no person is completely good. There is darkness hidden inside as well. Only you can answer if the love you share with this man is strong enough to accept both. However, I will ask the God of all things to help you. I will pray as my missionary father taught me. But, in the end only you can decide. Either your husband is trustworthy, or he is not. Both cannot be true."

Picking up the pillow from his side of the bed, she brought it up to her nose and drew in the scent of him. However, thoughts of him brought only confusion and she dropped the pillow back down on the unmade bed. Could she trust him?

How his words haunted her. Did she dare follow her heart? Or should her mind control what her heart believed? Usually she was not so easily confused. Grandfather said she possessed good instincts. She had a natural knack of knowing a person. She saw their inner truth. Yet with her husband she could barely think at all in a rational manner.

A knock on the bedroom door announced the arrival of the rest of her new clothes. Maggie laid armfuls of wonderful garments out all over the bed. They were beautiful. Silk and cotton day dresses of every imaginable color. Even a couple of serviceable wool dresses for her charity work this winter. Then there were at least four ball dresses. As well as a riding habit, two nightgowns of soft white linen, one with dainty blue roses embroidered along the modest neckline. Not to mention a dark blue cloak, soft cream shawl and delicate under things. Unfortunately there was also the dreaded corset and another pair of soft brown leather boots that pinched her toes just looking at them.

Feeling a bit overwhelmed by it all, she decided to let Maggie put the things away while she bathed. She had just slipped into the warm lilac fragrant water, when Maggie poked her head around the screen. In her hands she held an elegantly wrapped package cradled up near her ample bosom.

"Miss, they just delivered another box from some shop I have never heard tell of. Exotic Imports or some such thing. Sounds very mysterious to me.  Why even that silly boy who delivered it wouldn't tell me a thing.  Not that I be the nosy sort.  Goodness no.  I just thought it might be important with you being from China and all."

Sighing, Sarah sat up and held out a semi dry hand.

"Maggie I don't know why you insist on saying I'm from China.  I come from...oh, never mind.  Thank you.  It was most kind of you to bring it to my attention."

Sarah took the package reluctantly and was attempting to lay it down, when Maggie yanked it back up and shoved it back at her.  "Oh, no miss."

"You want me to open it now?  Here?"

Instead of retreating Maggie wiped her hands on her apron and sat down on the stool by the bathtub.  Leaning practically into the tub, she nodded eagerly, "Well, now is as good as time as any I always say.  No use waiting."

For someone not noisy, Maggie was doing a fine impression.  Sarah sighed.  She supposed there would be no putting her off.

As her wet hands touched the package, she took in the gold silk wrapping with blue dragons painted throughout.  She nearly hated to risk the chance of ruining the cloth, especially with wet hands.  Maggie seemed to read her mind.  A clean dry towel was thrust at her.  Obediently Sarah dried her hands; her curiosity peeked now as well.  Making up her mind, she handed the towel back to Maggie and began peeling back the wrapping leaving the gold box inside exposed.  Slowly, she slid the lid back and then gasped with unexpected delight.  For nestled inside the royal blue tissue was a shimmering silk pajama top and bottom that was the color of polished gold.

It must have cost her husband a small fortune.  From the intricate hand beaded pattern to the authentic corded clasps, she could tell it came from the Orient itself.  But, that wasn't what caused her to throat to close with emotion, or made her touch so reverent.  No, it was the kindness of such a gift.  A sign from Simon that he acknowledged the part of her that wasn't English and accepted it.

Maggie sat back, her bow shaped mouth hanging open.

"That's one of them China outfits. Now why would an English gentleman go and buy such a thing for his wife. It ain't decent, I tell you."

Sarah sat it lovingly down by the tub and beamed up at Maggie, "I know. Isn't it wonderful?"

Shaking her head in disappointment, Maggie retreated to finish putting the rest of her things away, mumbling the whole time about the master not needing to encourage her heathen ways.

But Sarah could think of only one thing and that was that maybe, just maybe she hadn't made a mistake in that hotel room after all.

The rest of the day passed fairly quickly. Sarah always enjoyed her visits to the orphanage. The way the children's eyes lit up at the basket of goodies and cakes Stella pulled out of the carriage. And then how they swarmed her skirts, laying precious hold of her legs as if she might disappear. How badly they needed to be held and loved. It humbled her. And she found herself saying a prayer of thanks each and every time for Grandfather. Yes, he had saved her life in more ways than one that night.

The little red-headed boy, Donovan, especially stayed on her mind this evening as she took down her hair and brushed out its thick honey-colored mass. Closing her eyes in pleasure as she ran the brush down along her scalp in slow easy strokes she remembered how happy he had been to see her. How proudly he still wore the string she had given him. In fact his disenchanted look had all but disappeared. Still, she knew he needed a home. She needed a place to belong. However, until she had one herself, she had nothing to offer him.

The small writing desk in the corner caught her eye. Its dark cherry wood glowed from the beeswax polish earlier that day. She felt drawn to it. How many days had it been since she had last put her feelings down in her journal? It was too many.

Making up her mind, she quickly got up and pulled a straight back chair over and sat down. Sometimes when things weighed heavy on her mind, writing helped. There was some magical balm that came from writing out her worries and thoughts on paper. For some reason, upon seeing them in print, it helped smooth out the confusion. Pulling out a sheet of paper, she began searching through the drawers for an inkwell. Opening a small drawer underneath one of the slanted shelves, she found a single crumpled page thrown haphazardly into the back, but unfortunately not the ink well she had been searching for.

She started to throw the crumpled paper away before continuing her search, but as her fingers opened to let it slip out into the wastebasket; she quickly clutched her fingers back around the shipping list. So much had happened last week she had forgotten all about it, or for that matter, even to question John about his strange actions that night at the gaming hall. Curiosity made her draw the lamp in closer, as she smoothed out its wrinkled surface.

Reading it made her arched eyebrows draw together in an uncustomary frown. It was a list of cargo shipments and times. All meant little to her. Perhaps when Simon came up to bed...her eyes locked on a single name. It was 'Henry's Folly'. Wasn't that the name of a ship belonging to Simon's company? She distinctly remembered the family joking about it. How Henry had spent a small fortune on the unusual design, only to find out it was too cumbersome for the much-needed swiftness of a cargo ship. Which was why it was only used in the summer months and early fall.

The time of departure from Mexico had been the middle of August. And that in of itself was unusual. What business did an English ship have in Mexico? She scanned the arrival dates. It was due to arrive back in England. She looked up, cold sweat popping up on her forehead. Tonight.

Deep in thought she slowly refolded the list, uncertain what to make of it. What was a list with Simon's ship on it, doing in a known smuggler's house? Was that the reason John left it lying there that night? He worried it would implicate his best friend in an act of illegal smuggling?

The sound of Simon's voice saying goodnight on the stairs brought her out of the dark thoughts struggling to drown her. No matter what the paper implicated, her husband was not one of the Sympathizers. It made no sense. After all, why would he send her to glean information if he were one of them? He wouldn't.

The tension in her neck was starting to give her a headache. Hearing footsteps in the hallway, she made her decision. Quickly she stuffed the list back into the drawer, covering it with the extra ribbon that had slipped from her hair and shoved it closed. Barely managing to shut the desktop and step away before her smiling husband entered the room.

"I see you got the present I sent you."

Did he have to look so sexy and carefree when her heart was breaking? It was extremely annoying. "Yes. It was most kind of you to think of it."

His brow furrowed as green eyes searched her face. "Is something the matter, China?"

"Of course not my husband, I am the most humblest of women that you would think of me." When he moved in closer, she took a step back.

He frowned. "I never thought politeness would annoy me so much until I met you. Now are you going to tell me what is the matter or not?"

Glaring at his attempt to bully her, she moved further from the desk, "I don't wish to talk about it Warrior."

"Because?"

"Because I...are you finished working tonight?" She prayed he would say yes. Maybe there was no ship.

He didn't pretend to understand her logic.

"Is that what is wrong with you? You're upset that I'm so late?" Simon smiled easily and pulled her into his strong arms before she could elude him again. Why was it the man never understood a word she was saying? But just as the thought brought frustration, her treacherous body leaned into him responding naturally to his touch. This aggravated her even more.

She shoved at his chest. "You are a most arrogant Englishman. And I would not get mad over such an insignificant thing. Warrior... stop that." She closed her eyes as Simon's warm breath along her neck caused a thundering in her veins.

"You know, a new wife is supposed to miss her husband when he goes to work. As a matter of fact, I missed you too. And if you would stop twisting about like a fish out of water, I'd show you exactly how much."

The huskiness in his voice made her breathless, "You are speaking illogically. After all, I know it is your duty to provide for me."

Pulling back a moment in confusion, he hesitated only a heartbeat before covering her lips with his own. But instead of answering the passion of his kiss, she turned her head away. She could not pretend everything was the same between them. It wasn't.

He took a cautious step back, although he never completely released her. Searching her face with a worried expression on his own, he asked seriously, "Okay, so now I know you're not the romantic type." When she didn't answer, he let go of her. His own temper was surfacing. "As it turns out, I do have to go back to work tonight. A shipment came in unexpectedly and it's important I be there. But unlike my practical wife, I happen to have missed you. So, I thought we could have supper together first before I go back. Is that all right with you?"

She tensed at the hostility in the words thrown her direction. Her own throat choked with tears. When she answered, it sounded more angry than hurt. "I'm not hungry."

Something in Simon's face changed. Reaching out, he gently removed a stray tear from her cheek, "Sweetheart, you're not making any sense. Has something happened?"

Pushing back from him, Simon's look of concern was nearly her undoing. "I don't want you to leave me tonight." She whispered, her heart was in her voice.

Relief washed over him, this he could understand. "If it's the meeting tomorrow I've been thinking that it might not be such a good idea after all. I mean that, China. I'll think of some other way."

Shaking her head, Sarah stepped over to the desk in indecision. Her hand reached out and touched its smooth surface. "No, it's not just that. It's more that I had hoped you would stay with me tonight. I feel unsettled, as if something bad is about to happen." When he started to shake his head, she laid a hand to his cheek, asking seriously, "Have the English not been taught the ancestor's way, how to respect a woman's knowing of things to come, like danger?"

Puzzled he started to say something then seemed to change his mind. Instead, he placed a gentle kiss to her forehead. She closed her eyes, trying to absorb the moment. Please God of all things, she prayed, don't let this man be a deceiver.

Seeming reluctant to leave, he gave her one of those endearing lopsided grins of his. Then, trying to make light of her gloomy prediction admitted, "No, as a matter of fact, I haven't. But that hardly matters. So far my dealings with you are unlike anything I have ever been taught." When his attempt at humor failed to produce the smile he was hoping for, he added, "China, there is absolutely nothing to worry about. And if anything ever does happen I promise you will be well taken care of."

Her head shot up, golden eyes studying him in sad wonder. "How can you think I care about such things? This is not the reason I worry."

"Isn't it?"

"No. I don't need your protection. And besides money can never replace someone I - have grown fond of."

He reached up and touched a finger to her lips. His own voice filled with tender emotion. "You know, you're not exactly doing your part to keep my male ego in tact. First you don't miss me, and now, from the look on your face wish I would keep my declarations of devotion to myself. "

She turned away. Afraid he would guess the truth. That she was finding herself more in love with him everyday and if he died, a part of her would too. It's strange how one moment, could change everything. If he had only walked in ten minutes earlier and said the exact same things, she would have been filled with such joy. Now all she felt was miserable.

Oddly enough her reaction didn't seem to surprise him. Instead he gave one eyebrow a self-depreciating lift. "Well, this is not going very well, is it?" Slightly ill at ease, Simon gave her a nose a final tweak before adding, "It's all right, China. This has been a crazy week for both of us. No wonder you're a little emotional."

"I am not emotional", she fairly hissed at him.

"Right. That aside, why don't we talk more tonight when I get home? But I have to warn you. I don't intend to give up on making you fall madly in love with me. It's a matter of principle now." His eyes held such promise. It was too much to bear.

Feeling his eyes boring into the top of her bowed head, she knew he would not leave until she looked up at him, or at least said something. He was looking for anything to explain her odd behavior tonight. Willing her pounding heart to slow down, she bit her lower lip to keep the tears at bay and raised her head.

With feigned indifference, Sarah gave a slight shrug. "I will wait up Warrior, even if it grows too late for such promises."

"And what is that suppose to mean?" Simon demanded.

His only answer was another shrug.

Searching her face, he knew there would be no further explanation for the unexplained sadness in her eyes. Dropping his arms, he stepped away. "We are going to talk about what has gotten you so worked up when I get back."

Sarah thought it sounded more threat than promise. And then he was gone. Leaving too much left unsaid between them.

She could not stop crying. The whole time she slipped out of the gift he gave her and into the dark blue pants and shirt of her former life – she sobbed. Even as she slid open the window to their bedroom, the night air breathing new life into her sad soul. Still, she cried.

Looking back longingly one last time at the locked bedroom door, she thought of Grandfather and shook off the temptation to go to him. She could not ask him to be a part of spying on her husband again, not tonight. Even if it meant death by her husband's hands, she couldn't bear for anyone else to know what she suspected to be true. That Simon was the very villain he claimed to chase.

A short time later, swinging out onto the old oak tree, she welcomed the feel of its rough bark on her bare feet. It felt good to be doing something, anything familiar instead of dwelling on things she did not understand.

Within moments she found herself once more on solid ground. Gathering up her sandals, she ran through the manicured lawn and waited by the street in the shadows. It was dangerous to be a woman alone on London streets at night. Recently there had been talk of a butcher who attacked women in the dead of night. Yet, for some reason, she felt numb determination driving past her fears.

She had thought of asking Simon out right if he was a smuggler, when he demanded she talk to him. But she didn't trust herself with the answer to that question. She had the heart of a woman in love. Willing to believe whatever he said, if only she could stay in his arms. No, her eyes needed to see what was true. Two countries and a war were involved. Children and families could be destroyed. Like her own was that dark October night. She knew what it felt like to lose everyone you loved because of one man's greed. This was why she could not turn a blind eye now even if it meant losing Simon.

She ducked behind the bushes as Simon's horse raced past. She would never catch up. A horse or carriage would be faster. She looked longingly toward the carriage house. Strange, she didn't even know if she could ride a horse. So much of her life had been erased that tragic night. Still, she had to try. Backtracking she sneaked into the small carriage building, gathering a horse blanket laid over a stall as she made her way forward. The soft lantern light threw a pattern across the opposite wall, where several reins and bits hung in uniform session along its rough exterior.

Trying not to think too deeply about what she planned next, she removed one of the bits from the wall and walked over to place it firmly into the nearest horse's mouth, quickly sliding the headgear over the horses' ears. She was shaking so badly afterwards that it took three tries before she was able to lift the latch on the stall and lead the ginger colored horse out of it warm hay scented haven. The horse neighed in protest, throwing its head back at her unfamiliar scent. Gently, she stroked the horse's soft nose and laid her head against his, speaking soft nonsense words in order to soothe him. In a manner of seconds they both relaxed.

Leading him over to some mounting steps, she decided against the blanket after all. What good was a blanket without a saddle? The memory, if she ever possessed it eluded her as to how to put them on. Besides if she knew how to ride well enough, she wouldn't need them. What if she didn't? Well, her inept attempts at securing the obstacles would hardly matter. Taking a deep cleansing breath, she jumped onto the stallion's back. Looking down, she noticed the way her body fit instantly to the horse. The reins held firmly and expertly in her left hand seemed comfortable and familiar, suddenly she knew.

She could ride. In fact, visions of jumping fences and chasing rabbits across fields with her father brought such joy to her spirit that it literally took her breath away. How could she have forgotten such a wonderful memory?

The horse danced in anticipation underneath her, bringing her back into the present. This was no time to reminisce. Simon would be too far ahead as it was. Quickly turning the horse out into the night and towards the Thames, she kicked him into a run. The two of them in a mad race with the thumbnail moon and few scattered stars in an ink black sky. They practically flew to the boat dock; brick buildings wheezing past at break neck speed. And never had Sarah felt more alive.

Soon the monstrous ships loomed in the distance and she slowed the thoroughbred down to a sedate walk. When she got within walking distance to Simon's warehouse, she quietly dismounted and tied the horse to some pilings behind a deserted building.

Now what? She couldn't very well walk up to Simon and demand to see his cargo. Nor could she stay hidden behind this building. As if on cue, her grandfather's voice seemed to call out to her. Telling her what she must do.

Face the tiger.

Knowing she really had little choice, she eased out and began making her way among the crates to the edge of the dock. Dizzy with fear, she pushed back past emotions of fear and helplessness. Reminding herself over and over again, that she was not a little girl of ten any longer. She was eight years older and a black belt in the martial arts...and wiser.

So she soothed herself until she reached the huge, wooden ship, with the name "Henry's Folly" peeling off its faded exterior.

There were at least ten men unloading burlap sacks. Although she could not make out the lettering on the sacks, there was no mistaking the puffs of white stuffing trying to work its way free of the bag. Her heart sank. It was cotton. Automatically she slid down the side of the warehouse and dropped her head into her hands. It was true then. Her husband was a smuggler. What else was a lie, his arms around her, his words of affection before he left?

She swiped at the tears stinging her eyes, and forced herself to rise on unsteady legs, anger urging her on. She didn't have time to feel sorry for herself. The only thing worse than a fool, was a coward. At least she was not that. Looking around the corner, she saw Simon supervising the unloading of the illegal contraband, while rough looking sailors struggled with the heavy sacks of cotton. It was now or never. She wasn't sure how much time she had before they began loading it all into the warehouse. Not much. She only prayed Simon had left his office unlocked. She needed proof, something to use against him. Her stomach turned.

The building was pitch black except for a dimly lit kerosene lantern on an old weather beaten desk in the far back corner. She was in luck. The door to the office was thrown open, piles of paper haphazardly covering its marred surface. Not bothering to shut the door behind her, she walked purposely through the doorway and into the building. Determined to try and talk some sense into Simon. But without proof...or for lack of a better name, blackmail...she knew he would never listen to her.

When she made it to the office she hesitated just inside the door. Something was wrong. The place was in shambles. File drawers open, things thrown onto the floor. It was as if someone else had already been here ahead of her, searching.

She heard rather than saw it coming. There was a loud explosion of sound. She barely managed to turn towards it, when she was tackled to the floor. Above her head, she saw the lantern explode and burst into flames. It instantly set the scattered papers on fire. Shoving at the heavy weight on her chest, it took a moment to realize it was a man crushing her into the floor. And whoever he was, he had just saved her life.

The weight lifted and she found herself jerked to her feet.

"We have to get out of here. Are you all right?"

John's face reflected concern and urgency. "Sarah? Can you hear me?"

"John? What are you doing here?"

The room was growing hotter by the moment and there were shouts coming from outside the warehouse.

"Could we perhaps talk about this later?" He threw an arm wide, indicating the room, "This doesn't seem like a good time."

Leave it to John to joke about their situation. But, nevertheless, she didn't resist the hand that pulled her towards a broken window in the back. Nor did she refuse the cup of his hands as he lifted her up to the window. She never once questioned him, her thoughts only of escape. A shred of glass cut her forearm as she crawled through the window, a soft moan of pain her only response. She didn't have time for much else.

The fire was out of control by the time John shoved her further out and into life saving fresh air. He climbed out after her, breathing in great gulps of air. His light colored eyes reflecting the fire's glow behind them. Without speaking they started running. She could hear people pursuing them. Still they ran. Until they came close to the water's edge, shadowy and covered with discarded drunks and trash.

"Can you swim?"

She nodded.

Suddenly she was shoved into the water. Behind her, she heard the splash of another body. A moment later John came up beside her and motioned to a far off buoy. It probably took no longer than four minutes to swim out to it, but their movements seemed deafening in the quiet dark water. For over half an hour they held onto the buoy, before their pursuers gave up looking for them, and slowly began disappearing back towards the warehouse to help fight the fire. Time had no meaning in the vast darkness of water. In the back of her mind Sarah wondered if Simon would be arrested when the police discovered the illegal contraband. John was quiet as well. He was lost deep in his own thoughts beside her.

She looked over at his normally blond hair darkened by seawater, and felt uneasy. He looked different tonight, older somehow. The times before when she had seen him, it was around the family. Around them his demeanor had been more open, more carefree. Observing this, it had crossed Sarah's mind to wonder why someone with his nature would choose the unlikely profession of English spy. That is, until tonight. Tonight he was different, more confidant, more controlled. His face was an unreadable mask. And she wondered if she really knew him at all.

But she was sure of one thing. If he hadn't been there tonight, at the warehouse, she would have been killed.

"Can you make it back to shore?"

Again, all she managed was a nod. Then he disappeared into the dark water, a silent and strong swimmer. She eased into the water as well, expertly gliding through the slight current and small waves. At last they were both on the dock again. She didn't realize she was shivering until John left for a moment and came back with a worn dirty shawl. No doubt bartered from one of London's homeless. Gently he placed it around her shoulders and led her back behind the buildings before he spoke again.

"Do you have a way home?"

"I rode a horse. It's tied up near the warehouse."

He nodded and disappeared again.

Within minutes he was back leading her horse to where she waited. Helping her up, he handed her the reins although he refused to let go until she looked down at him.

"I know this looks bad...as if Simon..."

She tasted blood where she had bitten through her bottom lip.

"He is not a smuggler."

She said the words with more conviction than she felt. John's face held sympathy and understanding. He handed the reins over.

"I wasn't here if he asks. Understand?"

And she did. He was sent by the government to spy on her husband. Yet a part of her still refused to believe Simon to be a traitor.

Surely, there had to be another explanation for what they both had seen tonight. Suddenly, she felt so unbelievably weary and brokenhearted. If only she hadn't followed Simon tonight. If only she hadn't found that awful note. Then perhaps she would be waiting right now for him to come back to her, blissfully ignorant and hopeful.

She looked away from the intensity in John's eyes. How could she betray her husband? Where did her loyalties lie now? She was so confused and weary of plots. She only wanted to go home.

She gave the shawl back to John. The smell was making her nauseous. "I won't say anything, but I need...need to know what you found in the warehouse."

"Sarah I hardly think it would do either one of us any good."

"I need to know."

John gave a resigned sigh. "Tomorrow night, then. Meet me in the carriage house at ten. Simon should be gone until eleven." He patted her sore arm and she flinched. "Sorry...about everything Sarah." With that final parting he hit her horse's rump. Once again she was sailing through the streets as if demons were after her. And in a way, they were. There were so many things running through her mind, so many unanswered questions. The cold air hitting her wet body took her breath away. Yet in a way the icy pain slicing through her body felt good. It overrode the pain in her soul. No, her only hope lay in that tomorrow might hold some answers for her. That is, if she could bear the sweet torture of seeing Simon tonight.

Reaching the house, she slowed the horse to a sedate walk and then slid off his back, leading him back to the carriage house. She used the time brushing him down to get a hold of her emotions before going back into the house. Simon wouldn't be back for some time because of the fire. And the police. She would need every minute between now and then to prepare. As Simon said, she was not a good liar. She laid a weary head against the horse's neck. This was a dishonorable land and it was teaching her its ways, or perhaps she was simply slipping back into what she already knew.

By the time she cleaned up and redressed into one of her new pale blue nightgowns, she had made up her mind what to do. She would finish what fate had given her, then she would leave this land and return to America. Her stomach clenched in gut wrenching pain, but she steeled herself against it. She must conquer her love and the pain it caused her. Or next time John might not be around to save her.

It was well after two in the morning when Simon slipped into bed beside her. He smelt faintly of smoke and lye soap. She forced herself to remain still, to remember to breathe evenly. Soon she felt his arms pull her into his chest and his own breathing evened. The slow steady beat of his heart soothed her and she finally drifted off to sleep.

# Chapter 12

She managed to avoid him most of the morning.

When she went towards the library to escape with a good book and noticed him walking down the hall, she quickly ducked into the parlor instead. Albert raised a bushy gray eyebrow up towards the heaven-depicted ceiling and picked up another spoon to polish. Desperately she placed a silencing finger to her lips. He seemed to take pity on her. For when Simon ducked his head in to ask about her, Albert coolly informed him it was his job to look after the silver, not his master's wife. Sending a grateful smile his direction she quickly exited out one of the open floor length windows and into the gardens.

She knew she was being ridiculous. After all, she couldn't avoid him forever, especially since he was the one escorting her to the meeting in half an hour. Still, she felt that the less she was in his presence, the less chance she had of blurting out the one question burning in her mind. Was he the smuggler evidence pointed him out to be? Yes, it was the one thing she most wanted to know and yet could never ask. For once asked it would change everything between them.

At precisely ten till eleven she steeled herself against his fierce frown and sailed past him and into the waiting carriage below. The whole time she was praying beyond hope that he would not get into the carriage with her. Her prayers could have been better spent. Feeling the carriage rock with his added weight, she jumped guiltily as the carriage door was slammed shut with a finality that shook her soul.

His eyes bore into the back of her head demanding her attention, but she refused to look his direction. She chose instead to study the scene out her window of a split milk cart owner arguing with a street urchin, his friends made off with a few bottles of ware.

"What is going on Sarah?"

"Those boys are stealing milk. Shouldn't someone do something? I am sure if we asked her, Sister Agnes would find room for them."

"Stop avoiding my question. Why have you been hiding from me all morning?"

Apparently the fight would not wait. The only thing she had accomplished by avoiding him was shortening its length. She let out a deep sigh. Suddenly so tired of pretense. Slowly she turned around to face him. Anger and hurt were written plainly for him to see. When she did speak, the words were a barely restrained whisper, yet the betrayal she felt was evident by the careful pronunciation of each word. "You lied to me."

Rather than act offended, he leaned in towards her on his forearms, hands clasped before him. "Okay. At least you're talking. Now, what have I supposedly lied to you about?"

How he could sit there so coolly handsome while her heart was breaking. Did the man not possess any sort of conscious at all? She barely kept from shouting at him, her voice now hoarse with emotion, "You lied about that shipment last night."

"If this is about me being late, I know I promised you I would be in early but there was a fire."

She waved his words away, "I followed you Simon."

A gush of air escaped his lips, and there was no mistaking the angry disbelief in his words. "You did what?"

"I followed you."

She felt her cheeks grow hot. Why did she feel so guilty when she had done nothing wrong? Perhaps because deep down inside she knew the truth, she was as guilty as he. For it mattered little to her conscious that he was untrustworthy. She was the one who made promises before the God of all things. To honor. To obey. That those promises were given to a fork-tongued husband was beside the point. Her own word must be true. And she had broken it last night. First when she had deceived him by hiding the list, and secondly by setting up the meeting with John. This made the two of them more alike than she cared to admit.

"You were unloading cotton, Simon. Southern Cotton."

The carriage pulled to a stop before Peter's house.

Simon was nearly too angry to answer her accusations. When he did speak, it was a harsh reprimand instead of denial. "Of all the stupid...not to mention dangerous...you should have come to me first Sarah."

"And you would have told me what? That you're a smuggler, or worse, a traitor like your father?"

He didn't say a word, but the intensity of his anger caused her to back away against the seat. His eyes glittering with rage.

"I don't know why I said that. To insult your family...of course it is not true about your father. I spoke with anger guiding my tongue. It is just that since meeting you, I seem to have lost myself. I have developed a tendency to act rashly. To say things. Grandfather says a man who cannot control his tongue is worse than a fool."

Ignoring her attempt at an apology, he asked cuttingly, "What do you intend to do, since it's obvious you don't trust me?"

She flinched at the coldness in his tone. "I don't know."

"I do. You are coming back home with me. Now. We need to straighten this whole thing out. These are dangerous men your dealing with today and there is too much at stake for you to spill out your uninformed opinions. Especially now that it's quite evident you act before considering the consequences."

It seemed as if they had been sitting there for hours but truly how long the carriage had been stopped, she couldn't be certain. A movement from the doorway caught her eye. Peter waved her direction. She gave a forced smile in return, her hand reaching for the door handle. "I have to go. Peter is coming down the stairs. He will see you and then I will be forced to say yet another lie. Or do you wish for me to tell him the truth?"

A solid hand engulfed her own, the strong grip restraining.

"For the last time, Sarah, what will you do in there?"

A long moment passed between them, a moment full of too many things left unsaid. Making a decision, Sarah pulled her hand away and pushed at the slightly open door. Her eyes never quite met his.

"I will honor my word. Your secret is safe. But tonight I will know the truth of things. And if what my eyes have seen is true, then I will sign your paper full of lies and leave England forever. This too is my word."

And with those damning words between them, Simon let her exit the carriage. Not a moment too soon.

John was there.

His eyes never left her. He studied her. She wondered what he thought about her injured wife act because he said very little to her directly as he nursed the gold colored brandy in his left hand.

"So, gentlemen...and ladies", Peter winked her direction, "what should be our course of action before the next House of Commons, any ideas?"

Whispered murmuring was the only response.

"What do you think Lady Conway?"

"I think," everyone quieted, "that Simon will vote against this idea of yours." She tugged at the collar of her dress. It was choking her with its high neck and billows of material.

"And why would he do that?" Hilary's father swiped at the sweat gathering on his pale forehead. "If the House of Commons agree to buy Southern cotton openly, he stands the most to win. Everyone knows his shipping company is practically bankrupt."

Out of the corner of her eye she noticed John casually switch his right leg up over one knee, a wary look on his face. As if waiting to see if she might really betray her husband to these men. What did he plan to do if she did?

She waved away the argument with a bored smile and rose from the settee. "I know nothing about his company. I only know he dislikes Peter and the rest of you. That alone will make him vote against you. At least that is what he was saying this morning at breakfast. Something about starting a war you can't win."

"By George, he is forcing our hand to break the law. None of us can survive paying the kind of embargo taxes the States are demanding. If we deal with the South alone we can bypass..."

"Father!"

The older man's flushed face grew redder. "I will not be silent any longer. The man must be made to listen to reason."

"Or, prevented from voting."

The quiet words were said from the back of the room. A large man in immaculate dress stepped forward and Sarah's mouth went dry. She instantly recognized him from the gambling party a week before. "If his wife truly wants to help, that is. I, myself, find it strange that both his best friend and wife are present at this meeting. I wonder what idiot thought of that little plan."

John rose to his feet and shrugged. "I fear, Sir, you have the wrong idea. I invited myself and was uninformed that Lady Conway would be here. Just because Simon is a friend of mine, does not mean we hold the same politics. As a matter of fact, the interruption of my gaming at your townhouse the other night caused quite a rift between Simon and me. Surely you remember that I lost a fairly good amount of my inheritance at the tables. Unlike Simon, I am not averse to lining my pockets with the America's misfortune."

"Why is it I don't believe a word you say? No, it is far more likely you and the honorable Lady Conway share far more than your mere interest in Southern cotton. Perhaps Simon's downfall would benefit you both in more ways than one. Or do you intend to have me believe any other reasons except illicit love or spying would bring you both here?"

John's grip on his glass tightened. "You slander the lady Sir."

The dark haired man walked over and looking her over as if she were beneath him, answered smoothly, "Have I? It has been my experience that given the nature of her sex, she is prone to deceit. An unhappy woman would be easy prey for a man such as you. And after all, who could really blame her after that touching reunion between our dear Hilary and Simon the other night."

Sarah felt as humiliated as he intended for her to. But she knew it would serve no purpose to defend her honor. How else could she explain being here behind Simon's back? Holding on to her temper she answered him coolly, "You Sir, are a man without conscious, the kind of man, who ignores the evil in his own soul by seeking it in others. If you will excuse me."

"Sarah, wait." Peter reached out to stop her from leaving.

"Let her go. Who knows perhaps she will find even more to hate her husband for which would be to our advantage…and yours John." John took a step forward, murder written on his face.

However, by the way Banister casually straightened his silk lapels his opponent's ire mattered little to him. "Speaking of which, I caught a glimpse of Hilary hurrying out the front doors a moment ago. You don't suppose she is off to Simon's arms while his wife is otherwise occupied? The mouse will play while the cat is away and all that." He sneered at that last line in Sarah's general direction. His slightly yellowing teeth distracting from his perfectly coiffed head.

"Now see here Banister, it is uncalled for to insult not only my sister but my guest as well."

Sarah forced herself to put down the untouched drink burning in her hand, swallowing down the urge to fling the contents into the evil one's face. Since arriving on English soil she was finding it more and more difficult to control such urges. She had had enough of both the lack of respect for other human beings through sarcastic wit, and the utter arrogance of the upper class.

She wanted things back the way they were, just her and Grandfather, alone in New York. The smell of Lee's laundry was permeating the air. The welcome sound of friends' laughter late into the night on the stairwell as they played cards and talked of moving out west in search of gold. Those were simple straight forward pleasures. No secret societies and past mistresses. Was it little wonder she had erased all memory of her homeland?

"You have it all wrong." Peter stood up, placing a steadying hand on her trembling shoulder. "Conway is the one to blame here. There is no need to attack his Lady wife. The man insults her along with my sister publicly and I as a gentleman refuse to sit idly by and do nothing. Sarah came to us in good faith. Why, she knows things about the South we can only guess at: towns, routes, even names of rumored Southern smugglers.

205

The fact that she lives in the man's house, is hardly her fault. I believe she would be a great asset to our cause."

"Perhaps." Banister's black empty eyes looked her over slowly, before he spoke again. "I wonder. Tell you what Lady Conway, if you're truly sincere about helping us than I am sure you won't mind having a little private talk with me in the library, before anymore is said in your presence."

"Now see here, man. You can't expect her to..."

The large man spun around, one beefy finger pointed at Peter's lean chest, "I call the shots here boy. And I say she doesn't get in unless I talk with her. Alone."

She was shaking. But it was not fear affecting her so. It was fury. Her head was pounding so fiercely, she felt dizzy. The last thing she wanted was to be alone with her husband's enemy. Surely Peter or his father would protect her in their home. It was only honorable.

But it was John who dared oppose the man. "I hardly think Simon would approve of his wife being alone with a man of your reputation Banister. Now would he?"

There was no mistaking the threat in his voice. And the large dangerous man towering over her simply gave a satisfied smirk. "Just as I thought... You are simply a spy for her husband. As usual nothing more than a pawn in Conway's little drama here." Turning to Peter, he ordered, "I want him out of here now. This meeting is over."

"But our plans."

"I said the meeting is over."

Sarah rose on shaky legs glad it was over even if it meant Simon would be in the dark about their plans. He had been right to be afraid for her and she had been foolish to think she could play deception games with masters of the craft. Peter started to help with her wrap, but was shoved out of the way. Banister's punishing grip on her arm caused tears of pain to instantly surface. Her instinct was to throw a well-aimed knuckle to his right temple. She knocked him unconscious. But, one should never use a weapon until it was truly needed. It was more effective that way. Besides she was supposed to be giving the illusion of being a defenseless, ill used

206

wife. She looked down as if afraid, although her eyes were glittering golden orbs of anger.

"You are hurting me Sir."

John took a step forward, but was held back by two men. Peter, although uncomfortable, stepped back out of the larger man's way. Banister leaned down to whisper in her ear with ale-laden breath, "On second thought, since you are so anxious to join our cause, I will oblige you. A test if you will. I will send instructions through Peter. And if you succeed in the little...um...assignment, you're in. And I owe you an apology. But if I'm right?"

She opened her mouth to object, but he only tightened his grip and pulled her up near his foul smelling breath. "You die and you're Lancelot over there along with you. So don't even think of defying me sweetheart, or someday I will come across you without your husband. And my pretty, I will do more than simply bruise your foolish pride. Do we understand each other?"

His hot breath on her ear, sent shivers of revulsion down her spine. She jerked free of him and gripped her hands into fists to keep from hitting him. Not trusting her voice, she simply nodded.

Laughing, he stepped out the way, giving her a shove towards John, "Do escort the lovely Lady Conway home John. And if you care anything about her, you will keep your mouth shut."

Rubbing her left arm where she was certain he had left marks, she soon felt John urging her gently towards the door. As if waking from a bad dream she felt the pull of the nightmare lessen once they got outside and onto the pavement. The bustle of London streets seemed surreal compared to the horror she had felt only moments ago. Slowly she came to herself and squeezed John's arm with cold trembling hands. Worriedly he stopped and pulled her behind a small tree. "Are you alright?"

She nodded, although her bottom lip tasted of blood.

"I am sorry you lost face because of me. The evil one made it seem as if we were ..." she blushed and looked off in embarrassment, "I am not usually in so much need of rescuing. It seems I am in your debt...once again."

He rubbed the warmth back into her hands, flashing her one of those charming smiles that surely felled many a young woman's heart. And she herself wasn't entirely immune. This was the John she knew. The other hardened and calculating man from last night was gone, hidden safely once more beneath the mask he had created. "You don't owe me anything. Simon asked me to watch out for you. I just didn't plan on showing my hand so soon in the game. What did Banister say to you in there? You went pale as a ghost."

For some reason she didn't want to talk about the evil man or his whispered threats. Not now.

"He told me to keep quiet. But, I don't understand why. It isn't as if I heard anything to repeat. Who was he anyway?"

John relaxed a little as he hailed a hired hack over to the curb. "His name is Richard Banister. He is involved in all sorts of illegal activity. The government has arrested many of his culverts, but they never turn on him. No doubt he is a greater threat than Newgate." She didn't doubt those words. The remembered feel of his cold indifference as he threatened her caused a tightening in the pit of her stomach.

"That among other things makes him a difficult man to convict. His connections go up to some very high places in government. I don't know if we will ever prove him guilty of anything. Simon has been after him for three years now, and let's just say, the feeling Banister had in there...well, it's mutual. He would relish a way to get to Simon, even if that meant using you. I think Simon was counting on that."

The whispered threat sounded in her ear once more. If John was right, Banister planned on using her to trap Simon. But, if Simon was already involved with the man, why should he bother? There was more going on here than she understood. Who was she suppose to trust?

A cab rolled up beside them and John helped her inside before giving instructions to the driver. At the last minute he leaned his head in and reminded, "I'll meet you in the carriage house at ten. Try not to be late. I paid someone to delay Simon's ride home, but I'm not sure how long we will have."

She nodded and attempted a smile, but worry wrinkled her dusk colored brow.

"It will be all right Sarah. I promise."

With that quiet reassurance, he waved the cab on.

What greeted her on the return home was a welcomed normal or normal for Simon's family, anyway.

Simon's mother was pacing in the hallway off the front door. Her embroidery of two redbirds left abandoned on the French end table in the parlor just visible through the open doorway. Worried about the poor woman's heart, Sarah immediately led her back through the doorway and over to the beige sofa. Then insisting she sit down, Sarah asked gently, "Is something the matter, my husband's mother?"

Taken aback by the way Sarah addressed her, Stella stopped her fluttering long enough to admonish, "Now dear, I told you this is England. You may call me mother, but not your husband's mother. It sounds rather...well, foreign. And you know tomorrow is the tea at Lady Ashworth's. I don't think she will understand all those heathen Chinese customs. You are English now after all. Although an orphan from the colonies."

"Mother...then. Tell me, why you were so upset a moment ago?"

"Oh, yes. Well, it's our Kate."

Immediately Sarah grew serious. Banister's threats still fresh on her mind. She readied herself for battle. "Is she hurt?"

"Oh, no, dear." She patted the side of Sarah's face. "She's fine. It's Hilary, that dreadful girl."

More confused than ever, Sarah let out a long deep sigh. She was trying her best to be patient with the dear woman. "Something has happened to Hilary?"

Perplexed surprise crossed the gentle features of her mother in law. "Goodness no. Whatever gave you that idea? No, actually it's my son that is in dour need of rescue. My heavens, I don't know where that boy's head is lately."

"Simon is in danger?"

Shaking her silver peppered head in sympathy, she explained patiently, "Now why would you think a thing like that?"

"But, you said..."

"You really should pay attention dear. No, it's something far worse than an accident. Oh, dear, and with Henry still at the office."

"What exactly is worse than an accident?"

"Why, that Hilary came over to see Kate. But, of course she didn't."

"Didn't what?"

"Come over to see Kate. It was only a ruse to see Simon, you see."

Unfortunately, she didn't.

When I told the forward chit that Kate wasn't available, she batted her pale eyes at me and asked for Simon instead. I ask you, what could I do? Good manners prevented me from throwing her out on her ear. So, I lied and said he was out. Then, the boy actually had the audacity to come sailing in at that precise moment and make a liar out of me. Why he was practically oozing charm. It was quite indecent. I tell you, I won't have such goings on in a nice English household."

Sarah was trying to focus on the teacup with yellow daisies encircling its lip, instead of the emotions churning up inside her. She must not lose her temper again. Especially since Simon's mother was in a fragile state of health. She must meditate. She needed to go outside herself and try to find a peaceful place.

"Where is the treacherous pale one now?"

Taken aback by the coldness in Sarah's tone, Stella pointed towards the back of the house. "Why, outside. They are in the garden this very minute and I can't find Kate anywhere. I have to think of some other way to stop him from becoming caught in that woman's clutches. If only Kate were here I could send her out to interrupt their little clandestine meeting before Sarah finds..." She suddenly gasped as if just at that moment remembering whom it was comforting her. "Oh, dear." Her hands fluttered nervously at the pearl buttons on the high-necked purple gown. "Did I say meeting? I meant to say tea. Yes, I'm sure it's nothing.

They are old friends after all. Perhaps she has never seen the garden. Or any garden for that matter. Why else would the creature be so pale?"

She was rambling again.

Sarah rose to her feet and gave her mother-in-law a reassuring smile. Although, she never did quite meet her in the eyes. The whole time calmly reminding herself that at least nothing serious had happened yet.

Her smile faded.

Visions of a pale ethereal Hilary wrapped in Simon's strong arms caused the blood to surge through her system. The thought of any arms other than hers, wrapping themselves around her husband, quickened her stride towards the doorway. Never mind she threatened to leave him less than an hour ago. Never mind the fact that Grandfather said, he who loses his temper, loses the fight. She was past being reasonable. Between too little sleep, being yelled at for catching her husband in a lie and finally threaten by some brute it would have taken all of two minutes to take out, Sarah was through with these English and their secret ways. Enough was enough.

For once in her eighteen years, she welcomed her temper. In fact, she hoped Simon was doing something dishonorable. She hadn't thrown anyone into anything in over a week now. And the urge was strong within her. No matter if Grandfather scolded her later about her lack of control. Or that it was childish, the truth was it would be well worth it!

"Where on earth are you going in such a hurry dear?"

Sarah spun around so fast her billowing skirts wrapped up her legs in a sea of dark brown satin.

"It so happens I just remembered something important I have to do before lunch. I won't be a minute."

Eyes big as saucers, Stella asked suspiciously, "And what would that be dear?"

Without missing a beat, Sarah sailed out of the room answering her mother in law's question over one small thrown back shoulder.

"I have to remind Simon that he's married. And I believe I'll use my heathen Chinese ways to do it."

She wasn't positive, but Sarah could have sworn she heard her mother in law snicker.

Simon was a head taller than the frolicking fish fountain along the stone path in the garden. And a head shorter than the trellis covered with yellow roses behind him. This made him easier to spot. Taking a deep breath, Sarah forced herself to glide up to the pair as opposed to barrel down on them. Hilary looked up first from her position on the bench and smiled ever so slightly her direction. The woman's skin was flawless. Her yellow hair reflecting the sun like spun gold. This only irritated Sarah further.

Simon was standing beside Hilary, one leg propped up on the bench much too close to be decent. To add to his crimes, her husband didn't even bother to rise, still resting casually on an arm that was laid across his leg. Oh, he looked suspiciously relaxed along side the pale beauty. So relaxed in fact, that when Sarah neared, he simply turned his head, his taunt jaw line the only acknowledgment of just how irritated he was with her intrusion. He cocked one eyebrow at her.

"Is there a problem Sarah? As you can see I have a guest."

She blushed at his cool dismissal.

"I just left your mother and I fail to see how upsetting her will further help humiliate me."

That got his attention. He slowly removed his leg and deliberately plucked a rose from behind him and handed it to Hilary. "I fear our talk will have to wait until another time. It seems my wife has, as usual, come to remind me of my duty."

Hilary, with help from Simon, gently came to her feet, and began addressing him as if Sarah were not standing two feet away. "Of course, Darling. Perhaps later, somewhere private where we could better escape your... how did you put it so charmingly? Ah, yes. Your obligations."

That did it.

Something must have snapped inside Sarah, because through a haze of emotion, she saw Simon move towards her. He was warning, no, more like pleading with her, "China, don't."

Hilary looked from his face to Sarah and back again, at first in confusion and then in sudden realization. Her eyes widened and one arm went up as she took a step back. Unfortunately the bench prevented more of a retreat. It wouldn't have helped anyway. Sarah was no longer mad. She was furious.

With a grace and speed defying the restrictive dress she wore, Sarah spun the shocked girl up over her shoulders and dumped her backside first into the small pond behind them. It all happened so fast, Hilary didn't even have time to scream, only sputter out a mouthful of disgusting algae and mud from a mouth that still hung open in shocked horror.

Simon squelched the grin threatening to surface and tried his best to muster a good mad.

"China, that is not the way we handle things in a civilized country."

She spun around and with two hands hiking her skirt up past her knees, delivered a sound front snap kick to his middle, sending him flying backwards and into the trellis. The wind knocked out of him, he could only look up in stunned surprise amid a bed of broken whitewashed wood and roses.

"Well, this may not be the civilized way one handles an unfaithful husband, but if I catch you with that pale snake of a woman again," Hilary's loud sobbing drew her heated stare. Instantly, Hilary toned down to a shaky whimper, "Let's just say, in China we don't believe in divorce. But, killing our enemies is considered honorable."

Hilary, sopping wet and terrified, weeds hanging off a sliding and disheveled hairdo, burst out in a fresh bout of tears. Sarah had no pity for the immoral woman. Her grandfather always said adulterous women should be run through with a sword or worse. She use to think that was a bit extreme, but now that she was involved with one – she felt that was too kind an end. Regardless, he would still lecture her on letting emotion dictate her actions. It had been a foolish thing to do and solved nothing. But, truth be told, it felt glorious.

"China, come back here!"

There was little doubt her husband had gotten his life's breath back, the roar of his words followed her all the way back into the house. And past the small group of house servants and family gathered at the French doors on the veranda. Stella was still gapping at her daughter in law, as Kate, who must have gotten home recently, opened her mouth to say something, only to shut it again. Without stopping to explain, Sarah threw shoulders back and head high as she sailed past them and up the stairs to her room.

Once inside, she wearily leaned against the door and locked it.

No doubt another reason her husband would be furious with her. And honestly, she no longer even cared. Yes, it wasn't until she removed the confining English clothes that she breathed a sigh of relief. Then after putting on Simon's gift, the beautiful gold Chinese silk pants and top, without fully understanding why, she fell to her knees beside the bed in true repentance for losing her temper.

And only once during her prayers did she peek up at the ceiling and shrug, admitting, "I am your most humble servant, God of my ancestors, but truth be told...I believe I would do it again."

The sun chose that particular moment to peek out behind the clouds and send a stream of light flooding into her room. To which Sarah, lifting her head to feel its warmth, smiled. It appeared God must have dealt with a few treacherous women Himself. This made her feel immensely better.

For some reason she slept.

It was mid afternoon before Simon's rattling of the locked door woke Sarah from her nap. Groggy, she sat up and stared at the door, willing him to go away.

"Sarah, stop being ridiculous and open the door. We need to talk."

Rubbing her right temple tiredly, she took a drink of cool water from a glass on the nightstand.

"Go away Warrior. I am much too tired to fight."

"Open the door or I break it down. Your choice."

The glass slammed down on the table, liquid splashing out the top.

"Fine. I'll open it, but, I will not talk to you."

She barely unlocked the door before being shoved back in its wake.

Simon looked once around the room before finally settling furious green eyes on her behind the heavy oak door. Even as thick as it was, the door was poor protection indeed against his barely restrained anger. But just as quickly, she saw him purposely reign in his temper, biting his lower lip and looking off before speaking to her. "I thought if I went to the club first it would help cool my temper."

She gave a slight smile at the exasperation in his voice. "Did it work?"

He started unbuttoning his shirt with short jerky motions. "No, it did not, China. And I thought we agreed you would stop reacting with physical violence every time I displeased you. Devil take it, woman, you can't go around throwing people into ponds and walls every time you get angry. It just isn't done. Do you have any idea how much explaining I had to do when I drove that weeping girl home? I still don't think she believed me when I said you pushed her, not threw, into the pond."

He jerked his shirt out of his pants and threw open the dresser to find another to replace the torn and dirty one hanging off his broad shoulders. Instead, he threw Sarah's riding outfit onto the bed.

"Change into that."

A mutinous look crossed her features, as she stepped out from behind the door. "I'm not going with you. It is a most bad idea. My emotions still rule my head. In fact, I have been thinking about our false marriage and since I didn't actually consent to it, well, I could probably sign the paper full of lies without..."

"Without your soul being eternally damned?"

A sick feeling in the pit of her stomach caused her to look straight past him and nod.

A great punishing sigh escaped his lips. "You're not signing any paper. Besides this is our destiny, remember."

"I no longer believe in destiny."

"Right. Look China, I don't have the energy to argue with you. Just get changed. I have to run out to one of Father's tenant houses in the country and I thought you could ride along with me. Mother suggested it and for once I agree. Perhaps we could stay at an inn and have that much needed talk tonight. It needs to be somewhere neutral. Mostly because I don't know how your going to take what I have to say and I would rather have you on top a horse, or surrounded by a room full of strangers when I start talking. Is that all right with you?"

She gingerly stepped forward. Relieved they would talk, and truth be told, excited to be riding again. "How did you know I could ride?"

"How else could you have found me so quickly last night? Speaking of which, what else did you remember?"

"Nothing. Just riding."

He nodded, his shirt coming off in a white blur leaving him totally exposed to Sarah's eyes. His chest strong and covered with coarse light brown hair, she felt her mouth go dry remembering how he felt against her. Automatically, she licked her lips in response. Their eyes met. There was no mistaking that he had caught her reaction to him. "Maybe the ride can wait."

Hurriedly, she scooped up her clothes and ducked behind the screen to change.

"No, it's getting late. We should be on our way. But what of your meeting tonight with the one who holds all your secrets?"

"I've changed my appointment to tomorrow. Tell me, is there anything you don't know about me?"

Suddenly serious, Sarah stopped struggling with her dress and answered truthfully from behind the screen, "I don't know how you are able to touch my soul like no other. I must say it displeases me very much. Usually I have more sense."

His deep laughter filled the room, like a welcoming balm to her emotions. Too soon it died down to a soft chuckle. "Ah, China. Let me tell you, it's not too great from this end either."

# Chapter 13

The horse felt good beneath her. The smell of leather and horseflesh was filling her nostrils with a welcome familiarity. Perhaps because it gave her hope that over time she would remember even more of her past, her parents, and growing up here.

As they left London, Simon looked back over one shoulder and then kicked his horse into a run. Not to be outdone, Sarah removed her hat and tucked it into the saddlebag, before turning the thoroughbred prancing beneath her towards the green countryside and Simon. By the time Simon slowed down his pace they were well beyond the city. Both of them were breathless and flushed with excitement. Simon reigned in the stallion he was riding, his arm muscles bulging beneath the strain, "You're pretty good. Who knows, with a little more practice, you might even catch up with me next time?"

Pushing back tangled hair, she gave a genuine laugh, "And who knows? Maybe next time I won't have to let you beat me."

Simon's laugh echoed across the rolling hills. "I believe you are sounding more English by the minute."

"I certainly hope not!"

Without thinking he leaned over and whispered close to her ear, "Me thinks the lady doth protest too much."

She turned, her eyes moving back and forth between the passion building in his eyes and the tantalizing lips just out of reach. He was doing it again, making her stomach toss about and her breath quicken. Without further thought she followed her instincts for once, and touched his lips with her own. His quick indrawn of breath was proof enough she had an equal effect on him.

After the kiss, Simon pulled away. He wanted to place distance between them. "We had better find that house before dark, there is talk of a storm brewing east of here."

Slightly hurt by his cool response to their kiss, Sarah nodded and followed him in silence.

Simon rode to the right of her, lost deep in his own thoughts. Perhaps it was better this way. She no longer wanted to talk about what happened on the docks the other night. After all, what could he possibly say to explain away the smuggled cotton? Or for that matter, why someone would try to shoot her…there was nothing he could say.

"Did you manage to find your grandfather before we left?"

She was surprised he even remembered she had been searching for him.

"Yes. He was in the library with his writings. It saddens me to see him at work sometimes. I guess because it means his task is nearing completion. I will miss him very much when he goes, even if it is the way of things."

Her horse stopped suddenly. Looking down she noticed Simon pulling back on its bridle, his knuckles white.

"What are you talking about? He would never leave you."

Taken aback by the fierce protectiveness in his voice she answered calmly, "Of course he will. My heart breaks within me. But, he will still leave. We both know his work will take him back to China one day. Since I am now a married woman I of course cannot travel with him. Now he only waits until the God of all things replaces what I have lost."

"And what have you lost, Sarah…your family?"

His hand accidentally brushed against hers and for some strange reason it made her want to weep. How could she explain what was in her heart, when he seemed so cold right now? "I've lost more than that. When I spoke the words to your holy man, your family became mine. So in a way, you are my family. No, it is my place in another's heart. This is what I have lost. When my family died God placed me in Grandfather's way and gave him a great love for me. Now Grandfather only waits for someone to… " she blushed, but whispered honestly, "Although I tried to explain it is not your wish, he still has hope."

Stunned, Simon let go of the bridle. It was several minutes more before he spoke again.

"You're talking about love."

She barely nodded, not raising her head. "Yes, but…"

"There is a stream up ahead. Maggie packed a light lunch for us. What do you say we stop for a moment? I think there are some things that need clearing up between us."

The gentleness and compassion in his tone was nearly her undoing. A moment before he had seemed distant and unfeeling. What was this man, villain or hero? The truth seemed somewhere in between.

Before long the trickling stream came into view, but a small herd of sheep blocked their path. Weaving in and out amongst them, they disregarded the sheep's deep protest at the interruption of dinner. Two babies frolicked in happy confusion in front of Sarah's horse. The dark brown mare danced around in nervousness, with Sarah tightening the reigns in case she reared. Still, those small woolly things made Sarah smile.

She supposed it was true what Grandfather said, 'That happiness hides in tears.' For what else could explain how a heart so heavy like hers, could still hope that somehow everything would be all right. That the man sitting so relaxed on his steed, smiling back at her would someday look at her like that every day of their lives. Some would say she was a dreamer. Perhaps she was.

On reaching the stream, Simon helped her down off the horse. His hands were strong and steady. Her own heart racing as she slid down the length of him. She tried hard to separate her mind from her undisciplined body. But, it wasn't working. Simon seemed to sense the war within and gave a seductive sexy wink. "It's perfectly normal to want me, you know. In fact, I rather like it."

Blushing she pushed back at the wisps of golden brown strands tickling one cheek, "But, I do not. Like it...that is. It makes me a weak opponent."

"Ah, China. But, that is how we differ. See, I don't consider you my enemy."

Bending down, he gently laid a hand to the side of her face, and then slowly and deliciously, kissed her. And it was if she had been holding her breath until that very moment. Her eyes closed. His kiss so sweet it was killing her. Treacherously, her body leaned in towards his warmth, remembering. Strong arms wrapped around her, as his kiss deepened. Then, suddenly he was gone.

Tugging on a hand, he led her over to a spot under an oak. "Much as I enjoy kissing you wife, it is time we talked."

Instead of leaving to fetch the basket, he sat down behind her with his back up against the tree and pulled her into himself, resting his chin on top of her warm sun drenched head. "So, let me explain about last night."

But instead, he talked about growing up in his family and his home and his dream of becoming a naval war hero. Of how he lost that dream, when his father was accused of murder. By the time he finished, the sun was beginning to set. The sun's reflection sending dancing ripples of color across the shallow creek. It was only then that he spoke of the night before.

"First off, you were right. It was cotton in those sacks. But, you were wrong about why I brought it from America. I was using the shipment to draw out a traitor. What I found out recently left me little choice. It seems most of the illegal shipments are coming out of Mexico, a place called Eagle Pass, Texas. With Parliament voting next week, I have to find out who is behind all of this before then. If I don't, it could mean war. And I don't think anyone here in England really wants to involve themselves in another Mexican war. Much less get involved in the trouble between the States."

"But you could go to prison if caught smuggling, wouldn't that be worse? Besides, how can you be certain that legal trade with the south would really start such a war?"

"There is nothing worse than war, China. And actually, yes, trade with the South would cause a war. Men are prone to do many things in the name of pride and money. Ironically, it seems that whoever is trading with Mexico is also against legal trade with the South. If Parliament votes against trade, he has a monopoly on Southern Cotton. If they vote for trade he would have competition from people like Peter. If that happened then Mexico would lose a valuable trade agreement they have between themselves and the smugglers. Someone in power, Mexico side, seems determined to keep that from happening, even if it means war to do it."

"But, I thought that was what you wanted, to stop trade with the South."

"What I want is to stop an enemy. But, even that has too high a price if it means a war, any war. If trade is legalized and we side with the South, it is only a matter of time before British soldiers will be involved in America's Civil war, while the whole time watching our backs for Mexico. But, if we do nothing..."

"An enemy wins and legitimate tradesmen lose money."

"Not only money. Businesses, homes, and England's economy will suffer. I fear it is rather like chess and he has just challenged my king with 'check."

"There must be something you can do."

Even though her statement was full of confusion and urgency, Simon pointed overhead.

"I know they are a simple bird, the swallow. Yet, I have a healthy respect for them. I remember being a boy at our country home and using a sling shot to fell quite a few of them before my father stopped me. For my punishment, I had to write down all the good qualities a swallow possessed."

His change of subject was frustrating, but years with Grandfather had taught her to be patient. That sometimes people needed time and distance to say truly what was on their hearts. Besides, today was the first time she had been given a glimpse into her husband's life before all the secrets, when he was simply a boy with a dream. Her heart yearned to know the man who was causing such havoc to her senses.

"It must have been hard, knowing the bird caused your downfall."

"I caused my own downfall. That was the point of the exercise. The bird was only doing what a bird does. The temptation was from within me. I was the one who ignored my upbringing."

This time she did turn around and look at him with wonder, her brown eyes flecked with golden light from the sinking sun. "It is a wise man who can see his own faults. He is not so quick to stumble over them."

"Let me guess, your grandfather?"

His grin lit up the inside of her more than the sun's decent did the horizon. "I told you he studies many ancient writings like the bible and Greek philosophers which makes him..."

"I know. A very wise man. Unfortunately, I am not. This is why my father used that small bird to teach me an important lesson. On what it truly means to be a man. Like for instance, taking responsibility for your own mistakes. Well, Sarah...I made one with you. I didn't trust you. Yet, I still forced you into becoming my wife without giving any part of myself to you. Instead, I just kept looking for a way to keep you out of this mess. Hoping I could send you back to America ignorant and in one piece, gain my freedom and then continue on with my life. Truthfully, I never even thought of you or your feelings at all. Except, how you could be of use to me."

Why was it that when he spoke, the words healed rather than harmed? Or why was it, that with his eyes looking so earnestly into her own, she simply wanted to touch him, to sit like this for hours, feeling the deep steadiness of his voice rumble in the comforting chest at her back. She turned all the way around, sitting cross-legged before him. "I have to admit it was not very honorable of you. However I have not been truthful with you either. I could have refused you. I didn't. Because," she looked down in embarrassment at her hands, "the truth is, I wanted to be with you."

Lifting her chin, he forced her to look at him, "Sarah, you wanted me because I set out to seduce you. I may not be wise in the ways of your grandfather, but I do know a few things about women. Do you understand what I am saying?"

Her small shoulders gave a slight shrug, "If you mean that you used your skill with women to bend me to your will, then, yes – I understand. But to tell you the truth, I think you must be not be very good at it. Otherwise I would not have kept throwing you into things for so long."

He shook his head at the teasing glint in her eye. "Have you heard nothing I've said? I've just admitted to using you for my own agenda. And now thanks to my selfishness, we are married. Permanently. But do you know what is even worse? Living with you has shown me how honest and trusting and beautiful you are. How I have probably changed everything good in your life. Yet, in spite of that, all I can think of is how blasted glad I am that you are mine. And how, even if it destroys us both, I never intend to let you go."

"I love you too Warrior."

She had spoken so quietly, the slight breeze carried her words to him. But, with her head down, he could not be quite certain he had heard her right. Gently he reached over and tilted her chin up. The only evidence his words had touched her, the wetness on her lashes.

"What?"

She smiled and even though the sky was aglow in evenings' last finale, it was no rival against her beauty.

"I said, I love you too Warrior. I, too am blasted glad you are here with me."

He threw back his head in laughter, hugging her to his chest. "It's insane, isn't it? Me, falling in love with a stranger. But I do love you, China."

She simply grinned in sweet contentment at being crushed in his powerful embrace. This must be what the verse in Grandfather's bible meant by, 'the two shall be one', for she had never been held any tighter. It was as if their very flesh and souls were merging into one entity.

Out loud she murmured, "You should not be so burdened about bringing trouble to me. Our lives are mingled now and my past creates problems for you as well. Grandfather says you can tell a man by the words he lives. I don't understand everything about you, but I do know some things to be true."

"Yes, and what would that be sweetheart?"

She could barely get breath enough to speak.

"Besides that you are crushing the life breath out of me?"

He laughed again, with deep, no holds barred laughter. "Is that better?"

It should have been once he released her, but she missed the strength of him around her. Still she sat back on two hands and watched as storm clouds started to gather just east of them. "Some. But, do you know what I think my English husband?"

The wind picked up his deep brown hair and ran its fingers through the dark mass, causing him to look devilishly disheveled when he asked, "No, what do you think my English wife."

"That despite how you try and hide the fact, you are a compassionate and good man. Only such a man would put himself in bondage for others. Risk his good name and fortune in the name of duty. And then marry a strange China girl from America in order to protect his family."

Now his head bent with the weight of her praise. After a moment's hesitation he lifted his head, the words of denial on his lips, when she held up a hand to stop him.

"If you will allow it, I would like very much to be both a true wife and friend to you. I want to share the keeping of your secrets." The words, although shyly offered sounded strong and full of promise.

He shook his head in wonder, studying the small hands engulfed by his own. Unconsciously, one thumb played back and forth along the inside of her smooth palm.

"Sometimes it is hard to believe your real, do you know that? I don't deserve you. However, for purely selfish reasons, I would be honored to claim you as a friend..."his eyes lifted to her own with unspoken promise, "As well as wife."

"You humble me greatly with so great a gift Sir Simon Conway."

Her heart skipped a beat when he leaned in and softly touched her mouth with his own. "Shall we make a pack then?"

Did she forget how to breathe? For all she managed was a nod. Then suddenly a thought came to her from the dark shadows of her past. Smiling she yanked her hand free and promptly spit into it.

"Whatever are you doing?"

Proudly, with chin lifted she held the hand out to him in friendship. "Now you spit in yours."

"I hardly think so."

A frown marred her sun kissed skin and furrowed her brow. "It's how a pack is made. I just remembered making such a pack with the milkman's son in my father's barn when I was six. You spit in your hand and we shake. Then we say, 'if I break this pack, may I die a thousand deaths and be eaten alive by worms."

He fluctuated between disgust and humor. Humor won out. Dutifully, he spit in his hand and together they quoted, "If I break this pack, may I die a thousand deaths and be eaten alive by worms."

After the pledge Simon refused to let go of her hand, but stared straight into her eyes and added, "And if Sarah Conway ever tells another soul her highly esteemed husband, Lord Simon Conway of the house of Lords, spit in his hand and shook on it, may she wear a corset each and every day of her life until she is thereupon eaten by said worms."

Laughter shone in her eyes, "Agreed."

"Agreed. Oh, and one other thing..."

"Packs over."

"This is just a request."

"All right then Warrior. What is it?"

"Do you think that the next time you remember something from your past it might prove a little more useful and a little less humiliating?"

A drop of rain fell onto their outstretched hands. But, even the threat of rain proved undaunted to her high spirits. Joyfully she lifted her face up to meet the cool air. Stating rather nonchalantly, "I'll try. But you know what Grandfather says..."

Love overwhelmed him, watching her embrace life. Even in a coming storm. "What does your esteemed Grandfather say?"

"Memories are like pieces of a puzzle. It is usually the odd ones that catch your eye first."

The breeze kicked up a little and Simon stood to his feet offering her a hand up.

"Does your grandfather say anything about being caught out in an English storm?"

She grabbed hold of his hand, her grip sure. "I don't think he ever has been."

Rolling his eyes, Simon yanked her the rest of the way to her feet. "Well, my arrogant wife, it looks as if you will be able to inform him since you are about to find out."

The rain landed in fat drops in random fashion all around them as they quickly made their way back towards their horses. Simon was still holding her hand as they reached their mounts. How she savored this moment of peace between them. To look at them now it looked as if they were any other pair of newlyweds out for an afternoon picnic. A rumble in the distance startled her right into her husband's side.

"I hate thunder."

"At least there is something my heroic wife is afraid of."

She blushed shyly in response to the deep timbre of his voice.

"We had better find shelter before it gets much worse. There is just one other thing I wanted to say before we race for the cottage."

"Yes?"

"I had hoped to explain in more depth about...however, as you can tell," he raised his voice over another clash of thunder, "that is proving rather impossible at the moment. So I will just have to say it. Next week, well, I will probably vote in favor of trade with the South."

So shocked was she by the announcement she didn't hear the clap of thunder only five miles away, or the flash of lightening across the now darkening sky. "But, the Sympathizers?"

"I needed to know which men were under the illusion of winning back the colonies through involvement of war. My traitor will not be among them. He stands to lose the most if his lucrative trade develops legitimate competition. No, he will not support England openly allowing others to participate in what he now has a monopoly on. Besides if I intend to be a thorn in his side, to draw him out, I have to make him believe I am a threat. Believe me he does not want trade with the South."

"But, why should he be a bigger danger than a vote for war?"

"This isn't about America. This is about England. I love this country, even the dark side of her. Believe me; no one really wants another war right now, especially the Sympathizers. They simply want legalized trade and there aren't enough in their group to pose a real threat, even with my vote."

"So you think the evil one is not a Sympathizer?"

"No, I don't. At first I did. Apparently I credited him with more integrity than he possesses. Thinking his politics were some vain misplaced attempt to get the colonies back. Now, I'm not so sure. My sources say he is already trading with the South and making a fortune, smuggling illegal cotton. It would hardly profit him to open trade up to cowards such as Peter and his father. Their many ships would put him out of business within a couple of months. But, if the North is lead to believe the traitor is acting secretly under Britain's orders...well, we will be forced into a war anyway. That is why he has to be stopped."

He gave her a hand up on the skittish mare. "I only hope our diplomat is persuasive enough to make Lincoln believe that we will honor both the ban against southern cotton and the higher embargo taxes on northern products. Believe me; it is to our disadvantage to side with the South right now. I am even sneaking one of the States' agents into the House of Lords next week. To further prove the culprit is acting alone without our consent."

Sarah noticed the storm clouds filling the sky now. The expanding storm is as real as the threat of war. What he said made sense. One wrong step and America would be in real danger of losing her freedom. And England would find herself involved in another Ireland. She knew that Americans would not give up their hard won independence so easily.

"But, what about you? You stand to lose everything if you vote for trade: like your respect, and your shipping business. Is there no other way besides voting against your heart?"

"No, there isn't. He has to believe that I am now a smuggler."

Sarah watched him mount his horse, the short-lived moment of joy fading. What would he do if he lost his shipping company? Those who did not know him would believe the worse. It was the way of people. So would those people that did know him.

"If your plan does not succeed, the evil one will have stolen more than money. He will gain honor in other's eyes as you lose yours."

"No doubt that is what he plans to happen. It only stands to reason that is why he is sneaking around, trying to convince others to vote against trade. The whole while crying out it is I behind the plot. If he succeeds, he will be a hero on both continents. Free to continue his lucrative smuggling business. England will be too caught up in a war they never really wanted and can ill afford. America too preoccupied to stop him."

"So, you are not afraid?"

He handed her his heavy coat, "We have to go Sarah."

"So your only way to defeat him is to think like he does?" She sounded resigned.

Simon urged their horses forward, but nodded, "It's my only choice if I want to catch him. However, all I have managed to do so far is to lose my investment and my office building. The only real progress I have made is finding out his contact in Mexico, which is how I obtained my cotton the other night. However, that tie is severed as well. The unfortunate man made the mistake of warning the traitor. He was gone before I could get there. But unfortunately for my contact, not before he slit the man's throat. I think the torching of my warehouses proved that my plan worked a little too well. You didn't happen to see anything out of the ordinary that night did you, maybe someone lurking in the shadows?"

John. Warning bells went off in Sarah's head. He said he was there to spy on Simon. But was he? A sudden pain in her head, made her reach up to rub her right temple. What he said made no sense. After all, John wasn't the one who had lied to her. Simon was. It had been John who had saved her life that night and her dignity the next day. Surely she owed him some sort of loyalty didn't she? At least until she could talk to him.

Besides, maybe this was simply a trick on Simon's part, to get a name out of her. She didn't know who to believe anymore. Or, why Simon would suddenly share so many secrets with her. In one conversation, the closeness she had felt towards her husband only a moment ago evaporated. Was her woman's heart deceiving her again? She needed time to think. Gently she removed her hand from her aching head. The stormy dusk hiding her features from his searching gaze.

She could tell he wanted to question her further, but the storm prevented any more conversation. The rain was now coming down in ice-cold sheets. Trying to avoid her husband's question, she kicked the horse in her flank. Urging her forward and away from Simon's probing stare.

They soon reached an overgrown path leading into the woods, so Simon took the opportunity to pull her under a group of trees in order to shelter them a little from the rain's angry onslaught and demanded, "What are you not telling me, Sarah?"

She knew her husband would not believe a lie. He dealt with evil men all the time and knew their ways. Yet she could not tell him what really bothered her either. She chose instead to share something he might already know.

"Someone shot at me that night."

A crash of thunder announced heavier rainfall and Sarah could barely see his reaction to her statement. Yet, it failed to distract from Simon's anger. It felt as palpable as the storm around them.

He ran a hand through his wet brown hair and shook his head at her. "Why didn't you tell me this?"

"I thought it might have been you."

"And why the devil would you think that?"

She would have to tell him everything, everything except John. Raindrops began to fall in earnest now onto her dress. Into her life. The wind whipping at what was left of her stylish hairdo.

"Never mind, we need to get out of this storm. The tenant cottage is not far from here. We can take shelter there. Can you handle the horse?"

The rain was coming down in sheets now. She had to shout in order to be heard.

"Yes. Let's get out of here."

The ride was a mere five minutes away, yet it felt like an eternity. The rain stinging her exposed skin. For once she was glad for the layers of clothing the English wore. Too bad she had left her hat on the ground in the mad rush for shelter. That too would have helped against the punishing onslaught of rain. Yes, between the rain and the dark it was

229

impossible to see much of anything, especially a small cottage hidden in thick English forest. Thank goodness the people inside the cottage were still awake. The soft glow of a lantern beckoned them forward.

Simon tied the horses out front and hurried her up on the porch.

Heaving a sigh of relief, she slumped against the rough planked door. Except now she began to shiver, wondering if she would ever be warm again. Automatically Simon drew her up under his sodden arm, trying to warm her as he knocked on the door.

There was no answer, only an odd peaceful silence. Another crash of thunder made her jump.

Simon pounded harder on the thick splintered wood.

Slowly, the door relented, creeping open from the onslaught of a pounding fist. The rusty hinges squeaking in protest. Hesitating only a moment, Simon pushed Sarah behind him and stepped into the cottage. Inside they found an unoccupied living area, warm from a dwindling fire. It was strangely quiet, the soft glow of a kerosene lantern the only light. In the center of the room, a note lay on the oddly square table. Its author apparently well taught, for the lettering was precise and rounded perfectly.

They looked warily at each other. Finally it was Simon who picked up the note to read its flowing script. Giving it a second once over he reacted by groaning and mumbling something under his breath about 'interfering', then throwing it back down on the table, before leaving to see about the horses.

Curious now, Sarah wiped her dripping wet hair out of her eyes, and gingerly picked up the note. A sad smile began to form as she read,

> *Dear brother and cherished sister in law,*
>
> > *Mother and I felt you both needed a little time alone. Somewhere far away from 'you know who'. So, we twisted father's arm to invent this little errand. Enjoy.*
> >
> > *Your adoring sister,*
> > *Kate*
>
> > *P.S. I absolutely forbid you to come home before tomorrow!*

Looking around, Sarah noticed the duck roasting over a still warm fireplace and the Sheppard's pie on the cupboard shelf. The ears of roasted corn stacked on a plate and one loaf of dark wheat bread. Everything set up for a feast. Why even a bottle of white wine sat in the middle of the table, a couple of French-cut, crystal glasses reflecting the faint firelight. The sight saddened her a little. It was a sweet thought but, there was still so much between her English husband and her. Secrets...a war and the fact they were practically strangers to each other. No, unfortunately, it would take much more than one night alone to fix what was wrong between them.

A part of her wished Kate were right and they could create a family together. Odd, how badly her heart yearned for it. A need that until Simon, she hadn't known existed. Sighing, she gave herself a depreciating shake of the head. As usual, simple common sense won out over the pipe dreams filling her normally practical head. Without further ado, she started putting things on the table. She might want love, but she needed nourishment and to keep her head. Otherwise, all she would end up with would be an aching heart and an empty stomach.

"The horses are bedded down for the night in a lean-to I found out back. If the storm doesn't let up I may have to...what is that smell?"

"Duck."

Apparently no matter his feelings about being manipulated by his family, he seemed, like her to be grateful for a moment alone. "Well, I guess a man doesn't have much to complain about if he gets to share a fine meal with a beautiful woman."

She smiled back at the mischievous grin he bestowed on her like a crown. His bad mood seemingly left outside with the horses. With his sexy charm turned full force on her, she found it hard to think about food. No doubt about it, he could cause any woman to forget most anything but him. That wayward thought caused a frown to appear. She only hoped his charm would be limited to her from now on. Otherwise he would be the cause of her throwing many more besotted Hilarys into ponds throughout their marriage.

She stopped jabbing at the poor duck and confronted her husband, "Simon, it appears as if your family believes our marriage is not...content."

Breaking off the dark end of one loaf of bread and smoothing on a thick slab of creamy butter, he raised an exaggerated eyebrow and took a bite. "You don't suppose it was that whole throwing Hilary in pond thing do you?"

His eyes shone teasingly at her around the hunk of bread he was stuffing into his mouth.

"Perhaps, but, personally I think it was my husband practically declaring himself to another woman and forcing me to throw her into the pond in the first place that made them have doubts."

"Now, China, you know I was only serving my country."

She swatted at his ducking head and snatched the half eaten bread away from him.

"You are a scoundrel, my husband. And I shall finish getting supper on the table, while you tend this dying fire."

"You're a bossy little thing, did you know that? Tell me, do you really intend on shivering in those clothes while you do it?"

Blushing she wrapped her arms protectively around her chest, "No, but I don't have anything else to wear."

"You certainly don't expect me to complain, do you?"

Good thing his words didn't warrant a reply. It was hard enough to remember to breathe when he pulled her into his arms like that, much less speak. She closed her eyes and gave in to the sweet temptation of his arms, before giving the disgruntled admission, "I wish you would just kiss me and get it over with."

His deep laughter caused her to open her eyes and frown up at him. "I fail to see what is so funny, my most arrogant of husbands."

"Oh, I don't know. It might be the way you invited me to kiss you. I've had more romantic invitations given me on a battlefield."

She shoved at his unyielding chest; "It is most difficult to think with you so close."

His finger doing a soft outline of her lips was extremely distracting. "Your problem is that you think too much, China. I can't seem to leave you alone for one minute before you change on me. What is it now? My family? The duck reminded you of ponds and erring husbands?"

Since he refused to release her, she stopped struggling and admitted, "It just seems as if we will never be, you know, normal."

He was trying hard not to smile.

"I mean we are not exactly normal are we?"

A grin slipped out on his face, as an eyebrow rose.

Flustered she tried again. "I just wish we could be..."

"Normal?" He suggested, not trying to hide his grin any longer.

Exasperated she flung out, "No. And stop grinning at me in that disarming way Warrior. What I mean to say is that I just wish we could be like other couples. Be ordinary. Go for walks. Have babies..." Shocked by what she had just said, she turned wide eyes up at him, and started rambling, "I mean...not that we can't...be ordinary...it's just that right now...would you stop laughing at me!"

"It's called having a family sweetheart. And if you would stop wiggling, I promise to get right on, making us extremely ordinary."

"Ohhh. Never mind."

Not to be put off again from holding her, he drew her back onto his lap. "What a paradox you are, China. So tiny that when I hold you, I swear you'll break. Yet, strong willed enough to fight any foe for something you believe in. Even if it's me and this sham of a marriage you were forced into."

Anger forgotten, she whispered against the mouth raining soft kisses along her left ear. "Simon, please. I can't think when you kiss me like that."

"Then don't." he growled almost fiercely, "I swear I can't be apart from you another moment. Do you have any idea how much I simply want to love you? Why do you fight me Sarah?"

She reached up and grasped his face, looking intently up at him. Reading the truth of his words and the pain it caused him to admit it, she gave in, pulling his head down to her own and kissing him, uncensored and full of passion. It mingled in with her own inner torment.

Suddenly, her feet were off the ground. Since Simon never slowed the assault of his mouth on hers, she wasn't exactly sure if he was carrying her, or she was floating across the room to the bed in the corner. Then she felt the bed sink beneath the weight of their bodies and watched in fascinated awe as her husband slowly got up and began unbuttoning his wet shirt.

The wet cotton clung to his muscular form; leaving little to the imagination, yet still the unveiling of his chest caused havoc to her insides. Her mouth went dry and she instinctively ran a tongue over her full lower lip. Another moment more, and she wouldn't possess enough mind to say what her heart demanded.

"I love you Warrior. And it terrifies me worse than the fiery dragons of my dreams, because you have the power to break my heart."

Sitting down on the edge of the bed, his damp cream colored shirt half undone, Simon gathered her up against the firmness of his warm skin. She felt his heart thundering in response to her nearness, although his voice remained soothing, as he tried to comfort her.

"I love you too Sarah. Trust me. I know it's insane to believe anything I say right now. All you've known so far is lies. But, this Sarah..." He kissed her eyelids gently. "And this..." His hand caressed her, as long fingers brought sensations too wonderful for words. "This moment is real between us. Not all of England can come between us here. Now. Don't ever doubt us, sweetheart."

With those words all evidence of the outside world evaporated. Soon the love between two souls became the only warmth in the small cottage. It, was the only reality. Even the dying fire and darkening room went unnoticed. For over an hour they simply loved and received love. And for once, with Simon's help...Sarah stopped thinking.

They must have slept for a little while. Sarah awoke to a rumbling stomach, as flashes of light from the storm brought the cabin in and out of darkness. Still, she resisted getting up and snuggled instead against the warmth of the husband beside her. His arm tightened and a gentle kiss to her brow told her he was awake as well.

"I wonder if I'll ever get use to you."

His soft chuckle made her smile.

"That doesn't sound like much of a compliment Sweetheart."

"I meant..."

"I know."

Her stomach rumbled yet again, only more insistent this time.

"What do you say we have some supper before I have my way with you yet again?"

Blushing, Sarah tried to pull away, but he only gave her a quick tight hug before swinging his legs off the bed. "Blast, its cold. Why don't you stay in bed while I start another fire?"

"Are you sure?"

He grinned as she burrowed under the covers. "If it means keeping you in my bed? Believe me, China, I'm sure."

She gave a sleepy smile and drifted off once more.

The smell of warming food woke her. She was hungry enough to eat a shoe if he'd offered it covered in Sheppard pie.

When she started to rise he came over, barefoot and shirtless, placing a makeshift tray of food before her. While she hungrily ate the fare, he leisurely poured a couple of glasses of wine. Studying her as she polished off the rest of the duck. It was only once her ravishing hunger had been appeased she noticed he wasn't eating. Horrified, she looked down at the few scattering of crumbs and licked clean duck remains and groaned, "Oh, dear. I hope that wasn't all of it?"

"It was."

"Oh."

Taking mercy on her crestfallen face, he handed her a half full glass and motioned behind him. "I ate earlier while you were sleeping. I do that a lot you know. Watch you sleep. I swear you must be the most beautiful woman I have ever known. Did you know I use to spend many a sleepless night when we were first married, trying to keep my hands off you and just watching you sleep?"

Too awed by emotion, she shook her head. "I can't really understand why. I'm rather common looking actually, but I must admit that I like hearing I'm beautiful. It's nice. I suppose that makes me just as vain as your other English ladies, doesn't it?"

He brushed a long dusty lock of hair away from golden eyes and back behind a sexy bare shoulder. "Sorry sweetheart, but you're nothing like any other woman I've ever known, English or otherwise. Now, are you done with that wine? For I feel a new hunger coming on, that only you can satisfy."

Morning came too soon.

Even though they both pretended to be in a good mood, they knew once they returned home this moment would end. Doubts and secrets would separate them yet again. And then there was Hilary. Sarah narrowed her eyes and jerked up the covers so violently that they untucked from the bottom.

"Is something bothering you, China?"

A fist pounded, rather than fluffed up the feather pillow in her hands. "No, what makes you think something is bothering me?"

"Well, you just ripped that pillowcase in two, for one."

"Oh."

He gently pulled it from her hands and laid it down on the bed. "Now, tell me what's wrong."

He looked so handsome, his day's growth of beard making him look sexy in an unkempt fashion. Today he looked less the rich nobleman and more the rugged adventurer spy. She folded her hands in her lap and mentally slowed down her breathing. Once she had control of her emotions she spoke. "It's Hilary."

"Yes?"

"I think you will have to stop seducing her."

"I see...well, all right."

Her head jerked up as a big smile lit up her features. "All right? Just like that?"

Helping her up, he placed two hands on her shoulders and nodded, "Yes, just like that. See, my wife is the jealous sort and has a tenancy to throw my lady friends into ponds. It draws too much attention to secret missions and such. Besides it does happen to put a damper on things to be so madly in love with the crazy woman. Not really the thing if you're trying your hand at seduction. So, now that is solved, is it safe to leave you alone with the bedding while I bring the horses around?"

Relieved she placed a light peck to his whiskered cheek. "I believe so. Oh, and Simon?"

"Yes?"

"Thank you."

His eyes looked deep into hers, and then they darkened to the green of a stormy sea. "You're welcome, wife."

His nearness set a spark kindling between them. His hands reaching out to caress her long tawny curls. Bringing up a hand full of the soft stuff, he filled his nostrils with her scent.

"Did I ever tell you, how much I love you hair? The way it touches me in the dark, slides through my fingers..."

He was a temptation her husband.

"We have to get back."

She didn't sound convincing even to her own ears.

"Later," was whispered against the throbbing of her throat.

He was making it hard to think.

"But, I thought you were meeting with the keeper of your secrets and I must meet with – the ladies."

She stopped herself just in time. However the abrupt ending of her sentence brought Simon's face up to search her own suspiciously. She tried to look away, but the intensity of his stare held her captive. Her husband's instincts were strong within him. She saw it in his eyes when he stepped away from her. The warrior was back. Hoping to sway his intention of questioning her, she tried to make light of her slip up.

"I only meant, well, there is the fall festival meeting today for the orphanage. Remember?"

"I remember. Now who else are you meeting with today?"

"I told you."

"You're a terrible liar, sweetheart. And I thought we had an agreement. No more secrets, remember?"

"I know, but this is different."

Not letting her off so easily, his eyes turned dangerous and dark before pulling her up hard against him, "All right, but, it'll cost you one question, answered honestly."

Her stomach fluttered in response, "What? I told you everything."

"I didn't press you yesterday, but I am today. Who was there with you the night of the fire?"

Suddenly her throat closed in fear and doubt. Had this whole night been only a way to get her to revile a name? Looking up into his intense and fierce face, she felt...heaven help her...she felt such tenderness and love. Yet, the secret he demanded, she had given her word to keep. She looked down and stepped out of his arms.

"It is not a name I can give. Not yet."

"If not now, when?"

The cold light of day chilled the warmth of her heart. "Tomorrow night. I made a promise."

The power of his grip caused her to look up. When he spoke, it was as a man use to having his word obeyed. "I'll give you until tomorrow, but then I will have that name. And under no circumstances are you to meet with this person alone. It's too dangerous. Do you understand me? This isn't a game Sarah. These are dangerous men we are dealing with, who have a lot to lose."

For a fleeting moment Sarah feared he might be one of them. But, it was too late to turn back now. She would have to tell him about John. Tomorrow. Between now and then she would have to ignore his other order bellowed at her with such force. She would still meet with John to warn him. Simon would just have to understand when he found out. Because she knew with certainty he would find out. He was much too cunning, her warrior husband, and she much too in love. No doubt she would probably be destroyed by this love. But, by all she held dear, she no longer even cared and that scared her most of all.

# Chapter 14

The ride back was uneventful. She wished the sun was out, but instead the heavy clouds threatened even more rain. Her clothes, still damp from yesterday, only intensified the desire to be once more back at the cabin and in her husband's arms, if only to hold off facing their individual demons, just for one more day. A touch of autumn wind brought her daydreaming to a halt, chilling her further.

"Cold, China?"

"A little."

He reined in his horse and pointed to a road not a quarter of a mile away, "Just past that bridge and another mile or so and we'll be home. Can you make it?"

The dark horse pranced underneath him impatiently. Simon's muscles strained from trying to hold the horse back, never the less his voice held a touch of concern when he spoke to her. It seemed that even as angry as he was with her, he still cared for her. He was a man full of contradictions, her husband. Then remembering how only moments ago she had thought the same about herself, she chided her wayward thinking and came up beside him.

"What are you smiling about?"

Leaning over, Sarah couldn't help how his nearness made her feel, how it made her want to erase the dark frown he was bestowing on her. She pointed over his left shoulder. "Nothing really, except I was just thinking that instead of walking..."

He cocked his leery head at her. "Yes?"

"I would rather race you to that bridge instead."

Then before he could comprehend her challenge, she kicked her horse into a full run. Gone was the seriousness of a moment ago as she tilted her face up with pleasure to the cool autumn day. The dampness of the morning all but forgotten as Simon's horse came thundering up behind her on the first bridge. Drawing her body even closer in to the chestnut mount, she urged the mare forward. Determined to defeat her much too confident husband, if only this once.

The city of London loomed just ahead. One more field and she would reach the second bridge first.

She felt, rather than saw, Simon's black stallion rush past and take the bridge not more than three paces ahead. By the time he reached the city he was a good six feet in front. Slowing down, Sarah pretended irritation.

"You know, of course, I let you win."

A raised eyebrow was his only response.

"I did. Everyone knows a warrior hates to lose. It is a fact. Since, it is a wife's duty to please her husband. And I am the humblest of wives." A feigned look of disbelief made her shrug in response, "Regardless, by losing this insignificant race, I have actually won a great victory."

"Is that so?"

The cobbled London streets added a soothing rhythm to her words.

"Of course. Now you will possess a false sense of superiority. This is a weakness, my husband."

Simon leaned over and nudged her chin up until defiant eyes met his. "Maybe. Or, just maybe, I am superior."

A satisfied glimmer from dancing golden eyes caused him to stare at her in awe. "And you my wife are much too beautiful for either one of our sakes."

Involuntarily she laid a hand to his chest. Whether it was to stop him from kissing her, or simply to touch him again, she wasn't certain. "Your words are like honey to the fly, my husband. So sweet, but still a trap. Nevertheless they will not sway my determination to defend myself from so cunning a warrior."

The sounds of London coming awake drew her attention away from the temptation her husband was to her. Street wares were beginning to line the streets as carriages hurried from townhouses to businesses lying in the heart of the city, and all were a welcome distraction from the sexy green eyes creating havoc to her insides. Reluctantly she withdrew her hand.

"Hot cross Buns!" A skinny man shouted, making her jump back as he held up his wares with one bony hand thrust up through the sleeve of a threadbare jacket. No doubt the dingy object was his only protection against the cold morning air. Sarah instantly felt a wave of pity for the poor man.

Recognizing an opportunity, he stepped in closer to Sarah's mare, shoving one of the warm rolls up towards her yet again. "Care for a nice warm roll, miss? Me wife just pulled them out of the oven."

Her heart went out to him. He was so thin; his body was nothing more than a leathery bag full of odd sized angles.

She reached over and accepted the barely warm roll. "Thank you, Sir. Simon, would you be so kind as to pay, I fear I left the money you loaned me at your father's home."

"It wasn't a loan. You're my wife now." When she raised her chin a notch to disagree, he shook his head, "Never mind. However, you should not reward rudeness Sarah."

The man grinned at her around several missing and tobacco stained teeth. Her stomach clenched in sympathy. She understood his desperation. Especially, since she had lived in tenement housing herself in New York. How easy it was for the rich to condemn the poor. People like Simon would never know what it felt like to be cold, hungry or desperate. She did. "You can plainly see the poor man is starving and hardly needs a lesson in manners at the moment."

Heaving an aggravated sigh, Simon tossed a coin the man's direction and continued walking his horse the last few blocks towards home. Sarah didn't bother to catch up. In fact she wasn't even speaking to him. However, once reaching the townhouse, Simon tried to get her to see reason. "Sarah, will you never cease feeling sorry for every riffraff that crosses your path?"

"And will you ever possess a heart? That coin meant nothing to you. But, it will probably feed that poor man's family for a week."

"Sarah, that 'poor man', was more than likely coming straight from the Opium Dens. He fairly reeked of it. No doubt his family will be lucky to see even a pence of what I gave him."

The lingering sickening sweet smell from the man's unwashed hand assaulted her senses when she brought up the roll to take a bite. Opium. Looking at the roll in disgust she dropped it to the ground and wiped her hand on the brown wool of her skirt. "You don't know that for certain." Her voice sounded shaky even to her own ears.

"No. But, then again you know nothing about the man either."

They had reached the carriage house and Sarah felt more confused than ever. He was right of course. She knew nothing of the man, nothing of this culture, or for that matter – even her own husband. Apparently just as her parents had not known whom to trust and died because of it, she was suffering from the same flaw of trusting too much. Even now she was choosing to believe Simon's words over her own eyes.

Out of nowhere a debilitating dizziness hit her squarely between the eyes. She grabbed the small horn on the English saddle to keep from falling. Behind her she could hear Simon's voice as if from a great distance, but could not make out his words. She clutched at her throat, finding it hard to breathe. What was happening to her?

It was the dream.

Suddenly all her old doubts and fears assailed her senses, and with them the nightmare of her dreams took hold and forced itself upon her.

Instantly her body tensed.

She would not remember. Not here. Not now.

Against her will, the familiar smell of cigar smoke and metallic blood became so real that it made Sarah gasp from the shock of it. Memories of her past were forcing themselves on her once again. Only this time she was awake. The dream was all too real. The fear was too paralyzing. And this time she could not simply awaken to end it. Her heart thundered inside her chest. The blind panic she knew from the dream world was back, strangling her with its invisible hold.

Eyes...so cold...the evil one... She began to shake. There was something about his eyes. Something important. She had to remember before it all disappeared again behind the wall of fear she had resurrected when just a little girl.

"Sarah!"

Simon was shaking her, his face intent and worried. "Are you all right? You're pale as a ghost."

"It's the dream."

How could she explain? Only Grandfather knew of her nightmares. The fear they evoked. Simon's hand stroked her hair, gentling her. She finally took in a cleansing breath of air and tried to gain some sort of control, slowly coming back to reality. When she did, her hands were shaking within her husband's strong clasp.

"Sarah, sweetheart, what happened?"

"It's the dream. It came to me, here. How is that possible?"

"What dream?"

The protectiveness in his voice was nearly her undoing.

"Sometimes in the night, I remember the time of my parent's death. The smells, sounds and odd things like expensive cigar smoke. But lately, just like a moment ago, my dreams have begun coming to me in the waking world. Grandfather says it is good to let the memories free of the dream world. He believes to remember my past, is to heal my present. But I'm so...I don't know."

"Afraid?"

Looking around, she noticed for the first time they were at the door of the carriage house. It was strange how time slipped by, when lost in the dream world. Almost reluctantly she pulled her hands free of his and slid off the horse. "It is more than that. I don't wish to remember. My mind is not strong enough. Not yet."

Within seconds he was on the ground beside her, gently removing the reins from her clenched fists and leading their horses inside. "Your grandfather's right, Sarah. Whether you want to or not. It is time to remember. If you don't, the man that killed your parents will never be punished for what he did. Is that what you want?"

The story he told of his father's partner held her thoughts prisoner. To speak of something held in secret for so long seemed impossible to begin. As if reading her mind, he shoved a horse brush into her hands, insisting, "Enough secrets wife. It's time to trust me."

She wanted to tell him. Yet the words stuck in her throat. So, rather than answer, she slowly began brushing the horse with slow even strokes, trying her best to ignore the angry male towering over her. When she refused to look up at him, Simon placed a hand over hers, stilling her actions.

"Sarah, how can we get past all of this if you won't let me help you?"

She ducked her head further, a blatant refusal to his plea.

Heaving an irritated sigh, Simon left her side and began the task of unbuckling the black stallion. She could tell he was still frustrated with her, yet he seemed to be giving her time to catch her breath and decide if she could trust him. Or for that matter, herself.

Silently she watched him talk softly to the stallion, easing the restless spirit within the finely muscled beast. The simple act brought tears to her eyes. She needed such comfort herself right now, needed someone to listen and to care. But most of all, she needed the strength of him, if only for a moment. She was so very tired of being strong.

Finally, reaching a decision, she spoke softly into the quietness of the barn. Finding some small comfort in the rhythmic pull of the horse brush as it slid smoothly across the animal's muscled side. "Remember the story you told me that night when we went for a drive about how your father was accused of murdering his partner?"

"Yes."

The only way she knew her words affected him at all, was the slow, careful way he hung up the English saddle. His back was ramrod straight and his muscles taunt.

"I think, no, I am nearly certain those were my parents. That my father was your father's partner."

He spun around, his face red with emotion. "Sarah that just isn't possible. They only had one child. She was found dead a week later. Washed up on the banks of the Thames, hardly recognizable –"

He stared at her. They both knew it was next to impossible to be absolutely certain about a body that long in the water.

"And what if, by some remote possibility it wasn't her? That would make her almost..."

The way he stared at her, as if calculating her age, she answered for him. "I'm eighteen."

Sinking down onto the stack of hay beside him, she earnestly pleaded with him to understand. "I know I should have said something that first night. But, when you said they found the body of the child, well, I thought maybe I was wrong."

"You still could be."

"Yes."

Both were silent for several minutes. The sound of the groom whistling as he headed towards the carriage house sounded intrusive and at odds with the feeling of doom both people felt. Finally, Sarah spoke up softly, almost afraid to actually say the words. "You could ask your father the little girl's name. Find out more about my - I mean her family." She studied the profile of his handsome face as he looked off, lost in thoughts, even she could not possibly understand. "I still can't understand why someone would want to harm me, a mere child. According to your story, they had nothing to gain. It doesn't make any sense."

"Maybe it isn't supposed to. After all, some men are without conscious Sarah. I certainly have run across a few in my line of work. Regardless, you will never find out the answer to that question by hiding from your past."

"But Simon, if you could have seen my destroyer, he was so evil. Hate I could understand, but from him I felt nothing. No emotion whatsoever. That is until he had me cornered behind the pilings. Then it was as if," She shivered. "as if, he actually enjoyed my fear. As if, it made him feel alive. Tell me why I would want to remember such evil? The echo of its dark shadow affects my dreams as it is."

She was crying softly now. Her body was chilled and trembling. Automatically his arm encircled her and drew her into his warmth. A soft kiss placed to her brow soothing some of the ache inside her heart.

245

"Don't cry sweetheart. I'll find out what father knows. And what he can't supply, perhaps the man I meet with later on can. He is known for finding out information no other men can. But before I do anything, I need to know if there is anything else you remember? It might help in the search. Even the most insignificant detail could prove helpful."

Someone had waylaid the groom on his way to the barn. The men's laughing voices over a shared joke, making a mockery of the subject so earnestly discussed between husband and wife. The sun was even trying to come out. How bright the few rays of sun penetrating through the slits in the wall were as they fell across the dirt floor. It was a warm invitation to come out of the shadows.

Why then did she felt so deathly cold inside?

Never before had she tried to remember details of that night. But, her warrior husband was right. The destroyer of her family did not deserve freedom. Not when he kept her a prisoner, chained to the past. Besides, how many other lives had he taken in the eight years since her parents' death? Grandfather's missionary father believed all lives were crossed for a reason. To resist one's purpose was like leaving a hole in a beautifully woven fabric. Someone else would have to repair the damage left by our indifference.

Saying a silent prayer for courage, she kept her eyes closed, concentrating on that night. The constant beating of Simon's heart in her ear was the only solace to her pain. Finally, she drew in a steadying breath and began. "I remember walking down a street. It was a cold night. But, my parents didn't seem to mind. I think they were like that. Warm. Beautiful together."

She couldn't finish. The words choked her. Simon squeezed her for encouragement. And after a few more moments she began again, "We were expecting a carriage, but rather than waiting for us outside the brightly lit theater, it was parked around the corner down a dark side street. I remember my mother commenting on it. But for some reason, none of us were afraid."

"Do you remember anything special about the carriage?"

"No. Except that when the destroyer came, my mother told me to run to it for help."

"But they refused to help you." It was a statement of fact. He was her warrior again.

"Yes. That's when I smelled the cigar smoke. And then I ran."

She was trembling again. She was going to be sick. "I can't do this."

"Look at me Sarah." She shook her head; trying to get away from the strong grip forcing her head up, "Look at me."

Finally, filled with hurt and anger, she did. But what she saw on his face overwhelmed her. His eyes held such compassion and silent strength, that all her anger instantly evaporated. Leaving her feeling listless and out of body.

"You ran. Then what? How many men were there?"

Nodding, she continued shakily, "There were two...no, three of them. But I only saw one up close. The only thing I can remember clearly are his eyes. They were full of light. Or so it seemed when he stepped out of the alleyway. And something about his boots."

"Boots? What about his boots?"

"It was odd. They were polished. I was little and hiding among the crates and barrels, but I remember thinking he must be one of 'The ton', like my Papa. Except that his coat looked like the other two men's. Dirty and patched." She felt exhausted and curled up further against his side. "That's all I remember. The next memory I have is of Grandfather carrying me on board the ship heading for America. For years, I remembered none of this. Then about a year ago, the nightmares began."

He just sat and held her for several minutes until her trembling ceased. Finally, he spoke with such regret in his voice that it tore at her heart, "I'm so sorry sweetheart. I wish that you didn't have to relive all of this, but I fear it is the only way to find this murderer."

"No, you were right to make me remember."

He rubbed his whiskered chin along the top of her head, interrupting her words, "Not only that. I should have asked you sooner. I was so caught up in my own troubles that I never even considered the suffering you must be going through not knowing what happened to your parents. I have been selfish and arrogant. Can you ever forgive me China?"

She pushed away from him, looking up.

So awed was he by what he saw on her face, that his heart swelled with choked back tears, which prevented him from speaking.

Simply put, she forgave him. And if that wasn't enough, trust, the real unadulterated kind shined back at him through her eyes.

The presence of it filled his soul with pride and paralyzing fear at the same time. For if what she said was true? Well, then she was in real danger. And he had helped put her there by making her his wife.

They barely had time to change before Simon was to meet with his father in the library and then head off to the Minister's for a briefing. Downstairs ladies were already arriving for the meeting taking place in the freshly clipped garden. Sarah had hoped to slip upstairs and avoid the meeting all together. Unfortunately Simon's mother waylaid them on the way upstairs. Informing her, as Sarah tried escaping one step at a time, that since she would be involved in the planning of games, a decision apparently reached yesterday at Lady Ashworth's, they would need her input. The whole while she was speaking, the woman could not seem to stop smiling up at the two of them. If that were not bad enough, in between sentences she would pause, as if waiting for something. It was to the point of becoming embarrassing.

Simon finally shoved Sarah up the last few stairs and commented warningly, "Mother it doesn't matter how long you stand there gawking, we are not going to tell you about our trip. It's personal."

"Why darling, I don't know what you're talking about. I wouldn't dream of interfering."

"Good."

"However, if you wanted to talk..."

"Goodbye, Mother."

Her face instantly fell.

Feeling uncomfortable about being so rude to his mother, Sarah stopped suddenly at the top of the stairs, adding "But we did have a lovely time. It was most kind of you to prepare it for us."

Knowing his wife, Simon began pulling her off towards their bedroom, "Oh, and Simon promises to stay away from the pale one. So you needn't worry any -" Simon jerked her through the door, "longer."

"Sarah, our personal affairs are no one's business but ours."

She watched him take off his jacket in quiet contemplation. "But she is an elder. It is extremely disrespectful to ignore an elder."

A heavy sigh filled the room. "Sarah, you don't understand my mother. She becomes overly involved. If you encourage her, she will suggest dates and times we make love in order to plan the exact arrival of her grandchild."

"Perhaps it is her gift."

"I hardly think gift describes it."

"Each soul is blessed with gifts. Your mother has a very caring heart. She cannot help wanting the best for us. Just as she cannot help going to the orphanage, or hiring inept servants so they will have a home. It is what the God of all things calls her to do."

Simon shook his head in wonder, "Do you really see the good in every instance? In every person you meet?"

A shadow of sadness crossed her features. "No, not everyone."

He knew she was referring to the man who had stolen so much from her. Slowly Simon came up behind her and gently pulled his damp coat away from her body. "Sweetheart, I'll find him."

Her slight body trembled. And all he could think about was ways in which he would like to warm her. He didn't suppose he would ever get use to how his body reacted to her. How deeply she affected him. He ran an index finger slowly around the rim of an ear. "You know, I've been thinking."

"About what?" The breathlessness in her words sent passion shooting through his body. He began placing soft kisses down the side of her throat.

"That perhaps you're right. Maybe I should include my mother in our love life after all. I am sure if we asked, she would much rather you attend me and work on that grandchild than attend any meeting."

"Simon, you must stop."

"Stop what?"

Sarah knew she should pull away from the hands helping her undress. If she didn't, she would be even later to the meeting. No doubt everyone would think her most rude. He kissed the corner of her mouth. Would wonder...his mouth covered hers in a deeply possessive kiss. It literally melted away any resistance she thought she had.

Unfortunately, she didn't need any.

Kate's knock was resistance enough.

Apparently, when one was absent, the rest of the group chose an ambassador to search them out. From the loud banging coming from the other side of their bedroom door –this time it was Kate.

A frown marred Sarah's usually sunny disposition as Kate once more banged on the heavy oak door.

Simon grinned down at his aggravated wife and gave her a hard fast kiss.

"I think it's time we moved. Either that, or marry off my sister." With that said, he threw on a dry jacket and opened the door.

"Well my dear sister, what a surprise. Tell me do you have something against obtaining a niece or nephew, Briar? Because, you are definitely not helping."

Blushing Kate stammered, "Simon you are incorrigible. I only wanted to check on Sarah. To tell her the meeting will be starting any minute."

Sarah spoke up quickly, stating logically, "But I don't see why I have to attend. As I told your mother, I am deeply honored to be asked but must refuse, I know nothing about this gathering of women."

"Tsk. Tsk." Kate admonished. "Everyone knows you're in charge of the games this year. Better finish dressing." Then glaring at her brother, she added, "And Father wants to see you in the library. Now. So don't think you can detain Sarah from her duty a moment longer."

"But, my husband's sister," Sarah argued as she threw on a robe, "I cannot see how I can be in charge of something I never volunteered for."

The last sentence was shouted at Kate's retreating back. She simply waved a hand back over one shoulder, "Oh, and don't forget your speech."

"Speech? What speech?!"

With that little tidbit of information thrown Sarah's direction, Kate left in a whirlwind of pink satin. Off, no doubt, in search of another unlucky soul to torment.

Simon's unabashed laughter filled the room, "Seems to me wife, you had better get down there before you are 'volunteered' for something else."

Shoving her irreverent husband out the door, she warned, "Then perhaps you'd better go down as well, before your mother volunteers you for something."

His face went ashen. Visions of chattering women ordering him about wiped the smile completely off his face. "Not funny Sarah."

She batted her eyes innocently at him; "I would catch Kate if I were you."

He was gone in an instant.

Quickly washing up, she threw on clothes while peering out at the richly adorned carriages pulling up outside. Her gut was churning. There were so many of them. In fact, there was so many, that there was no real place to park all the carriages. So each pulled up, emptied richly dressed women at the foot of the curved stone steps and set out yet again. She dropped the curtain back in place with a sigh.

She hated these gatherings of ladies, even if it was for a good cause. Maybe Grandfather was right and it was just that she had been a free spirit for far too long. Regardless, she doubted whether she would ever understand or even want to, the unspoken rules of the ton. She supposed if her parents had lived she might be use to it all. But she wasn't.

Walking over, she sat down at the dresser. Laying down the pearl handled brush and looking at her reflection in the mirror, she wondered for the thousandth time. Did she look like them? Where did she get her small boned frame and thick mane of honey-streaked hair?

Talking with Simon today left her feeling melancholy. Wishing she could remember. Oh, not that night, never that. Just to remember what it felt like to be rocked in her mother's arms. Her father's laugh, those simple, heartfelt things.

She gave a wry grin at herself in the beveled mirror, the scalloped edging making her reflection a framed picture of sorts. Who was she kidding? She had absolutely nothing to prove who her parents were. Not one photograph. Not a single person that even knew she existed. Maybe Simon was right. Those people who were killed so long ago? Who was to say they were her parents. The odds were a million to one that fate could have brought her here to the very house that would hold the answers. Still...

Golden eyes stared back at her, lost eyes.

Her head went down on crossed arms and she moaned softly into their depths. She just wished all of this would be over. What was the purpose of remembering anyway? It only made her long for things impossible for her to have.

"Oh, God of all things", she prayed brokenly, "I know you are the master of our destiny, but I am so confused. So afraid."

As if an answer to her prayers, she felt the locket slip from her neck. Lifting her head, she gingerly fingered its smooth golden surface. The name Sarah engraved within a circle of roses. As if someone had cherished and loved her once. Wiping at tear filled eyes, she gave a weak smile heavenward. "You are right, of course. It doesn't matter if I am afraid. To not remember is to forget two people who loved me and died trying to save me. I will not fight the awakening of my past. From now on, I will fight with, not against you."

Courage gathered around her like a cloak. Funny, she no longer dreaded what was to come, even the ladies. Quickly, amid the hectic activity downstairs she finished dressing and headed out into the hallway.

She had barely taken a step when she noticed her grandfather practically running down the hall towards their rooms as if the fiery serpent Satan himself was giving chase. And from his wide eyed expression? Satan was gaining on him.

The sound of ladies laughter drifted up the stairs behind him.

Understanding made the corners of her mouth turn up into a knowing smile. Of course it wasn't the ancient serpent at all that her warrior grandfather feared, but something much worse...the ladies charity group. Yes, they were kindred souls, this ancient China man and lost English girl. He was just luckier. He could escape to his room.

"Hello, my grandfather. Is something, or someone chasing you?"

A slight tug at the corner of his mouth belayed the stern rebuke he tried to give, "I have fought in wars, killed a tiger with only a knife to aid me, and even saved one small troublesome English girl. Do you doubt my courage?"

"Well, you were running."

His grin and quick look behind him, made her giggle.

"They are only women, Grandfather."

"Ah, I suppose. If you say so. But there is a reason I remain unmarried. I find no enjoyment in puzzles that have no solutions."

"Or perhaps, no puzzle has intrigued you enough to try."

"I have a very meddlesome granddaughter indeed." Turning serious, he looked more intently into her red-rimmed eyes. "Is everything all right Little One? Your husband is not the cause of your tears?"

"No, it is just my past that insists on intruding on my present. And now the warrior asks something of me that I can't do."

"What is that?"

For just a moment she nearly confided in him about everything: her doubts about Simon, John, and the smuggled cotton. But, her heart would not let her. Grandfather must be free to go back to his homeland. The only way he would leave, is if she could be strong enough without his guidance. The pupil must leave the teacher, so both could fulfill their destinies.

"It is nothing. I'd better go, Grandfather."

He looked as if he might press her further, but she gave him no opportunity. Sailing past, and not quite looking him in the eye, she gave a light kiss to his weathered cheek, "Do stop scowling Grandfather, I promise I am fine. I must fight my own battles now."

But, as she hurried down the long hall and made her way downstairs, she felt his eyes on her back. As always, watching and protective.

She was late.

Once outside, she slipped into a wrought iron chair at the back. Kate caught her eye and waved. Then when she was sure no one was looking, cut her eyes to the podium and pretended a bored yawn. Sarah smiled back.

In the midst of another long speech, Sarah's stomach growled. She was starving. And unfortunately the ladies had just finished brunch. Dishes of half eaten food lay in heaps on delicate hand-painted periwinkle China. She shook her head at the irony of it all. This was supposed to be a meeting to raise money for the orphanage's fall festival. Yet, the leftovers alone would have fed the Little Ones for several weeks.

She ignored the gnawing pain in her stomach, and tried to concentrate instead on what was being said by Elizabeth's mother adorned in a huge silly hat with one ostrich feather sticking straight up.

"Ladies, as you know it is once more time to fulfill our Christian duty to those less fortunate than ourselves."

Well coiffed heads nodded in agreement, their backs straight, clothes pressed and clean.

A strange whispering from the hedge to the right drew Sarah's attention. She peered into its thorny depths, but seeing nothing, once again returned to what was being said.

"However this year, my daughter Elizabeth has a wonderful idea. Instead of the usual festival, she proposes..." her gloved hands clapped together in barely restrained enthusiasm, "that we have a mask ball instead. Isn't that a delightful idea? Now all we need is for someone to volunteer to-"

Sarah was already to her feet when a small wiry red headed boy with twine encircling one wrist burst through the bushes, wagging a bony finger toward the horrified lady at the podium. A small three-year-old girl followed shyly after him, one small hand fingering her too short jacket.

"Hey, you can't take away our festival. That's thievery, it is. I'll tell the bobby and he'll fling you into Newgate right alongside my mum. At least her only crime was selling her favors, not stealing from helpless orphans."

"Oh, my, who is that horrible little urchin shouting at me in that rude manner?" Elizabeth's mom swayed prettily, putting the back of a pristine gloved hand to her forehead.

Another woman, who Sarah did not recognize, screamed in horror. "He's got a knife! Someone do something."

Sarah rolled her eyes. This whole thing was getting entirely out of hand. "Donovan! Put that down."

Unfortunately the redhead couldn't have heard her if she had been shouting in his ear. He stood transfixed in surprised shock as the flurry of women scattered in all directions, Sarah's firm practical voice lost in the growing uproar. Then he did something strange. She caught a mischievous grin, right before he raised his arms high overhead, waved them about and...Growled. It sounded like something that rather resembled a cross between a pirate and a wild animal.

Elizabeth fainted, along with several other ladies.

This was not good.

Knocking a chair out of her way and trying to push her way through terrified ladies, Sarah shouted. "It is ill mannered to growl at the ladies, Donovan." Which sounded ridiculous even to her, "And put that stick down at once before someone gets the wrong idea."

But, it was too late. Everyone all ready had the wrong idea. Right before her eyes he was snatched up by a burly stable hand and the offending stick wrenched painfully from his grasp. "I'll teach you some manners, you ungrateful little street rat."

Her breath coming in short gasps; Sarah planted her feet in front of the huge man dangling the squirming boy from one beefy arm and demanded quietly, "Put him down at once."

The fires of adrenalin had already caused the man's huge upper arm muscles to bulge and the small boy was turning purple from the ever increasing tightening around his middle. Still, he managed to choke out a few defiant words. "See, Miss Sarah, I told you they don't care nothing about orphans. But, me sister is going to have her festival or else I will find me a knife and cut their bleeding hearts out!"

The dark giant shook the boy and roared; "Watch your tongue boy, before I yank it out of your head."

Sarah sighed mightily. She was going to have to interfere again.

The noise outside was becoming annoying. What were those ladies doing anyway?

"And so you think it's useless to try and save the business by trading in a more lucrative commodity?"

"Son, your warehouse burned to the ground. It would take a miracle to save the business now."

Simon hated to deceive his father, but it was necessary. He poured a glass of brandy and took a deep swallow of the stuff.

"I was thinking... cotton."

His father jumped from the leather chair as if it were on fire, "Are you completely insane?!"

"Father-"

"Besides it being illegal to trade with the south, there is the very real danger you could find yourself murdered by some other criminal when you encroach on his territory. No. I absolutely forbid it."

"Then what do you propose I do?"

Realizing his son was serious; Henry sank back down on the chair and shook his head in defeat.

"I don't know son. But I do know what it is like in prison. What it is to have no one trust your word again. All the money in the world cannot buy back a good name."

Putting his glass down on the over sized desk, piled high with ledgers and folders stuffed with paper, Simon walked over and placed a comforting hand on his shoulder. "The court cleared you of any wrong doing Father. You have to stop blaming yourself."

Emotion clouded the older man's eyes as a shaky hand patted the one on his shoulder. "I know. But I am to blame, regardless. If only I hadn't been late that night. I was so worried about those infernal ledgers...if I had been there on time, then perhaps none of this would have happened."

"Or you might have died right alongside them."

"Maybe that would have been best. At least it would have been with my honor intact."

Simon went to pour his father a fortifying drink. "What was he like, your partner? I was away at school during most of those last few years when you worked together. I barely remember him."

His father automatically took the drink offered him and stared off into space.

"He was a good man. I still find it hard to believe he was stealing from the company."

"Could it have been anyone else?"

"What?" He looked up, nearly surprised to see it was only Simon standing there. Then, after taking a slow swallow of his drink, he continued, "I suppose. There was me of course, and then there was the accountant..." His hoarse laugh seemed very telling.

"Who was the accountant?"

"Me again."

He could tell the memories were painful for his father and aged old protectiveness made him want to end the discussion. But, he owed Sarah at least this much after all he had put her through.

"Was there any other family members who stood to gain from his death?"

"If so, I don't know of them. The lawyers said there were some long lost Irish kin in America. However I never met them. Anyway, it hardly matters now." With disdain, he threw down the rest of his drink and rose from the chair. "That racket outside is driving me mad. Where the devil is Albert anyway?"

The moment was passing and Simon had saved the most difficult question for last.

"And the little girl? The one they found dead."

"Son, I really don't want to talk about this anymore. And about this whole cotton idea... well, I think it best to side with the southern sympathizers when parliament meets and vote for trade. But, I wouldn't do anything as foolish as trying to do it without the government's sanction. But if your even considering this because of me? Don't. If the business goes under, your mother and I would be fine. I have made some rather sound investments recently and should-"

"Father, the little girl's name?"

The two men stared at each other. The tension in the room was mounting. Then, as if Simon had only imagined the trapped look in his father's eyes, he shrugged and headed for the door.

"Was it Sarah?"

One hand on the knob, head bent down in despair, he spoke so quietly, Simon had to take a step forward to hear him.

"Yes, that was it. Sarah. If she would have lived she would have been Lady Sarah Adams."

Simon stopped breathing. It could still be just a coincidence...a strange trick of fate...

His father turned around and his eyes were full of pain. "She would have had golden brown eyes like her mother's and wavy light brown hair like her father's. And yes, she would have looked very much like your Sarah."

And in that instant, he knew what his father had probably suspected from the very beginning when a small English girl had stood up on his table, dressed in Chinese silk pants, and been introduced as an orphan named "Sarah."

He knew that his partner's daughter had somehow managed to survive the massacre of her family on that cold and deadly October night and he had been given a second chance to redeem himself.

When his father left the room, the quiet was deafening.

His father knew who Sarah was. So why pretend differently all this time? It didn't make any sense. Except, maybe it explained why his usually sensible father would find it so easy to accept some unknown orphan as his heir's wife.

But, why not tell her? Why all the secrets?

Albert came running in, caught himself and skidded to a stop in front of him.

"You called sir?"

Too weary to play this game again with his butler, Simon snapped back, "No, I did not call. So, why don't you simply tell me what is going on here"?

"There is no need to shout Sir. I just thought you might have called to ask about your wife. But it certainly is no concern of mine if she goes to jail or not."

"What?! Speak English, man."

The commotion outside was escalating.

"It seems Sir, as if some ill-mannered young woman in a purple hat with fruit bobbing off of it suggested doing away with the fall festival this year. A young man, who your wife claims as family, threatened everyone with a knife. When Toby tried to help...that would be the stable hand, Sir. Well, your lady knocked the wind out of him. He landed on Mrs. Hawthorne who demanded the young boy be thrown in jail. Lady Sarah then threatened the officer bodily harm if he did. They are taking her away now. With the young gentleman in tow, I might add. Oh, what do you expect me to do about the young miss in the kitchen?"

"I am sure it's no concern of mine. It appears I have to rescue my wife from Newgate at the moment."

"Apparently it is, Sir."

Shoving an arm in his coat sleeve and reaching around Albert to retrieve his hat from the mirrored hat rack, because asking Albert to hand it to him would have wasted even more time, Simon headed out the door.

"Albert, stop speaking in riddles. I'll be back in a couple of hours."

"As you wish, Sir. But, I am not trained to deal with small children. And sadly I will be forced to resign if you cannot be more forthcoming about adding children and wives to your household. From now on I would appreciate it if you would advise me before hand, so that I might prepare. Might I also request that you acquire them in a more traditional English manner next time? Perhaps then I would have amble time to prepare the household and hire the proper staff."

The man drove him crazy. "I don't have any children. But, if I do 'acquire' them, it will be none of your business. Do we understand each other?"

A huge sigh blew past the butler's lips. "As you say Sir, only according to your wife, who announced it at the meeting-you do. Two, to be exact. The young man who growled at the guests and the small girl he claims as his sister. Her name is Lucy and according to the young lady, loves cook's oatmeal cookies."

"I do not have...oh, never mind. I'll take care of this when I get home. Surely you can manage not to misplace one little girl until then."

The butler's "Very good Sir", was drowned out by the slamming of the front door. His master, no doubt, had other more pressing matters to attend to.

# Chapter 15

That evening a very subdued Sarah sank into bed, exhausted beyond belief. Supper had been a nightmare. Between Stella's worrying about the fund raiser, Kate's weeping over the spoiled plans for a mask ball and Henry's unexplained sullenness, Sarah thought she would never make it upstairs to her own room. Not to mention she now possessed the problem of one red headed boy, who her husband absolutely forbid she refer to as family again, who needed a place to stay. After a rather loud discussion on the way home from the law offices, her husband finally agreed to allow the boy to learn a trade. Albert's to be exact.

If she didn't comply the poor little fellow would be tossed out on his ear. To be honest she was thankful her husband had bothered to bail them out of prison at all. He had been so furious with her that he had barely spoken since 'the unfortunate incident', as her mother in law liked to refer to it. No, having Donovan go back to the orphanage was the least of her worries. After all, he was one very fortunate little boy that her husband had a compassionate heart behind the steely look of disapproval he was bestowing on her right now.

So rather than locked away somewhere, Donovan was to learn a trade in the household. Albert was to teach him the impeccable manners of a butler. Which she secretly thought had something to do with punishing Albert. Otherwise why would Simon have announced his decision while daring the stupefied man, standing so ramrod straight, to argue with him. She didn't know who she felt sorrier for, Albert or Donovan. And the dear sweet three year old who trailed behind her brother? Maggie promised to watch over her in nursery until a more permanent home could found.

Meanwhile the closeness she had shared with Simon in the cabin seemed to have evaporated. Watching from the bed as he changed clothes, then began gathering his notes from the desk, she gave a heartfelt sigh. She missed him.

"Simon."

He seemed intent on his task, or ignoring her, one. She cleared her throat. He continued what he was doing. No doubt about it, definitely ignoring her. In fact, he didn't even bother to look her direction, only pausing long enough to grab a scarf and drape it around his neck.

"Simon, I want to explain what happened."

"Sarah, do you have any idea how angry I am with you? I can't talk right now. Perhaps in a couple of hours when I cool down and don't feel so close to throttling you, I'll be in a better humor to listen. I'll be late, so don't bother waiting up."

He sounded so put out with her, that she felt truly sorry for complicating his life even more than it already was.

She raised the covers a little more around her chest hoping he wouldn't notice the satin rope loops and buttons of her Chinese shirt bulging beneath the unusually prim nightgown. It happened to be choking the life out of her at the moment. It couldn't be helped. He would be even more furious with her if he knew she intended to follow him tonight.

She hated deceiving him again, but she doubted he would understand why a Chinese belief required she do so. No matter how many times she explained it, he somehow failed to see that it was her duty to protect him from now on. She yawned sleepily. If only he would cease being an undercover operate, she might get a little rest.

Her wishes hardly mattered. There would not be much sleep tonight. Besides, John sent a note over asking her to meet him at the carriage house around eleven. It was another deception. However since she had given her word, she had no choice, even if it was behind Simon's back. No, she doubted her English husband would understand any of what she planned to do tonight.

The rumble of thunder in the distance and the stillness of the night boded ill, and mirrored her mood.

As if reading her mind, Simon suddenly stopped and turned at the door, demanding fiercely, "I need your promise that you won't follow me through this door."

"Simon, I..."

He slammed it shut and walked over to the side of the bed. She smiled weakly up at him. He did not return her smile. Rather, he leaned over until her head butted up against the backboard, the carved antler of a stag digging into her scalp. Her smile disappeared.

Then slowly and firmly he demanded, "I want your word Sarah."

"It is impolite to shout at people. And I don't know why you are so angry. After all I am the humblest of wives and only wish..."

"Repeat it back."

She looked down and toyed with the appliqué on the deep chocolate colored quilt. "I promise."

"You promise what?"

"You offend me by doubting my honor husband."

"Say it."

She heaved a heavy sigh, "Fine. I promise that I will not follow you out that door."

"Good." Then his anger seemed to dissipate a little as he raised her chin with an index finger and looked deeply into her eyes. "I only want to keep you safe. You do know that?"

"I know."

Pleased with her answer, he nodded before giving a quick kiss to her mouth. "Don't wait up."

She counted to ten before throwing back the covers and pulling her cream colored gown up over her head. She struggled with the tangled mess a moment before freeing herself and flinging it over into the corner. She almost wished he had made her promise not to follow him out the window either. Then perhaps she would have had an excuse to stay in bed and off the dark London streets.

Mumbling to herself, she gathered up her shoes and threw them out the window with practiced ease, grumbling the whole time about Simon and his secret meetings. She had a bad feeling about tonight. The opened shutters let in cold clean air that smelled of rain. The stars were obscured now by gathering rain clouds just north of the garden. No, none of it boded well. Evil was about tonight.

Nevertheless, she was determined. Perching herself on the ledge, she inched out with one foot towards the tree. With a sudden bang, the bedroom door burst open. A weeping, distraught Kate entered the room without so much as a knock. Sarah's shoulders slumped in defeat. Her husband's family seemed to have a problem with privacy, mostly hers.

Trying to slow her pounding heart, and hoping Kate failed to notice she had been about to escape out the window, Sarah slid softly to the floor.

Apparently Kate was not that distraught. "Sarah, how many times must I tell you, a lady does not climb out her bedroom window? It just isn't done. Besides, where are you going this time of night anyway? Why, it must be near ten in the evening."

Sarah opened her mouth to say something, but what possible explanation could she give? That she was out chasing Simon, who was really an agent for the crown? Hardly.

As usual her sister in law didn't wait for a response. Kate drew her own conclusions. With eyes widened in alarm, her rag curled head shook from side to side taking in the obviously empty room.

"Oh, no. Where is Simon?"

"He went out."

"Your following him again, aren't you?"

"Yes, but it isn't what you think."

"Oh? No wonder your acting crazy. You poor thing. And to think, I thought he had changed his ways. Doesn't he care what another scandal will do to this family?"

This was getting out of hand, as usual.

"Well, I am going to march right back downstairs and tell Father about his philandering. He has to be stopped once and for all. After all, it is ridiculous for you to have to go out every night to fetch him home."

Quickly, Sarah hurried over and shut the door hindering Kate's retreat and the rest of the household from hearing their conversation. The young girl was shouting loud enough to wake the ancestors. "My husband's sister, you are mistaken. Simon is not out prowling the night for women. He has promised to stay away from Hilda."

"Aha!"

Sarah jumped back. "What?"

"Her name is Hilary. Which only proves my point. He deliberately upsets you. And to think you actually believed him?"

"Yes, and I still do. So, as this is of little importance, you must return to your room and I will-"

Kate sidestepped Sarah's outstretched arm and peered out the window. "If you're not chasing Simon, where are you going?" She leaned further out, "Oh, my. That is terribly far down, isn't it?"

Peering out over Kate's shoulder, Sarah noticed Simon leaving in a hansom cab. She would never catch up with him now. A glance at the clock showed ten fifteen. Still forty-five minutes until she had to meet John. A flash of lightening furthered her resolve to remain indoors, at least for a little while longer. Perhaps the extra time was better spent calming Kate's fears.

Reaching up, she barely managed to stop Kate's nervously waving hand from side cocking her in the head. Then very gently she led the young girl over to the rumbled bed.

"Come, my husband's sister, let us talk with each other."

"But, I thought you had to climb out the window. Now, you have time to talk? Something is definitely odd here."

Smiling sweetly, Sarah insistently tugged on her sister in law's hand, slowly bringing her down on the bed beside her. "I have never gotten a chance to show the gratefulness in my heart for last night. It was a lovely trick you played on us. It was good to be alone with the warrior for a little while. Things have been so complicated lately. Ever since...well, since..."

Laughing at Sarah's loss of words, Kate finished with a nervous giggle, "Since coming to England? Or since loving my brother?"

Now Sarah blushed, "I didn't mean to say that." Seeing she wasn't fooling Kate in the least, she relaxed her shoulders and shrugged. "Your brother and I? Well, we are much like the American tornado. When hot air mixes with cold it is never a good thing. All you can do is pray that the chaos takes a turn away from you."

"I wish there was some way I could help. I still think that if we went down and talked with Father…" Suddenly a worried crease formed on her brow, "But I suppose if Simon is off meeting someone in secret, it would only cause more trouble." Suddenly she snapped her fingers, "What we really need is a plan."

Great. The girl held on to an idea better than a sea turtle to his supper. That was all she needed, Kate's interference could get someone hurt. Rubbing her right temple where a headache was beginning to form, Sarah accepted what she must do.

It could not be helped; she would have to share her past with this young girl. Otherwise her misplaced sense of heroic intervention would cause more complications. Simon would not be pleased. But, she sincerely doubted he would like the 'plan' his sister came up with either.

"Actually, he is investigating my past."

"Your past? But, I thought you were an orphan. I mean, I assumed you didn't have a past."

A raised eyebrow flustered Kate even further, "I mean, of course you have a past. I just assumed you didn't have any idea what it was. You know, all very mysterious and tragic rather like "Jane Eyre."

Sarah ignored her rambling and got up, handing Kate a dark green ribbon and brush from her dresser. "Would you mind braiding my hair? The length of it makes my arms grow tired when I do it myself."

"Oh, yes, of course. However, you really must relent, and accept a lady's maid Sarah. It is quite the thing, you know."

"I like doing things myself."

Busy running the brush through her hair, Kate seemed lost in thought a moment. "You know, I for one don't think it is all that terrific knowing one's relatives. I certainly wish I didn't know a few of mine. Take my cousin James, for instance. He is such a horrible boy. Do you know he actually blamed me when he broke his own arm? I tried to tell him not to ride Father's favorite thoroughbred. And I certainly would never have told him to jump it into a bog either. I might have told him to jump off a cliff, but never with father's horse. Because of his antics the poor thing had to be shot and that was mild compared to what I received because of his lies. "

Settling down in front of her sister in law, Sarah closed her eyes in pleasure as the gentle tug of the brush lulled her into a peaceful trance. Kate separated the thick mass into three parts, and then asked gently, "Do you think your parents came from here?"

Sarah gave a soft sigh. She had to be careful what she revealed. Kate was what others called, an open book. There existed no secrets in her world, which meant she would have trouble keeping someone else's. "I believe so. My grandfather found me at the docks here in London, so it is only logical to believe this was once my home. Besides, lately I have started remembering bits and pieces of my past. This is one of the reasons the warrior goes into the dark night, to gather information."

Reaching the end of the braid, Kate tied it off with the silky ribbon. "Oh, how very heroic of him. Although I have to admit it is easier to think of one's brother as a scoundrel, than a romantic figure. It must be all those toads in my bed growing up, and the nickname "Briar" he bestowed on me.

"Briar?"

Her task done, Kate leaned back on her hands and admitted, "He used to claim that all my sneaking around and spying on him was choking the life right out of his social life."

The look of hurt innocence on her sister in law's face forced a knowing grin from Sarah.

"And were you?"

Kate grinned back and batted long eye lashes, "Well, only once in awhile. I suppose the time I told Father about the smoke coming out of the stable, some might call interfering with his social life."

"That does not sound like interfering to me."

"It is, if Simon was the reason for the smoke."

"Oh, no."

"Yes. Father's best cigars. And if that wasn't bad enough, John and my brother were selling the rest of them off to the servants. Seems, they were gathering money to bet on a horse at the Sunday races."

Sarah's laughter made Kate explain further, "I was only five at the time. Father made the two of them work a month in the stables until they had paid him back for the cigars. Then they had to do three weeks alter boy duty and donate their pin money for the entire month to the church as penitence. But the worse part was Father's lecture on the sins of gambling. There is nothing worse than facing one of father's long disapproving talks about the Conway honor."

Turning around and resting her elbow on the bed, Sarah tried to imagine her big strong husband as a scolded boy. Then something Kate said caught her attention. "Was John staying here at the time?"

Silence greeted her question, and then Kate sighed in a resigned way, "I guess it would not be gossiping, since you are one of the family now. John is our cousin. His father, my uncle, was a scoundrel to say the least. I believe at the time he came to live with us, his father was off smuggling slaves from Africa. But of course, we only found that out much later when father had to hire lawyers to get him out of Newgate. He was lucky it was an English ship that caught him, instead of the Americans. They still hang smugglers there. Very barbaric. But, you know how those Americans are."

She gasped, a dainty white hand flying to her mouth in horror. "Oh, I didn't mean you Sarah. I mean you're actually English and not some American ruffian."

A raised dusky eyebrow halted Kate's explanation and sent her off into a fit of giggles. "I suppose I sound very much like the haughty aristocrat from England."

"A little. But then, Grandfather thinks the English are silly empty-headed fools. He says we talk much and say very little. I suppose every culture thinks they are superior in some way or another."

"Do you realize this is the first time I have ever heard you refer to yourself as English?"

Stunned, Sarah shook her head in wonder, "I wonder why?"

"Maybe this is starting to feel like home to you. Or maybe it's because you're in love with my brother."

The conversation had turned to a subject Sarah definitely didn't want to discuss. She feigned a yawn. "I really have to get some sleep, dear Briar. Perhaps we can talk more of this later."

"But you still haven't explained why you follow Simon out windows. Or, why most of this sneaking around is done in the middle of the night."

Trying her best not to peer anxiously at the clock, Sarah rose on cramped legs and explained. "I have good reason to believe my parents were killed the night my grandfather found me."

"Oh, how awful for you."

"Yes and unfortunately not many villains give up secrets in the light of day."

"No, of course not, but..." Sarah helped her up and opened the door, gently guiding Kate through it.

"Well, I am most exhausted, dear sister", she gave a very real yawn, "we will talk of this another time."

"Yes certainly, but, Sarah I am still very upset with you. None of what you have told me explains why you made such a scene this morning positively ruining any chance for a mask ball. I so wanted to go."

"It was the orphans. They really love the festival. And it is highly unlikely the poor tenant farmers have clothing suited for a ball, now do they?"

Sarah could see how instantly distraught the young girl was at the slight reprimand. Her sweet disposition would normally never allow even one soul to be left out, especially the children. Sarah knew how much Kate loved the orphans by the way she lit up each and every time she visited them. No doubt she had been so lost in the romantic idea of a ball that she had completely forgotten about how dreary an orphan's life really was.

"No, of course not. Oh, heavens. To think it never even occurred to me. I guess I am behaving rather like a spoiled aristocrat after all. I never even once considered the children. I suppose I was caught up in the excitement of the moment, still that is no excuse and I will certainly bring it up the next meeting."

It was ten minutes of eleven.

"Could we talk of this tomorrow, my husband's sister? Touring one of London's prisons and having my husband, who is quite as good a lecturer as his father, has really exhausted me." Which was true.

"Of course. But one more thing. Mother asked me to speak to you, as well. I am to remind you that hitting people in England is frowned upon, especially by a lady, and most assuredly in public, even if they do deserve it. Why, she hasn't stopped wringing her hands all evening and Father has fairly paced a path clean through her new rose carpet."

Contrite, Sarah bowed her head, "I am truly sorry if I caused them to lose face in front of their friends."

Kate's easy way of making people feel better was turned full-fledged on Sarah. "Oh, never you mind. It really wasn't what you did, but what Elizabeth's mother said. Something about brawling was for uneducated ruffians and never ladies. I tried to explain to them that you were from America, therefore..." Sarah's frown made Kate clear her voice and begin again, "It's just that I know Simon, and I don't believe he will ever grow use to the idea of pulling his wife out of prison, or his lady friends out of ponds, so perhaps you could try a little harder next time to behave more, well, English."

"I'll work on it. Good night Kate."

And then before Kate thought of another excuse to keep from leaving, Sarah shut the door and turned the skeleton key in its lock. A glance at the clock telling her, she had less than five minutes to make it to the carriage house. Thanks to Kate's unexpected visit, she would be late.

Blowing out the candle, Sarah shimmied down the tree and landed with a graceful jump to the ground. The grass felt cool and damp from the light rain falling soft around her. Shoving on her sandals, she ran like the wind to meet with John. Now that two days had past, her questions had mounted. No, she would not rest easy this night unless she found out exactly why he had been following Simon.

The carriage house was lit only in pale moonlight. She hesitated at the doorway in indecision. For one instant the logic of her husband's words made her doubt the decision to meet with John alone. The building was eerily deserted and she uneasy. It wasn't that she doubted her ability to protect herself, but as Grandfather said, only a fool believed they were indestructible, and she was not a fool.

Finally it was John's beckoning whisper that drew her into the building's shadowy depths. And honor. She had given her word.

"John, is that you?"

"Yes. Over here behind the carriage, I have pulled up some old trunks to sit on."

Her eyes growing accustomed to the faint light, she managed to make out his beckoning arm towards the back of the building. Perhaps it was the guilt of knowing Simon would disapprove, or that they both came to this place to discuss his loyalty – whatever it was, she felt like a traitor, a deceiver. And she held very little illusion, that if Simon found out, he would never trust her again.

She hesitated once more, uncertain whether to move forward. For if she did, there would be no going back.

John seemed to sense her reluctance.

His comforting hand found hers in the darkness. She shivered, whether from her damp clothes or his touch she wasn't certain. Gently he pulled her forward into the shadows. Once settled on a trunk with John's coat used as a barrier against the rust covered exterior, Sarah brushed back a damp tawny curl and tried to ignore the warning bells going off in her head. Or for that matter, the sick empty feeling in the pit of her stomach.

"What's wrong Sarah?"

He reached up and gripped her shoulder in concern, only to jerk back and swear under his breath.

"You're freezing. Did you run out here in this weather? I should have canceled this until tomorrow."

Then suddenly, from the semi darkness a scratchy wool blanket enfolded her. She buried herself in its warmth and began to relax.

Thank you, my husband's friend."

"Why do you do that?"

"What?"

"Mention Simon whenever you are with me. As if to remind us both that you belong to him."

Her heart beat a little faster and the blanket, welcome before, seemed stifling.

"John, I do belong to him. And I should go back to the house before he comes home."

"Why did you come if you are afraid to be alone with me?"

His whispered words were too near her ear, a challenge, as he knelt down before her.

"I'm not afraid. It's just this seems wrong somehow, disloyal."

His hand stilled hers. This too seemed wrong. Awkwardly pulling back her hand, she rose to her feet trembling, "I can't do this."

"Sarah, we aren't doing anything wrong."

"We are deceiving my husband."

John rose and placed his hands on her shoulders, giving her a light shake. "He is deceiving us. You know that as well as I. It is why you met with me tonight. Why you feel the same thing I do when we are together."

"No."

"Yes." His voice sounded tense and frustrated, but never the less, he let go of her and stepped back, "Then go. But I fail to see how ignoring the truth will help him any. It seems all women are the same, weak and cowardly, especially when it comes to facing the truth. I thought you were different."

Shocked by his hostility, Sarah blushed in anger. "I am neither weak, nor a coward."

"Aren't you? Then why not talk to me, try and help your husband, or at least admit what you feel for me."

"I don't feel anything for you."

"Don't you."

Frantically she tried to imagine what she could have possibly done to mislead him so.

Shamed, she straightened her shoulders and said as calmly as possible, "I never should have agreed to come here."

Now he was pacing, she caught a shadowy glimpse of him running a hand through his hair in aggravation. Finally, he stopped in front of her, his words so close she felt, rather than heard them. "He is a traitor Sarah."

"No, you're wrong. You have mistaken his actions, just as you have mistaken mine."

She shook off his words like a cold rain in winter and turned to leave. He caught her before she could escape. His arms strong and unyielding like his words. "I wish I were wrong. Surely you haven't forgotten he and I have been best friends since childhood. He has saved my life more times than I can count. But, a man changes. Circumstances change."

"Stop it." Her words came out more a plea than a demand.

"I didn't know how to tell you. The government has suspected him of treason since before he left for America. And heaven knows how I have tried to ignore my feelings for you. You're his wife for crying out loud. Blast if I don't feel more the traitor than he is. But, now...well, it's too dangerous for you to stay here with him."

"Too dangerous? But you of all people know Simon. He would never hurt me." her words trailed off in confusion and despair. Memories of that day in his hotel room and being shot at in the warehouse flashed across her heart. Could it be true? Was Simon a traitor?

Gently, he helped her sit back down and began pacing again, "I didn't want to believe it either. I argued with the minister for over an hour the other day. But, the truth is I found a list of shipments carrying smuggled goods at Banister's house a few weeks ago. Unfortunately some of Simon's ships were those named. We are talking about illegal contraband; cotton, French wine, the list is endless. I blame myself. Maybe I should have shown that list to my superiors instead of leaving it at the gaming house. Or, maybe I should have interfered sooner, stopped him somehow."

"But Simon says that he is working with the government to draw out the traitor. It is why he had the cotton at the warehouse that night. To force the traitor's hand."

"Think Sarah. What does the government care about illegal cotton trade? You are comparing a war to some petty thievery. No, what the minister fears is that Simon plans to use his contacts to force others to vote for trade with the South. To blatantly force our country to take sides. It will mean war."

Confusion and hurt were overwhelming her. "I can't think."

"Listen", he knelt down before her, his hands taking hers, "I need...no, England needs you to be strong. I have to obtain proof of some sort to present to the minister. I need his documents. I need you to get them for me. I know it is dangerous, but there is no other way. He suspects someone has been following him even now. I don't want to send you back there even for one more night, but the minister reminded me of my duty tonight. So even though every fiber of my being demands I get you as far away as possible, I can't. Not yet. Because, unfortunately, no one else can get as close to him as you can." He gave her a light shake, "Sarah are you even listening to me?"

"I can't do this thing. You ask me to betray my heart."

He cradled her face in his hands, his tone softening, "Then change your heart", and before she could stop him, he kissed her gently on the lips.

"John, get your hands off my wife. Now!"

John immediately dropped his head and rose slowly to his feet. When he turned around there was a gun aimed straight for his heart. He looked Simon in the eye, unflinching, "What do you intend to do? Shoot me."

"It had crossed my mind."

Shaking like a leaf, Sarah tried to step between the two old friends. "Warrior, please, you can't do this thing. It will harden your heart. Grandfather says-"

"Shut up, Sarah. I am not in the mood for one of your grandfather's quotes right now. See, I've just discovered my long time friend and wife sharing a very touching moment and who knows what else, so believe me, my heart is the least of my worries."

His eyes were cold and his voice colder. Sarah held her middle, trying to ward off becoming sick. Simon would never believe the truth now. That she had not returned John's kiss, or even welcomed it. Besides, it hardly mattered. They were both traitors, him to his country and her to their vows.

Oddly, it was John who defended her yet again.

"Simon, this is all my fault. Sarah was an innocent in all this. I was simply bringing her a note from Peter. When you weren't at home, I thought it better to meet out in the carriage house."

"Did you also think it better to deliver the note with a kiss?"

"No, that was not my intention. I lost my head for a moment, but I swear to you it won't happen again."

"No, it won't. Because the next time you even speak to my wife in private...I will kill you. Do we understand each other 'cousin'?"

Sarah wondered if only she saw the fierce anger in John's eyes at the reference to blood ties. He looked like he wanted to strike Simon; instead he looked off and nodded.

"Good. Now get off my property."

John snatched up his coat from the trunk and turned to leave. Simon grabbed an arm as John sailed past him, "First, the note. Where is it?"

Jerking his arm away, John reached inside a jacket pocket and flung it at Simon, "This is not over between us."

Lowering the gun, as he watched John leave, Simon's voice held a note of regret in it, "No, I don't believe it is."

Then without further ado, John stormed from the carriage house. The half broken door banged softly in his wake. Then it was quiet, too quiet for Sarah. It seemed odd that this strange day full of emotions and revelations, should now end in a deadly calm. It was Simon who broke the silence between them.

"Kate saw you run in here earlier. Perhaps next time you plan a clandestine meeting with your lover, you will be a little more discrete."

"Warrior."

"Don't call me that. Ever again."

Her heart sank. He walked past her and lit a lantern, hanging it on a hook in the wall. It was only then that he ground out in anguish. "What did you think? That I wouldn't discover it was John you were protecting? How could I have been so blind? No doubt he was there with you the night of the fire as well."

He sounded like he hated her. She closed her eyes to stop from crying, but his words demanded she accept the change in his feelings toward her. "Don't you dare weep now. I've had quite enough of your theatrics to last a lifetime. Was John with you, or not?"

So much like the wounded warrior was her husband that her soul ached to comfort him. But she would not lie. "Yes. He saved my life that night when someone tried to shoot me. We escaped to the Thames and hid in the waters until it was safe."

"Who else was there?"

Her body started shaking with cold. Funny how her mind seemed to drift above her body, separate, watching. Simon took off his coat and laid it over her shoulders, a welcome protection against the bone-chilling cool of the evening. Its interior warmth from Simon's body instantly soothed her. The lingering smell of him still residing in its depths. She stepped back and answered in a monotone voice, "I don't know. Simon, please believe me when I say... "

A fist slammed into the wall beside her. She didn't even jump.

"How long have you been lovers? Since that night?"

She willed herself to look deep into his eyes, at the hurt and betrayal she had put there. However because of what Simon had said yesterday. That what they felt for each other, was the only real thing that existed. She accepted the truth, for it hardly mattered if he was a traitor or not, she loved him. She couldn't stop loving him, even now. Not even if he had been the one who shot at her in the warehouse that night. "I have known no other man but you, nor will I ever. You know that Simon."

"Do I?" He turned away and angrily swiped at his eyes. When he turned back around, his face spoke volumes. His hair was long and wild. His green eyes smoldering. Then, before she could react, powerful hands yanked her up against him. His chest was solid and heaving with emotion.

"The man kissed you. You're meeting with him in the dark. And you have lied to protect him. Tell me, would you believe you?"

She forced herself not to give in to her tears or all would be lost. She needed to make him understand. Believe. "My husband says that when you look into the eyes of the one you love, truth resides there. Look into my eyes Warrior. Tell me what you see. Because when I am lost in yours, I see hurt and pain. But, I also see love. So even though John says you are a traitor and that you are deceiving me. I believe you are telling me the truth and it doesn't even matter that it was he who saved me that night, or protected me at the Sympathizers meeting...I still believe..." she choked tears back. She must not cry.

"What Sarah? What do you believe?"

"That he has to be wrong. My mind tells me not to trust you, but my heart already does. I did not kiss John. He kissed me. And I am nearly certain he already knew you stood there in the shadows. So, I have to ask, why would he deliberately anger you like that? Unless, it was more about dividing us."

Powerful arms shook her a moment, "What you are asking from me is impossible. To trust a woman I barely know and doubt not only my cousin, but a friend as well. For all I know, both of you could be in this together."

Biting her lower lip, Sarah refused to cry out in pain. His fingers were digging into her upper arms, making tears gather in her eyes. Then suddenly, she saw something change in his eyes. Anger turned to passion and suddenly his lips descended and claimed her own in a searing possessive kiss. As if to erase all trace of another's touch. Her legs gave way to the relief of having him need her. If this is all he could give right now. It was enough. As his kiss deepened, she clung to him, silent tears falling down her cheeks.

Tasting her tears, his hold gentled and using the very hands that a moment ago had caused her pain, he molded her safely against him. His whisper, hoarse and with an edge of desperation, "You belong to me, China. Only me. Remember that."

And then as he laid her down on the soft new hay, he claimed that promise with his body. The storm picked up and lightening flashed, filling the barn with electricity, neither seemed to notice. For it seemed to match the passion filling their hearts. Nor did they think again of the damning letter left by John as it drifted from Simon's hand and floated to the dirt floor. Or even traitors and impending war. The only thing left that mattered were two lonely people and their desperate need for each other.

The covering of night lasted not nearly long enough.

Soon it was dawn, and Simon left her side to dress as pinkish light filtered in through the cracks in the walls. She noticed in a sleepy haze, the light disappearing briefly as massive shoulders shadowed some of its faint light, then when Simon moved, they reappeared again.

Reluctantly she opened her eyes. Once adjusting to the light, she noticed Simon lost deep in thought as he read a note in his hands.

"I wish this was all over."

Distrust still resided in his eyes when he looked down at her. "As I do."

Suddenly ill at ease by her state of undress, Sarah shyly gathered his cloak around her. "If you would turn around for a moment I could dress."

His lazy seductive smile made her blush. "And miss looking at you one last time?"

What she wouldn't give to see a smile like that greet her every morning of her life, instead of the mistrust she read in his eyes earlier. He was hot and cold, this husband of hers. She too weary to fight with him.

The sound of Donavon and Toby coming through the yard, made her gasp in horror before jumping into an empty stall for cover. Simon only laughed and went out to run interference.

They had thought to sneak up to their rooms. Unfortunately, what looked like the entire family, had gathered for an early breakfast. Simon tried to act as if it were perfectly ordinary for them to be coming in at dawn. Almost casually he pulled her reluctantly into the dining room, retrieved two plates from the sideboard and handed her one.

Sarah gave everyone a weak smile, but the way they were staring at the two of them was a bit unnerving. Even Grandfather studied her over the top of his small round spectacles, curiosity in his Chinese mother's black eyes. She smoothed out the wrinkles in her dark linen trousers with shaky hands. Simon on the other hand ignored them. Filling his plate, and landing hard in one of the chairs, he stabbed a forkful of omelet and pointedly asked, "Is there a problem here?"

"Well, it's just...um..." Kate broke out in laughter.

"What?"

"Simon dear, you and Sarah have hay in your hair. Did you actually sleep in the carriage house last night? That is hardly necessary and entirely inappropriate, given your station in life. Speaking of which, Sarah you must not go around in those indecent clothes any longer. I hardly think that it is appropriate attire for a lady of the realm, or any lady for that matter, to be seen in trousers."

The only one not saying anything was Henry. Finally, he cleared his throat.

"Son, you do have a bedroom."

Simon refused to even acknowledge that remark.

Sarah, on the other hand, believed she would never be able to look these people in the eye again. Her life was over and if the floor would just swallow her up, her torture would end.

The book her grandfather had been reading shut with a resounding thud.

"My study of the English culture does not mention this subject. Usually, the English speak of married love as if it were a shameful necessity, instead of as a way for two souls to become one as the people in India believe. I would be most interested in hearing if you believe as the Chinese, that this subject should not be dis-"

"Grandfather!"

He winked, pushed back up his spectacles and resumed reading, "as I assumed. Very much like Chinese culture."

"Henry, remember what we discussed last night. I think this is as good a time as any, under the circumstances."

He looked ill at ease. His gray sideburns rose up and down with the working of his jaw. "Your mother thinks...and I agree, that you and Sarah should have your own home. It seems we all could use a bit more peace. I mean privacy. So, we are deeding over our country home, "Primrose estate", to the two of you. It is a wedding gift of sorts. The paperwork should be completed by the end of the week. And then you can begin acquiring an heir...I mean...Dash it, you know your duty."

"I may be wrong, but from my granddaughter's blush and your son's rumbled jacket, it seems as if they need very little encouragement in that regard."

Kate and Stella's gasp drowned out whatever else Henry meant to say. Flustered he finally managed to raise a glass of juice and toast the two completely embarrassed people at the other end of the table. Simon's mumbled thanks lost in the commotion.

The breakfast ended not soon enough to suit Sarah. Her appetite gone, she suffered through the next few minutes before excusing herself and heading upstairs. She needed both a bath and some blessed privacy.

The maids brought in hot steaming water for the tub, as Sarah waited on the bed in her robe. Simon was using the spare room to bathe and Sarah was glad for a moment alone with her thoughts. In an hour she was suppose to discuss plans for the fall festival with the nuns. Apparently, she would not be allowed to anymore of the tons' meetings. Her mother in law tried not to shame her with the news; still it only further proved she did not belong here in this country, where the rich thought little of the poor among them.

And there was still Lucy to worry about. Maggie could not watch over her indefinitely, so a home would have to be found soon. If only Simon's heart would soften then the small ones could stay here. After all, most working families were too poor to take on another mouth to feed. She did not understand why so many rooms must lay empty here in this vast house while the orphanage was packed with more children than rooms.

The last bucket of steaming water topped the brass tub. Sarah expected everyone to leave. They didn't. Instead, Maggie stood wringing her hands, trying to work up the courage to say something. Sarah's hope to have a few moments of peace seemed just a pipe dream. Still, she smiled warmly and tried to sidetrack the maid, by dismissing her in the best 'mistress of the house' voice, she could muster.

"Thank you Maggie. That will be all."

"Yes, mum. I was a wondering Miss Sarah?"

Apparently, she wasn't very good at even pretending the role of mistress. Maggie looked even more worked up than usual. A warm flush came to her freckled round face.

"Yes?"

"Is the master so very romantic then? The maid at the Featherstones says her mistress doesn't even share a bed with her husband. I told her it weren't like that at this house. That the two's of you were like a pair of regular lovebirds, you were. Why, everyone downstairs is still talking about how the two of you came slinking in from the carriage house at dawn all starry eyed and-"

"Yes, well, if that is all I believe I'll take my bath now," And she might just drown herself in the process. Was the whole world aware of her and Simon's private affairs?

"Now there's no use getting all full of color Miss. I think it is ney on wonderful. Very Irish of you. We Irish admire passion, but it is a rare quality in the English. Imagine, an English gentleman actually in love with his wife. Why I told Harrison, tis' good for the soul to see the two of you together."

"Just because a man and a woman share...well, it doesn't mean he's in love Maggie."

Maggie busily laid out a towel and placed a drop of scented bath oil into the tub. Humming happily, despite her mistress's scolding, she continued rambling, "Yes, mum. Still, if Lord Simon isn't in love than there is no explaining why his eyes light up every time you walk into a room, now is there? All I know is that it wasn't that way 'fore with any of his other lady friends. The master always looked a bit like a caged hunting dog, all trapped and bored. But, since you came and announced your destinies being entwined and all, he looks free like."

She let out a sigh full of romantic longing. "I guess it's too late for the likes of me to find a man like that."

Trailing a finger in the cooling water, Sarah asked hesitantly, "Do you really think my husband holds love in his heart for me? He seems more mad, than in love, most of the time."

Maggie tsked, tsked her. Then, jerking the robe off an unsuspecting Sarah's back gently shoved her towards the tub. "Now look at that, all our chatting and the water is losing heat as fast as the blarney stone in winter," to which she grabbed up one of Sarah's hand's from covering herself and plopped a bar of scented soap in its depths, in a no none sense fashion. Then, remembering the sponge on the dresser threw it unthinkingly at her mistress's head. Sarah's instincts were automatic as she caught the sponge in mid flight.

"Don't you mind the master; he's in love all right. Can't say why, but most men act all puffed up like that when they be fighting what's in their hearts. There's just no explaining the way a man thinks. Do you need me for anything else, Miss?"

"No, thank you." She still could not get use to complete strangers helping her dress and bathe. Why, they acted the whole time as if she were fully dressed and out for a stroll instead of bare and freezing in a bathtub. The English were a strange people. It seemed the richer you were, the more helpless you became.

"Very good. And if you have time to drop by the nursery, I am sure the wee one would love to see you."

"Actually, I was thinking of taking her to the orphanage with me for a visit. I am sure she will have childhood treasures she had to leave behind. Besides, it will give her a chance to say goodbye to her family."

"I wasn't aware orphans had treasures, or families, for that matter. But, that is neither here nor there. What I mean is, well, do you think that's wise mum?"

"For Lucy to visit her home? "

"Oh, it's not Lucy I'll be a worrying about. It's your weakness mum."

Perplexed, Sarah leaned a little out of the tub to better hear Maggie. She was muttering now under her breath as she headed for the door, a frown marring her plump features, "There'll be no telling how many more wee ones you'll be bringing back home with you. You mind my words. Very much more of you visiting the poor and soon all of London will be having a fall festival for us."

And with that dreaded prediction thrown back over one shoulder, Maggie shut the door snugly and left Sarah to her bath.

A knock on the door a half an hour later drew her up out of the bath and quickly toweling her body off as she hurried tried to find the robe Maggie had efficiently hidden from her. In the midst of her frantic search, a massive bed leg stopped her progress with painful repercussions. Yelping in pain, she dropped to the bed, rubbing her aching foot and shouting, "I really hate everything English right now, especially this huge ugly bed!" To which she slapped a fist against the mattress in frustration.

Immediately, the door flew open and her husband stood transfixed in the doorway. Whatever imagined danger had lured him into the bedroom when she yelped in pain was replaced by a much stronger instinct. Desire. Speechless, his eyes traveled over his wife's scantily clad body. Her damp hair hung in limp curls down her back, as drops of water glistened on her rosy, fresh washed skin. Whatever he had meant to say was lost to him. His lack of self-discipline, totally frustrating him.

He had a mission to complete. Not to mention, that right now he couldn't trust anyone, especially her. She was a stranger to him really. A stranger who less than eight hours ago he caught kissing his cousin. Yet, that knowledge didn't seem to stop him from wanting her. From needing right now to take her into his arms and forget everything else but how she felt against him.

"There is no need to glower at me. As you can plainly see, it is you who interrupted me."

"It takes you a half hour to bathe?" He demanded unreasonably.

She flung her foot to the floor and winced. Then hobbled up, clutching the towel up against her, "Yes, it does. Now is there some reason you came in here, my most arrogant of husbands? Or, are you simply annoying me? Because, my throat aches with the want to shout at you."

"When are you going to start acting like a lady?"

"I suppose when you start acting like a man and not some angry dragon, who constantly breathes fire, to hide what is really bothering him."

The tick in his jaw was probably not a good thing. But, she couldn't help herself. The last two days had her emotions raw and begging to be released. She flung back her damp hair, and dared him to take a step closer. Something in her eyes must have warned him, she meant business. He blew out an angry gust of air and began rubbing the bridge of his nose trying to gain some ounce of self-control.

"Sarah could you please put some clothes on. I can't think with you standing there like that. I really didn't come in here to fight with you."

"Well, all right, then." the man drove her crazy with his conflicting emotions. One minute he acted like he wanted to kill her, the next he was admitting being attracted to her. No wonder she couldn't remember being English. Being Chinese was so much saner. "It isn't as if I asked you here Warrior. Now if you would kindly leave for a moment perhaps I could find my clothes."

"Don't be absurd, we are married, after all." A warning look sent his direction caused another sigh to escape his lips. "Fine. How is this?" Dutifully, he turned his back and leaned one arm up on the cloth-covered wall. "I don't have time for unnecessary niceties. We need to go to Dunson's Law office this morning. After, I have to go by the warehouse on the way back. There is something I need to show you."

Where in the world were her clothes? There was something really unnerving about standing only in a towel, while the man she shared a bed with leaned impatiently against the wall not three feet away. She pulled out another drawer and began flinging clothes in the middle of the floor. At last she gave a heavy sigh of relief at finally finding her under things and hurriedly put them on. But, between her wet wrinkled fingers and the delicate tiny buttons, she was having an awful time finishing the business. "Stupid English clothes."

A slight chuckle came from the man leaning against her wall. "Do you need some help?"

She glared at his back. "No thank you. One should never invite a wolf to guard the sheep."

"This is true. However if memory serves me right, you're no sheep. More like a wild lioness. I'd say the wolf was in graver danger."

Flustered she yanked down a dress of bright yellow from the sea of new clothes and stepped into it. "The mother of my husband has asked that I go to the orphanage with her today."

"Besides the fact, that I am the husband that will not be a problem."

"It is kind of you to offer to escort me, most honored husband, but I plan on making my journey alone."

"Oh, but I insist, most obedient of wives."

He grinned as her exasperated groan filled the room.

"Don't worry about the good sisters. I'll send one of the servants with a message that we will be late. Are you decent yet?"

"Yes."

"Good." The words died on his lips. She was more than decent, she was glorious. With anger's fire making her eyes golden brown. She looked very much like the small fiery lioness he had accused her of being. And she took his breath away. Heaven help him, he didn't even care if she was in love with another man, or a spy for America. The man in him wanted her, needed to hold her and to hear her laugh, even to listen to those inane Chinese quotes of hers that were starting to grow on him. Yes, he would give up nearly everything, if only he could spend a lifetime loving her.

Rolling his eyes in disgust at himself, he wondered what had happened to the dedicated patriot who had stopped feeling anything eight years ago. Was she angel, or temptress, his wife? Only time would tell. But, one thing was for certain, he had to refrain from touching her until this whole mess could be sorted out. He had to stop playing with fire for both their sakes.

Her anger had cooled by the time she finished pinning up her hair in a loose French knot. He knew this because her eyes had turned a soft brown once again. Her voice more controlled with just a hint of sultry in it. He doubted she was even aware of the purely feminine way she enticed him.

Spinning around, she asked, "Do I look like one of your English ladies now?"

"You are an English lady, China. But you did forget one thing."

Well-placed hands rested on slim hips, once more the lioness. "I refuse to wear that object of torture you English invented to keep your wives from breathing."

"It's called a corset. And I like you without it. No, you forgot something else."

She followed his eyes downward to her painted feet clad only in Chinese slippers.

"Oh."

"Yes, not quite the English lady. And today I have need for you to be."

# Chapter 16

Dunson's law office was more welcoming to her this time. Apparently her husband had said something to the lawyer. His thick lenses could not hide the darting glances her husband's direction, or the lowering of eyes when speaking to her. There was no more talk of annulments, only property and a new will.

Sarah shifted in her seat uncomfortably. Finally, when it came to her husband's last wishes upon the event of his death, she could hold her tongue no longer. She stood up and bowed respectfully to the keeper of her husband's English laws.

"I regret that I must be leaving."

The sound of papers rustling and the clearing of the lawyer's throat, made her blush deepen.

"I beg your pardon, Lady Conway, but this will only take a moment. If you would allow me to read the last paragraph, we will be nearly done here."

"It is bad Karma."

"Sarah" Simon's voice warned.

"Bad Karma? I'm not sure what you mean."

Simon groaned. Would he ever be able to deal in facts where his wife was concerned?

"She means it is bad luck to talk about my death." Simon ground out as he snatched the papers from the stunned lawyer and forcefully scribbled his signature on the last page, "Just sign the thing, China."

The stubborn tilt to her chin was not a good sign. Nor the folding of her hands in mock humility.

"I promise not to die, all right? Now pick up that pen and sign your blasted name."

The lawyer shoved his chair back, the rollers gliding him well out of the way. He had once before experienced the Earl's wrath. Apparently the little lady, standing so serenely before him hadn't. She didn't even flinch when the ink well slammed down on his newly polished mahogany desk.

"To speak of one's death is to invite heaven's notice. Maybe the God of all things will think you prepared to leave this life. You have already cheated your time once. It is foolish to take such a chance. Besides, since I saved your life, I am now responsible to keep you safe. I cannot sign your death sentence."

"Sir, perhaps another time." The glare sent his way caused the lawyer's voice to trail off in uncertainty, "Unless now is better for you."

Drops of ink spattered the cuff of Simon's lawn colored jacket. That was Sarah's first coherent thought when he reached out and pulled her up against him. His threats low in her ear. "I mean it Sarah. Sign that paper. You're my wife and I need to know you will be taken care of if I die. Not to mention the fact, it puts the country estate in your name as well, should something happen. Surely, even your superstitious mind can understand the importance of that."

The secretary came in; her bun was as severe as her disposition.

"Is there a problem Mr. Dunson?"

Her calm demeanor rivaled the scene before her. The Lord and his lady were in a passionate embrace, but not of the romantic sort. The honorable Sir Dunson, of Dunson law offices, was shoved up against the bookcase, his beady little eyes wide with shock. It only took a moment for her to make up her mind. In no none sense fashion she sailed in and inquired politely, "Perhaps I could help."

Sarah stepped back from her husband and answered with a tiredness the secretary only too well understood, "It seems my husband wishes me to sign a paper that prepares for his death. I do not wish to sign. And the keeper of the Law only wishes us to leave."

With a short nod, Miss Carmichael lifted the paper in question, and studied it for a long moment before turning to the man cowering against his law books. "Is it not usual for some husbands to speak for their wives in this modern England?"

The thin man's face lit up as he sat forward a little in his apparent excitement, "Why yes, if the wife is uneducated or unable to sign for herself, because of a disability of some sort."

"Then what is the procedure?"

"Then a witness notarizes the husband's signature. It is all perfectly legal."

"I possess no disability."

"What is my wife's supposed disability?"

"Superstition. Her reasoning is neither valid nor logical, but based on fanciful reasoning, a form of uneducated insanity if you will."

"Excellent, Miss Carmichael."

Sarah expected Simon to deny the preposterous statement. She glared at the woman she had thought a kindred spirit and folded her arms in defiance. These people were the ones insane. Imagine signing a piece of paper for every transaction imaginable, past and future. Even a man as stubborn as her husband would see how pieces of paper only took the responsibility away from people to honor their word. In America, most things were agreed upon with a handshake. This talk of death was ominous and wrong. She wanted no part in it. With a haughty look thrust on the lawyer, she turned to leave, fully expecting Simon to follow.

Which, he might have done...had he not been signing the paper at the time.

It was the last straw.

"I am no longer the keeper of your destiny Simon Conway. Our paths are no longer one." Then she rounded on the other two totally shocked and confused people hovering at the desk, "And another thing, I'll have you know that I hold you and you family name responsible for this great wrong you are doing. From now on future generations will shudder when they think on this day and your part in it."

Turning on her heel, she walked out of a room; so silent it rivaled a tomb.

After a few shocked moments the shakey solicitor croaked in disbelief, "Sir, I beg your pardon, but did your wife? Well, it certainly seemed as if she..."

"Cursed you?"

"Why yes, Sir."

Unbelievably his client grinned and slid the paper back across the desk at him. His name scrawled in bold black strokes. "I wouldn't let it keep you up at night Dunson. It was her great-grandfather who was Irish, I'm sure it won't hold."

The shocked man started to nod then stopped suddenly, his eyes widening in fear, "Sir?"

"Good day Dunson. It has been a pleasure Miss Carmichael."

Whistling, he left the office in search of his wife. Because one thing he knew for certain. She might try and cut off their ties to each other, but she certainly did not want him dead. Otherwise she would have signed the papers. So, spy or not, it was a start.

Remembering his man's shocked expression when his wife's fiery temper reigned a curse on his head, he began to chuckle. Yes, she might only be Irish by association with a half-breed China man, but heaven help anyone who crossed his sweet wife again.

"Are you speaking to me yet?"

Sarah sighed and shifted in the soft leather seat. The words she wished to speak forced back down behind a tightly held mouth.

A soft chuckle filled the too quiet carriage. "All right then, I'll do the talking. I felt it important to show the world that when I die, you inherit my fortune. I think it will prove to those who question whether I trust you, like Peter and the sympathizers, that I do. And it also gives a reason why you would betray me if Banister checks my papers. Money is usually an enticing incentive for betrayal even among husbands and wives."

"This is a dangerous game, Warrior. Only a fool chases a storm."

"Maybe, but I have little choice. You're the one who speaks so much about destiny. Perhaps this is mine."

Sadness made her voice tremble, "This is not destiny. This is choice. You can choose to fight another way. You take a chance with my life, yours and even our future. Can't you see I have lost everyone I have ever loved and now you ask me to not only consent to your death, but also be a part of it? I won't. I can't."

For once she saw her words penetrated the cool exterior he presented so much of the time. Simon dug out a cheroot and lit it. Slowly, trails of smoke emptied out the carriage window. It reminded her even more of that long ago night that took her family and changed her destiny. Why was it that others seemed to have more influence over her own life than she did?

"I'm sorry, China. You're right, of course. Maybe I do have a death wish of sorts. But it doesn't mean I enjoy putting you through this. It can't be helped."

His words held a sort of tenderness within them. Turning, she watched the strong man she had fallen in love with remove his hat and defeated, lay his head back against the seat. She reached out to comfort him, but pulled back at the last moment. They were worlds apart. He refused to discover her world. And she hated his.

Perhaps when Grandfather left, she would go as well. Maybe her destiny had always been to only find what she had lost. Not fall in love with a warrior. Perhaps it wasn't destiny at all, but her own will that had caused such heartache for the two of them.

If so, then maybe the right thing to do was leave. Start again. No more nightmares. No more visions of death. No more Simon. She closed her eyes in pain.

Who knows, maybe this time spent with Simon, would be enough to last a lifetime without him. But, if that was true, then why did her heart clutch in despair at the very idea of leaving him?

His hand reached over to cover hers. She felt the energy of his soul. At that moment, her heart knew that she could never leave him. She was only fooling herself to believe she could. Yes, even if it meant her own death. But perhaps there was something she could do. Tiredly, she pulled her hand free and began removing her tan gloves.

Determination fired up her brown eyes to a golden hue. "I will help you. But, I require a promise Sir Simon Conway. It is a promise that must not be broken by English trickery. A promise made between a man and a woman before the God of all things."

"What kind of promise?"

Clearing her throat, she sat up a little taller and turned towards her slightly amused husband. But seeing the strength in her beautiful face and the trust she was placing in his hands, the smile died before it ever began. He couldn't help running an index finger along her sculptured jaw line. "You're so very beautiful, China. Even angry and defiant, you move me in ways even I can't understand." Her blush made him smile. Then as if waking from a trance, he nodded his agreement. "It doesn't matter what it is. I promise if it is in my power to give, it is yours. You have given up too much as it is."

"I want to return to America."

It was as if cold water had been dashed in his face. He could agree to anything but that. Fear fueled him to demand, "You want a divorce? I thought I made it clear the other day that there will be no divorce."

"I want you to come with me."

"What?" The word was uttered in shocked whisper.

"I want you to come with me."

"Sarah, I can't just leave. I am an Earl. There is the shipping company, not to mention that America is involved in a war at the moment. Why, the whole idea is ludicrous."

This time she would not be put off. This was their only chance for a future. She leaned in closer. He could smell the scent of jasmine and fresh air. She was so near, visions of her barely clad in a towel, overwhelmed his good sense. He took a deep breath and slid back over to the window, flicking out the rest of the cheroot. "This is my home Sarah. I'm English. And, even in spite of all those inane Chinese quotes, so are you."

"Don't you see? We will never be free unless we leave here. The government will always have one more job for you to do. I will continue to be haunted by the past. Too much has happened that cannot be undone. I can't be English and I'm not Chinese. Don't you understand? I am an outcast here. But in America, everyone is an outcast. We could start over. Go anywhere. Be anything."

The carriage rolled to a stop in front of the warehouse. Yet still his wife waited, so innocently full of hope for his answer. Her soft golden strands highlighting the brown, being lifted free of its pins by the brisk September wind off the water. He flung the door wide open and reached for his hat, and then turned on her in frustration. "Sarah, you ask too much. Moving to America will not solve anything. I can't escape who I am. Do you really believe it will be so different for us there? Think how we met. I was in a fight for my life as a spy. It's who I am."

"What about, who I am? I cannot live so dishonorable a life. Wondering every time you walk out a door, if you will live or die that day."

"Sarah stop shouting."

He slammed the door closed again, shutting them off inside the carriage.

"I will not stop shouting. You said whatever I asked."

He felt trapped by his own words. Visions of him leaving everything he had rebuilt since his father's imprisonment overwhelmed him. "Surely you can't be serious to hold me to such a promise. It's absurd. How would I make a living? Where would we live? Do you expect me to run a laundry in China town? Or perhaps live by my wits alone, like some homeless no name..."

"Orphan?" She finished for him.

Their eyes met and held. "Sarah, I didn't mean it that way."

"No, don't touch me." She swatted his hand away before she burst into tears, "I want to go home Simon."

"Not like this."

Harrison's head popped down through the open window, careful to avoid another bout with the door. "Don't you worry none, Miss Sarah, old Harrison will take you home." Then giving Simon an evil blurry eyed glare, he added, "I warn you lad, it wasn't too long ago I was quite the boxing champ on Scurry lane."

"When was that? At the turn of the century?" Simon drawled sarcastically before closing the window shade in the old man's face. A loud 'humph', was the old man's response before mumbling loudly from the top of the carriage something about beating that young upstart within an inch of his life with one hand tied behind his back.

"Now as I was saying..."

"I hope you didn't hurt his feelings."

Incredulous, Simon's green eyes widened. "His feelings? What about him minding his own business? In case you hadn't noticed, the man threatened me. Last time I checked a man is entitled to have a private discussion with his wife."

"But we were not having a discussion."

"What?"

"I said, you were shouting at me. Not discussing. And I thought it was most heroic of him. The brave, older servant facing his insolent young master." Simon looked like he wanted to throttle her.

"This is a ridiculous conversation. Now we are going inside that warehouse and you are going to play the good, if not slightly materialistic wife, do you understand me? According to John's note, this is supposed to be where you receive further instructions from Banister. And since there is no telling who will be watching us, you have to get a hold of yourself."

"At your warehouse? But, how can that be unless..." Her voice trailed off in a hushed whisper, "there must be a traitor among your people."

"Exactly, and I am most interested in learning who he is."

Flinging open the door, he stepped outside the carriage, fully expecting her to follow. However, when he turned around she was still sitting ramrod straight, her now gloveless hands clutched in her lap.

"Now what are you doing?"

Not moving her body, her eyes cut quickly to his and back again, her voice sounding hoarse with determination. "I am waiting for your answer. Do you intend to honor your word to me, or are you a liar as well?"

He was back inside the carriage and up in her face, his muscular chest heaving from barely restrained fury.

"No one calls me a liar. You will guard your tongue wife."

She knew if she backed down now it would be impossible to save him. "Then you will come with me to America after we discover the evil doer and he can do no more harm?"

"Sarah, it is not that simple."

He physically slid away from her, his walking stick splintering in two when he struck it against the seat before them. She knew with certainty at that moment that if she forced his hand in this, he would never forgive her. Yet, if she did not, he would die. If not now, then on some future assignment his government forced him into. No, she would not lose him.

Much bolder than she felt, she concentrated as her grandfather had taught. She drowned out all things; the sailors' shanties, the sound of the water hitting the dock, everything, except the determination to save him. Then once she had her emotions in check, she turned golden eyes calmly to his and answered. "It is simple. A man is worth no more than his word. Even if it is given to an unwanted English orphan."

Anger spent, Simon shook his head at her steely determination. "All right. I will go to America with you, but only if you help me finish this one last assignment. No more questions. No second-guessing. No going off on secret rendezvous. I want it all Sarah, your complete trust. Do we understand each other?"

Her heart filled with joy. Yet, she remained calm, solemnly promising, "Then, yes. You have my word Simon Conway."

"And, one other thing."

Her hands were trembling now. "Yes?"

"Many an English wife has been known to change her mind."

"Yes, China, wives as well."

"If you change yours, or break your word to me, I want to be released from my promise."

Graciously inclining her head, she agreed. "But, Simon?"

"Yes."

"I won't change my mind."

His face drew in closely to hers. "Perhaps, but I certainly intend to use all the methods at my disposal, to try and change it for you."

Goosebumps broke out along her arms and she was thankful for long sleeves, otherwise her husband would be aware of how his seductive threat affected her. Rather, she bowed her head, nodding submissively, although her words were anything but submissive, "As you wish. However, I think experience proves, that I don't respond well to unwelcome advances. Therefore, I sincerely hope there will be a creek or trellis nearby to break your fall."

She wasn't certain, but when he helped her out of the carriage, she could have sworn she caught the trace of a grin. Men were confusing creatures. You try and save them. They shout at you. You threaten them. They smile. And then they say women were hard to figure out. Hardly.

The sound of rebuilding drowned out whatever else she might have retaliated with. Amazingly, the warehouse seemed partially intact. Only the storage end with the main office was burnt past recognition. It looked crippled and smoldering, dying with all its undisclosed secrets forever mingled among soot and ash. Its' blackened remains were being pulled down by a team of horses, as other dockworkers sawed new boards in the distance. Her hand squeezed Simon's arm in sympathy. How would her husband ever recover from such a loss?

Unconsciously, she searched out his hand and wrapped her own around it. "Your warehouse looks so defeated. Marked, as if the echo of evil still resides here."

"Evil only wins when good men cease to fight. Come on, I want to show you something, China."

Dragging her over to the new makeshift office, he dug out a rolled up set of plans from one of the file drawers. His face seemed transformed. Gone was the look of the tired warrior. In it's place the young adventurer. She peered down to see what had him so excited. Studying it intently, she looked up in wonder.

"It's a ship."

"My ship, to be exact. I know it is a costly project at the moment. Still, I think once I am reimbursed for the lost cargo..." His voice trailed off into an embarrassed cough, "I don't know why I'm showing you these. It's a silly dream of mine, left over from my younger days, when I dreamed of adventure on the high seas. I suppose, if we do go to America, I might very well have to build the thing. That is, if England doesn't want her."

Her hand stopped him from his task of hurriedly rolling it back up. "No. I would like to hear of this ship. It seems different somehow."

"It's because of the sails. See, for such a small a ship, the sails are broader than usual and I've added an extra mast. That one extra sail and the shallower body, makes it much faster than any regular cargo ship. Right now, because of the war with France and threat of war with the Americans, well, I thought a new faster ship was in order. I have hopes to sell it to the Navy."

The interest in her eyes encouraged him to continue. "Just think, a small enough ship that could slip past the enemy to deliver cargo, soldiers. Or perhaps it could be used in apprehending smugglers, or spies. Anywhere close to land it would be invaluable."

The irony of his words caused her to laugh. "Do you mean to tell me you have designed a ship to catch spies like yourself?"

His answering smile warmed her heart. "I suppose that is where I got the idea. I thought of calling them guards of the coast."

"Hmmm...Coast guards. I think it's an ingenious idea."

He continued rolling up the plans, giving a slight shrug of embarrassment. "Let's just hope the minister agrees. Otherwise, I am afraid if I can't recoup my losses, there won't be much I will be able to offer you. Other than Primrose estate and this." His arm gave a sweep of the burned remains of his building. "Well, it's hardly a fortune, is it? I guess what I am saying is, if I don't manage to stop the man who did this? Ironically I may have no other choice than leave England."

He shrugged, "If that happens, maybe the North will be in need of one inexperienced ship builder to help fight their war."

Leaning against the desk, in total disregard of her light yellow dress, Sarah watched him place the plans in the bottom of a file drawer carefully, as if he placed something precious in its depths. Never had she felt such a bond to this man. It was as if he had given her the greatest of treasures, his dream. Shyly, she fingered the quill pen stating softly, "Actually I think anyone would be honored to have you. Be it as a shipbuilder, or husband."

Turning serious, he faced her, folded arms across his chest. Out of the corner of her eye she noticed the whiteness of his knuckles, as if he fought not to reach for her. She wondered why. His arms would have been a welcoming balm to this exhausting day.

"I wonder if you really understand Sarah what I am trying to tell you. If I am unable to stop the traitor, I will be left with hardly anything. We will have to start over somewhere. But at least here, I have property. In America I will have less than nothing. That is why I became so angry a moment ago. The thought of having nothing to give you when you have already lost so much. Well, it is past bearing." He turned away to better control his emotions. After a moment, his head whipped around, his eyes hardened with anger, "Because of me, you could have died here in this place and I still am no closer to finding out who is responsible. I have failed you. And heaven help me, I will probably fail you again before this is all over with."

Her love for him only intensified, "And I will fail you. It is the way of things. But, it doesn't change the fact that I can't imagine a life without you in it."

His shoulders instantly relaxed at her words, although he tried to make light of them "You know of course, it's just the destiny talking."

"Is it? Actually, I think it must be a touch of insanity. For I fell in love the moment you rolled those sexy eyes at me in the hotel room, when I refused to pick up the gun. There you were in a fight for your life, and still you managed to find the humor in it all. So, you see, although being there was not my choice. Loving you is."

"Sarah."

Such love was in that one word, tears welled in her eyes.

"No, wait. I can't think when you touch me and I have to finish what I have to say."

"Okay sweetheart."

"I can't pretend I don't love you. It's not my way."

"I know."

"I want to be free of trickery and lies between us. I don't want to pretend I care for money and not you. But most of all, I want to run away on that ship you will build, to anywhere but here, somewhere safe. To a place where people will not take away the one precious thing that the God of all things has given me, love. I don't want you to be a spy. And I don't want to sign a paper that tells heaven you are ready to leave. I am never going to be ready."

"Sweetheart, stop."

Tears were coursing down her cheeks. "I am afraid for you. I cannot lose my family again. My heart will not survive this time."

"Hush, sweetheart. I'll go to America. I'll do whatever you want, only please stop crying and let me hold you. You're breaking my heart."

And then his arms were around her. She couldn't stop crying. It was as if all those years of lost tears had found their way back; tears for her parents, tears of a long forgotten childhood, and tears of loneliness from not belonging.

"I don't want to be strong any longer. And you're right. I do want to remember. I want to remember my parent's touch. The way their skin felt. I want to know if they read to me, or even scolded me." Through hiccups and tears, she clutched at his soaking wet shirt, "Because if I can forget them so easily, maybe I'll forget this moment with you. Or Grandfather. Or..."

His hand stroked the back of her head, his whispered words of comfort soft against her ear, "Hush, sweetheart. I won't let you forget. I promise."

"But, what if the evil doer kills you? What if Grandfather dies during his travels? Then I will be alone again."

In the back of her mind she knew she was being illogical, not at all in control of her emotions. But, strangely enough, as Simon quietly shut

299

the door to the office and settled her down on his lap, she no longer cared. She welcomed the feelings buried deeply inside for so long, welcomed the flood of them washing over her, healing her.

Simon just held her for a long time. His arms were so strong and tight that had she not needed their security, she would have felt frightened by their intensity.

At last, after what seemed hours, and also minutes...her tears eased. Silent tears replaced the gut wrenching ones that had rolled freely down her cheeks and onto her husband's chest. Until at last, she had emptied out the last of the sadness inside her heart. Only then was she able to feel something other than pain. She felt Simon.

She felt the warmth of his chest and the steady rise and fall of his breathing against her cheek. She heard the sweet sound of his heart beating, blending with her own. Even the sounds outside the office were becoming louder, more distinct.

She sat up, embarrassment coloring her tear streaked face. "I was wondering my husband, if you happen to have a handkerchief?" she swiped at her nose as fresh tears threatened to fall.

She felt the lap beneath her shift, and then a freshly starched handkerchief appeared in her hands.

"Thank you."

He was so quiet. How she regretted falling apart like that. Here amidst intrigue and shattered plans, was no time for breakdowns. She should have controlled herself. Once upon a time, she would have.

"It's all right Sarah."

His gentle understanding was nearly her undoing.

"But, your workers. Grandfather says my cries are loud enough to wake the ancestors. No doubt, right now your people are wondering if you are beating, or leaving me for a mistress. For no other news would distress a more reasonable wife. I am deeply ashamed, Warrior. To cause such loss of face to one's husband, is a disloyalty."

He lifted her chin, forcing her to look at him. Surprisingly traces of his own fallen tears had left marks on his handsome face. Yet, he grinned at her, belaying the sadness still residing in his eyes. "I have to admit you are pretty loud."

She tried to rise but, he pulled her back down, saying seriously, "You have nothing to be ashamed of. For heaven's sake Sarah, you lost your entire life. I think it is a miracle you kept your sanity at all. Much less shed a few tears."

"But there are others who have suffered worse. Donavon for one is all alone and he is just a boy. Then there is Albert with his haunting dreams of past wars. I am mourning over something, I can't even remember."

"Perhaps. Yet, I doubt anyone you mentioned, has remained as untouched by his or her pain as you have. Anyone else would have become a suspicious and bitter person. Not to mention angry. I'm angry for you and it wasn't even my life that got taken away."

Their hands touched, palm to palm.

"Instead you're warm and funny. And so giving that I have about decided it would be easier to move in with the orphans, rather than wait for you to sneak them over one at a time."

Her smile of tenderness flooded his senses. Yet, when she tried to shake her head in denial, he continued. Forcing her to see what he saw everyday in her presence.

"I still can't believe you married me, a stranger. I was so full of anger, that it made me selfish and blind. Still, you have protected and loved me. Not only me, but also my entire family. Then there is that crazy half-breed China man. He loves you so deeply, that he actually threatened my life if I ever so much as caused a frown to cross your face, much less if I made you cry. I suppose it is a good thing for me that you broke down here instead of around him. I guess what I am trying to say is this. You might forget me. But, I can guarantee, there is no possible way I could ever forget you."

Never had words touched her heart so deeply. For once there was no doubt in his eyes when she stared in them. Awed, she bent down, her eyes never leaving his as her lips spoke softly against his. "You trust me then, Warrior? Truly? You believe me about John?"

For a moment he hesitated. How old had he been the last time he trusted anyone? Before his father was jailed? Before the government promised more than it delivered? It certainly was before the House of Lords. A place where men's loyalties changed with the exchange of monies.

It had been a long time. He had thought he could trust John until he found him kissing Sarah. Did he trust her? He loved and admired her. He craved her. He needed her.

A resigned look entered her golden brown eyes. She turned her head away. At that moment, he felt as if he had been gut shot. He would not do this to the only woman he could ever love. With steely determination, he turned her back around. He was neither gentle, nor kind. When he spoke it was ground out roughly between terse lips. But, she heard the promise behind the words. "Yes, I trust you. My life depends on it."

And she believed him.

No further instruction came.

Simon had left twice on pretend errands, but no one sought her out. She felt responsible. After all, it hardly seemed likely that she was in a loveless marriage when half the workers had witnessed her emotional breakdown. Not to mention, the passionate kiss that followed. Because of her, Simon had reached a dead end. That is, unless she did something before they reached home.

"Simon, I think you should stop here."

He had been quiet for quite awhile, no doubt trying to form another plan. Without asking why, he knocked on the roof of the cab and Harrison stopped immediately in front of a ladies' hat shop.

"You need a hat, now? Last time I checked, you have to wear them first."

She ignored his sarcasm and pointed excitedly to the tearoom on the left. Its mauve coloring and rich green drapes beckoned the elite inside. "Heldi just went in. If we hurry, maybe there still might be a chance to salvage your plan."

"I thought you didn't want me seducing 'Hilary'. And quite frankly, I don't think I'm up to being tossed across the room like a Caesar salad in front of half the ton."

"I have no intention of tossing you or anyone else for that matter. I can hold my anger against the albino snake woman. Grandfather taught me."

"Albino snake woman? Sarah, I don't think-"

"Simon I want this to end and the only way that is possible is to draw out the evil-doer. Is this not true?"

"Yes, but... "

She spoke matter of fact, replacing the confining gloves and gathering up an armful of billowing skirt. "Are you coming or not?"

The carriage door swung open and a wary Harrison popped his head around its edge. A scowl wrinkled his weathered forehead. "Are you two having one of your fights, or getting out? I got errands to do for your mother and the day is near gone as it is."

Simon's sigh was loud enough to blow the wiry old man over.

"We're leaving." Mumbling, Simon snatched up his hat and cloak. Sarah only caught a stray word or two as he exited the carriage in front of her. Something about the women in his life surrounded him with project people.

She smiled as he lifted a hand to help her out, before sending a wink Harrison's direction.

"Did you say something Warrior?"

"Yes. As a matter of fact I did."

"And?"

Both wife and man servant stared at him. His wife's lips were twitching and Harrison's scowl held a look of defiance. No doubt whatever he said would accomplish nothing. Harrison would still hit every pothole in the city of London. And would no doubt finish him off one day by dumping him over the bridge in the dead of night when he was too far gone in his cups. And Sarah? Well, she would do exactly as she pleased with, or without him.

"I said, let's get this over with, shall we?"

Then before his common sense took over, he snatched up her arm and pulled her into the tearoom.

Sarah dug in her heels, stopping suddenly just inside the door.

"Oh, Simon, look."

Perplexed he searched around for the source of her excitement. "Look at what?"

"This." Her arm swept the restaurant before them, "Isn't it absolutely beautiful."

This was one of the things he admired most about his China bride, her ability to appreciate moments, places and people, even those she had no wish to emulate. For the first time in his life, he really looked around him.

The chandlers hung from the ceiling, their cut glass sending a rainbow of reflected colors from the afternoon sun out over the red plush seats and polished oak tables. The carpet beneath their feet was cushioned and softened their entrance into the restaurant. For just a moment he, like Sarah, stood there soaking up the beauty of the building and its brightly attired occupants.

When she suddenly began to back up a little, Simon's worried voice whispered in her ear, "Is something the matter, China?"

Answering in a slightly frightened voice, she asked, "Do you suppose I really was a part of all this before my parents died?"

"They are just people Sarah."

His words put things back in perspective. She shook off the slight feeling of homesickness in her soul. "I know. I just can't imagine seeing such beauty. It surrounding me and not remembering."

Handing their coats to the attendant Simon pulled her hand through one arm, "But do you know what is even harder to imagine?"

"No, what?"

"You see the beauty. They don't."

In wonder she looked about at the bored expressions on the faces of nearly every person in the room as they passed insincere flattery back and forth. Sadly, she commented, "I guess Grandfather is right, after all."

Simon pulled out a chair and motioned with a nod for her to be seated before asking, "It seems about a lot of things. But, tell me, what does the wise China man have to say about English tea rooms?"

She waited for him to be seated then confided, "Most people don't appreciate things unless they are taken away. If my parents had not died, I would be no different than these people are. This would simply be another lunch. Instead, it is an experience I will always treasure."

His hand felt warm as it reached for her own across the table, forcing her to meet his eyes. "I don't believe that. Sarah, knowing you, it wouldn't have mattered where we ate today. You would have still enjoyed it. People rarely change who they are. So whether you were born in a palace or fisherman's hut, you would have been the same. As another wise man once said, most of the world is viewed from the inside out. And you, my wife, can't help seeing the beauty. For that is what you are, beautiful."

The love shining in her eyes, made him want to gather her up and take her home. Raising her hand to his lips, he placed a slow sexy kiss to the inside of her palm. "I have to warn you, if you keep looking at me like that? The albino snake woman will have to wait."

His words caused havoc to her insides. Not to mention, she could have sworn the room temperature went up at least ten degrees.

"Excuse me Sir. Perhaps you would like to look at a menu."

Both people lost in each other's eyes didn't even bother looking up. "We'll have the Salmon and two glasses of white wine."

"Very good, sir."

For half the lunch, Sarah seemed to forget why they had come into the room to begin with. Simon was being charming, entertaining her with tales of his youth, and funny stories about the goings on in the somber House of Lords.

That is until Hilary came over, a handsome stranger by her side.

"Why Simon, I thought that was you with your blushing bride. How are you darling?"

Sarah took in a deep cleansing breath of air before looking up and smiling. Or at least she hoped it was a smile. Not that it mattered. The woman acted as if Sarah didn't even exist. Calculatingly, she moved in closer to Simon on 'darling', pretending not to feel Sarah's eyes boring into her back.

Pointedly turning her back further to Sarah, she addressed Simon intimately, "It's been a long time. I must say it is particularly bad of you to ignore old friends just because you're now shackled with a wife. I am sure your young bride wouldn't mind you coming over sometime for a visit. Now would you dear?"

Narrowed eyes were Sarah's only comment.

"I mean marriage certainly hasn't stopped her from visiting my brother. Although I must admit I find it a little odd that John shows up a few minutes later each and every time as well. A coincidence, I'm sure."

Simon caught Sarah on the way up from her seat, capturing one hand and tugging her back down.

She tugged back hard.

He smiled and remained unmoved. His eyes studied the pale beauty's now seemingly innocent motion over to the town's biggest gossip. The whole room seemed to be listening in on their conversation. With a bored expression on his face, Simon asked coolly, "Are you trying to create a scene Hilary? Because we both know I am not the jealous type."

Her musical laughter grated on Sarah's nerves. She especially did not like the way the woman's well-manicured finger slide along her husband's jaw. "Are you not? Odd. You used to be. At least with me."

The last words were whispered into his ear.

The young man at her side even blushed at her boldness. "Perhaps, we should be leaving Miss Atwood. Your brother is no doubt cooling his heels, as we speak."

She barely glanced in his direction. Her words still directed at Simon. "Yes. It is probably a good idea. I wouldn't want dear Peter upset, seeing as we have our yearly moonlight sail in a couple of days. He is the Captain, after all. Do come, if you can, Simon. We've missed you."

The battle beneath the table belayed the calm her husband displayed to their audience.

Then, as the afterthought it was, Hilary turned back around and threw out, "Oh and of course you are invited as well dear Sarah. If it is not too past your bedtime?"

"In China, your tongue would be cut out and fed to the dogs."

"Sarah," Simon warned, "you promised."

"I beg your pardon?"

Fire was shooting out of Hilary's pale blue eyes. Her body stiff with indignation.

Even the young man at her side grew a shade paler, his freckles more pronounced.

"It was very good to meet you and your wife, sir. Although, perhaps, we should be leaving now."

"Perhaps, you should." Simon agreed.

Sarah only glared. Something between a threat and a promise passed between the two women rivals.

Then before the two women bent on destroying each other could utter another word, Hilary's companion whisked her away amid a sea of whispers, and not a moment too soon. Simon had lost his battle under the table with Sarah and she had risen to her feet. Chest heaving and fists clenched.

It seemed as if all eyes in the tearoom were focused on the two of them, waiting expectantly.

Simon politely rose to his feet and wiped his face with the napkin. Motioning to the shocked audience surrounding them, he suggested, "I believe, China, it would be a good time to exit. It appears as if you don't know how to hold your temper against the albino snake women, after all."

She opened her mouth to argue, when she caught his wink.

Instantly her anger began leveling off. It was hard to argue when he was right.

With an arrogant toss of golden brown curls over one shoulder, Sarah observed casually while gathering her things. "I don't know. Maybe that was holding my temper. She still possesses a tongue, does she not?"

Simon's amused laughter followed her out the door.

# Chapter 17

Two days had past much too quickly for Sarah.

Struggling to keep her voice down for the sake of the little girl resting at her feet, she felt herself choking on words. In fact, she would be shouting at her husband right now if given the chance. However the small child was not fooled by their barely restrained voices. Big blue eyes cut back and forth between the two beautiful people in the bedroom.

"Why can you not wait for me?"

"Sarah we have been through this before."

The sweet urchin looked up and tugged on Sarah's skirt. Sarah ignored her, choosing instead to interpret the tug as access to her lap. Without thinking, the little one was plucked up and soothed into quietness. "I do not trust her. Let me send Grandfather with you."

"Absolutely not. China, I am a grown man. I don't need a wisp of a girl or ancient China man for that matter, to protect me. Now let it lie."

Stubbornly Sarah looked down, pretending submission. The whole time she racked her brain how to prevent Simon from boarding that boat with Hilary. She had a bad feeling. There was evil in the air and a full moon tonight. No good ever came on such a night.

The little girl tugged on the ribbon at her throat. "Excuse me Lady Sarah."

"Yes, Lucy?"

"Donavon says you are taking me back to the orphanage to live tomorrow, not visit like you said. Will I have to give back my new dresses, or Polly, my kitten? She is awfully worried about it. I tried to tell her the nuns couldn't help, but like her. Especially since God sent her to be my kitty. I don't think she believed me, though. She cried till Maggie came in and held us."

Both adults looked over her head at each other. Sarah's expression was full of sadness and Simon felt his own stomach clench in response. Instantly he was down on one knee before Lucy, awkwardly patting the hands held tightly together in a lap so small, his own strong hand dwarfed it. "Don't you want to go back to the orphanage?"

The stiffening of Sarah's body was her only response. Lucy simply looked up at him through big blue eyes. Wisdom beyond her years made her answer truthfully, "I'm supposing I have to. It is where little girls and boys live, who don't have families after all. I'm just worried about Polly. She is new at being an orphan and a bit scared."

"What if I could find you a family? Until then, perhaps you could stay with us for awhile. What do you think?"

Identical smiles from the two girls nearly knocked him over with the hope residing on their faces. Lucy, who was still innocent at three, took him at his word. "I would like that very much kind Sir. But do you think they will adopt Polly too? Seeing as she doesn't have a mother and all?"

"I don't see why not."

Suddenly the little girl leaped from Sarah's lap and into his arms. "Thank you ever so much. I'm glad Donavon was wrong about you. He is such a silly boy."

"Wrong?"

Quickly coming to her feet, Sarah cleared her throat and tried to pry Lucy's arms from their stranglehold around Simon's neck. "Lucy it is impolite to repeat gossip. Run along and don't forget your robe on the chair. It is time you were off to bed."

Simon placed a hand on her arm, halting the hasty retreat. "I think Lucy has time to answer a simple question, don't you moppet?"

A heavy sigh escaped his wife's lips. "You're not going to be pleased."

"I seldom am, but that is beside the point." Looking down at the small blond haired angel, he restated, "What did Donavon say about me, exactly?"

A worried frown puckered her forehead, uncertainty now causing her to shift from one leg on to another. "Well, I'm sure he just didn't know about you finding me a family."

"Yes, go on."

Forgotten was the drama of the day, all their thoughts now centered on one little girl twisting her hair around a chubby finger. "He said that you were a rich lord and didn't care if'n I got me a home or not. And that if it wasn't for Lady Sarah we would both be in Newgate. What is Newgate?" She was now warming to her subject.

"A prison. What else did dear old Donavon say?"

Eyes wide and deadly serious, she leaned in closer, crooking a finger and beckoning him closer.

Dutifully, he leaned down to better hear the rest of her tale.

"He said more than likely it was you made us orphans to begin with. But, that's just silly. The drink made me an orphan. At least that's what Sister Elizabeth says."

Sarah looked off, trying not to laugh at the fascinated look of shock on her husband's face.

"Really, how interesting. I suppose this Sister Elizabeth is right about most things?"

"Well...she thinks so anyway. At least that is what Sister Mary says when the door closes."

No longer able to hold back, Simon let go. Mind releasing laughter washed over him. The sound of it was deep and cleansing, especially to Sarah's ears. And when at last, Simon could catch his breath, one hand to his side, her husband clucked the innocent under the chin and winked, "Do you know what I think?"

"No, Sir."

"I think whoever gets you for a little girl, will be extremely lucky.
"

"I ever do hope so. I use to wish so hard each and every night on a star for a family. But Donavon said it was awfully silly to wish on stars and Sister Elizabeth said it was a sin. So, now I send a prayer up to heaven and my Papa instead. The star just reminds me."

Her heart in her throat, Sarah stroked the little girl's hair. "We'd better go now. We just might have time to make a wish before Maggie finds us."

Lucy's head whipped back in anticipation. "Does that mean I really get to live here until I get me a family?"

"I don't see why not. That is, if Sir Conway really meant what he said."

The words were an invitation. She was offering him, no matter how shyly, a chance to participate in her world. Given that, how could a man with any kind of a heart turn such an invitation down.

"Of course you can stay. At least until we find you a family." Sarah had no doubt the 'until' was for her benefit.

"Oh, thank you ever so much! I promise to be extremely good. And don't you worry. If that mean old Donavon tells anyone else about you making orphans I'll kick him in the shin."

"I'd appreciate that." Simon had a bit of a smirk on his face. "Yes, I'll just add you to my long list of defenders. Let's see..." His hand touched the top of her head, then went up to caress Sarah's smooth copper skin, "One old China man, one little girl and one young woman who believes in destiny. Who could ask for a better army than that? I certainly couldn't."

Strangely enough, he meant every word.

"I believe, granddaughter of little hearing, that your husband said he did not wish for you to follow him."

"I know, Grandfather, but he doesn't know the danger he is in."

The trees were blocking her view of the channel. It couldn't be helped; she would just have to move in closer to have a better look. Besides, she wasn't exactly interfering, it was her duty. Okay, maybe she was interfering a little. Those stupid trees were still in the way.

The old red-haired China man raised an eyebrow and crossed his arms, refusing to budge.

"This is most unwise."

Not afraid in the least of being seen, Sarah resorted to climbing up on the Rock embankment. The rocks begin sliding down in deafening announcement. When at last she found an outcropping of rock she sat down with a little satisfied sigh. At least she could see now.

"I do not trust that woman. She is planning something."

"No doubt, it is the seduction of your husband. However, there can be no seduction of a man if his heart belongs to another. Do you question his loyalty?"

"Of course not." She shot back a little too quickly.

"I see."

"No, it's not like that."

Where was that full moon anyway? The cloudy night was keeping most of the night light hazy at best. The shadowy yacht down below was bathed in weak moonlight as the clouds moved out of the way for a moment. Climbing down on her belly, she peered into the shadowy light, hoping to catch a glimpse of the people down below. Music trailed upwards. A single stringed instrument accompanied a man's voice. The words lost long before ever reaching her ears.

"It seems an awfully small dinner party if you ask me."

"Jealousy is not an attractive garment."

Her grandfather's voice sounded very much like her own conscious. Not wishing to talk about it, she scooted back up and pointed down below. "I am only pointing out the danger. After all, a man who refuses to acknowledge danger-"

"-is as blind as the mole. Both are in danger of falling into the cunning one's net." He finished for her. "Speaking of falling. If you continue to wave your arms about, your presence will no longer be hidden."

Her foot slipped as if on cue, sending her skidding forward. "Great" was the last thought she had before trees started sliding past her. Frantically, she groped for any passing object to slow her fall. Yet, still she tumbled forward.

Relax. She kept repeating the words to herself, and forcing her trained body to be loose. It was her only hope in not breaking something, not that she didn't deserve the outcome. She found it strange how one's thoughts continued to flow even when tumbling down to meet certain death. Thank goodness, she had the sense to bring Grandfather along this time. At least there would be someone to carry her dead body home.

Suddenly a huge pile of dirt and grass hit the side of her body. It was no doubt an animal home of some sort. Instinctively she latched hold of a root sticking out the top, it was not enough to stop her completely but it was close.

As she hung suspended over the surf below, bloody and scrapped beyond recognition, she realized this was not the best plan she ever had. In fact, besides the time she saved Simon and married him, this was a close second to the worst one.

"Granddaughter, do you still live?"

Her grandfather's hoarse whisper was like music to her ears. Mostly because it meant she was still unbelievably alive. "I'm over here. Please hurry."

It took only a few moments for him to unwrap his belt and use it to pull her back up to the ledge and safety. He didn't have to say a word as she stood trembling before him. His muttering in Chinese as he lifted her to safety and the now heavy silence as he studied her said it all.

Ducking her head in submission, she tried to explain the unexplainable. "Don't be angry with me. It is only because I am trying to protect him as you taught me. His life is my responsibility after all, so after he made me sign that paper called a 'will'…even if I didn't actually sign it. Well, now heaven's taken notice of him again. It's hard to explain."

The look of disapproval had changed into one of confusion.

Desperate to explain, she rattled on.

"Then I didn't get the note, because of my loud weeping. Of course I had to fix things. But, there she was whispering in his ear and I couldn't help myself. It is all perfectly reasonable really."

"I do not understand your words. Did the fall affect your logic?"

"No. I'm trying to explain."

His sigh stopped her. Gently, he led her over to a soft patch of grass and newly fallen leaves. The small yacht was within sight below, bobbing quietly on the dark sea. They sat in silence awhile watching the shadowy figures walk about. Then two people separated from the others and took a walk along the shore. She leaned in, peering into the darkness and trying to make out who they were, almost afraid her intuition was right.

Surely Simon possessed more sense than to take the snake woman into the night alone. A shaky hand ran through tangled curls.

"It is your husband. Notice the way he walks. With the pride of his ancestors."

She was glad she wasn't alone tonight. Her grandfather was right, of course. She wasn't thinking clearly. Hadn't been thinking clearly since becoming Simon's wife. This was why she was finding it extremely irritating to be in love. There was very little logic in it.

"Is something troubling you Little One?"

"No. Just thinking."

"One can only hope."

Sarah grinned at his exasperation. Yes, she had been wise to ask him to come with her. His voice soothed her. His presence comforted.

"Thank you for coming, Grandfather."

"We are family. Now tell me, what is our purpose here."

It was her turn to offer a heavy sigh. "I have absolutely no idea."

A soft chuckle was his only response.

"So much has been happening lately. I don't know even where to begin. I should have asked for your help sooner, but I didn't want you to dislike my husband. To tell the truth, I wasn't sure if I even liked him." She turned back to better see his reaction, hugging scrapped knees up to her chest. "Can I tell you something from my heart?"

"Always, Little One."

"It isn't very wise or noble. In fact, well, it proves I am no better than all the other weak willed women you taught me to despise."

He didn't argue with her. Simply leaned down on clasped hands to listen.

"When I first married Simon, I didn't really care what the truth was. I wanted to stay with him, even if it meant I had to lie to myself."

"And, now?"

"And now..." her voice trailed off. From somewhere deep inside herself a reservoir of past integrity forced her to continue. "And, now?

Well, the truth is, I still want to stay with him. But, I cannot if it means lying to myself. I had to be here tonight. Not to protect Simon, but to know the truth of things. He told me what he is doing here. I only came to see if what he says will be the same as what my eyes show me. I guess I am testing him."

The crickets were cheering her on. The surf pounding below, urging her to finish. Yet, her grandfather sat silently, not judging. Just listening.

"I tried to pretend it is because I thought him in danger. Which he is, but in truth, it is purely selfish. I doubt his loyalty. Even now, after I urged him to trust me. Not quite the brave trusting girl you saved eight years ago, am I? Perhaps my English heritage is stronger than my will."

"Perhaps."

"You're supposed to disagree."

Studying the sea, he stretched out his legs and leaned back on covered elbows. "It grows late. What will you do?"

They both knew they were talking about more than time.

"What do you think I should do?"

"This is not important. What I think."

"No. But I wish you would tell me what to do anyway."

He grew quiet, then in a hushed voice, he began telling her a story. "Once, a long time ago in America, there was a very foolish child who gave up her blanket to a homeless woman living under a bridge. This gift caused much grief to her grandfather who had to share his last remaining blanket with the small child throughout the winter."

Sarah noticed a ship coming into the harbor. Its lights quickly doused to keep from being seen. Still, she listened respectfully to his tale.

"When asked why she would give her only blanket to someone who probably was better off than she was, she answered wisely."

He had her full attention now.

"What did she say?"

"She said the woman did not have a family. Therefore the little girl was richer than the woman. She could afford the loss. Well, I think that little girl is even richer now, for she knows love. She can afford to trust."

Her heart swelled with understanding. For the first time that night she felt at peace, even though nothing had truly changed. "You are a very wise man, Grandfather."

"Sometimes. Why do you suppose that ship chooses the covering of night to come into this cove?"

Her worried eyes scanned the shore below. Where was Simon? Thanks to her grandfather's words, she no longer feared him falling prey to the pale one's beauty. Now she had a different worry. She worried more that he might be alone down there.

"It might be one of the evil doers ships. Simon came here tonight in search of answers. He thinks Hilary has some connection to England's traitor. Apparently there are smugglers from America that wish to cause problems for the English. Involve them in the war."

"There is a rowboat coming to shore."

She stood up and looked around for a quick way down the cliff's embankment. "Stay here. I have to make sure Simon is safe. Once he is, I'll come back to you."

The old man ignored her dismissal, taking the lead himself down the rugged cliff's side. His movements were sure and agile, even at sixty years of age. Sarah obediently followed him down, trusting in his ability, as she trusted in his wisdom. She had known in her heart that he would not leave her. However, watching him carefully descending the rugged landscape, she wished she had never asked him to come in the first place. He would give his life for her. This she knew. Yet, she could not help thinking that if only she had not come into his life eight years ago, he would be finishing his book right now, relaxing in front of a warm fire, and teaching pupils. Not climbing down cliffs to fight off smugglers.

Once their feet touched damp sand, Sarah hugged the side of the cliff. They used the shadows to hide from the men exiting the rowboat, not thirty feet away. Her grandfather's hand pulled her down and back into a shallow cave. His face was calm. His demeanor was that of a warrior.

She followed suit. She forced herself to calm her mind and still the fast beating of her heart. Purposely she slowed down the rapid intake of air coming into her body. She must become invisible. She must focus. She must listen.

The words the men spoke were in a foreign unfamiliar tongue. Their skin was as dark as the Italians in New York. Their bodies were small and stocky. Hilary and Simon emerged from the shadows ahead of them, her hand resting easily on the crook of his arm. One of the men stepped forward and doffed his sailor cap before asking something in the strange tongue, to which Hilary angrily replied back in the same language.

"Is there a problem Hilary?"

Hilary's face cleared as she lifted seductive lips up close to Simon's ear. Yet the whisper was loud enough for them to hear. "These men are looking for Peter. Some sort of business. I told them he is back at the house, but they refuse to leave without talking to him first."

"Perhaps I might be of service."

Did Sarah only imagine the look of cunning that crossed briefly across the young woman's pale features? The moonlight choosing that precise moment to peek out from a cloud, accenting her lily-white skin and ice blue eyes.

One of the men, wearing an odd official looking frayed uniform, took a couple of steps forward. His words were rapid with urgency.

A wave of Hilary's hand ceased his words instantly. She paused a moment, than seemed to make her decision. Turning to Simon and resting her hands on his chest she whispered in fear, "Simon these men claim soldiers are after them. They say they possess a cargo that belongs to Peter and if caught we will all go to prison. Do you have any idea what they are talking about?"

Simon's eyes grew cold. His voice was deadly calm. "Ask what cargo they hold."

"But Peter would never resort to smuggling."

"Ask them."

Once more words were exchanged. A skinny man standing nearest to Simon began tugging at the bandanna encircling his dirt-encrusted neck, his other hand clenching in repressed hostility.

Something was wrong.

Hilary dropped her hands in shock, "He says, the shipment is cotton. Oh, no. Simon if we are caught with such a cargo we will do more than face prison, more likely swing from the hangman's noose. What was Peter thinking?"

Dragging her forward, Simon ordered, "Tell him to bring the cargo here to this place. We will hide it in the narrow cave a few feet up the cliff. You remember the hideout we had as children."

"But, Simon... the soldiers."

"I'll worry about that. Tell him. We only have a few moments to spare if what he says is true."

She began speaking rapidly. Interrupting, Simon turned her back around to him. His hands, crushing her upper arms. "Tell him, first I wish to meet with his captain."

"Are you insane?! These men could kill you. And besides, there is no time."

Sarah stepped forward to stop him. Her grandfather placed a restraining hand to her shoulder, while shaking his head. With all the will power she possessed, she stepped back beside him.

"They have to return to the ship anyway. Someone will need to show them where the small inlet is in the dark. It only makes sense that I would be the one to go with them."

"Then I am going as well."

"I prefer to go alone. It is too dangerous. Besides, someone has to tell the others what is happening. I only hope the Captain speaks English. I have mastered some Spanish, but this language is different somehow."

"They are from the Republic of Mexico. Simon, this is not a good idea. I should be the one to go." He was already shaking his head no, "Alright, then at least let me get Peter first."

Simon held her hands close to him, jerking her up in his urgency. "I don't want you hurt. Besides, your blessed brother was who got us into this trouble to begin with. Let me help you."

"Oh, darling, how brave you are." then unbelievably Sarah watched as Hilary reached up, fully intending to kiss her husband.

The few lights on the boat out at sea flickered a warning to the shore.

Simon turned his head, causing Hilary to kiss his check instead. He pressed a light kiss to the hand he still held and demanded, "Now Hilary. We are running out of time."

Disappointment shone in light blue orbs, but she turned obediently to the men waiting. After a few more words, the men nodded in understanding. Then the long haired sailor with the huge machete attached to one leg, motioned for Simon to follow. Just before Simon climbed into the boat, Hilary gave a trembly smile and blew him a kiss. Tears of gratefulness gathering in her eyes.

"Do be careful Darling."

"Go warn Peter."

And then he was gone. The semi dark night swallowing him up as the small boat rowed toward the ship waiting at anchor. Hilary watched a long moment before turning at last to leave. Her lace covered silver skirt billowed from the sea's breeze behind her, as hair pulled loose from its diamond combs, swirled eerily about her face. She was beautiful in a dangerous sort of way. She looked more ghost than flesh and blood woman.

But, that was not what unnerved Sarah the most.

The albino snake woman…was humming.


They had been running hard for the last four minutes.

Keeping the ship on their left, Sarah and her grandfather dodged and climbed over obstacles as they frantically tried to keep up with the ship. They would never find the inlet otherwise. Neither one said a word. It would have required too much effort. The last thing said by

Grandfather, before they took off in the same direction as the ship, still haunted her with each agonizing step she took.

"They were told to kill him."

Sarah's heart was pumping blood at breakneck speed, trying to keep up with the demand she was placing on it right now. Every other instinct she possessed, turned off, except that of fear. She felt both cold and faint at the same time. But, still she ran. They were Simon's only hope. No one else knew where he had gone, except Hilary, of course. But her reaction left little doubt what she intended to do.

Let him die.

And her friend Peter? Where did he fit into all this? Right now, it hardly mattered. She only wished John could have been trusted for back up tonight, or at the very least was still following Simon like he had been ordered. They needed more help against so many men.

The ship stopped moving. Thank goodness. The sounds of men weighing anchor and trimming sails carried across the water. But, thankfully there were no gunshots. She knew logically that there were more ways than one to kill a man. However she still clung desperately to the absence of gunfire and the hope that a shipment really did exist. Its existence alone would guarantee Simon's safety to shore. No one else knew the caves. No other soul left on the beach to guide them. Unless it was all a trap, then her husband would die this night, while she waited hopelessly on shore.

"We must prepare."

Sarah only nodded. Her mind was screaming things like, "prepare what?" They had no weapons. Not even a rope to use for making a bludgeon. Behind her the China man gathered several rocks, tying them up in the end of his tunic. At once Sarah followed suit, even though the sound of a boat being dropped in the water caused her to miss her footing. The few precious rocks she had gathered, scattering across the beach.

"You must concentrate."

"Yes, Grandfather."

There was no more room for mistakes. Time was their enemy as the oars could be heard slapping against the waves. Those blessed oars.

There must be a shipment, otherwise why would they leave the ship? Simon was safe. He had to be. Sarah placed a hand to her heart and said a prayer of thankfulness, as the sound of groaning men rowing toward shore made her eyes fill up with grateful tears. Looking up, she noticed that tied to two small boats was a makeshift barge stacked high with wooden crates. These no doubt contained the illegal cotton.

Yet in spite of everything, all Sarah could think of, as she climbed higher up the side of the embankment and ducked behind some jutting boulders, was that cotton was the cause of so much sorrow. To the slaves of the South, it meant backbreaking labor. To the men losing their land, it was a loss of heritage. To a country losing its fathers and sons, there would be such grief, that it would be hard to ever bond together again. And now thanks to her, it would be the reason Simon died tonight, if she and Grandfather could not stop it.

The small craft skidded up on shore, its bow delving deep grooves into wet sand. A huge dark man climbed out of the first boat. Soon at least ten other men stood on shore looking around. As if waiting for something, or someone. Sarah didn't care about anything else except where her husband was. Her eyes began frantically searching the group for Simon. He wasn't there. Tears clouded her eyes as anger choked her. They were too late. The snake woman must be sending someone else to meet them. She clutched at the sharp rock in her hand so tightly that the edge began to cut into her palm. She didn't even feel the pain, so great was her heartache.

A single drop of blood fell to the ground. It was a testament to her resolve. She would seek justice from whoever came to this place tonight.

Suddenly a man with hands tied behind his back was dragged out of the boat and deposited on shore. The ugly one with the anchor tattoo kicked Simon once in the side before roughly standing him up between two other sailors. Sarah felt her knees go weak. Thanks to the God of all things, he was alive. Battered and bleeding, but alive. The moon was so bright now that it cast the shadows of the men along the shoreline.

Simon stood silently, swaying slightly. His eyes speaking volumes even before the cloth around his mouth was ripped off and a huge bowie knife shoved up against his throat.

"So, my friend, it seems we are at an impasse, you and I. You do not wish to tell me who else is with you. And I? Well, I have the upper hand and do not choose to tell you anything. Therefore one of us is no longer necessary. I believe that would be you. That is unless you have changed your mind about giving me a name."

The speech was in broken English. But at least it was English.

Grandfather began to cut his silk belt with the small knife he kept inside the waist of his pants. He handed her one half, then rolled his half into a rope with a makeshift pouch in the middle. In seconds he had made a sling.

Sarah instantly followed suit. She remembered felling many a small rabbit, or squirrel outside the city for extra food during their time living in the tenements. She had just never used a sling against a human being before. She prayed that her strength would be enough to help Simon escape.

"Well, gringo?"

Even from up above him, Sarah could sense Simon's fury. His words were curt and challenging. "Get it over with."

Then he spat at the man. That small act of defiance caused the angry captain to dig his knife deeper into Simon's flesh. Sarah watched as her husband's lifeblood began to ooze out from the fresh wound in thick red drops.

It was now or never.

She heard, rather than saw, Grandfather begin swinging his sling through the air. It swished loudly around his head as he swung. Only the oceans' roar drowning out the sound, kept them undetected by the group below. She felt the small stone whiz past her ear, lifting the hair as it sailed straight for the man holding Simon.

It was a direct hit.

Sarah began building up momentum with her own sling.

"What is going on?!" The Captain barked out orders. "Find out who is out there. Now!"

Simon wasted no time taking the opportunity offered. Ducking his head, he rammed the bearded Captain in the stomach. Both men flying back into the rock encrusted shadows.

A shot rang out down below. Sarah took that man out first. The others scattered, shooting wildly up into the cliffs over their shoulders. Sarah picked up another rock from her pile. The boulder it rested on, her shield. Grandfather was already sending his second shot at the huge black man's knee. He crumbled to the ground moaning in pain. Five other men were diving back into the rowboat, loosening the cargo ropes and frantically fumbling about for an oar.

All the men were shouting in Spanish now. Their words not understood by the determined young woman bombarding them with stones. A tap on her shoulder drew her attention, as Grandfather motioned below. Two men were battling now in the surf. Simon was being overpowered, his tied hands preventing him from any real defense against being drowned by the snarling Captain shoving his head back down under water for the second time.

The only advantage Simon seemed to have, was his strength of will. That will was the only think keeping him alive. Sarah watched in helpless terror as her husband battled furiously under the salty surf. Then after what seemed an eternity, at last he pushed his head up out of the water, knocking the surprised man backwards into the water. For a moment, both he and Sarah could breath. One breath and then he was down again.

"He is too far away. I will have to climb down to them." Her grandfather's voice sounded so matter of fact that it belayed the terror going on down below.

Shaking her head, Sarah pointed to the men left on shore now gathering together. Cautiously they began heading for the two men struggling for dominance. "Grandfather, I will have to go. Your aim is truer and there are too many for us to fight by hand."

He nodded. Neither found it strange that a young woman would be the choice to face the evil ones. Life was full of tests. This one was Sarah's.

She only hoped she would not be too late.

A front snap kick to the Mexican man's side sent him cart wheeling into the waves.

Sarah hardly glanced in Simon's direction. His gasp of air reassuring her, that he lived. She waded out a few steps just as the man managed to rise to his knees. A pearl handled knife pulled free of its sheath.

"Sarah get out of here!"

"Not now Simon."

The Captain slowly rose out of the surf. His front silver tooth was gleaming in the moonlight, as he smiled evilly at her.

"Ahh. Senorita, such a waste. It is a shame I will have to kill you. You have such spirit. Such beauty."

"Words of flattery from lying lips are like drops of poison from a crystal glass."

"Sarah I mean it. Get out of the way."

Her eyes never left the evil smile of her opponent, Sarah hissed back in aggravation, "Shut up Warrior. I must pay attention. He has a weapon."

"I can see that. Move."

One moment she was standing there and the next she was drinking salt water, the air knocked from her lungs. A sound like thunder echoed through the water covering her head. Simon's weight held her underneath the ocean's icy depths, drowning her.

She shoved at him. Slowly he rolled to one side and she struggled up on hands and knees, coughing up seawater and drawing in much needed air. And when she could finally catch her breath? She felt only one thing. Fury.

Never mind that the evil man who had threatened them lay face down in the surf dead.

Never mind that they were no longer alone. An unknown man, fighting the waves in order to reach them.

"What is wrong with you, Englishman? You could have gotten us killed!"

Simon looked as furious as she felt. He lay on his side, the waves jarring his body as they rushed to shore. His face was swollen and bruised. His lip cut. Massive shoulders straining to keep the rest of his body from tumbling over in the surf. "I could have gotten us killed?! What part of move did you not understand?"

"Could you two do this another time? The regiment has a few questions for you both and I have to a body to retrieve."

Surprise made Sarah sit slowly back down in the shallow water. "John?"

"The one and only." He smiled and blew at the smoke still curling from the barrel of his gun.

"How did you find us?"

He shrugged and replaced his pistol to its' holster, before using his knife to cut loose the ropes binding Simon.

"He has orders to follow me, remember? It seems to have come in handy this time."

"That is an understatement. Especially seeing as smugglers were about to cut you up for fish food. Tell me cousin, did you really intend to let your slip of a wife die trying to save your miserable life?"

Green eyes the color of the sea, narrowed in on John. Then moving past him, Simon held out a swollen hand to Sarah. "I can take care of my own wife."

"It looked rather like she was taking care of you."

John was no longer smiling. Both men lost in a childish clash of wills over who saved who. It was ridiculous. Sarah pushed past both men. Shivering with cold and delayed shock, she began wading toward shore, doing her best to avoid looking towards the red colored water and bobbing body of the man who had nearly taken her life. She only wanted to go home and crawl under a pile of covers and forget this awful night ever happened.

On shore were several lanterns swaying in the strong breeze that had picked up over the ocean. Men's voices were shouting orders and gathering up scattered cargo. But all she cared about was finding the one person that mattered most to her. Then she saw him. Grandfather's lone figure stood at the water's edge waiting for her. Her haven in the storm. With heartfelt gratefulness she silently sent a prayer up to the heavens, for as terrible as this night had been, she still had her family.

The clock on the mantle read two o'clock in the morning.

There were still soldiers milling about outside Peter's country home searching. Peter was suspiciously absent, while the guests had all been questioned and sent home. Not one had seen Peter since the party started, or anything else for that matter. That is until they heard shots coming from somewhere down the beach.

With the sailboat party participants all gone, only seven people were left remaining. All of them were sitting in the drawing room; the sergeant and his lieutenant, Grandfather, Hilary, John, and sitting on either side of the warm fire, Simon and herself. Their shoulders were covered by a blanket. Their bodies, chill and damp. At least Simon had a drink and a cheroot to warm him further. Sarah, only her temper.

The snake woman was lying again.

"And you're sure you don't know why those men attacked Sir Conway?"

"No lieutenant. We were sharing a moment of privacy," She blushed prettily, pretending to avoid looking directly at Sarah, "when those horrible men accosted us and forced Simon onto their boat. I rushed to find Peter, but he had disappeared. Thank goodness you and your men showed up when you did. Another minute longer and Simon might have perished."

Sarah noticed there was no mention of her own impending doom, which didn't surprise her.

"I am at a loss Miss Atwood why you did not retrieve help from those at the party."

"Well, I...you see..." Hilary's words stumbled out awkwardly, until Simon interrupted.

"That is partly my fault Lieutenant Farrell. I specifically told her to go and get Peter."

"And why would you do that Sir?"

"By all appearances it looked as if the cotton smuggled in on the Mexican ship was his. I had no wish for Hilary, or myself to be caught up in something illegal. Personally, I felt I could handle Peter better by myself, after the men left. Try and talk some sense into him if you will. End this quest of his to get rich quick. His family has suffered a great financial loss since war began in the States. No doubt the federal blockade set up along the South's coast has further frustrated his efforts to obtain the much needed crop. His family trade is manufacturing linen, and unfortunately linen requires cotton. Preferably, cheap cotton."

Sarah shifted in the blanket and leaned forward. Her words were calm and exact. "Peter is not responsible for this."

She chose to ignore the heavy sigh coming from her husband. Wiping a wet curl from her face, she continued, "The woman named Hilary is," she motioned to the pale beauty sitting across from her. She knew her words must seem ridiculous to the Sergeants. Especially seeing as the snake woman now wore the look of innocence and moonbeams. Even as she was accused, insincere tears were wetting her ivory cheeks.

"She is the one who wished my husband's death. No doubt she knows more about this night than she chooses to reveal."

"Of all the gall. I have suffered the loss of a brother, not to mention my near abduction and now I am accused by a woman, who is obviously only jealous, of being a traitor. Well, I won't stand for it. No, I won't stay here one more moment and have my character slandered. If you will excuse me gentlemen, I will be upstairs if you have further need of me."

"I think that is best Miss Atwood. If we need anything else, I will send someone up for you."

Throwing her head up in mock bravo, with lip quivering prettily, Hilary inclined her head, "Thank you sir. And thank you too, Simon. I never would have been able to endure this awful night without you."

327

Why was it that Sarah suddenly felt the overwhelming urge to give a standing ovation for the pale one's performance? As if on cue, all the men rose to their feet as she exited the room. A silent tribute to her beauty and acting ability, no doubt.

Once Hilary was gone, the lieutenant turned a questioning look her direction. "Now, Lady Conway. Perhaps you could enlighten us as to why you think Miss Atwood is involved."

"Lieutenant, I am sure my wife is just overwrought."

"I most certainly am not. And with the exception of Grandfather, I appear to be the only one here not smitten with the dear Miss Atwood." She jumped ahead, interrupting Simon's attempt to silence her, "If you would have been thinking straight Warrior, you would have observed that the snake woman knew the foreign tongue of your enemy perfectly. Not to mention, that if she was so near swooning, why she did not so much as scream when being 'accosted'? For someone supposedly terrified, she acted most calm to me."

A look of respect briefly crossed Simon's features, but it passed so quickly, that Sarah wondered if she had only imagined it. With a contemplative air, he studied the drink in his hand, before sitting it down on the small end table. "All right. Let's suppose your right."

"There is no supposing, as you like to say. My granddaughter speaks the truth. The snake woman who lies, told the men to kill you. Their language is not unknown to me. It comes from the country Mexico. A fact you are well aware of, my granddaughter's husband."

Simon's eyes never left Lee's, neither denying nor confirming the accusation. All the others in the room now turned to the small redheaded China man. He sat silently. His dark eyes taking in the scene before him. Waiting until the time to speak again presented itself.

John rose to his feet and walked over to the door looking up the stairs before firmly shutting it, so they would not be overheard. "Are you certain Sarah?"

"I am most sure. I also know those men were waiting for another. It is well known evil seldom walks unaccompanied. The woman without honor, no doubt employs, or is employed by this same person."

"Why didn't you speak up sooner, man?"

The Lieutenant sprinted to the doors, calling over one shoulder, "Sergeant gather the men from outside. I want them to search this entire house. Meanwhile, we have to get that woman back into town before she can warn her partner."

John rose to help, his jaw taunt with anger.

"She played us all for fools. Don't worry, Sarah, I'll get to the bottom of this." That said he quickly went in search of the Lieutenant.

Sarah started to follow him out the door, but paused when she realized something. Her husband still sat, one foot propped casually on the opposite knee. Oddly enough Simon wasn't bothering to follow. Instead, his eyes never left the small wiry man sitting calmly before him.

The old Chinese man merely stared back at him before stating blandly, "They are no doubt wasting their time searching the house, are they not, my granddaughter's husband?"

Sarah jerked her body back from the doorway. The blanket slipped down to land in a pile at her feet. "She's gone? But how?"

Giving a shrug and wiping off his hands, Grandfather rose. His eyes accusing as he faced Simon. "Ask your husband, granddaughter. For it is he, who has bestowed her with freedom."

Furious tears were wiped from Sarah's fire reddened cheeks. Her chest, heaving gloriously under the wet silk of her tunic. "Is this true Warrior?"

Shouts of confusion were coming from the second floor landing. The sounds of men running back downstairs, answered her question long before her husband gave voice to the damning words, effectively crushing her heart.

Drawing on the cheroot he had been smoking one last time, he flicked it into the flames. No, he never even flinched before looking his wife straight in the eyes to inform her dryly, "I had my reasons, China."

# Chapter 18

Kate and her mother shook their heads at the sight before them. They were supposed to be discussing the mask ball with Sarah, of course. Only Sarah was preoccupied at the moment, practicing that strange form of dance learned from her grandfather. She called it self- defense. Yet, it looked more like dancing to the two women watching. That is, except for the sudden movements and odd issuances. Yes, it was becoming more and more difficult to discuss their plans amidst the strange guttural sounds coming from the beautiful woman's lips.

A growl rose forth from deep within Sarah's chest pushing the women back a step. Then when the sound erupted to a sharp command in another language, it caused a shriek of surprise from the two women watching.

After another such explosion, Stella tried once again to gain her daughter in law's attention.

"Dear, do you suppose you could do this another time? Preferably after our discussion?"

"I cannot." Then remembering her manners she added, "My most honored mother."

Stella sighed. Her daughter in law had been like this all morning. Distant. Simon was not much better. Last time she checked, he was still locked in the library, having given strict orders not to be disturbed. Whatever had occurred last night definitely put the two young people in a foul mood. Regally stepping out of the way as Sarah performed a roundhouse, she reminded, "You do realize dear that this mask ball is not to cancel out the fair don't you? Katherine and I talked to the ladies this morning and they agreed –"

"I swear to you Sarah, the orphans will have their fair. I told Mrs. Oxford that some of the proceeds from the charity ball would have to be used to fund – "

"Kate, you are interrupting again."

She automatically shut her mouth, "Oh, yes. Sorry about that mother."

Sweat was gathering on the cloth band around Sarah's head. Her hair now damp with perspiration. Stella sat down on the stone bench behind her. Her perfectly coiffed head cocked sideways in order to speak to the young woman now doing stretches. It was becoming more and more difficult to get the young woman's attention.

"We simply," the older woman's stomach got a small cramp bent in the middle as she was, which caused her to sit up quickly rubbing at the offending muscle before continuing, "we thought it might be a good opportunity for you to make peace with some of the ladies. Child, I really must insist you at least desist in making that awful sound while I am talking to you."

Unmindful of the distress she was causing her mother in law, Sarah obediently laid her head neatly alongside her right knee. Without uttering a sound. Seemingly effortless, she switched to the middle and then to the other knee. The older woman raised her voice a notch, speaking to the back of Sarah's head.

"I can understand you refusing to speak of the ball, but at least could you tell us? Well dear, Kate and I were wondering if something unpleasant occurred last night between Simon and yourself."

Sarah popped up quickly, causing the surprisingly agile woman to instantly rare back in order to avoid being trounced upon by the young woman who jumped smoothly to her bare feet.

Never quite meeting the older woman's eyes, Sarah moved her arms in slow figure eights. "Why do you ask?"

"Well dear it seems rather obvious to me."

"It's because you're both in such an awful mood. Why Simon has scarcely said a word to anyone all morning. And you've been doing that strange Chinese thing for over two hours now. Something is definitely wrong. Father said it was none of our business but, then again, when we heard about Hilary's disappearance at the meeting this morning we thought-"

"Thank you Kate. I do believe Sarah gets the point."

Stopping what she was doing, Sarah thoughtfully took the hand towel from Kate's clutches and began wiping her face. "Yes. I am most upset with the warrior."

Both women waited, rapture written on their faces for her to continue.

Instead, Sarah smiled warmly and began walking off. "About this mask ball, I believe I shall wear the costume of my ancestors. Simon should wear one that represents one of his. A dragon. Does that answer your question?"

"Actually, Sarah, I was referring to your disagreement. Did you say dragon?"

"I humbly ask your leave, I am in need of a bath."

"Yes, but you didn't really answer our question at all." Kate shouted back at the young woman's retreating back. However, Sarah was either extremely deaf, or pretending to be. She never even turned around to acknowledge the statement.

Absolutely stunned, they watched in surprised wonder as she waved over one shoulder at them, before heading back inside.

"Can you believe she just walked off like that? She didn't even tell us a thing."

Stella began to chuckle, her hazel eyes twinkling. "Oh, but she did Kate. Didn't you hear what she said about Simon's costume?"

Confusion threw Kate's arms up in mock surrender. "Yes, something about a dragon, I believe."

"Think dear. A dragon is a rather large fiery serpent."

"Oh. I still don't quite understand how that... "

"With a forked tongue."

Hooking her arm through Kate's, she pulled her along, heading straight back for the house. "Our dear Sarah just called your brother the worst sort of a snake."

Disbelief filled her voice, "And that makes you smile?"

"She's still here, isn't she? Even furious, she stays. And that can mean only one thing."

Totally confused now, Kate asked, "Which is what exactly?"

"That our dear Sarah is at long last in love."

The glass of cool well water soothed her parched throat as her mind too full to dwell on any one particular problem at the moment, took in the scene outside. Looking out the kitchen window Sarah noticed Kate and her mother in law coming back inside. Quickly emptying the rest of the glass in the sink, she escaped to her room for blessed privacy. She just didn't feel up to yet another bout with her husband's family. She was weary past thinking.

But on the way past the library, she slowed her steps.

Raised voices were finding their way through the thick oak doors and drifting out into the hallway. Instinctively, Sarah slowed. Curiosity was drawing her in closer to the massive double doors. She could have sworn she heard Simon say her name, his voice strong and insistent.

Hesitatingly, she leaned in closer to the slightly ajar door.

"Father it's important I learn more of Sarah's family."

"Son, I have already told you everything I know. Besides, we can't be entirely sure that your wife is the same Sarah."

"You're sure. Why is that?"

His father's hand shook with emotion as he replaced the volume of accounts back down on Simon's desk. He finally took in a fortifying gulp of air before answering the uncompromising man who was his son. "I've seen the locket she wears around her neck. It was the first Sarah's. As it so happens, I was there when Edward gave it to her for her tenth birthday." He looked off in sadness. "That was a week before they were all killed."

Sarah gasped. Touching the locket at her throat, she leaned heavily against the door. Her eyes closed, her ears open.

The stunning admission caused Simon to drop down into his brown leather chair. Placing a weary head into his hand, he demanded, "Not all of them were killed, or so it would seem. Tell me father, what really happened that night?"

"I told you."

His head snapped up in anger. "I know what you told me. Now I want to know the truth. She is my wife now and your daughter-in-law. She deserves to know who she is."

Henry turned water filled eyes on his son. His pride was holding him hostage. His shoulders were back, his body stiff and unyielding. Yet Simon had never seen him so broken. He didn't have to say anything. From his father's expression, Simon knew the truth his father refused to say.

His hands gripping the arms of the chair, in some unconscious effort to sustain him from the blow that was about to be dealt, he looked up. When he spoke, it was in a furious whisper. "It was you, wasn't it? You're the one who gambled away half the business, not Sarah's father. Tell me Sir...what kind of man steals from his partner and then lets his memory be tarnished? I am simply curious. Was the murder a botched effort to save your own precious hide?"

"No. It wasn't like that. I can explain."

"Can you?"

"You don't understand. We had lost two ships at sea and were in danger of losing the business. I was simply trying to recoup our losses at the gaming table when the investors choose that particular time to take a look at the books. When Edward died there was nothing I could do to save him, but I could save my own family. I did it for you son."

Simon waved a hand to stop him from speaking. "Save me the heroics. Just tell me, did you have them killed?"

Horrified, Henry leaned forward on the desk across from his son, saying in a voice choked with pain. "Of course not. How could you think it of me? He was more a brother to me than my own flesh and blood."

A sob drew the two men's attention to the open doorway.

Sarah stood there looking more like an angry lioness, than wounded victim. One hand still clutched the door knob behind her back. The other covered her mouth holding back the suffocating tears threatening to escape.

Simon came to his feet. "Sarah. Sweetheart." His words were more a plea, than an endearment.

"You hid the knowledge of my family from me. How could you?"

Henry's large frame swayed under the onslaught of her words. "Sarah, Simon knew none of this until a moment ago. I kept it from him. It shames me to admit so cowardly an act, but it is mine alone."

His long graying sideburns quivered from the effort to keep his emotions in check. Sarah took a long searching look at the man before her. His hands were outstretched, and his voice held a slight quiver to it. And yet, she felt nothing. Numb.

Lightheaded, she felt the room grow dark, her body trying to separate from the scene surrounding her. Surely fate couldn't be so cruel as to place her in the very villain's house that killed and then marred her parent's good name. She lowered her hand from the door and forced herself to look her enemy in the eye. When she could manage to speak, her voice asked softly, "If not you, then who did kill my family? Who tried to kill me?"

Simon moved from behind the desk, in a moment he would be on top of her. She stilled him with a hand. "No, don't." Then raising her head a notch, she repeated calmly, "Do you know who did this thing?"

Oddly enough, she felt no hate towards the barrel chested older man. It was as if she were a stranger, unemotionally noting the look of pain in his eyes and the deep intakes of air he was taking. No doubt it must have cost him dearly to admit such an unscrupulous act to his son. But, she needed to know it all. He held at least part of her memories intermingled with his own. Whether he wanted to or not, he would help her.

Simon had never been so proud of her. She had just heard devastating news. Yet still, she bravely fought for control in order to finish the thing. He had not seen such courage since the war. In spite of her false bravo, he knew the truth. What it was costing her to stand there so serenely. He felt her hurt as if it were his own. Every instinct in him wanting to go to her, but he respected her wishes and stood silently in the background watching and waiting, while the two people he cared about the most in the world confronted each other.

"No. But, I am as much to blame as if I myself struck the blow. See, I was the one who was supposed to die that night, not your father and certainly not Ann. I was to pick your family up after the play; only I was at the gaming halls instead, deep in my cups and refusing to leave. So, instead I sent my wayward brother out with a message for the coachman to pick them up without me. No doubt seeing my coach parked there, the ruffians assumed it was me they were killing. I had already been threatened that if I did not get the money owed my creditors before the week was out, I would pay dearly."

The memories of her mother's tortured screams blinded Sarah with gut wrenching pain. Instinctively, she reached up, with both hands pressing against her temples. "Stop." Her words a mere whisper, as images flashed across her mind of blood, smoke, banging on the carriage door, the sound of footsteps chasing her through the dark night, and finally, brilliant green eyes closing in on her, an impartial assailant whose only desire was her death.

Suddenly, her golden eyes snapped open. Fighting the panic she felt inside, as first one man's face, then the other overlapped, she tried to understand what it all meant. Two pair of sea green eyes stared back at her. Why hadn't she ever noticed before? The room was spinning out of control. Simon's worried voice barked out orders as it loomed ever closer to her. Only one clear thought surfaced through all the confusion and pain filled haze.

It was her husband's eyes. They were a brilliant green.

Sarah slept through supper. Her drug induced sleep brought back the nightmares. Now the memories of that night came flooding back and with them, the terror as well. She moaned softly, tossing on the feather pillow.

He was reaching for her again, the evil one. His face half hidden in the shadows except for two piercing green eyes that seemed to glow in the darkness, taunting her.

She screamed for Grandfather.

"Sarah stop, it's all right. I'm here sweetheart."

336

Simon. The arms holding her instantly soothed. His voice calmed the havoc of her soul. Slowly she ceased her struggle against the phantom of her dreams. Still groggy, she tried to focus on her husband's face, or something, anything tangible in the real world. His eyes were a dark color in the semi darkness. The candlelight on the other side of the bed putting him in the shadows. For a moment, she could nearly forget what her mind had registered shortly before passing out, but not quite.

Sitting up, she gently began pushing herself away from the man who now held her hand in his firm grip.

"Why are you looking at me like that, China?"

She avoided the question. Instead she nervously ran a hand through the tangled mass of curls falling in disarray down her back.

"I was dreaming of that night."

They both knew what night.

"Sarah, I know you've been through more than any human being should the last couple of days. But I have to know what you remembered in there. Before another night slips past us, I think we should talk about this. Be honest with one another."

"Like you've been honest with me?"

He jerked as if she had slapped him. Why was it, she wondered, that although she only spoke what was true, it pained her to hurt him? No longer able to look him in the eye, she turned her face.

He released her hand. Standing slowly to his feet, she could feel his eyes on her. Feel his anger. Not until she heard him walking over to the fireplace, did she dare turn back. She watched in numb fascination as his chiseled face flickered in and out of darkness, making it hard to read his expression. His words however were easy to comprehend.

"Sarcasm hardly becomes you, China. You're sounding more the English wife, after all."

"Am I?"

He looked so...so untouchable. Once more, he was the handsome lord, surrounded by his riches. The French brocade chair and massive Italian marble fireplace was an apt backdrop for the presence of the power he exhumed. His massive chest and trim waist were covered in a pure white linen shirt, opened at the throat to reveal the tanned fit body beneath. Dark brown hair too long to be fashionable was pulled back and tied with the same leather strap he had worn in the hotel the first day they met, a reminder of the untamed adventurer. Instead of the tight pants worn by the ton, he chose rather the looser cotton pants worn in America. Although they were simple, few men there could have afforded the special cut, or pressing his pants possessed. His boots were polished until they shinned, even at this late hour of the day.

A flash of another pair of polished leather boots rose unbidden to her aching head. It could not have been Simon that night. He would have been a mere boy of seventeen. No one that young could be that evil. Besides, how could she possibly love someone this much that possessed such a cold heart. She couldn't, could she?

Her feelings were as jumbled as her groggy mind. "What was that in my drink? I feel out of sorts."

"Laudanum. The physician thought it might help. You suffered quite a shock."

"It leaves a bitter taste in my mouth. And I don't care for how it makes me feel numb inside. Grandfather says some feelings must be born, otherwise they poison the body."

He didn't comment only changed the subject. "Why did you faint? Did you remember something else?"

She licked parched lips and wished for a sip of water. Most of all, she wished Simon would stop asking questions she was not prepared to answer. For the one thing she had remembered, clear green eyes...still haunted her too much. The uncertainty of whom she could trust choked her voice; instead she chose the safer route. She chose truth, or at least part of it. After all, it had been used too seldom in this house of deceivers. "Before passing out, I did remember something."

Concern made his own voice rough in return, "Yes?"

How could she trust him? His father had lied. Simon, himself, admitted he kept the truth from her, for how long she did not know. Silence filled the moments. The ticking of the mahogany clock was the only breath of life in the room. Finally she spoke.

"I don't think I can trust you Simon."

When his hand slammed down on the mantle, she jumped.

"Enough of this, Sarah. I thought we were one. Our destinies were written in the stars. Isn't that what you said? Heaven knows I shall remember that moment for the rest of my days. It certainly changed my life. There you were standing there in the middle of our sitting room. Proudly facing the rest of us, like some beautiful exotic warrior, sealing my fate with your words. Do you have any idea the havoc you have brought into my life?"

"Simon I never meant to hurt you."

"Not to mention, the unfathomable joy."

Dumbfounded, she asked almost reverently, "Joy?"

"Yes, joy. Before heaven dropped you into my lap, I was perfectly content to believe the world was full of deceit. I was living in shadows, and so unbelievably lonely. You taught me that things like honor and loyalty still exist. Yes, even love. Not the kind found in lit ballrooms, but the kind that shines from your brown eyes when you look at me, warm, open and inviting."

His words brought tears of wonder to her eyes.

"Yet, when it really matters, you withdraw from me. How can I help fight your dragons Sarah, when you hide them from me?"

She ached to touch him as his words touched her, but he was wrong to think she believed in people. She didn't. Not with things that really mattered, like her life and her heart. She watched as Simon paced in front of her. She knew the strength of him. He would not give up without acquiring something from her.

Finally reaching a decision, she scooted back until her back touched the headboard and with bowed head, spoke from her heart.

"Your words are hard to believe. My parents trusted your father and he betrayed them. My mother trusted whoever was in that carriage and it nearly got me killed. How can I be sure you speak the truth? How can I know?"

Instantly he ceased pacing and dropped down on one knee before her. "Because I love you Sarah. That is how. You know this. How can you compare me to some monster that took your life in every sense of the word? Tell me what you remember. Let me help you end this thing."

"Don't you understand? I can't remember. I only know that my mother screamed for me to run to the carriage. That they refused to help me. But most importantly of all, that they were not the strangers your father believes."

She pulled at a lose thread on the coverlet, lost in her own dark thoughts, Simon all but forgotten. She was no longer frightened. She had learned something tonight about herself. A truth that was against everything her adopted grandfather had taught her.

Although the evil one's face was still lost in the recesses of her healing mind, it would come out to the light of day. She would remember. And when it did? She yanked out the stray thread. She would make him suffer as her parents had suffered. She shook off the traitorous thought that had plagued her sleep and her soul for so long now. It was the knowledge that she burned with the need to destroy him.

It was wrong to hate. It would only destroy her in the end. Yet she did. Resigned, she sat up straighter and pulled an overstuffed pillow into her lap, as if for added protection, a wall against the man kneeling before her.

"I am not feeling well, my husband. Perhaps we could talk of this another time, when I am not so weary of heart."

She was breaking his. He stood to his feet. For just a moment he had thought she might confide in him. Instead she had pushed him even further out of her life. Her brown eyes were cold with indifference.

"Stop being the polite distant wife. If you're still angry with me, then have out with it."

"You kept your father's secrets from me."

"All right. Then, shout at me, call me names, but don't sit there so unbelievably indifferent. I can take anything, but that."

A tear slipped from one eye and rolled silently down her cheek. The pillow clutched so tight that her hands ached.

"I don't understand you at all. Not just the hiding of truth about my parents, but everything. Simon, I was there in the shadows last night.

I saw Hilary. I saw you touch her." She must not cry. She must think about the sound of the candle flickering and sputtering to stay alive, as she tried to survive this heartache. She must think clearly.

"If you were there earlier, then you know nothing happened."

"Do I?"

He dropped down on the bed and grabbed her upper arms, determined to make her listen. "I swear to you that she means nothing to me. The woman nearly got me killed."

"You let her go. Do you deny it?"

The accusation in her voice caused him to let go and begin pacing again in frustration. "No. But, there is a lot you don't understand."

"Then explain it."

He pushed back hair that had escaped the leather straps confines. "Don't you see she is the only lead I have? As your grandfather said, there is someone else involved. And without him, I have nothing. He has been one step ahead of me for two years now. You can't possibly understand what it's like chasing him for so long now. Even I don't know any longer if it is for my country, or my own personal vendetta that I must find him. I just know that I am close, so close, I can nearly taste it."

How she wanted to believe him. If her head were not pounding so horribly maybe she could test his words for truth. As it was, she did well to separate the words he spoke. Try to soak them up for dwelling on later, once her head cleared from this fog. Pulling her knees up to her chest, and laying her throbbing head down on them, she moaned softly.

Instantly, the bed gave way to his weight beside her. His strong hand massaged the taunt muscles of her neck. A soft kiss to her temple further weakened her resolve not to melt in his arms. Yet, she could not. Must not. Because of the very words he spoke. Time was running out. She needed answers, or the nightmares would invade her reality. She had felt danger last night and today. It was real danger, not the imagined one of her dreams. She felt it as surely as if a storm were brewing.

Slowly, she lifted her heavy head and pulled his hand into hers. She may not understand all he spoke this night, but she did need him to answer one important question and it was the most important one of all.

341

Her eyes glassy with pain, she asked honestly, "Why did you keep the truth of my ancestors from me?"

He gripped her hands so tightly, she winched. "I couldn't tell you anything until I understood how my father fit into all this. When I realized he knew who you were, at first I was shocked. Then the more I delved into past accounts; I began to suspect something else, as well. That it was my father who gambled the business away, not yours." He let go of her hands and gave a self-depreciating little laugh. "To think, I sacrificed half my life in order to clear his good name. That makes me more the fool than he was."

"You wanted to believe in him. That is not so very foolish."

"Isn't it?" It was his turn to look off. Not willing to see the disgust he knew his next words would bring. "To make matters worse, I very much feared he was the murderer that October night. That he, not some masked stranger, had welded the gun that took your parents lives. Tell me, how do you tell your wife that?"

She touched his face, softly pulling it back around. She wanted him to see what she said was true. Her only goal now, was to soothe his pain. Her own was not important any longer. "Your father could not have done this thing. I was there."

Tangible hope flickered across his face. Suddenly, it was him turning to her for comfort. Yet, within the time it took for a spark of hope to find life, it was quickly blown out. When he did speak, it was matter of fact as he was once more the impartial British agent. "How can you be so sure? You said yourself everything is lost to you about that night. Except for bits and pieces you are no closer to the truth than I am."

Impatiently pushing back a stray lock of hair that had fallen over one eye, he demanded, "Did you know that everything your father had left after his death went to pay my father's gambling debts? My father walked off with half the business still in tact and his good name. In fact, if I hadn't married you, everything I have now would legally belong to you."

He gave a wide swoop of his arm taking in the omnipotent room full of expensive furniture consisting of deep browns and rich golds.

Shocked, Sarah blinked back the enormity of what he was saying. "But you saved the business, not your father."

"I could have done none of this without your inheritance. So, invariably, all I have is yours in the truest sense of the word." Trying to lighten his words, he joked sarcastically, "I guess the very fact I married you instead of doing away with you is proof I am not my father's son."

Too late he realized his poor choice of words.

Sarah pushed back the covers and slipped out around him, refusing to look at him as she crossed over the bare floor. The coldness of the wooden floor seeped into her being. Just as his words seeped into her mind. The open French doors beckoned her out onto the balcony. She only wanted escape. But, it was not to be. She flinched when his voice broke her mind's swirling.

"I didn't mean it that way China. I did not shoot at you that night. Think. If I wanted to kill you, I could have done it anytime. Not wait until some dark night at the warehouse."

The cool breeze was easing her headache. Her heart however was not improving. His words were stifling, strangling the life out of any hope still flickering in her breast.

"Simon, I can't think anymore tonight."

"Sarah"

Spinning around, her glorious hair falling all around like a golden streaked cape, only intensified her beauty to him.

"No! Don't speak anymore. Please, stop."

He was on his feet and holding her arms in a death grip in a matter of seconds. Giving her a light shake, he spoke with urgent intensity, forcing her to listen, "Sarah, I love you. You have to know me better than to believe that I could ever hurt you."

Going limp, she looked him straight in the eye. The sad emptiness he found looking back at him, made his legs go weak. Defeated, he let go and took a step back. "I see."

It took every ounce of will power she had not to reach for him. To say what he wanted to hear. But, she couldn't. Not anymore.

"I need time to think Simon."

Anger held in check, he looked off into the dark night before answering her.

"All right. The House of Lords vote is tomorrow. I could stay at the club until the mask ball at the end of the week. Three days. Will that be enough time?"

They were talking so casually. As if discussing the change of staff, not the state of their marriage. Her own voice sounded unemotional and tired. His voice was so cold that it chilled her.

"Yes."

"I will ask only one thing from you in exchange."

Wanting peace at any price, she nodded, "All right."

"I want you to stay here at the house the next three days."

She opened her mouth to argue, he cut her off with an intimidating stare. "This is important. I don't know who shot at you, but until I do I want you safe. And that means no secret meetings off the premises, or following me. It is the only way I will agree to leave tonight."

Knowing if he stayed, she would be helpless to resist him, she leaned against the open door. The glass was cool and steadying. With strength past what she possessed she stayed where she was and answered sadly, "I give my word, Warrior. At least, until the ball."

With a short nod, he turned from her and was gone. It was then, facing the solid door he had exited, that she finally gave in to all the emotions running rampart through her body. Sliding down the glass behind her, she landed in a sobbing pile of sheer lace and broken dreams.

The next day passed in relative quiet. No one asked after Simon. Servant's eyes shifted away from her, no doubt knowing more than they let on. Even her in-laws refrained from mentioning his absence.

Henry was particularly subdued. Once as he was passing her on the stairs, he hesitated as if to say something. Dressed immaculately, as usual, in a dove gray suit, his face reddened before clearing his throat. But, when she turned around, one step lower than the other, as if in indecision herself...he bowed slightly and resumed the climb downstairs. Both were apparently choosing to avoid the words left unspoken. A part of her wished he had said something and explained things. But, there was nothing left to say.

Later that afternoon, the Lieutenant came to question her once more. He reported there still was no sign of Peter or Hilary. It was his opinion that both had fled the country. No doubt bound for America. Regardless, the seasoned soldier wasn't taking any chances. There was a guard posted outside for her protection, at least until she could testify at the hearing.

Throughout his visit, Sarah sat perfectly erect in the small Elizabethan chair as if in a daze. The soft red velvet of her gown matching perfectly with the glowing cherry wood that made up the parlor. Her hair caught up in ruby combs, soft and curled. Even her shoes, the finest kid leather, were the very height of fashion. No doubt she appeared the perfect epiphany of an English noble, and she had never been so miserable in her entire life.

She missed Simon.

She didn't even have the heart to go to Grandfather. He knew her too well. And she didn't want to say out loud to anyone, how she really felt. Instead, she opted to spend the rest of the day in quiet seclusion. She read the same paragraph twice over before giving up, and beginning to pace once more. She would have welcomed the night when it came, if she could have slept. But the absence of the warrior was evident all around her. She felt trapped. Held captive by her promise to Simon, but most of all, she felt terribly lonely.

The next morning, Maggie came in tsk-tsking her.

Throwing wide the heavy drapes of brown velvet, she informed her mistress in no uncertain terms, "Enough moping my lady, your husband has need of you."

Excitement momentarily vanquished the unfamiliar depression that had descended on her the last couple of days, "Simon is here?"

Giving her a knowing smirk, Maggie placed hands on ample hips. "No, he isn't. But, no woman leaves a man alone to face what he be a facing now. So, get your skinny body out of that bed and go to him. Word on the street is a thousand pounds will buy his head on a silver platter. The master swayed the vote yesterday. Gave quite a speech I hear tell. Thanks to the master, there will be no legal trade with America. Southern cotton is off limits and half the ton is up in arms."

Maggie's words were upbeat and confidant, proud even. Sarah felt proud of him too. She was glad that he had changed his mind and relieved that his honor was more important than his need for revenge. Yet she could do nothing to help him. Sinking back down onto the feather bed she answered truthfully, "I cannot go to him Maggie. I gave my word."

"Oh, pshaw. When has that stopped a woman from doing what she needed. How many times have you climbed out that window, on some loophole you found in giving your word?"

Surprise widened Sarah's eyes, "How did you know?"

"We servants have our ways." Then she winked. "Now up with you, Master Simon is facing the reporters today in Hyde Park. He will need protection and I know no better person for that, then you and them heathen Chinese ways of yours."

"But he has the police." Even as she argued the point, covers were quickly discarded. Her feet barely touched the ground before grabbing up lacy under things from Maggie's outstretched hands.

"And a fine help the Bobbies will be too. They always seem to arrive after trouble's had a seat and made itself at home. Where were they I ask you when the Master was captured by those no account smugglers?"

Hurrying to dress behind the silk screen, Sarah racked her brain, trying to find a way around her promise to Simon. He said, 'she could not leave, or follow him', but maybe... Maggie heard a snap of fingers, as Sarah's beautiful face popped up over the screen. "Grandfather. Simon didn't forbid me from sending him. Maggie, could you please find Grandfather for me, and have him meet me in the Library in about five minutes?"

Maggie ran around the screen and snatched her up in a bear hug. Apparently Sarah's state of undress was of no real importance to the enthusiastic woman. "Oh, Miss. I told the others our dear Miss Sarah would think of something. I'll get right on it."

Then leaving in a whirl of enthusiastic mayhem, she exited the room. In her wake, the screen lay crumpled at Sarah's feet and the freshly ironed peach satin dress trampled past recognition. Sarah sighed. Apparently the maid wasn't called Messy Maggie for nothing. Then, without further ado she stepped over the screen and continued dressing. There was much to do. Simon needed her. And right now, she didn't want to dwell on how that made her feel.

It was nearly noon before Sarah began to worry.

She hadn't heard anything from Grandfather since sending him to protect Simon. Too restless to wait any longer, she decided to pass the time with Lucy. Climbing the curved staircase, she smiled. Lucy. The child's sunny smile and wise ways always managed to cheer Sarah's heart. She was just the medicine Sarah needed this long, long day.

Catching a hold of herself before reaching the nursery, she smoothed out the wrinkles in her dress with one nervous hand. This would never do to worry the little imp. The child had the gift of insight and seemed to have an uncanny way of knowing what was on another's mind. For once in her young life she was free of worries and Sarah had no intention of changing that.

Reaching the door, Sarah gathered her spirits and forced a smile. There would be plenty of time to find Grandfather later. Besides she was through worrying about Simon. A groan escaped her stiff lips. Who was she kidding...she would never be through worrying about Simon. Not as long as one of them drew a breath. And with that telling admission still fresh on her mind, she pushed open the door and went inside.

An hour later, after rereading the story of "Cinderella" for the third time, Sarah closed the book and suggested, "How about playing outside for awhile? The sun has been calling my name all morning. Why, just look at those rays reaching out to us through the window. I have no doubt that if we succumb, and lay on our backs atop Mr. Garth's freshly cut grass...well, it is said on a beautiful day, if you peer really hard up into the sky, you just might get a glimpse of heaven itself."

Lucy's jumping up and down was answer enough. However her squeal of excitement suddenly died. Her face grew thoughtful before saying words that tore at Sarah's heart. "Oh, I hope that is true. Who knows, maybe you will even get to see your mummy, if I pray really hard. You seem especially sad today. I get that way too sometimes when I think no one will want me for a little girl. Did Simon make you sad? Donavon says he erases smiles, did he erase yours?"

Tweaking the end of her nose, Sarah smiled affectionately at the barrage of words, "No. And you must not listen to Donavon about Simon. After all, he is probably still sulking about the warrior's lecture on his lack of good manners at the Ladies tea the other day."

"Did he lecture the big lady with the funny hat too?"

A giggle escaped Sarah's stern look, "I hardly think so. Although I agree that she could have used one of Simon's lectures."

Lucy fell into a fit of giggles before landing in a pile on Sarah's lap.

A short time later, hand and hand climbing down the stairs, the small girl turned big blue eyes up at Sarah. "I've been thinking Miss Sarah, if Donavon is wrong about Master Simon, could he be wrong about me never being adopted? I mean might someone want me for a little girl, like Master Simon says? If I'm very, very good."

Sarah bent over and raised the tiny hand up for a kiss. Then she looked deeply into Lucy's expectant face. "How could anyone not want a sweet girl like you for a daughter? Why they would be blessed indeed. Grandfather says children are like salt. They add flavor to a dull world."

The smile she bestowed on Sarah was bright enough to rival any feeling of gloom that might still be lingering. "I rather like that, Miss Sarah."

Giving her a hug, Sarah rose and stretched the kinks out of her body from sitting most of the day. "We'd better hurry. Donavon plans on visiting the orphanage with you and Lady Conway, after your nap this afternoon. And that leaves very little time for woolgathering or peeping up into heaven."

They only stopped once on their way out the door. Gathering a curled up Polly from her warm place in front of the kitchen embers, Lucy chatted on unceasingly. Questions on heaven were high on her list of topics. "I hope when God gives me a family they have a baby boy. Mine went to heaven right before I was sent to live with the sisters. Sister Elizabeth said he got too cold. If I get another one, I'll share my blanket with him each and every night. Do you think maybe I'll get to talk to my baby brother today? If we see heaven and all, I mean." Then her light eyebrows knit together deep in concentration. "Can babies talk in heaven?"

Sarah laughed and swung the little girl up into her arms. "Of course they can, and much better than down here."

The sun did wonders to lift Sarah's spirits. After a game of ball, Lucy settled in to playing with Polly, the kitten. Sarah choose those moments of peaceful solitude to cut flowers from the garden, the whole time imagining how much brighter the nursery would be full of children and flowers. The smell of roses completely covered the small garden. Yet, with all the beauty and peace surrounding her, she could not take her mind off Simon.

Sitting around doing absolutely nothing all day was as foreign to her as the clothes she wore. The kitten attacking a silver ribbon dangling from Lucy's dress forced a giggle from the child and drew Sarah's attention. She walked over, settling down on the grass, her peach dress splayed about her in a shiny sea of satin, as a lap full of yellow and white roses added more beauty to the scene.

And that is precisely the picture Simon took in, walking down the stone path leading to the two beautiful ladies. One was a smiling fairy with blond hair, the other a dusky-skinned enchantress who had stolen his heart. The anger he felt earlier dissipated even more when he heard their laughter. How he missed his China bride. The need to take her away from here and make slow sweet love to her until they both forgot all that had happened over the last week overpowered him. Instead, once reaching her, he stood stiffly, with hands clasped behind his back, waiting for her to notice him. It didn't take long.

"Simon!"

The joy on her face was a balm to his ego. Unbidden his own smile answered hers.

"Hello, China. Miss Lucy."

The moment did not last long. Almost instantly, he saw her smile start to fade. Their harsh words two nights ago, intruded on the joy of seeing him. It was obvious from the way her smile slowly evaporated and she began shredding a rose in her lap. Seemingly lost deep in concentration, but noticeably avoiding looking directly at him. His face took on a more serious expression, as he ran a frustrated hand through windblown hair.

Gathering what was left of the flowers from her lap, she started to rise. Simon's firm clasp lifting her easily the rest of the way up from the ground and drawing her chilled body against his own heated one. Breathless, she regained her footing, and took a step back. Looking up at him, she frowned.

Any hope she had that he did not notice how he affected her diminished when she noticed his satisfied smirk.

"Did you miss me sweetheart?"

She chose to ignore his attempt at seduction. "What are you doing here?"

Looking around at the open area for the first time, Simon's frown deepened. "I thought I told you to stay inside."

"It was too beautiful a day for staying inside. Besides you said not to leave the house. I haven't." Leave it to her to be so frazzled from a simple touch. She was rattling again. Then, before she could guard her words, she blurted out, "I thought you weren't coming home until tomorrow."

Coming up between them, Lucy tugged on Simon's coattail, her young voice full of irritation. "Are you going to take Miss Sarah's smile away again? It took ever so long to coax it back, you know."

Confusion momentarily threw him off balance, "Her smile? I wasn't aware I was the villain responsible."

"Her eyes had lights in them, until you started talking. Do you know what I think Sir?"

His lip twitched. "No. What do you think?"

"I think you talk too much. You have that scary kind of voice that just erases smiles."

"And what do you suggest I do instead?"

"Well..." she placed a chubby finger to her chin, as if contemplating the dilemma, and then very seriously she suggested, "Miss Sarah always likes it when I hug her. You could try that."

His eyes darkened with passion as they bore into Sarah's. "I'll consider it. In fact, maybe I'll start work on it right away. I promise you moppet that even if it takes a while, late into the night if need be, I'll return it. Is that satisfactory?"

Pink dusted Sarah's cheeks at the mere mention of Simon working on her smile. Simon on the other hand was grinning from ear to ear. "Will there be anything else I can do for you?"

"Polly ripped my ribbon." Lucy informed him, holding up the offending cat as if to prove her point. Distracted, she seemed totally unaware of the undercurrent of emotion between the two adults thanks to her innocent suggestion.

"So I see. Maybe you should take her into the kitchen. I think cook has some fresh cream sitting on the table. That should put Polly in a better humor."

Nodding seriously, her tight curls bouncing, the child squeezed the yellow tabby happily. "Thank you Sir. Polly does prefer cream to most anything else." Then she turned blue eyes the color of the sky above on Sarah. "May I be excused, Miss Sarah? I don't think Master Simon will steal anymore of your smiles, now that he understands things."

Rumpling her curly head, Sarah smiled warmly, "Of course not. See you at supper, darling."

Then as they watched, Lucy stumbled off, the large kitten held tightly in chubby arms, his feet dangling. Admonishing him the whole way on his poor manners, the little girl gave kisses to the culprit before turning back to wave and entering the open kitchen door.

Simon chuckled. "She is a sassy little thing. I don't know who I feel the most sympathy for, me or Polly. Although, from the looks of things...my money is on Polly."

351

"Grandfather says the tighter you hold on to something, the more chance you have strangling the life out of it. But I guess he never felt so alone in the world like Lucy does. I think that sometimes things do disappear if you let go."

He studied the curve of her face, the soft beauty of her and wondered if she was talking of Lucy, or herself. Doing instinctively what came next, he reached out and took her free hand into his. He felt her physically flinch and it turned his stomach. He didn't want this distance between them. He didn't want her afraid. "Let's take a walk, China. I am sure cook has a vase, or some such thing. Those flowers look as bad off as Polly did."

Sarah relaxed a little. Her smile was genuine. "I would like that."

Their hands comfortably intertwined, they walked towards the house. Simon was just raising his fist to knock, when Cook yanked open the door. "Master Simon. I can't tell you how worried Miss Sarah has been all morning. She bothered all of us about if we'd heard anything. Now why you would be telling the cook your whereabouts is beyond me. Still, we are all" to which she looked pointedly at Sarah, "glad to see you home where you belong.

Sarah blushed. Sometimes the woman talked too much.

Simon gave her a look before cocking an eyebrow.

"Is that so?"

Taking the flowers, she fussed at Sarah further for missing lunch and tried to force a small beef pie on the two of them. With her throat closed in embarrassment and her stomach churning, Sarah couldn't have eaten a bite. However, Cook was a dear sweet soul and she hated to hurt her feelings, as if she would have taken no for an answer anyway. The past two mornings the dear lady had sent up Sarah's favorite green tea with various offerings of food, trying to get her to eat something. No doubt aware, as all the staff was, of her and Simon's estrangement. She could hardly act ungrateful now.

Simon, sensing his wife's dilemma and foreign to how he would normally have handled things, smiled charmingly at the frazzled woman. Automatically, he took the pie before it slid out onto the ground.

"We are most appreciative, my good woman, however I had plans to take my wife out for tea to celebrate..." he paused at a total loss for a moment. Sarah's grin widened, seeing her usually calm husband at a loss for words. "To celebrate our one month anniversary?" He finally managed, before trying to hand the pie back. The cook shoved it back at him, ignoring his attempts at diplomacy.

"Now Sir, what kind of outing would Miss Sarah have with all of England out to give you a piece of their mind." She admonished, the whole while gathering a couple of forks from the counter.

"I assure you it won't be a problem." His voice raised a notch in order to be heard when she disappeared inside once more and came out carrying a couple of linen napkins. She stuffed them into his coat pocket and plucked up a huge bowl full of batter and began whipping it into shape.

"Oh, go on with you Master Simon. Sounding so offended, like one of them heroes in the romance novels." She sighed. "It makes me wonder why I settled on my Mr. Harrison. He is nay on the most unromantic soul a body could marry. Why, you've fired him half a dozen times yourself. He is not an easy man, my Richard, but love is a strange force. Now take that there beef pie and you two have a little picnic instead. I insist."

"Well, I'm sure Harrison is an imbecile to not appreciate a good woman who can cook."

The small round woman, her gray hair sticking out at odd angles from hours in the hot kitchen giggled and swiped at him dangerously with a batter dipped wooden spoon. "Oh, Master Simon, get on with you." And still giggling, she shut the door on the two of them.

Simon left holding the pie.

"Well, China, I suppose we can't fight fate, or well intentioned cooks for that matter. Now, if only I had a bottle of wine, we could..."

The back door swung open, a bottle of wine and two glasses thrust out at them. Simon obediently let go of Sarah and took the offering. The cook's wink raised an eyebrow, before the door shut firmly back in place.

Lifting the objects up in mock surrender, Simon noted, "Well, Harrison may not be a romantic, but his wife definitely is. So, tell me Lady Conway," to which he bowed beautifully, as if asking her to dance at the King's ball, beef pie and wine glasses not withstanding. "Would you care for a picnic in the Gazebo with your smile-stealing husband?"

She curtsied deeply, loving this side of him, and thoroughly charmed. "I would be honored, Sir."

The garden seemed transported into some enchanted forest. Monarchs danced before them, as the sun's rays reflected on the small pond lying in their path. Lily pads covered its' outskirts. The sounds of frogs plopping into the murky water, reminded her of another time someone else had been plopped into the very same water. She frowned. Hilary. The memory made her all too aware, as they crossed the small footbridge that so much was still left unsettled between them. But, for now, Simon's flirtatious mood was contagious. No doubt he was as weary of fighting as she was.

When they reached the secluded spot, surrounded by daisies, he placed two strong hands at her waist and lifted her up on the Gazebo. Eye level now, he slowly leaned in and kissed her sweetly. Effectively melting the walls of steel she thought built securely around her heart. How she loved him. And how she wished she didn't.

The lunch was delicious. The wine relaxing. Simon, unbelievably charming. She hated it to end, but knew it must. None of this changed the decision she must make tomorrow. Looking off over the garden, she wondered what to do. If she were a different kind of woman, she could be happy never knowing the truth about her husband. But she wasn't a different woman. She was Lady Sarah Adams Conway. And for once she wanted to choose her destiny, not have it chosen for her.

"What are you thinking?"

He looked so relaxed, one knee pulled up with an arm resting casually across it.

"You are a most handsome man, Warrior."

She didn't think it possible, but he blushed. After a moment, he remarked, "I hardly think you were dwelling on my good looks. Tell me,

China, what has you so lost in thought? It's rather a blow to my ego when I have been doing my best to charm and dazzle you and you have been someplace else."

With simple honesty, she shrugged. "I was wondering why you are here with me? What I am going to do about us? How to find the rest of my family?" She smiled, "And how utterly charmed I am right now."

"Are you always so honest?"

"I try to be. Besides, my husband of many great secrets, has said I am not a very good liar."

Leaning in closer, he reached out and ran a finger along her delicate jaw line. "You're not. Do you have any idea what a rarity you are? The thought of losing you makes me fluctuate between anger and heart stopping fear. I know I can't make you stay with me sweetheart. But, then again, I can't let you go either."

Her voice, a breathless whisper, warned, "Simon, you mustn't."

He pulled her forward, hand clasping the back of her neck. They were so close now, that she was finding it hard to breathe again. And when he kissed her? It was earth shattering. His passion was as palatable as the taste of wine on his lips. For one glorious moment she let herself soak him up. Saturate her being.

Somewhere in the outer reaches of her consciousness, she was aware that her wine glass had disappeared. That her husband's arms were now encircled around her, as he slowly began to press her down to the floor. The innocent kiss was now turning wild and fully out of control. Fighting for some sort of control before she was lost to him again, she shoved at his chest. "Simon, don't."

His words were tempting as he reigned kisses down her neck, "Are you sure that is what you want, China, for me to stop?"

She fought back from love's passionate haze, her heart pumping furiously. Her senses were all too aware of every part of him. With a sheer strength of will, she broke his hold and nearly his wrist.

Automatically, he let go.

When she gained enough courage to look up at him, his green eyes were glazed over with frustrated desire. "I sincerely wish you would find some other means of coping, every time I kiss you, besides violence. If you are trying to dissuade me, it's working."

Rubbing his wrist, he watched as she tried to regain her own senses. His sarcasm lost on her.

"Simon, I can't do this." She put a trembling hand down and started to rise.

"Sarah, you don't have to go." He looked disgusted. Whether it was with her or him, she couldn't tell. "Here."

She looked down at the envelope he had drawn from his jacket. It's beige, neutral paper looked innocent enough, but the force of the word 'here', held a promise of life changing information.

"What is it?"

The envelope was pressed into her hands. "It is answers sweetheart." He rose to his feet and buttoned back up his shirt. Amazingly, she realized he was not angry with her at all.

"Where are you going?"

"In case you didn't notice, I can't keep my hands off you." His green eyes were full of love for her. "And apparently you're not too keen on the idea. To save me from being black and blue and you from falling into my arms again, I'll leave like I promised. Only before you make a decision about us, I felt you needed all the facts, or at least the ones written on paper. Inside is also a copy of the statement I made to the press today. If you still feel the same way tomorrow after reading it, I'll let you go. No strings attached. However, I have to tell you, I will probably spend a lifetime loving you. Regardless."

Questions bombarded her mind and heart.

"Wait."

A slow sexy smile dimpled his cheek, "Tomorrow. And then, if you'll have me, I plan on doing a lot more than talking. I do have orders to work on those smiles after all." He took a single step down, and then turned back around, his face like flint. Gone was the charmer. "One another thing…"

Wary, Sarah asked, "Yes?"

"I can take care of myself. Those words 'Don't follow me', well, they also include your grandfather. This whole thing is my problem. I don't want anyone else hurt, understood?"

Biting her full lower lip, she nodded.

"Good. Until tomorrow then, Sweetheart."

And then once more, he was gone. But this time, as Sarah looked down at the envelope in her hands, he had left something wonderful behind. He had left her answers..

# Chapter 19

The envelope burned in her hands.

She wanted to open it immediately. Here alone in the privacy of the garden, the place where Simon had given it to her with love shining in his eyes and in his touch.

The scented breeze lifted soft curls at the nape of her neck, reminding her so much of Simon's kisses. The imprint of his strong hand where he had held her was still warm to the touch. Around her were scattered remains of their impromptu lunch, physical evidence of their afternoon together; otherwise she would have wondered if she had dreamed the whole thing.

Slowly she sank down upon the bench. Her legs curled comfortably to one side, she pried the envelope open and pulled out the thick legal documents from its richly adorned interior.

The first page was in Simon's handwriting. His strokes were bold and confident, with the precision of many years in the schoolroom. It was the press release. She read, and then reread it again, to make certain. There was no mistake. He had, in front of the whole city, released not only her real name but cleared her father of any wrong.

Apparently Henry had stood by his side and admitted freely that her father had not been guilty of gambling half the business away. Together, they had both publicly welcomed her into the family, declaring her true title to the world. She was Lady Sarah Ann Adams Conway, heir to the Adams fortune, or lack of one.

She closed her eyes and breathed deeply. For the first time in eight years, not only she, but also the entire world knew who she was. Henry and Simon had spoken the truth, and restored honor to her father at a great sacrifice to their own. Warmth towards the two men who were now her family engulfed her soul. It had been a courageous act, fitting of a warrior.

With a grateful heart she pulled out the next paper. It was a birth certificate, hers. October 7, 1849. In less than one month, she would turn nineteen. She soaked up the information. From her parents legal names, to the property entitled her. Every morsel of information filled up the too long empty hole in her soul.

The next few pages contained more information about her family, but, most important a name. An Aunt. Her Aunt. She put down the paper, her eyes closing with joy. Here was someone who knew more than words on paper. Someone who knew of her past. Knew things, like how her parents met, and her mother's favorite color. This was the answer to her prayers, what she had wished for, her family back.

In this one small stack of papers was everything she hoped for.

Yet if that was so, then why did her heart feel too full? Her lungs constricted? It was as if she could bear to read no more. Regardless, she seemed drawn to do so, the compulsion too strong. Even if her heart burst from all the emotion washing over her, she had to read further.

When at last managing to face the papers again, she drew them closer in towards the fading light. Was it hours or only minutes she had sat there? She poured over the information, again and again looking for anything that might spark a memory. The world no longer existed. Only the very real numbness in her legs, forcing her to get up and walk around periodically, reminded her this was all very real.

Finally on the last page, was the address of her father's solicitor. Although, if what Simon told her was true, there was nothing of her father's small fortune left. It was now all invested in the burned warehouse by the Thames, and one small floundering shipping business. Even that was in a way fitting. For as her father's fortune had been entwined with Henry's, hers was with Simon's. Unwittingly, her father had supported a gambling habit. And she? Possibly a smuggler. In some unbelievable way, it was as if she were destined to repeat the same scenario as her parents. Only this time, the players and scenes were different and she prayed the ending would be too.

It had to be.

For no matter the words staring at her from the stark white paper, she remembered none of it. No great white light. No sudden blinding insight, no memory. And none of what was written here, explained who killed her parents or why.

Nothing in the envelope explained her husband's actions. For example, why he would pretend ignorance of Hilary's whereabouts? He said she was his only lead, which made no sense to her logical brain. He would not let her go if that were true. Unless. The practical part of her brain, not so taken with the warrior's charm, knew he would not have let Hilary go unless he knew either where she went, or else planned a meeting at a later date. It would have been foolhardy otherwise. And Simon was not a fool.

"Hello beautiful. Or, should I now say, 'Lady' Sarah?"

"John." Sarah jumped guiltily, as if Simon's friend could read her thoughts and knew of her doubts about the warrior.

"I usually get an entirely different reaction from the ladies."

His suave nature and teasing tone brought a smile to Sarah's lips. "I'm sorry, my husband's cousin. I assure you it was only my own awakening that startled me. Simon brought me information about my family. I seem to have lost track of everything else."

"Even time?" He admonished lightly, his dark blond hair reflecting the twilight.

Surprised, Sarah looked around. It was nearing dark. The stars less faded in the darkening sky. In wonder, she shrugged, "It appears so." Then remembering her husband, she frowned, "You are not supposed to be here John. I mean, with me. Simon will be most displeased."

"Will he? What if it is he I am searching out?"

"Oh. Well, Simon is not here. He is staying at the club tonight."

"I know."

"Then why are you here?"

His words sounded sultry, full of hidden meaning. Remembering what happened the last time they were alone in the dark, Sarah cleared her throat and rose quickly to her feet. She forced a smile and remarked casually, running her hands down the front of the impossibly crushed dress. "Poor Maggie will be most upset that I have ruined the English dress. If you will excuse me, my husband's cousin, no doubt she is looking for me this very moment."

"Sarah. It's all right. I promise not to ravish you."

Her golden eyes turned dark, "Simon will not like you being here."

"So you said. I have a solution. Don't tell him."

He took a step closer and she automatically put up a hand. "John."

Sighing, he shrugged and leaned back against a stone pillar. "Hey, you can't blame a guy for trying. But, truly, I just wanted to see how you were doing. It has been quite a day. I must say Simon certainly has turned the town upside down with his vote today. Not to mention his statement to the London papers. Then at the front door this afternoon, I am greeted with the words, 'Master Simon is at the club and Miss Sarah is in the garden'. It doesn't exactly sound like you've had an easy time of it. So, I thought you could use a friend."

His understanding brought a sweet smile to her face causing her shoulders to relax instantly. She suddenly felt very silly being so nervous around him. Of course they were friends. They were more than that really. At least in the Chinese culture. A life saved was a debt for a lifetime. "Thank you. But there is nothing to worry about. As you say, so much has happened. But most of it is good. Simon and I just needed time to think. It is a wise person who reflects before embarking on a journey."

He studied her intently. "Just remember if you need a first mate on your journey, I'm here."

She immediately looked down in order to break the impact of his eyes boring into her own. Confused she clutched the envelope to her chest and attempted to brush past him.

He casually blocked her exit with one arm, asking, "So, did the information about your family help clear things up?"

"I beg your pardon?"

"I mean do you remember anything more about that night? I don't mean to pry, but Simon said you think someone murdered your parents. That the man responsible might have been someone they knew. The man, at the very least, used Uncle Henry's coach to hide his identity. If you ask me, that is quite a lot to forget. Even for a child of ten. Did the papers stir any memories?"

His words caused her pause, more than his arm barring her way. "How do you know so much of these things? About the coach? My lost destiny."

There was a slight hesitation before he answered, "It was only your memory that was lost Sarah, not your destiny. This is your destiny. Here. Now."

"You haven't answered my question. How did you know?"

When she refused to be sidetracked, he admitted, "Simon told me. He confided in me today and asked if I could find out anymore about your long lost relatives. I've spent all afternoon knocking doors and inquiring of servants. It seems a waste of time to me, surely if someone had seen anything they would have come forward years ago. But it seemed important to him that I try."

"Unless, they were threatened somehow. Whoever did this thing, my father knew them. So it only stands to reason, someone else might have too."

She felt his eyes studying her in the dark, as if weighing how much he should tell her. "It would seem Simon agrees with you. Something about your mother telling you to run for the coach convinced him."

Going over that night again with John seemed to sap her last bit of energy. "It doesn't really matter, does it? Because regardless, I can remember nothing of that night, or the evil one who participated in it. Perhaps, I never will."

"Perhaps. But maybe it's for the best. I can't see how remembering your parents' death could be good for you."

More comfortable with John's easy manner, she put the papers down and stretched her arms out in front of her, rolled her neck, to ease the ache there. "It is not their death I want to remember, but their lives. Besides, there is still a murderer walking around free. I fail to see how that is best for anyone. But what I feel about it one way or another hardly matters. The memories stay hidden in the shadows of my dreams."

She gave a weak smile. "Grandfather says I must try to search the dark places. Draw out the beast. Maybe then he will not frighten me so. I do not know, sometimes monsters are just monsters even in the light of day, or dressed in tailored clothes. They are still just as frightening."

"No doubt, however Sarah-"

"I really do not want to talk of it this, especially this late. It brings the nightmare."

"What nightmare?"

"What did you come to see Simon about?"

He took the hint, his laughter filling the too quiet night. "All right then. Subject changed. That is the one thing I love about you Lady Conway, your refreshing bluntness."

"Would you stop laughing, someone will hear."

"Sorry." Only he hardly looked it, pushing off the pillar with one shoulder and offering her his jacket. "Shall we?"

She started wringing her hands, "I don't know. Simon-"

"-will be displeased. Yes, so you say. Would you stop worrying? Simon is not himself lately. I assure you, my actions are above reproach. I just want to make sure you make it back to the house safely. Besides I have a favor to ask of you." When she still hesitated, he added, "I promise to slip away into the dark afterwards and no one will be the wiser, even our disapproving Simon."

It felt silly to deny him. Besides, Simon had warned her against being out alone. Surely even in one of his jealous moods, he would see the innocent necessity of John's company. Resigned, Sarah allowed him to slip the jacket onto her shoulders, her eyes dark and searching. "Do you always ignore Simon's instructions?"

"Not always. Do you?"

His wiggling eyebrows made her laugh. "Point taken, my husband's cousin."

"It's John."

"What?"

"My name. It's John. You can stop calling me, 'my husband's cousin'. Believe me, I haven't forgotten you're his wife, as badly as I would like to. I came, because I have information about Simon."

Sarah looked down. "All right..John. I guess I am a little nervous. I can't help but feel I am being a deceiver by being out here in the garden with you. If Simon asks I will have to tell him the truth. I am not good at hiding things."

He stopped and turned her around, forcing her to look at him. "There is nothing to be nervous about, or to hide. I will behave myself. I promise." He crossed his heart. Then noting how her eyes still swept the garden, he added in a teasing tone. "However, I must say that if Simon ever happens to get captured by Mexican smugglers again, I will not be so quick to save him."

His words had the desired effect on her. He had saved Simon and her, was it really only three nights ago? Despite everything that had happened, they were family after all. And even in this barbaric country of deceivers, family meant something. Trying to lighten the tension between them, Sarah teased back, "And I thought it was me you saved."

"As a matter of fact it was."

The words spoken so casually held such intense meaning behind them, it sent her senses reeling. Her heart pounding, whether from his words or the implication she didn't know, Sarah chose to ignore both. Instead, she changed the subject once again. "You said you had information about my husband."

John was not a fool. Her tone was short and matter of fact brooking no lead way for his evasion, or further flirtations. He took one last look around as if for spies hiding among the primroses. Then bending down, his deep voice became so soft, that she strained in closer in to hear.

"I am to follow him. It is believed he plans to meet with Hilary very soon now."

The frogs' serenade surely drowned out his words from listening ears. Their footsteps sifting through fallen leaves sounded louder than usual, further covering up their conversation. Yet, despite all of natures camouflage, she was certain that if anyone were near they would hear every whispered word. She leaned in even closer, John's deep voice still carrying easily.

"Then either I help, or arrest him. I imagine that is up to him." He placed a comforting hand over Sarah's trembling one. "I know I sound rather cold and unfeeling, but I assure you the last thing I want to do is arrest Simon. I owe that fool my very life many times over. And not just since we started working for the government either. You can't imagine how angry it makes me that he has put not only me, but you in this spot."

Sarah heard genuine frustration in his voice. "Do you have any idea how many fights he has fought on my behalf, or how many young eyes he blackened just to protect my honor at school? Believe me, it is not easy having a father who is a known coward and a wastrel to boot. All of London was well aware of how he threw away his portion of the inheritance on cards and drink. I suppose I should have been grateful that he denied my birth. But, I wasn't. Being the illegitimate son of a fool is hardly an improvement." He shrugged, his face devoid of feeling. "If it had been left up to my dear father, my mother and I would still be trying to survive on the back streets of London."

Sympathy erased her fears. How strange life was. She would give anything to remember her past, while he on the other hand could never escape his. She stopped to place a comforting hand to his wind chapped cheek, "I had no idea you too knew the pain of losing someone."

He jerked as if she had slapped, instead of caressed him. "Losing someone? Hardly. More thrown away, I'd say. At least your parents loved you and were willing to die so that you could escape. My father refused to acknowledge either of our existences, especially mine. That is until my mother, for once in her sordid life, did the courageous act of going to his solicitor and threatening to expose him if he did not at least set up some sort of trust for me."

The anger radiating from him was so thick it was palatable. Then as quickly as his temper surfaced, it eased back down into the depths of his soul. She shuttered. Such pain. How awful that underneath that carefree front, dwelt a hurt and angry boy.

"But you are not like your father. You have a home with Uncle Henry, a profession, even friends. Grandfather says the pull of one's ancestors is very strong. That it takes a great man to live his own life apart from them."

Letting go of her hand, John turned away and said softly, "I am hardly great, and maybe not so different from my ancestors. After all, here I am spying on the two people to whom I owe a great deal. I hardly think that makes me the better man."

She stood there in silence. He was right. Life was hardly black and white. But he was wrong about not having a choice. "John perhaps you could have someone else follow Simon. Then you would not feel so torn. Maybe you could even help clear his name."

He cut her off angrily, "Believe me, no one wishes things could be different more than I, but they can't. Don't you imagine I have tried to think of some other way out of this? But it is no use. Perhaps we all do have a destiny that can't be escaped and it is just foolish to try."

"I don't believe that. Every man's destiny is influenced by choice. Whether yours, or another's." Her voice drifted off into uncomfortable silence.

John pretended not to notice the sympathy on her face. As if it confused him further and dampened his resolve. "Look, I didn't come out here to talk philosophy. Just to let you know what was going on."

"I think you came out here for more than that."

"What?"

"Why tell me any of this? I am Simon's wife. It makes little sense to tell me your secrets. That is, unless there is some other reason."

She gathered her wits and tried to dispel the feeling of being found out. As if Simon, himself were watching the two of them. John gripped her hands so tightly she winced.

"I forget you're not quite like other English girls, are you? All right then, the truth is I came in an effort to protect you. I don't think you understand how dangerous this all is. I want you forewarned, in case Simon tries to use you."

"He would not."

366

She was grateful for the darkness and the cool autumn air. Both helped cover the way her hands trembled when she withdrew them from his grasp and clutched at John's huge coat wrapped around her.

"Sarah, you're not being logical."

"And you are slandering my husband's honor."

Heaving a great sigh, John took a step back, clearly at a loss how to get through to her. "I only want to help."

"If that is true, then we will not talk of what you think my husband might be doing. Only what you know for sure."

"All right." He drew out his gloves and shoved his hands into their soft leather interior. "What do you want to talk about?"

Wishing better to understand the man she had married. Not to mention, bring their conversation around to something more comfortable, she asked casually, "What was Simon like when he was a boy? Our marriage happened so quickly that I hardly know anything about his past. And you, as his friend, knew him best."

John looked up from his task at the beautiful woman trying to make amends and finally gave in to her charm with a half smile of defeat. "A man could hardly refuse when you look at him that way."

They passed a white iron bench. Smoothly, John twirled her around into its depths.

"Whatever you wish, 'my cousin's wife'."

She laughed softly at his barb. "Oh, I suppose it would be all right for you to call me Sarah."

He raised an eyebrow. "Are you sure Simon will not be 'displeased'?"

"How very ungallant of you to mock me." She teased back in a false English tone. Foreign from her usually forthright manner of speaking, John rolled his eyes.

"Now tell me about Simon."

The bushes rustled in the light October breeze and both people jumped guiltily. Adrenaline made Sarah's heart pound and John shout out, "Who goes there?"

Once more Sarah caught the cool confidence of the man she knew no better than her own husband. When no one answered, John motioned for her to be quiet and prepared to go in after the intruder. As if sensing his intentions, a shadowy figure finally emerged from the bushes. Surprised, Sarah shook her head. Apparently she wasn't the only one intimidated by the fierceness in John's tone.

"It's only me. For goodness sake John, there is no need to bite my head off."

To both their surprises, a shrub covered Kate stepped out into the faint moonlight. She gave a sheepish grin. Leaves were stuck to her dark hair, and her fawn colored dress dirt smudged and sporting a tear in the right sleeve.

John's eyes narrowed in on her. "How long have you been standing there?"

The young girl's chin rose a notch. "Long enough to know you are shamefully flirting with Sarah. Simon will be-"

John rolled his eyes heavenward, "I think we all know how Simon feels. But, that hardly excuses your conduct, does it Briar?"

"I thought I told you never to call me that again. I am quite grown up after all."

The words spoken from the scraggly haired urchin standing before them caused Sarah to choke on suppressed laughter. "Kate. Do come and sit down. John was just going to tell me what Simon was like as a boy. Now Simon could hardly object to that, could he?"

Indecision wrinkled the young woman's forehead. She looked from Sarah to John and back again. Then her innocent trusting nature won out. She shrugged her shoulders and plopped down alongside Sarah. "I suppose your right. After all, how could anyone really be jealous of John? He's well, John."

"Thanks ever so much Briar. Your flattery knows no bounds."

Kate looked ready to start another argument. Wishing to continue their conversation, Sarah laid a soothing hand on Kate's. "So what is your favorite memory of Simon?"

Distracted by Sarah's question, Kate turned her back on John's satisfied smirk. "I guess it was our tree house."

"Our tree house? I believe it belonged to Simon and me. You were an interloper."

"John." Sarah warned in an exasperated tone.

He bowed in defeat and thoughtfully looked about the garden as if there might be even more unwelcome souls lurking in the shadows.

"Personally, I hardly think a tree house belongs to anyone. However, I did love sneaking up there at sunset. It was so quiet and peaceful."

The word 'sneaking' was not lost on Sarah. No doubt Kate had indeed been a thorn in the young boys' side. Still, Sarah felt for Kate as the younger sister. She must have been as lonely as Sarah growing up.

"You can't imagine how magnificent it was being huddled up among the branches of that great ancient towering oak. It was like sitting on top of the world and spying down on the people below. I always wondered if that is how God feels looking down on us. Him seeing us, but we remain unaware of Him."

"Could you stay on the subject Kate? I have some things I still wish to discuss with Sarah."

Frowning, so that her rosebud mouth pinched up in a wad, she drooled, "Anyway."

John sighed impatiently, but kept quiet.

"The rope ladder always reddened my hands, but it was worth it. In fact, I always considered it my special 'constant'. Always there. Always strong and guiding me upwards. At least, until that awful day. How I would have gladly given anything for the familiar pain."

"What happened?"

Kate's eyes widened with remembered fear. "I don't know how exactly, but the rope was not there when I got ready to climb down. I panicked. I called out so long, that I remember my voice became hoarse and raw. It must have been hours by the time I finally gave up and just dissolved into uncontrollable sobs. For you see, there was no moon that night."

369

"It was not that dark, or late."

"I was seven." Kate shot back at John, as if that explained everything. "Anyway," she continued once again, "I decided to try and climb down like the boys did sometimes while playing pirates. I had no choice after all. Being as the owls would soon be flying about."

"The owls?"

John answered Sarah's question in a bored voice, "We made up a little story"

"Hardly, little. You said that if seven-year-old girls were out after dark on a moonless night, that owls often mistake them for rabbits. They swoop down with their claws extended and snatch them up, flying off until they reach the sea."

"It was a harmless joke. No one thought you would be silly enough to believe it."

"You said they would carry me off to the top of the cliff and feed me to their young!"

Sarah quickly wiped the grin from her face when Kate turned back around.

Suspiciously, Kate eyed both people for signs of laughter. Finding only John's disinterested expression and Sarah studying her intently, she continued.

"As I was saying, I had no choice."

John snorted.

"I didn't. Well, anyway...I got stuck half way down. I was stretched out belly down on a thick extended branch, the ground swimming beneath me. My skinny legs dangled, but just out of reach of the next limb. I could not climb up, or down. You can't imagine how relieved I was when at last I heard Simon's voice calling up to me. I started crying and laughing at the same time. I still don't know how he managed it, but somehow he found a way up that huge tree. Then together, we started down. His hand guided me. His words were calm and reassuring. He was so patient. I guess that was the moment he became my hero."

"Why didn't he call your parents for help?"

"Oh, he knew I would get in trouble."

"Which you deserved."

Kate slapped her leg in frustration, "John, who is telling this story?"

When he shrugged, she turned once more to Sarah, "In fact, he never told on me. I guess I pretty much adored him after that. And, well, he has been looking out for me ever since. Protecting me from danger and some people's," she glared at John, "humorless pranks."

Sarah nodded with understanding. "He snatched you from heaven. In China, it is believed that if a person saves you, from then on your lives are bound. The warrior became your protector. It is the way of things."

"Warrior? I never thought of it like that, but you know, it makes sense." Eagerly, Kate asked, "Is that what happened between your grandfather and you? He saved your life and now he must guard it?"

"Yes. He fought the evildoer who killed my parents. Because of him, my destiny was changed."

"If he fought the man, surely he must remember him." John interrupted.

For some reason, Sarah was reluctant to involve John further. Whether it was because of Simon, or years of suppression, she didn't know. And despite the seemingly lack of interest on John's face, there was a wariness creeping along her spine. Something was not as it seemed. Maybe John was right and they were not alone in the garden. Whatever it was, she no longer felt comfortable talking about what grandfather had discovered.

Rather than answer him directly, she laughed uneasily. "I am afraid it was many years ago. A night so dark, that even the few scattered stars were covered by clouds."

Her voice trailed off. She thought of Grandfather. Surely he must remember something. John was right. One did not fight hand to hand and not peer into his opponent's eyes. Perhaps if she could find some old pictures of the family, Grandfather might recognize someone.

A lantern bobbed on the back veranda, the light splintering through the vine covered stone baluster encircling it. A muffled call reached their ears.

"We'd better go back inside. And you had better disappear, before Simon finds out you were even here." Kate pointedly looked past John into the dark night.

The bobbing lantern was drawing nearer.

Sarah tried to push John toward the shadows of the garden. "She's right. You have to leave. Now."

"Sarah, first you have to promise me something."

She had made more promises than she could keep the last couple of days. One more would surely make little difference. "As you wish. But then, you must go."

Kate shifted uncomfortably back and forth in indecision. "I'll go see, if I can do something." She threw up her hands in frustration, before throwing over her shoulder. "Honestly John, sometimes you act just like your father. Flaunting convention and expecting the rest of us to cover up for you."

Sarah felt John's hand tighten around her upper arm. Wishing to soften Kate's words, Sarah whispered, "I am sure she did not consider her words. But you must go. I want no more arguments with Simon this night. I am simply too weary."

He nodded as if in agreement, but pulled her with him behind a fledgling cherry tree.

"There is only this one thing. If Simon asks you to go with him to meet Hilary, don't go."

"I can hardly refuse. It is my destiny to protect him."

He shook her gently. "Must you always argue with me? Don't you understand? I may be forced to take care of things. I don't want you there."

His words were ominous, suspended between them, demanding to be recognized. But she was afraid that once acknowledged, they would somehow become undeniable. She sucked in air, her voice a horrified whisper. "What are you saying?"

"I don't want you there. Not just for your sake, but for Simon's as well. If he were thinking clearly, he would not keep putting you in danger like this. Does he really care so little for you?"

His words were like a slap in the face. With a trembling hand, she pried him loose from around her arm. For as his fingers dug into her flesh, his words dug into her soul. With more control than she felt, her words sounded strangely calm and clear. "Fear guides your words, therefore I will forgive them. You understand little of what is behind my relationship with the warrior."

Shaking his head, John brushed a lock of hair out of his eyes. "I'm sorry Sarah. I am just worried about you."

Kate was talking furiously just out of earshot. Vaguely, Sarah heard the approach of Henry and his daughter, the latter talking endlessly about the lace on her Queen Ann costume for the masquerade ball. Still, Sarah stayed rooted to the spot, feeling the need to change John's mind. Only she couldn't really. Her husband and John were distant now because of her. Even now, she wondered what else John knew and wasn't telling her?

Instead, she looked into the familiar Conway eyes, their worried depths revealing his true feelings. She glimpsed, for just a moment, the hurt little boy covering his pain in class clown antics and the man who even now tried to shield her from the truth. He believed he would have to kill Simon. He didn't want her there if he did.

Kate was losing her battle of distraction. Her words were now easily understandable. A few more feet and they would be discovered. Yet, John refused to let go of her hands, demanding her promise with his eyes.

"I've heard enough of lace daughter. Now, where is Sarah, confound it?" Then an oaf was heard as Henry must have stumped his toe on something. "What in blazes is a stone fairy doing in a good English garden anyhow!"

Sarah could not promise to stay away. It was impossible. Her grandfather's teachings were strong within her. Her memory already lost. If she had no honor and no beliefs, then she had nothing. She would be nothing. She took a step back and raised her head a notch calling his bluff. She would not make a promise she could not keep. Even if Simon did not ask her to go, she would follow him. It was her destiny. Yes, even if that meant stopping John from killing a traitor.

Apparently her thoughts were evident. John took a step back as well, until the shadows swallowed him up, leaving nothing but his words to haunt her. But before he left, she did not imagine the sadness and resignation, lurking in his eyes. Yes, it was as if some monumental decision had been made for the both of them. A brush of cold English air sent goose bumps scurrying over her body. She had chosen a side, Simon's. In doing so, she must now suffer the consequences.

"I'm sorry Sarah."

With those final words, John left. His coat still protecting her from the English cold, but nothing could protect her from the meaning of his words. It was not an apology for past wrongs, that he offered her. No. What he apologized for, lay in the future. And that chilled her blood more than any winter blast ever would.

After supper and dodging more questions, Sarah slipped off into the library where Grandfather was engrossed in his writing. Books lay open all over Simon's desk. His papers shoved out of the way, some littering the floor in haphazard fashion. Sarah automatically squatted down and began gathering up the strays. Simon, no doubt would be displeased enough to know Grandfather had taken temporary residence at his desk, much less left it in such a mess.

Very few but Sarah understood that Grandfather wrote where an idea surfaced. As if it resided there alone. And he did not surface until spent. Even now, as she crawled about on her knees, he continued scribbling away. Her grandfather, so lost in writing, never even acknowledged her presence when she pushed at his leg to retrieve one bill of sale from under his shoe.

Finally, once the scattered papers were stacked neatly on the file cabinet, Sarah cleared her throat. Glancing at the mahogany clock, its hands indicating twenty minutes had already passed, she cleared her throat again. This time, a little louder. Her grandfather's spectacled face looked up in surprise to see her standing there, waiting.

"Ah, Little One. I did not sense your presence. What time is it?"

Sarah laughed. Why did it always feel wonderfully safe around him? As if nothing ever changed, even time. "I think, Grandfather, your books have captured your mind and stolen your hearing. I have been in the room this past twenty minutes now. Or then again, maybe you are simply becoming too old. Your instincts are becoming as rusty as a hinge on an old battleship."

He raised a reddish eyebrow. Then pushed back his manuscript, and removed his spectacles. Rubbing the bridge of his nose, he asked, "Do you know what I believe, my most disrespectful granddaughter?"

Eyes twinkling, Sarah answered, "No. What?"

"I would rather hear little and understand much, then hear much and understand little. Who were you talking with in the garden?"

Shocked that he knew about John, she sank down on the embroidered seat across from him, "How did you know?"

He slowly placed his small-framed glasses down on the desk and serenely pondered that question before answering. And when he did, he answered simply. "I am aware of everything. I am a very wise man after all."

Seeing the amazement on her face, he gave a slight smile, "And I saw you out the window."

"Grandfather, that is not terribly funny. Not with all this talk of spies and ancestors lurking about."

"A woman who has nothing to hide, is afraid of neither. What secrets hold you hostage, Little One?"

She blushed at his subtle reprimand. Thoughts of John's conversation and even more telling, what he didn't say, was still fresh on her mind. "John came to warn me. He says my husband is a deceiver. That it is possible he could be dangerous."

"What did you say?"

Unable to sit a moment longer, she quickly rose to her feet and tried to explain, "I defended him, of course. But, although my heart pounded with denial?"

"Yes?"

"My mind sees the truth of things."

"And that is?"

She sighed, standing a little straighter, before forcing the words through her lips. "It is possible."

"I see."

His voice sounded so serene, neither judging nor denying. Even as he listened, his movements were slow and thoughtful. Finally, after a long pause in which she had been holding her breath, he added, "He is not the evil one who attacked you that night long ago, if that is what you fear granddaughter."

Relieved Sarah sank down on her knees before the old man. Tears of relief shone in her golden eyes. "I was so afraid it might be true, but if not him, then who?"

The China man seemed suddenly years older than his sixty odd, as he patted her hands resting in his lap. Then slowly he arose and crossed over to the window. His reflection was solemn in the dark beveled glass. At long last he turned back around to face her. "I am not completely sure, the truth is still hidden from me. However, there is one I suspect."

"Why didn't you say something sooner?"

"To you, Little One? Do you not know that the evil one would destroy you if he thought you knew his identity? For some reason right now he chooses to remain unknown. Therefore your ignorance protects your life."

"Can you not tell me anything else? Surely such a man as he could turn in a moment. Change his mind. Then how safe would my ignorance be?"

Tapping a thoughtful finger to his nose, the old man nodded. "Yes, knowledge is power. However your face betrays your thoughts. It would not be safe for you to be aware, at least not until I am sure."

She started to argue, but his look quelled her instantly.

"I will tell you this however. The man does have a mark of a warrior on his arm. This I remember."

"A tattoo? What kind? Where is it?"

The China man raised his hand in mock surrender. "Slowly, Granddaughter. It was very dark that night. Yet when we were doing battle, I ripped the sleeve of his knife hand in an effort to take his weapon. It was then I noticed the mark. It was the serpent wrapped around a moneybag. A single word beneath. An odd word my stilted English did not recognize."

"Twister." Sarah finished for him, her voice no more than a whisper. Her face drained of her normally healthy glow.

Lee barely managed to reach her stricken form, as her voice whispered over and over, the one word her brain remembered. He gently guided her onto the sofa. Her face was ashen, and her hands ice cold. "What did you say granddaughter?"

"That night," she closed her eyes remembering her mother's screams. The fat one's voice yelling, and then there was a woman's voice calling out angrily from inside the carriage. "There was a woman inside the carriage. I did not remember until a moment ago. She called the one who chased me...'Twister'."

She was shaking. The China man placed a glass of sherry in her hands. "Drink this, Little One. It will help warm you."

Still not use to spirits, she sputtered as the liquid burned its way down her throat. But true to his word, after a bit, the shaking did ease. Fortified, she forced herself to continue. "What does it mean, Grandfather? What kind of name is it?"

The lamplight flickered on the wall, as the wind picked up outside. The sound of fallen leaves swirling against the window further added to the eerie feeling inside of her. It seemed as if at long last her nightmare had come to life. No more did it hide in the shadows. Good or bad, she had drawn it out into the open. Vaguely, she noticed her grandfather shifting through his papers and mumbling to himself in irritation.

"What is the matter?"

He brushed back a strand of wiry hair from his long pigtail and said triumphantly, "I know this word. I just cannot remember its meaning. It is in these papers somewhere."

Now forgotten as he hunted through scattered notes, Sarah placed her half empty glass onto the table and rose on shaky legs. "I will help you look."

He looked up suddenly, as if just then taking in her wrinkled clothes and stricken expression. Instantly, he stopped what he was doing and embraced her, letting her rest a moment against his steady breathing. Gaining comfort from the familiar sound of his heartbeat against her ear, she began to relax. Finally, after her breathing evened, he lifted her chin and spoke to the trusting child within her. "This evil has lain dormant for many days now. One more will hardly matter. We will both sleep on it. Then, tomorrow we will solve this riddle."

Grateful for his common sense and that she was not alone, Sarah gave a weak smile before bowing in respect. "As you wish, my most honored teacher and protector."

"And you will not let the evil one steal your dreams this night."

It was not a question, and even that further comforted her. "I will not. For I have a great, if rather ancient warlord, who guards me well."

He grinned slightly at her proud words. Knowing her trust in him was great, he bowed in return, promising, "I will gladly give my life to protect yours Little One."

Catching his look of promise, her eyes shone with heartfelt love. "And I yours, Grandfather."

There was no more to be said. If evil came this night, he would have two worthy opponents and that is all anyone could hope for in a world of treason and lies. One true and loyal friend. It would have to be enough.

So, after climbing the massive stairs that seemed to grow higher with each tired step, she entered her room and slipped off the wrinkled mass that barely resembled a dress. Then, lying only in her chemise, she curled up under the thick gold and brown coverlet that still smelled of Simon and slept. Her last coherent thought was of her husband.

He was not the green eyed one who killed her parents after all. Tomorrow he would come home to her. Surely with Grandfather's wisdom and Simon's strength, they would find the one called 'Twister'. Then the nightmare would no longer haunt her. At long last, she would have the life stolen from her, returned. Her parent's memory restored. And for once when she awoke in the mornings, she would finally know who Lady Sarah Adams Conway really was.

# Chapter 20

The sound of birds arguing out the window drew Sarah from her sleep. The room was chilly and the sun unusually bright for October. It was a good day to be alive. There was a deep feeling of joy welling up inside her heart this morning, as gingerly she pulled back the covers and slid slender legs to the floor. As if this would be a day of new beginnings.

Humming to herself, she went about her toilette. Only the cold water in the pitcher looking dauntingly back up at her threatened to ruin her renewed optimism. For a moment she thought about pulling the bell rope by her bed and asking that warm water to be sent up. But that would be a hardship on the staff downstairs preparing for breakfast. Shaking her head at how quickly one adapted to luxury, even at the expense of another's comfort, she decided against it. She was not that encroached in the ways of her husband. At least, not yet. So, holding her breath in anticipation of the assault of cold to her senses, she splashed the water as quickly as possible over her face.

She was so lost in the act of torture, that she never even heard the door open and someone step into the room.

"If you planned on seducing me, China, it's working."

"Simon!"

Taken by surprise, she spun around and Simon had to remind himself to breathe. With damp ringlets softly framing her face and droplets of water trailing down into the top of her pink ribboned camisole it took every ounce of willpower he had to resist taking her right back to the rumbled bed where she had obviously just risen from. Oh, he would touch her. It was asking too much of a man, not to. Just not right this moment. There was still so much he wanted to tell her. Explain.

She nervously bit her lower lip trying to regain some semblance of control.

He lost his.

Her eyes widening as he started moving towards her, she held up a restraining hand. "Simon, I wanted to thank you for your gift."

He didn't stop, or even slow down for that matter. He had the look of a warrior in his eyes. One she recognized at once…and it nearly made her smile.

Her own breathing was becoming short and rapid. And when he reached her, she meant to say something wise and aloof. Yes, that is what she intended. At least, that was what she told herself, until his dark head dipped down, his tempting mouth barely out of reach.

At this point, all she could manage was, "You're back." And even then she wasn't exactly sure if she had said the words, or breathed them.

"Kiss me, China."

And those beautiful words stole what little will power she had left. Not only stole, but threw out all the reasons why they must remain apart. In fact, to be honest, she couldn't even remember one of them. Whether her walls had been chipped away during their impromptu picnic in the garden yesterday. Or whether, the envelope he left behind had caused the change. She didn't know. But now all that remained between them, was this unquenchable need that only he could satisfy.

Obediently, she stretched on tiptoes and touched her lips softly to his. Then the room swirled around her and heat wrapped her in its arms, as Simon groaned deeply in response. His answering kiss was more desperate, more passionate than anything she had ever felt.

"I need you Sarah. I know there is so much that needs saying." He looked deeply into her eyes, his breathing shallow. Then he gave a self depreciating grin before admitting, "But the truth is, well, right now talking to you is the last thing on my mind."

She wished he would keep kissing her and stop trying to be so noble. With her heart in her eyes, she answered simply and honestly, "I need you too and I don't feel like talking either."

Suddenly she was lifted in strong arms, his assault on her senses mind jarring. Then she felt the bed give way, as he gently laid her down on top of it before slowly starting to remove his jacket.

"Simon"

He gave her a heated look and shook his head, "Don't ask me to stop."

A slow sexy smile reached out and touched him, right before her hands pulled him in closer. Then very deliberately she started undoing buttons, "I was just going to say...you're taking too long."

It was all the invitation he needed. Soon both were past the point of no return. Soaking each other up as a desert soaks up a warm summer rain. They had been alone for far too long. Every touch seared. Every kiss branded. And as the world fell away and they into each other's arms, they both knew this time was different. As if, there was the promise of a kind of loving neither had ever known before, one born of trust.

Yes, Sarah thought, as strong hands slid possessively down her body. From now on they would face the world with all its joys and heartaches together. Some might call it a romantic pipe dream, but she knew the truth. It was much more than that. It was destiny.

They missed breakfast.

They would have missed lunch, as well, if not for the unceasing pounding on their door.

"Sarah. Can you hear me?"

"The dead could hear her", mumbled a still groggy Simon.

Grinning at her husband's complaint, Sarah sat up, pulling the sheet up along with her. Simon started distracting her, placing sweet sexy kisses along one shoulder. Blushing, she called out in a voice, gravelly with spent passion. "I am awake, my husband's sister."

The doorknob rattled, "Well, open up. The seamstress has been cooling her heels down in the parlor for the last twenty minutes. We still have our final fitting. Or did you forget?" She rattled the doorknob again. "For heaven's sake Sarah, what in the world is taking you so long?"

"Well, I am not exactly dressed. I mean, properly. For...you know... dressing."

"You are making absolutely no sense Sarah." Exasperated Kate shouted through the door, "Are you going to let me in or not?"

"What my wife is so delicately trying to tell you, dear Kate, is that she is not alone."

A horrified gasp was heard from the other side of the door then dead silence. Kate's embarrassment so palatable, it was felt through the thick oak door. When she did speak again, it was at a far greater distance away. "Well, then. I'll just be going. But, do hurry Sarah. We have the mask ball tonight and there is much to be done. Not to mention, father is searching for you Simon. So I suggest-"

Groaning and sitting up the rest of the way alongside his wife, Simon massaged the bridge of his nose and interrupted, "Unless you're out of here in exactly one minute Kate, I will open that door."

Another, more horrified gasp than before, made Sarah roll her eyes at Simon. She didn't know who he was embarrassing more, her or Kate. But apparently the threat worked. The sound of his sister's hasty retreat left little doubt that entering the room was no longer a priority.

Sarah slapped at her husband's muscled shoulder. "Warrior, I shall never be able to go downstairs now."

"Really?" With a look of devilment in his eyes, he bent over and whispered. "Well, then I guess we shall have to find something else to do to occupy the time."

She laid a restraining hand on the solid wall of chest pushing her back down onto the bed. "And what of the seamstress?"

He was nibbling on her ear now. She closed her eyes in response to the temptation.

"And then there is the ball tonight."

"Are you going to stop talking anytime soon sweetheart, because your wasting that poor woman's time cooling her heels in the parlor. You see, before I let you go? I fully intend on having my way with you at least one more time."

So she did. Stop talking, that is.

She was starving when they emerged from their room an hour later. Unfortunately, they still had not spoken of the ball, or what she had discovered last night with Grandfather. To make matters worse, Simon took one look at the hustle and bustle of activity downstairs and decided to abandon her to his family.

With a quick peck to her forehead as she protested, he promised to see her later. Then before she could stop him, he left by the servant's stairs, leaving her to face the knowing glances and sly grins that were sure to come from Kate.

"Traitor." She whispered to the now empty hall. Sometimes the way he disappeared reminded her of the phantom warriors of Grandfather's stories. The ones who gave impossible orders to save the kingdom, then left the responsibility of accomplishing the task to their followers. Perhaps he was not flesh and blood after all, but some spirit sent to tempt her. Steeling herself for the long day ahead, she descended the stairs, her mind lost in thought about all she must accomplish before the ball tonight.

The most important one being, finding Grandfather, before Kate found her. No doubt, it would take the better part of an afternoon for the two of them, shifting through all his papers to find what the name Twister meant. So far, it was their only lead.

Once reaching the bottom of the stairs, her stomach instantly started growling. On second thought, maybe she would first have something to eat. Then, find Grandfather. Peeking around the corner, and seeing several people in the parlor, she sighed happily. Now just a few more steps and she would be feasting on cook's rice pudding.

The aromas of a just cleared lunch assaulted her senses and beckoned her forward. Her mouth watered in anticipation, and she would have made it too. If it hadn't been for Kate, blocking her path.

"Oh, there you are. Honestly, mother is fit to be tied. The seamstress already left, so your costume will just have to do."

"Kate, could we talk about this later. I'm famished. I promise to be right back after I get something to eat."

As she drug Sarah away from the dining room and into the parlor, Kate admonished her, "Oh, no you don't. There is no time for that. The dance master is here. Since this will be your first function as a hostess, mother thought you could use a little more instruction. Most of the ton will be here and last time you seemed a little..."

"Inept?"

Kate blushed and pushed open the door. "You just need a little more practice."

Sarah's stomach protested loudly. Putting her hand to it, she remarked logically, "Believe me, my husband's sister, it will not help. I have tangled feet."

A soft giggle came from Kate, "It is two left feet. Not tangled ones."

A frown marred the young woman's features as she was yanked into the room. "This is not possible. Two left feet."

"I didn't mean literally, I meant...oh, stop confusing me. Mr. Jacobs is waiting."

A small wiry man with glasses looked up from his pounding away at piano keys and nodded her direction. The ticking of a meter on the piano's polished top irritated Sarah's already taunt nerves. This was not in her plans.

"I hate the dancing ritual."

"So you said last time too, dear. Don't be silly." Stella chided, coming up and giving her a reassuring hug. "No woman truly hates to dance. You're just a little nervous. That is what these lessons are for, to build up your confidence."

"One can only gain confidence if one improves," mumbled a disgruntled Sarah. But, as she had been taught by her grandfather to respect her elders, she obediently followed Simon's mother over to the Piano.

They had barely gotten started when Maggie's headless body hurried in, almost tripping over the Persian rug gracing the middle of the room. Her voice bellowed out through the hugest bouquet of flowers Sarah had ever seen. "Where will you be a needing these things put, Miss?"

"Oh, I think the dining room would be appropriate, what do you think Sarah?"

Besides thinking she wished she could be carried into the dining room herself, she hadn't a clue. "I am sure they will look most appealing, my husband's mother."

A small frown puckered her features as Stella leaned in to whisper, "You must call me mother, or Stella dear. Remember we discussed this earlier. It makes you sound a little foreign otherwise. And the ton is very peculiar about foreign people. Although some, like the French, do seem to pull it off."

Interrupting Stella's confused rambling, Sarah answered meekly, "Yes, my husband's...I mean honored mother."

"No, dear. Just mother will do. Now where were we? Oh, yes. The lesson."

"I really don't need dance lessons."

"Where is Simon? Don't tell me he's left already."

"Well, actually he has."

"What is that boy thinking? He knows we have the benefit tonight?"

No doubt he was thinking about his escape from the dreaded Mr. Jacobs, thought Sarah.

Albert chose that particular moment to enter the room. His back, ramrod straight in disapproval, announcing, "Sir John has arrived, madam. He asks permission to speak to Lady Sarah. And despite being informed she was otherwise occupied, he insists on waiting." He threw an accusing look Sarah's direction. "Refuses to budge, I believe were he exact words. I then reminded him it was highly improper to be visiting a married woman in private. To which he responded, in a most ungentlemanly fashion."

"Albert," Stella scolded, distracted by the sheets of music she had been picking through. "John is hardly anyone to be wary of, he is family after all. By all means, show him in."

For once Sarah was glad for John's insistence on seeing her. The dreaded dance lessons would have to wait, which was a good thing. And perhaps, he would even know of someone nicknamed Twister. But first she would steer him by the kitchen and get a huge hunk of cook's brown bread with a thick pat of creamy butter.

Kate stepped in front of Albert, halting him instantly, "I don't think that would be such a good idea right now, Mother. Sarah has dance lessons, after all. And we both know what a poor dancer she is."

Although Sarah raised one eyebrow at the insult, she decided to use the slip up for her benefit. "Kate is right, my hus…Mother. I possess the problem of many left feet. Besides, there really seems no point whatsoever in the hopping about and twirling, you English call dancing. Perhaps I could perform one of my Martial Arts forms for the party instead."

"Absolutely not!" shouted a thoroughly shocked Stella.

"Oh, I didn't mean to say that you were that horrible." apologized Kate, wringing her hands in agitation.

Getting a hold of herself, Stella reprimanded slightly, "Sarah, child. I hope you do not intend to refer to your own class of people in that foreign manner tonight, or do anything…well, not normal. Tonight is important."

Exasperated, Sarah ignored the comment and continued, "I fail to see how stopping me from seeing John would be unwise. After all, he is-"

"A wonderful dancer. Of course, why didn't I think of it sooner?" Her mother-in-law interrupted, grabbing one of Kate's arms and pulling her deftly out of Albert's way, "Send John right in. He can be Sarah's dance partner. Everyone knows there is no better dance partner than John."

"But, mother," Kate looked a little put out. "Simon doesn't want John dancing with Sarah."

Albert sighed and turned back around to wait for further instructions.

Stella waved him on, "Go on Albert, what are you waiting for?"

Rolling his eyes, he turned to leave.

"Wait. Don't you dare get John. Simon will be furious."

Albert stood perfectly still and studied his gloves a moment before turning back around and waiting.

"Don't be silly dear. Now why in the world would Simon object to Sarah dancing with John? Why, they are practically brothers." She looked over one padded shoulder, and commanded. "At once, Albert."

This time he simply looked to Kate, who was shaking her head insistently.

Sarah sat down on the stuffed Victorian chair and toyed with the cherry decanter. Even the dark red liquid looked good to her right now. She was so hungry. Simon, no doubt, was enjoying a nice lunch at that restaurant he had taken her to the other day. Visions of baked fish and flaky rolls made her head swim.

"Because he's jealous, Mother, that is why."

"Well, that is just ridiculous."

"Perhaps, but do you really want to mess things up between Sarah and Simon, right now? I mean this morning I caught them actually...together." Sarah blushed at the goofy face Kate was making in an effort to make her mother understand what she meant by 'together'.

Her mother looked back blankly.

"As in, they missed breakfast."

She still started to turn away, but Kate grabbed her upper arm and blurted out. "He told me to go away, or else he would open the door. It was a threat. Because...they were...alone."

Understanding was now beginning to dawn.

Sarah, on the other hand, knew beyond a doubt she would die of mortification right then and there, if Kate did not shut up.

"Then they didn't come down for another hour."

"Ohhh...I see."

As did Albert and the dance instructor, no doubt.

"Am I interrupting something, Aunt?"asked John.

Awkwardly, Sarah looked down at the suddenly extremely interesting pattern of pink rosebuds on her new day dress. Her hunger now replaced by nausea. If by some miracle, she ever did make it back up to her room, she would curl up under the covers and die of humiliation.

John's eyes were now boring a hole into the top of her head. A guilty blush crept up her neck. What she felt guilty about, she couldn't imagine. Surely even the English could not have created a rule against a wife spending time with her husband.

Feeling ridiculous, pride lifted her tawny head. Her eyes met John's cool green ones. Eyes so like Simon's, yet so different. His were so light they resembled cat eyes. Simon's were dark green like a storm tossed sea. However, regardless of the difference, both men spoke volumes with them.

She wondered if she only imagined the hurt she saw in his. It nearly seemed as if, by being with Simon, she had betrayed John's trust somehow. And then, just as swiftly the look disappeared. His devil may care attitude returning. Rather than leaving, like she thought he might, he walked over and stretched out a hand in invitation.

"If I heard correctly, you are in need of a dance partner. I happen to be available, so I would consider it a privilege to partner such a lovely lady given the opportunity."

Her hesitation caused him to whisper a challenge for her ears alone, "What about it 'my cousin's' wife? Unless, you're afraid to be in my arms, that is."

Tossing her long loose hair back over a shoulder, she smiled warmly up at him. "According to my husband's mother, you must call me Sarah. And no, I am not afraid. And yes, if I am to endure the dancing ritual, I would be most honored to endure it with you. But, believe me, you're the one who should be afraid. I really can't dance."

"What of Simon?" Kate whined.

Even Stella now looked apprehensive. "John, perhaps this is not such a good idea after all. We wouldn't want to cause any trouble right before the benefit. The Bishops are the worst gossips, and you know Simon is not always rational when it comes to Sarah."

John's hand crushed Sarah's, as he answered tartly. "I was not aware that assisting Sarah with dancing lessons, or coming to the house, was in any way 'causing trouble', as you like to put it. Sarah is like a sister to me. As you are, Briar. But if it makes you both uncomfortable. If I am no longer welcome here in your home. Well, of course, then I will leave."

The room went deathly quiet. Kate's face was ashen. Stella's ashamed. It was evident to Sarah, they all had offended him terribly. She, by not being totally honest about her feelings for her husband, and the two embarrassed women by acting as if he were nothing more than a disposable orphan, taken in for charity purposes. She felt both his shame and his fury.

Apparently, despite the persona of him being included as a family member, he had spent a lifetime being an outcast. Never quite good enough. Wearing Simon's cast-offs. Sharing his family. And now even being rejected by a woman he imagined himself in love with.

Sarah's compassionate heart went out to him. Determined to fix the rift, she rose quickly to her feet and kissed John's cheek affectionately. He looked at her, a question in his hard eyes, but she only smiled back before placing her hand into his, her other hand on his stiff shoulder. "I would love to dance, John. And who knows, maybe with you as my guide, I will not be so hopeless a pupil, after all. Although, I gravely doubt it."

Her voice was both warm and tender. Her offer of friendship was sincere. After all, he did not deserve to be slighted because of Simon's jealousy and her confusion. Besides, in a way, this misunderstanding was partly her fault. But this was a day of new beginnings and she would start again with John, her friend.

It took only one dance for Sarah to know they were right about John. He was an excellent dancer. He performed every dance beautifully, guiding, teaching, and once his good humor returned, making her laugh. Unfortunately, she was also right about herself. Her dancing improved not one wit. Even Kate cringed as she watched Sarah go the opposite way on the minuet, for the third time in row.

Finally after an hour of such antics, the dance instructor rose from the piano bench, his face red and his skinny body shaking with righteous fury. "No. No. No. You must glide across the floor young lady, not stomp. And the man leads. This never changes."

"Really Mr. Jacobs, I hardly think one should yell at one's student. Sarah is trying after all." But even Stella's protest sounded weak and slightly sympathetic to his plight.

Gathering up sheets of music, the upset man began stuffing them haphazardly into his satchel, "Be that as it may, madam. If I were you, I would reconsider allowing her on any dance floor, especially one with people on it." With that said, he stormed out of the room and out the front door.

Shocked faces turned to Sarah in sympathy. However, it was John's twitching upper lip that was her undoing. She shrugged. "Well, that certainly went better than I expected."

To which the whole room burst out laughing, Sarah most of all. Then accepting a kiss to the back of her hand from John and a hug from Kate, she started for the doorway and freedom.

"Thank goodness that is all over with. Now if you will excuse me, I'll be in the kitchen getting something to eat."

"But, dear. There are still the seating arrangements to be discussed, quests to welcome, baths and hair to be done."

Sarah stopped and spun around, determined to put an end to this whole farce. What she intended to do was find something to eat, even if it was one of those huge bouquets of flowers adorning the house at every turn. Their cloying sweetness was making her a little nauseous at the moment, but she would manage if she had to.

Next, she would locate her grandfather. Time was slipping away and she still was no closer to finding out who Twister was than last night, when she had went up to her empty bed. At the moment she was tired, hungry, and disillusioned with the whole of English society. And the thought of an entire evening with her race, filled her with the same dread as facing the dark one from her dreams.

But strangely enough, none of those thoughts found a voice. Just one look at the expectant face of her mother in law, silenced all she was about to say. So, rather than stomping her foot and demanding freedom, she instantly reverted back to the teaching of her grandfather. She tested her words before speaking, so as to cause no insult.

Bowing respectfully, she answered calmly, "I would be most honored to help, my husband's mother. Later. For if I do not find nourishment soon, I shall surely pass out. Then Simon will have to carry me upstairs in front of our guests. And although unfamiliar with all the English customs, I believe this is not one of them."

With that said she left the room. And this time, no one stopped her.

A short time later, Sarah sat in, what she was sure was the most glorious kitchen in all England. Readjusting herself on the rough wooden bench, she continued to eat what she would swear was the best bread ever baked. As she gulped down another mug of sweet milk and took a huge bite of Cook's dark brown bread, she sighed happily.

"Heaven sakes, Miss Sarah, one would think you hadn't eaten all day."

"I haven't. And this is wonderful."

The cook's laugher filled the cozy kitchen, as servants whizzed past. Some were carrying freshly plucked chickens. Others bowls full of sauce and chopped garden vegetables. A passing maid gave her a quick curtsy, before gathering up the sparkling wine glasses sitting next to her and heading for the dining room.

Sarah swallowed the mouthful of bread choking her, as her eyes followed the maid out the door and up the staircase. The thought of masked balls and a room full of strangers was making her stomach clench up in a knot again. Smiling wanly, she laid down the last slice of bread and remarked almost to herself, "I seem to have lost my appetite."

Needing some advice, she turned to the good-natured woman pounding the dough down on a wooden slab. "Mrs. Harrison, about the ball?"

Wiping her unkempt hair out of the way with a floury hand, the cook barely glanced in her direction. "Now, Miss Sarah there is no need to get yourself all worked up. None of those so-called ladies can hold a candle to you. Why, you'll be the envy of every woman there. Mark my words, they will take one look at the way the young master adores you and they will be a asking your advice on husbands."

"I don't think adore is exactly the right word."

"Pshaw. Why, the man looks at you like you were a slice of my best Shepard pie. It's fair romantic, it is."

Sarah didn't know if she liked being compared to Shepard pie. Besides, if Simon felt anything for her, it was gratefulness. Or, maybe attraction, but not love. Sadly, she added almost to herself. "I've no wish to be envied, Mrs. Harrison. Grandfather says a man envied, creates many enemies."

"Maybe he's got the right of it. Still, a lady does like to be admired. All I can say is that I hope that Hilary woman dares to show her face here tonight. It would please my old soul to see her have some color for a change. Even if it be a lovely shade of green."

Shocked, Sarah threw her legs back over the bench and leaned forward. "Hilary? Is she back?"

"Oh, you didn't know?"

"No. Simon never mentioned it. Was she arrested?"

Now it was the cook's turn to look shocked. "Why, no. Why would you think so? Now, I did hear tell that they took her over to Scotland Yard for questioning. But, it would hardly warrant arresting the poor thing. Seeing as she was kidnapped and all."

"Kidnapped? And they believed her?"

"You say some awfully strange things Miss Sarah. Why would a woman lie about something as serious as kidnapping? No, it seems some more of those smugglers that nearly did away with Master Simon were holding her and her brother in a cave along the coast. Not more than two miles from their home. If you can believe it?"

Sarah didn't.

"Why, the whole staff has been talking about how they barely escaped with their lives. It is a wicked old world, that's plain for my old eyes to see. I mean, her coming in all disheveled and that nice young man a deep gash in one shoulder. It's a wonder the two of them weren't killed. Now where are you off to Miss Sarah?"

"To find Grandfather. Thank you again for the wonderful bread."

"You're welcome, Lady Sarah. And you don't worry none about the benefit, or what those uppity gentry think. To all of us here on the staff, you're a true lady. Always so thoughtful and polite like. We are glad the young master had the good sense to fall in love with you. I must say I did have my doubts about his sense before you came along."

Warmed by the cook's sincere words, Sarah automatically bowed. "I am most honored, and would be more than humbled to be called friend, by so generous a soul as you."

Rising from her bow of respect, she took in the flustered cook's embarrassed widened eyes, and groaned. When would she realize it was against the English laws for her to befriend a servant? Frustrated with both the system and her inability to learn it, she pulled back her shoulders and stated simply. "I've shocked you again Mrs. Harrison. I do apologize. But, I am not sorry for my words. They are true."

Instantly the cook's shocked look turned all motherly. She reached out and patted Sarah's cheek, leaving behind a floury hand print. "Now you don't worry about a thing. I know you were raised by that mixed up China man. You'll learn our... I mean, your old ways. It will just take a little time, that's all." Then, leaning in as if confiding a great secret, whispered, "And I am honored to be your friend, as well. Even when you learn your place and don't speak of it, I'll not forget."

Hands clasped. It was an unspoken pledge of friendship.

"Now get on with you. There is not much time before the ball and I've work to do."

Smiling, Sarah hurried out of the kitchen, in search of Grandfather. Funny how quickly a person's feelings could take a turn. When she first arrived back on English soil all she could think of is how badly she did not fit in. How much she missed America. But something had changed. She had changed. And as hard as it was to admit, this was becoming her home. In a way it felt rather bittersweet. As if in order to gain her place here, some other things would have to be left behind.

So, it was with mixed emotions she finally located Grandfather in a spare bedroom on the third floor. His legs crossed in meditation. His writings scattered all over the floor about him.

Her eyes instantly teared up in response to the sweetness, his dear old form evoked. She would miss him most terribly, when destiny called him away. Quietly, she sat down across from him. Her eyes closing. Instantly, her breathing began to slow. Through long deep breaths, she began to erase all worries from her mind.

But, instead of the traditional chanting done by her grandfather's ancestors, she prayed very like the heathen English she swore never to be. No, rather she prayed as her grandfather had taught her, as his missionary father had taught him. It was a compromise of two cultures blending into one.

And when she prayed? Her prayers were as simple as her heart, just that the God of all things would show her the path. His path. For no longer did things seem clear. Only her love for Simon was strong and certain. Yet, even in that, there was still so much she did not understand about her husband. A part of her desperately wanted to force Simon to come away with her to America. Although a more logical part, knew he never could. Besides, the truth was, nothing could be resolved by running away. You always took your problems with you.

"Are your prayers over my granddaughter?"

She opened her eyes to his quizzical look. "Yes, my honored teacher."

Nodding his approval, he picked up his small round spectacles and a sheet of writings next to his leg. "Good. I have found the reference."

Her heart raced as she rose to her knees to peer over the top of the paper. "Oh. That's wonderful. What does it mean? Does it clear things up? Do you think we know of him, or-"

Looking up at her over the top of his glasses in disapproval, the old man reminded, "A patient man listens first, and then speaks. It is the way of wisdom."

Feeling reprimanded, Sarah sank back down on her feet and waited for him to continue.

"That is better. I know you are anxious Little One. But all things have their own time. They cannot be rushed."

"Yes, Grandfather."

Picking up his writings, he continued on in a calm voice, "The name Twister is an English slang. It refers to one who deceives another in order to steal from him."

A feeling of disappointment caused her 'oh', to be half hearted.

"It is a clue."

She barely refrained from shouting her frustration. She had expected...well, she wasn't sure exactly what she had hoped for, but certainly not this vague clue. That the evil one who killed her parents was also a thief was hardly surprising. How did that make finding him any easier?

Feeling her grandfather's eyes on her, she looked up and nodded serenely. "Thank you. I am deeply humbled that you searched so diligently for the answer. Now if you will excuse me, Grandfather, I have to get dressed"

"I see you can still control your emotions when forced to. This is good. There is more on this name."

Hope brightened her expression, yet she sat perfectly still waiting.

"The name is attached to a group of young evil doers on the back streets of London. They are normally referred to as 'Knockers'. That is all I know. However, your husband holds many secrets of the evildoers. Perhaps he will know more."

Excited to have some avenue to pursue, Sarah forgot all about restraining her emotions and threw her arms around the China man practically knocking him over backwards. His responsive laughter was like a dash of color into the drab room.

Lovingly he pushed her off him, before scolding, "It is plain to see Granddaughter, you will never truly be a child of heaven."

Wrapping her arms around him in a bear hug, she added, "But I will never be completely English either. So, you will just have to stay here with me. Otherwise who will save me from myself?"

He placed a gentle kiss to her forehead.

"You have it wrong Little One. It is you who have saved me."

She stilled at his heartfelt words. Her eyes tearing up at the mere thought of him leaving her.

"When will you go, Grandfather?"

Now it was his turn to become quiet. The squeeze of his hand on hers conveyed both his love and the hardness of his words. "Soon, Little One. There is still much to discover in the world. It is my destiny to know the wisdom of the world. Besides, if I do not go now, how will I ever gain the strength to leave you?"

"I still wish you could stay."

"As do I."

The room felt cold and dreary once again. Their unwelcome thoughts sucking out what joy once filled the small room.

"Now you must go and prepare for the foolish English celebration."

She smiled, rising to her feet with him. "I think you forget it is supposed to be a benefit for the orphans. Not a celebration."

One disapproving eyebrow shot up at the word benefit. "If you say it is so. However, when a person is poor, he rarely benefits from another's celebration. He only wishes for a slice of bread, not a party."

Those were exactly Sarah thoughts as well. For even the two orphans that resided in the house were banned from the party. No, her only consolation was that the fair would be held next month as originally planned. That would be a celebration all of them could enjoy. And who knows, perhaps tonight would not be a total waste. That is, if she were clever enough. Rich people did need servants didn't they? They just didn't usually grow their own.

"I know that look, Little One. What are you planning?"

She blinked at him innocently, her long lashes a distraction from the gleam in her eyes.

"I am your most humble granddaughter; your ways are strong within me."

It was then the China man grinned with her. Knowing his granddaughter, the party might prove more interesting than he first thought. Perhaps he would help in the kitchen after all. Close by. Just in case.


"Oh Miss Sarah, aren't you just beautiful, all sparkly and quite the Lady." Maggie beamed bringing in fresh hot water for Simon's bath. Or at least Sarah assumed it was for him, since she had bathed over an hour ago.

Sarah ignored the comment, her eyes transfixed by the flow of steamy water as it cascaded into the elegantly molded interior. Her voice choked a little as she asked nonchalantly, "Is the warrior back then?"

The only response she received was a shake of Maggie's finger, before saying, "Warrior, indeed. You've got to watch yourself and them China ways tonight around the gentry. Not to mention the new help." She glared at Ann, the new maid, as she fairly tripped over herself in her haste to clean up the mess left by the mad rush to dress her. "This is your first party and you wouldn't want to be making the wrong impression, now would you?"

The young ladies maid, Ann, blushed prettily and curtsied, saying honestly, "You don't have to worry none about me mum. I think it is wonderfully romantic to call the handsome Master, Warrior."

This earned her a grateful smile from Sarah, and a scolding frown from Maggie.

"Now don't you be encouraging her, it will only bring her heartache around the gentry. They can be brutal to those who are not one of their own."

Wishing only to slow down her heart rate and the telling flush thoughts of Simon evoked, she asked again, "Is Simon downstairs?"

A second pail of steamy water poured out into the copper tub.

"Maggie."

"Oh, all right Miss Sarah. Yes, Master Simon is home. And yes, he is headed up the stairs, not ten steps behind me. For the life of me, I can't figure you gentry out. One minute you're lying abed till noon, the next you're blushing like a new bride when a body just fills a bathtub. Speaking of which, you need to leave before he gets in here. You're supposed to surprise the man with your costume. It is part of the fun. If you like I could bar the door while Ann sneaks you through the dressing room."

"It is an impractical rule. We are married after all."

"All the more reason for surprises, if you ask me. Do you want to know what I think?"

"Not really."

She laughed heartily with a sparkle in her gray eyes, "What I think is, the Master flusters you a bit. Nothing wrong with that. At least them China ways haven't messed with your woman's intuition. But a man does like a chase every once in awhile. It's in his nature."

Forcing herself to unclasp her tightly held hands, Sarah replied sternly, "Maggie, don't you have something else to do?"

"Oh, no Miss. Not a thing. Do you know I think I just might get married myself one day. Only I'll be hiding in the dressing room. Believe you me."

As if on cue, Simon entered the room and Sarah could nearly swear she stopped breathing. He was so handsome. So strong. His dark brown tousled hair and chiseled features, brimming with fresh air and exercise. She didn't think she would ever get use to just being in the same room with him. Looking at him.

It seemed as if Simon was equally affected, for he too stood there, his eyes devouring her. If not for the soft giggle of Ann, they might have never come out of their trance.

Simon cleared his throat. Then as if realizing they were not alone, looked around at the besotted maid, who at the moment was smiling with a goofy dreamy expression at the two of them. He frowned. Then when that failed to uproot them, sent a warning glare Maggie's direction.

"Oh, right Sir. We'll be leaving now if there isn't anything else. That is unless you would like me to send Albert up to help you dress."

"Only if you want to be a party to murder." He remarked drolly. "I've had quite enough of inept servants for one day."

"Oh, yes Sir. I mean, no Sir."

She started curtsying madly in her nervousness. Too late Sarah saw the impending doom about to befall, as empty buckets swung wildly about her husband's head. He dodged twice, but failed to avoid the one that landed unmercifully on his foot. Furious, he let out a roar.

"Would you watch what your doing woman!"

Too late he realized that yelling was not a good choice. Taking in the maid's horrified expression and her confused whirling of the last remaining bucket. Which just barely missed knocking him out. He rethought his technique and grabbed her shoulders, saying more calmly, "I believe that will be all Maggie. Thank you."

Blushing furiously, she began curtsying in rapid succession on her way out the door. "Oh, yes Warrior...I mean Sir. What I meant to say is, if you need any help with your bath..."

Ann's gasp, made Maggie cringe as her face went from red to white. "Oh, I didn't mean to imply I would be helping...I meant, that is to say..."

"Goodbye would probably be a good idea right now."

"Oh, yes. You're quite right. Good-bye Sir. And to you, my Lady."

With that the two maids practically ran from the room.

Once the door slammed, Sarah burst out laughing. She couldn't seem to stop even when her sides were cramping in protest. Even Simon was shaking his head and grinning. "I guess it is too much to hope for, that we will ever have any semblance of a real servant in this house."

Sarah stifled another bout of mirth and with golden brown eyes dancing with laughter said sadly, "Probably not. It seems as if your mother insists on hiring infirm ones and I am filling the leftover slots with orphans."

His good humor evaporated instantly, "That reminds me. We need to lower the shelves in the carriage house."

She bit her finger to keep from laughing, especially given the fact that the look on her husband's face was now one of total disgust.

"Let me guess. Donavon can't reach them."

He was shrugging out of his jacket and for the first time she noticed a huge gash on his forehead. "Oh dear. What in the world happened to you?"

He stilled the hand that was automatically reaching out to touch his wound, "That boy, you call a groom's helper, very near killed me. That's what happened. He was hopping about on some dilapidated old crate, trying to grab at the grooming tools. Like an idiot, I stood around watching him, because he insisted he could do the job. The whole thing was ridiculous. That boy belongs in an orphanage, not my stables."

She could just imagine the scene, Simon glowering with impatience and Donavon proudly stubborn. "You didn't hurt his feelings, did you? After that terrible incident with Albert and then being demoted to the stables I would hate for him to lose face again."

Exasperated Simon pulled off his boot and dropped it to the ground. "Why is it, my dear loving wife, that every time a servant wounds me, you ask if I hurt their feelings?"

"I'm sorry Warrior. It is just that you are prone to losing your temper and saying things you don't mean."

"Yes, I do lose my temper. Only you are wrong about one thing. I know perfectly well what I am saying at the time and mean every word of it." He started unbuttoning his shirt. "Especially when a nine year old boy knocks an entire shelf of tools on top of my head."

"Oh, no."

"Oh, yes."

Running to the door, she smiled sweetly back at her husband, "I'll just go and check to see if he is all right."

"You will do no such thing, China. He's fine. The boy should be an acrobat. Do you know he managed to dodge every single tool? How, I'll never know because, I certainly wasn't able to."

Suddenly, she felt such love for the handsome man frowning up at her from their bed, a big purple knot decorating his forehead. It wasn't many men who would put up with nine year old orphans assaulting them. Much less a bucket swinging Maggie, and still retain a depreciating sense of humor.

"I missed you today."

Taken aback by the adoring smile she was bestowing on him, he tried his best to stay mad. "Sarah we have to talk about this. You know he is too young to work in the stables. He could get hurt."

Unmindful of her dramatically hooped dress, or softly curled hair, she started placing tempting kisses to his face.

"Kissing me senseless will not work, Sarah. I won't change my mind."

"All right. Then he will no longer be a groom's helper." She ran a hand slowly along his upper arm muscles "Perhaps the solution is to adopt him ourselves."

That brought him to his senses. He jumped to his feet, and let out an exasperated hiss.

"I swear, China, you don't listen to a thing I say."

Now she was mad. Every time she even mentioned adopting the children, he reacted as if the idea was ludicrous. It was the only time his prejudice showed through perfectly. Obviously, he felt they were not worthy, simply because they had the misfortune to be born within the bowels of London.

"Maybe if you ever said something that made the least sense, it would be a little easier to listen."

"Now what are you talking about?"

"Hilary." And as if that explained everything, she turned her back and started rummaging through drawers.

Floored, he dodged a flying corset, and demanded, "I don't know why you think shouting a name at me, is an explanation of any kind. We weren't even talking about Hilary." Hit in the face by a pair of stockings, he stormed forward and spun her around. "I ask you again. What are you talking about?"

The last two days of raw emotions had finally caught up with her. She knew it was irrational how very angry she was. She also knew it had been her idea, that he left her alone all week. But he kept disappearing. Meanwhile, she was left all alone to figure out her feelings about him, the children, the evil one and even Hilary. Now there was this stupid party they had to go to.

"Speaking of not listening. I hate dancing, do you know that? Not that anyone in this entire house seems to care, but I do."

Now he really looked confused. "You're making absolutely no sense. And why are you changing clothes?"

She jerked at the lacing of her 1700's costume. "I never wanted to be an English wife. I never asked you to marry me. And I certainly don't want to host some extravagant ball, so your rich friends can spend a fortune congratulating themselves on their supposed act of charity. So, if I have to live a life not of my choosing," She was completely stripped down to her underclothes now, which was not helping with his train of thought. "then I will at least go to it, in the clothes of my ancestors." That said, she slid on the shimmery gold outfit he had given her. While, he on the other hand, watched with a mixture of admiration and frustration.

"You know you can't wear that."

She shoved a braided stick through one of the rich red loops. And when she was done? He was speechless. She looked magnificent. The golden color with red and green highlights, accented her skin tone and beautiful topaz eyes. Speaking of which, were looking defiantly up at him at the moment. Her small chin jutted in the air, as if daring him to deny her beauty and the rightness of her choice.

Instantly, his heart fell. She was right. He had stripped her of her identity, forced her into this marriage, and kept secrets from her. What had he really expected his lioness to do, when he was now threatening to kick out her orphans?

He sighed. Precisely this. She was clinging to the only solid thing in her past she could remember, the only thing safe and constant. Well, he would not be the one to take it from her.

With a tenderness she did not expect, he took one of her hands in his. Then turning it over placed a slow gentle kiss to the inside of one wrist. "You're right, China. You look beautiful, if not a tad defiant. And I'm sorry I yelled." When she continued to eye him warily, he added, "By the way, you can also stop giving me that look, your orphans can stay."

His words soothed her wounded pride. Nodding, she took a step back. "I am sorry also. I guess I felt a little abandoned today. It has caused my emotions to guide my words."

A smile quirked his lips, "Really? I hadn't noticed."

She wasn't giving in to his charm quite yet. "I am wearing this."

"All right."

"We are not sending Donavon or Lucy away, ever."

403

His answer came with a condition attached. "I agree. But only if you promise, they will be the last ones. I don't want to transfer the entire orphanage into our home. Understood?"

The words, 'our home' warmed her soul. But there was one last thing she needed from him. "You have my word. However, I would wish a promise from you as well, my husband."

He hated when she became polite. Wary, he asked, "Such as?"

"That there be no more secrets between us."

"Sarah I can't promise that."

"It is non-negotiable."

He turned away, slamming his hands down on the dresser. Then, dropping his head down in defeat, he groaned, "I will tell you everything. After tonight. I promise."

"Because tonight you're meeting with Hilary?"

His head shot up, anger evident in every fiber of his being. "Who said anything about meeting Hilary?"

"You don't have to. I heard she and Peter showed up yesterday, claiming they were kidnapped. It just makes sense you would plan on meeting her tonight. That is the whole reason you let her escape wasn't it?"

The words lay between them like a gauntlet.

"Yes."

The back of her eyes stung with unshed tears. "Do you believe she is innocent then?"

"Sarah"

"Do you?"

He turned back around to lean on the dresser. His arms crossed in front of him, as if to ward her off. "No. But, she might lead me to the one behind all this. I've explained this to you before."

Sarah mimicked his posture. Arms crossed stubbornly and shoulders thrown back. "Then I want to help."

"Absolutely not."

"Simon, you will need someone to watch your back."

He waved off her warning, "I don't want you following me and that's final." Seeing the mutinous look on her face, he reached out and gently pulled her unyielding form into his embrace. "China, you have to trust me on this. Last time you nearly got yourself killed following me." She began shaking her head, he stilled her with one hand cradling her face, "Besides, John will watch my back. That's where I went today. To explain everything to John and set up the meeting with Hilary."

How she wished to remain firm and unbending like an ancient oak, yet his touch was softening her resolve. For once she looked hesitant. "John will be with you?"

"Yes. And if I recall correctly he was the one who saved us both last time. Now do you feel better?"

John's whispered words of warning in the garden gave her pause yet again. "So you are not involved with, the 'others'?" She bit her lip trying to find a way to ask the question without offending him.

He seemed to read her mind. Automatically, he drew back. The tenderness on his face evaporated. Once more he was the proud warrior, challenged by an enemy. She hated to hurt him, but it was a matter of life or death. His.

"The word is smuggler, Sarah. And no, I'm not."

His words should have brought relief, but the look of angry betrayal in his eyes only brought sadness. Still, she had to know.

The room got deathly quiet. Twice now she had accused him of betrayal. Whatever he once felt for her surely must have changed. As Grandfather said, there is no wall as impenetrable as the lack of trust between friends. She felt sick. Looking back at him hoping to explain, she noticed he had already dismissed her. Walking over to the window, his stiff back to her, one arm threw back the curtain.

"My bath grows cold and half of London is arriving downstairs. Why don't you go to Kate's room, until I am done?"

"Simon, there is a reason I asked." She drifted off, knowing nothing she said would ease his hurt. Her heart in her eyes, she willed him to turn around, but he didn't. Finally, knowing there was little else to say, she bowed, saying softly, "As you wish my husband."

She wasn't certain why, but his stance stiffened.

"Seldom are things as I wish wife. I'll see you downstairs."

Or as she wished, either. Nodding, she quietly exited the room, her soft slippers gliding over the plush rug and onto the wood floor of the hallway. As the soft gave way to the hard, a part of her wondered if his heart would ever forgive her, or for that matter if she would ever forgive herself.

# Chapter 21

Kate's chattering did nothing to ease the knot gathering in the pit of Sarah's stomach.

"Did you know that Elizabeth's cousin, Tom Rutledge, is supposed to be back for a visit? He's been in India with his regiment this past three years. He says everyone there," Kate tilted her head at Sarah taking in the way she was still absently nodding her head and pulling distractedly at the gold tassels on a red velvet pillow, "rides cows and drinks yak's milk."

A vacant nod was her only response.

Exasperated, Kate snatched the pillow out of her hands. "Are you even listening to a word I've been saying?"

"What? Oh, most certainly, my husband's sister."

Cocking her elaborately coiffed head in disbelief, Kate asked sweetly, "Then what did I say?"

Caught, Sarah sighed before guessing, "Something about Elizabeth riding on a yak I believe."

Throwing the small pillow her direction, Kate admonished. "Honestly Sarah, this is supposed to be fun. You are acting like a prisoner preparing for the gallows."

"Maybe I feel a little like one," she mumbled.

"I heard that," Kate scolded. "Now tell me what has you so down in the mouth."

Sarah shoved off the bed and began pacing the room in agitation. "You mean besides spending the entire evening with perfect strangers pretending they are my friends, while listening to hours of gossip and talk of mundane things?"

"Really, if you would only try to fit in, I am sure they will adore you as much as I do."

"Or if you like, we could talk about the fact that I hate the dancing ritual." She stopped in mid-stride directing her comment straight at the young girl only one year her junior but years apart in life experiences.

"I am sure you'll get better."

"Before, or after, I take out half the dance floor?"

A smile threatened to break Kate's valiant effort at maintaining a certain amount of seriousness. "But a masquerade ball is so much more than dancing, or gossip. There is, well...eating for instance and..."

"Yes?"

Kate burst out laughing. "Well, maybe it is mostly gossip and dancing. But it is also very lovely. There are scores of handsome men, all dressed up in mysterious costumes. Did you know, one can flirt quite outrageously when behind a mask? Then there is the game. We only have until midnight to figure out who is who by asking questions and noticing little clues about their behavior. Did you know that the one who guesses the most correct identities, wins a new pair of horses from the Bishop's best stock?"

"I thought this was about the orphans."

Kate blushed guiltily. "You are not giving this whole thing a chance. Believe me, there is more to life than saving orphans and climbing out windows after my brother."

Realizing Kate was right. She was being argumentative. Sarah sighed heavily, "I know. It's just that this is all so new to me. I hadn't planned on staying in your England. Sometimes I still find myself wishing for home. Even the old laundry in China town and our cold cramped rented room on the sixth floor, at times seems like heaven."

Rather than chide her further, Kate tried to lie across the bed in order to bridge the gap between them. However, her hoop skirt and tight corset made the simple act near impossible. Slapping at the garment several times in a vain effort to flatten it, she finally asked, "Is that where you met my brother, at the laundry?"

Taken aback by her direct manner in pursuing what had happened in America, Sarah tried to distract her by asking a question of her own. "Do you not wish to see more of the world? I cannot imagine so small a life as yours, especially with the spirit of curiosity strong within your soul."

A light dimmed in Kate's eyes, as her war with the hoop skirt came to an end, the hoop winning. She looked rather sad and dejected like a painted doll stuck in an elaborate wired trap. "It isn't as if I have a choice, now is it? No English lady does really. All we can hope for is a well turned husband and children."

With perplexity shinning through golden eyes, Sarah reached over and silently helped untie the hoop, motioning for Kate to stand. "Everyone has a choice, even an English Lady."

That said, she helped Kate step out of the hoop.

"You do not know our ways."

"Perhaps this is true. However, do you not know the story of Pocahontas?"

"No." Kate breathed a sigh of relief as she was freed from the tortuous garment.

"She was an American Indian Princess who lived many years ago."

Transfixed Kate obediently turned around as Sarah began to unbutton her. "Oh, I think I remember her now. Do you mean the one who married an English man and came over here to live?"

"Yes. Grandfather's writings include her story. She too, had the spirit of an explorer, as you do my husband's sister."

"Coming here hardly takes courage. Who wouldn't want to be civilized and live in England?"

A tawny eyebrow rose at the young woman's arrogance.

"I'm doing it again aren't I?"

"You repeat many words, but have few of your own."

Truly repentant, the young girl slid the heavy dress off her shoulders. "Do you really think I am like this Indian princess?"

"Yes, I do. She too protected a people who were not her own. As you do the orphans and me. She even dared to marry one of their kind and learn their ways. Then she boarded a giant wooden boat and sailed across an ocean that she could not see the end of, only to arrive in a place full of strange customs and teachings. That is bravery."

"What happened to her?"

"She died of an English sickness not long after coming here."

Tears welled in the young girl's eyes for a woman she had never met. "So it was all for nothing, her bravery?"

"Everyone dies, Kate. But not everyone lives. She lived."

Kate stood a little taller, as understanding grew within her heart. "I wish I could dare to live so brave a life. But I don't know how I could. Or even how to begin."

"Grandfather says most of life's greatest gifts come in odd packaging. Maybe it is not in the searching of a thing that one finds it, but being aware when it trips you up."

As if for the first time, Kate looked down at her scantily clad and costume free body. Her face when it looked up again was filled with awe. "It's strange, but I didn't even realize you had freed me of my costume."

"It was stealing your breath."

"But what will I wear instead?"

"What do you want to wear?"

"Well..." She perked up and then biting at her lower lip, started circling Sarah. "What I wish I could do was wear something scandalous like what you have on. I think you are very bold to wear such an unusual costume. It looks so, unencumbered. Sometimes I envy you. You are always completely confident in yourself. Tell me, where did you get it? It certainly isn't the costume Mother and I picked out for you."

Sarah ran her hand over the gold silk jacket that reached her knees and looked down at herself, taking in the loose pants and intricate embroidery. Almost lovingly she adjusted the high collar, saying proudly, "It is a gift from my husband."

"Simon?" Kate's eyes widened in shock. "He gave you a Chinese dress for a present? I must say, America must have loosened him up quite a bit." Then a little wistfully, she added, "That is my dream you know."

"What is?"

She shyly picked at the ribbon of her camisole. "To go to America and meet some darkly handsome Indian, or outlaw."

Sarah's laugh filled the room. "I do not think it would be exactly as you are envisioning. Outlaws are violent men. Indians aren't all that romantic either. Besides, I haven't met one yet who thought well of the English. Seldom is the idea of love, the same as the act of love."

"Still, it makes me wish I could be bold enough to try. But of course, I couldn't."

Seeing Kate looking so forlorn in her camisole and powdered hair, Sarah had an idea. "Why not?"

"Why not, what?"

"Why couldn't you go?"

"Well, for one I don't think father would agree to it."

"In fact, why not begin your journey by dressing as I am tonight."

Fear made Kate stammer, "But how? I certainly don't possess anything even remotely similar."

"I have other clothes. They would not be so richly adorned, but they are equally as...how did you phrase it? Ah, yes. Scandalous."

Biting her lower lip in indecision, Kate ventured, "Do you really think I could?"

"Certainly. Besides this is supposed to be a game of deceptions, is this not so?"

Hope turned Kate's normally pretty face, radiant, if not still a tad bit hesitant. "Of course I could explain to Mother how I was simply assisting you in confusing our guests. I mean, with both of us dressed in this fashion, no one will know for sure who is who. Why, the more I think on it, the more it makes perfect sense. What a wonderful idea!"

She was already tugging off her wig, sending powder flying everywhere. "We had better hurry. Simon will be coming to get us any moment."

Sarah's was no match for Kate's enthusiasm. After sending Ann back into her room for another suit of clothes, Sarah got to work. It took far longer to free Kate of her previous costume than it took to redress her. However in a very short time, Kate stood strangely clad in the free moving blue cotton jacket of Sarah's ancestors. Simon would correct her on the wording. But, truth to tell, her grandfather and his ancestors were more real to her than the blue blood flowing through her own veins.

Blushing shyly, her sister in law asked hesitantly, "So, what do you think?"

Sarah smiled. "I think you will honor the memory of my people."

An answering smile of pleasure burst forth and touched Sarah's heart.

"And I am honored as well." Automatically, she bowed. As if the suit of clothes dictated her actions. Taken aback, she shot up with a rather awed expression. "How odd. I don't know why I did that."

"Some things are past understanding. We simply accept them."

Nodding, her loose hair falling softly down her back, Kate became suddenly serious. "But, if we are to pull this off, I will need more than your clothes."

It amused Sarah to think only thirty minutes earlier Kate could barely imagine even wearing such an outfit. Now she lapped up every aspect, as hungrily as a starved man his first hot meal in weeks.

"I will teach you. What would you like to know first?"

The young girl's hands folded humbly at her chest, as demure hazel eyes slid away, not quite meeting Sarah's. "I think for my first lesson."

Sarah waited, wondering at the twinkle in her sister-in-law's eyes.

"It would please me to know, my brother's wife, how one throws an unwanted suitor from a balcony. After all, who knows if this Thomas Rutledge will turn out to be quite the prize Elizabeth claims."

To which Sarah burst out laughing.

A short time later, after several lessons of teaching Kate the fine art of throwing a man, both girls fell into an exhausted fit of giggles onto the bed. Which is exactly how the new maid found them a short time later. Two beautiful women dressed in oriental clothing, sweat and laughter covering their faces. Yes, amid rumbled bedding, they looked almost charming, as if they having tea, rather than wrestling about like two young ruffians.

Remembering how Harrison grumbled about the gentry and their strange ways, Ann now understood what he meant. But, seeing as she was new at working in such a grand house, she simply curtsied and asked politely, "You rang my Lady?"

Blowing a stray strand of tawny hair out of her eyes, Sarah nodded, "We will need brown dye, Ann. I believe that Mrs. Harrison will know where to find it."

She didn't even raise an eyebrow. Just simply replied, "Will there be anything else Miss?"

"Oh, and tell Simon not to bother coming to get us. We wish to..." Kate giggled, before finishing rather solemnly, "surprise him."

There would be no doubt of that, thought the young maid.

"As you wish mum."

Then shutting the door, Ann could have sworn she heard the sound of a picture tumbling to the floor and then a muffled oaf as if a body had actually been slammed into something. She shook off the insane notion that the two young respectable women were actually wrestling.

About that time, the sound of classical music drifted up the stairs filling the hallway with richness and composure, as if to deny what her eyes had taken in. With a shrug, Ann went to retrieve the dye.

Another thud, then a series of giggles followed.

Taking a deep fortifying breath, Ann tried to appear dignified before taking the servant stairs down into the kitchen as smells of sweet meats and pasties wafted up through the doorway. No doubt about it. Harrison was right. The gentry were a strange lot.

Descending the stairs into the fairy tale beauty below, Sarah hesitated a moment to catch her breath. Even when Kate looked questioningly over at her from the two holes in her elaborate mask, Sarah could find no words to explain the awe of what she was seeing, nor how very frightened she was of it all.

The candelabras' soft light lit up the golden picture frames and reflected off the full-length gilded mirrors lining the walls of the ballroom. The polished wood shined underneath, as the swirling dancers in an array of colors, glided gracefully over its polished surface. Fairy people in a make believe world. However, no matter how it overwhelmed her, she realized Kate was right. It was exciting. She felt her stomach tighten in anticipation. Automatically she began searching the room of people below.

"You should not be so obvious, Sarah. An English lady knows it is to her advantage to have a man give chase. Men do love a challenge."

As if on cue, Simon came into her line of vision. He was visiting with a fair Genevieve and a hefty King Henry. What a handsome knight he made, in make believe steel mesh and an elaborately carved sword by his side. His outfit of dark green and gold cloth, truly set off his coloring perfectly. The cut of his shirt more than enhanced the strength of his broad chest and muscular arms. Only his dark brown boots were of the present period. His absolute refusal to trade comfort for effect was one of the reasons she loved him so.

They had reached a small round table by the door, decorated with masks and silk ribbon. Scattered on its lace-covered surface, lay several small slips of paper, each with a leather pad for writing. Kate picked up two and slipped one into Sarah's hand.

"Now remember, you may answer questions about your character, but not your true identity. Then at midnight, everyone will turn in their slips of paper and unmask. The one with the most correct answers wins."

Simon was walking over to them. Kate shoved Sarah the opposite direction.

"And under no circumstances should you be seen with Simon. You will give us away."

Sarah planted her feet. "If people are to wonder which of us is which, we will both have to talk to him."

Sighing heavily, Kate warned, "Fine. However, we both have to treat him the same or it will never work."

Remembering the distance in Simon's eyes when she had left the bedroom, Sarah didn't think distancing herself from him would be a problem. "I will do my best."

When reaching the two lovely ladies, Simon raised each of their hands and placed a chaste kiss on each. Then with a touch of humor in his voice, he admonished, "Kate, has father seen you yet?"

Her mask started to come down in agitation, before she caught herself and jerked it back up in place, hissing, "Simon Conway, you are not suppose to say my name out loud, you'll ruin everything."

"Hardly. I am afraid rumors of my China wife will dispel any doubt that she resides in at least one of those costumes. Especially, since everyone saw the two of you come down the stairs together."

His unmasked head came up slowly meeting his wife's eyes. "Besides such beauty in a room full of average is hard to disguise."

Sarah thought he was mad at her. Yet the way he was staring, made her melt inside and made Kate's orders harder to follow. "You're not masked." She sounded a little breathless even to her own ears.

Kate stomped her foot. "Why are you uncovered? Simon just once I wish you would cooperate."

"Someone had to greet the guests. I was chosen."

"Oh. Well, I suppose that will be all right then. But now you must disappear so we can mingle. Besides, you're looking at Sarah that way again."

"What way is that?" He asked never taking his eyes off his wife.

"As if you could...honestly Simon. Go away!"

Instantly Sarah's stomach, which had just settled down, was churning once again. Her only thought was that if they were required to remain separate all evening, she would be alone in this crowd of strangers. She tried to still her thoughts. A feeling of panic made her hands shake slightly. She gripped them together, hiding them in the wide sleeves of her jacket. "Perhaps I should unmask as well. It would be rude not to welcome our guests as husband and wife."

Kate took no notice of Sarah's suddenly pale features, or how her voice had turned to a thready whisper. "But you can't, everyone will guess who I am. Besides, I am quite sure Simon can manage on his own for one evening. Can't you brother?"

He felt, rather than observed, his wife's panic. And oddly enough he too felt more danger here, then on that windy coast four days ago when pirates held him hostage. If only she would trust that he would protect her. It still stung his pride that she didn't. Unfortunately, until this whole thing was over with, there existed no real reason for her to.

His gut wrenched. Leaning forward and whispering in her ear, his voice invoked confidence. "Courage China, I'll be close by."

His much-needed words soothed her nerves. Gratefully she smiled up at him and valiantly tried to sound less worried than she really was, "Thank you my husband. I am certain danger will find it hard to touch me this night, with you as my protector."

Impatiently rolling her eyes, Kate tugged at Sarah, frowning hard at her brother in the process. "Heavens, listening to the two of you one would think you were going into battle instead of a dance floor. And believe me, the only one in danger out there will be the unfortunate gentleman who asks Sarah to partner him." Then determined to separate the two, Kate dragged Sarah into the ballroom.

Thoughtfully Simon watched as they disappeared into the sea of gaily dressed people. His worried look and stiff shoulders gave evidence to the fact that he, like his wife, very much believed this was no simple masquerade. His instincts were honed sharp. An intangible edginess haunted him. And the one thing he had learned over the years, was that his instincts were never wrong.

Two hours and five dance partners later, Sarah needed a break. Her feet were aching and a growing uneasiness made her impatient. Both with the men and their insignificant talk of her beauty, and the endless noise filling the ballroom.

A welcoming breeze lifted a stray curl from the back of her neck. She closed her eyes. It felt cool against her sweat covered skin. When she reopened her eyes, she realized it was coming from an open balcony door propped back to let cool moist air in from the outside. She could faintly make out the sweet fragrance of the garden, as it blended in with the rose water worn by the women, and the delicious smells coming from the dining room.

Suddenly, the room full of people seemed to drown out the beautiful music of the musicians. It was if their life energy was sucking up all the beauty of the evening, leaving behind this empty, strained feeling. She put a hand to her aching head.

"May I claim this next dance from a most mysterious, and may I say, enchanting Lady from the Orient?"

Sarah barely smiled. You would think since she had stepped on the man's feet twice and in confusion grabbed up the wrong partner halfway through the last minuet, he would have given up on the idea of dancing with her. However, even with his large peacock mask covering most of his face; his eagerness was oblivious, not to mention irritating.

"Well, actually, I feel a little unwell at the moment."

Just as she thought things couldn't get worse, he whipped out the dreaded leather pad, and poised his writing utensil. "One question first, my beautiful Lady."

She groaned. Having long since given up her own slip of paper with the list of supposed names, she had nearly forgotten the silly game. It seemed especially pointless, given the fact, that all the masked people at the ball were relative strangers to her. Which was precisely why she had left her blank list by the potted plant, an hour ago. Her only regret being that everyone else had not seen fit to do the same thing.

Answering endless questions about the Far East was giving her a horrible headache. For just a moment, she was tempted to make up an outlandish statement, just to shock him into leaving. Unfortunately, he probably wouldn't know the difference. Even now he was leaning in closer as if she were deaf, using the opportunity to gaze adoringly into her eyes. Which only irritated her further. Where was a balcony when you needed one?

Bulging red rimmed eyes from too much drink were far from enticing. The fact that he was scribbling away furiously with the wrong end of a pen, not exactly giving the impression of intellect. She sighed impatiently. His attempt at flirting would have been humorous, if it were not so aggravating. She was fast learning that hiding behind a mask brought out the worst in people. So far tonight; she had been propositioned, flirted with, and forced to endure long-winded views on everything from politics to sordid gossip. Rather than finding the evening exciting, as Kate said, Sarah found the lack of human integrity depressing.

"So, tell me, my little enchantress. Whatever possessed such a lady as yourself, to associate with those yellow moguls from the East?"

Ire turned her voice to ice, "My past has not yet returned to me. But I must say, being in your company has helped open my eyes to some of what drove me to seek them out. "

Flattered, he stuck out his chest, and used his pen for emphasis, "I am pleased to have been of service. But, what about my presence brought inspired you?"

She opened her mouth to tell him bluntly exactly what she thought of him, when he waved her into silence with the feather end of the quill. Managing to swipe her nose in the process, as it moved past. "Let me guess. It is my civilized manner."

"No. The Chinese are far more polite, even to their enemies."

A frown wrinkled the loose folds of skin along his forehead, "Then perhaps it is my superior intelligent."

"No. Like the mule of America, you are stubborn and cunning, but that hardly makes you wise."

"Now see here"

"However, this ball has helped me remember that your people hide behind many masks. That what you represent is not always what you are. See, in other cultures, the evil ones are easier to recognize. Perhaps that is what I sought out among the yellow Mongols. Honesty."

She knew from his sputtering, that he knew he had just been insulted, but was not sure exactly how. Taking advantage of his momentary confusion, she added, "However, I am sure you are different. You, Sir, are exactly as you seem."

"Why, thank you." He purred, bending down to retrieve his pen. This caused his wig to flip forward, effectively knocking his jester hat over his eyes. When he finally managed to straighten his costume, and shove the hat back, Sarah was looking serenely back at him. All evidence of her barely contained laughter, erased from her smooth expression.

The strange man began nodding inanely at her, as he scratched some words onto his paper. Then looking up, he proudly announced, "It is just as I first suspected. You are Miss Kate Conway. Any idiot could tell by your answers you know nothing about the Orient."

The orange and red jester snatched up her hand and placed a wet kiss to the back of it.

"I believe the Lady is speechless."

She snatched back her hand and said evenly, "Only at your ability to reason. Now if you will excuse me, I do not wish to dance with one who possess the same level of skill in the art of perception, as I do on the dance floor," Grandfather's stern warning about treating all people with dignity else you lose your own, made her draw in a fortifying breath before adding more politely, "Although, I am most honored by your request."

Her worry that she had offended him seemed unwarranted. She wasn't even sure he understood she had just insulted him. He smiled a huge discolored grin and offered, "Perhaps I could get you some refreshment then? I have just a few more questions to ask. Every good detective should double check his theory."

Her headache was increasing in strength. What she truly wanted, was for him to leave her alone. She tried to look down at her lap in order to avoid letting him see her irritation. But his pointed red and black shoes with the huge bow on top were making it hard to take him seriously. She quickly looked up in search of Simon. Or for that matter, anyone who would see fit to rescue her.

"Why don't you leave the lady alone, Johnson. Even across the room I can see that you're making a fool of yourself, again."

Simon's deep voice was music to her ears. She looked past the indignant sputtering of her companion and gave a relieved smile to her husband. His only acknowledgment, a slight nod her direction before taking the pad from Johnson and stuffing it into one of the oversize pockets on his jacket. Then, spinning him around, gave a slight shove the opposite direction.

"Now see here man, you can't just start shoving people about, even if it is your party."

"Apparently I can. Now unless you wish to call me out, I suggest you find some other helpless female to bother and not my wife."

The poor man's face went from red to ashen. "Wife? Oh, I do beg you pardon, Conway. I assure you I would not have been so forward had I known. Why, everyone here knows you're a crack shot." He then turned his apology her direction. "I hope you can forgive me, Lady Conway for my remark earlier. I am sure wearing pants will be all the rave next season. Especially those, who like you, fill them out so becoming."

Eyes narrowed, Simon reached out and grabbed a handful of orange ruffled shirt and jerked him forward until he was standing on his tiptoes, eye level and shaking. "I didn't...that is to say..."

People were beginning to stare.

Sarah laid a hand gently on top of Simon's. "You are wasting your anger on a fool, my husband. Let us talk in the library. Then you can say what is on your mind."

Conflict rose in Simon's breast. He would have dearly loved to slam a fist into the wide-eyed face of Johnson, yet Sarah was right. He was angry about something else entirely. And they were causing a scene. Besides, the soothing action of her hand gently brushing across the back of his was taking the total joy out of hitting someone anyway. Not to mention, reinforcing the need to be alone with his wife.

He looked up at his wife's calm demeanor, her mask now removed. The unspoken words between them causing Simon to loosen his hold on the trembling imbecile. Then, disgusted with the whole experience, he growled. "Don't just stand there, man. Get lost, before I change my mind and throttle you after all."

The poor man did not have to be told twice. Tripping over his pointed shoes, he stumbled away. Not once completely turning his back on the man twice his size. Within seconds the music started back up and their guests went back to gossiping. Although Sarah was fairly certain they were now the subject of conversation.

She slid her hand into Simon's. "Not having a good time?"

A squeeze to her hand made the roughness of his voice less intimating. "Hardly. I've been dealing with ridiculously dressed people pretending they don't know each other. Never mind, that they have lived and breathed within the same circle for years. The only one a real mystery here, is you. Or at least you were until now. Unfortunately, your unveiling will not make my sister any happier with either one of us."

"Oh, I think she has forgotten all about trickery. She left out the balcony door a moment ago with 'Don Juan'. Although I am not sure this is wise. Isn't he the man known for his seduction of woman?"

The aggressive worry emanating from Simon, turned from her to the empty doorway across the ballroom. She groaned. Now if she didn't stop him, he would cause a scene with Kate, who would react by erupting into a bout of tears. None of which boded well for spying. When would she learn to keep her thoughts hidden?

Sarah forced a smile, saying lightly, "Although to be honest, I hardly think he could be much worse than that man you rescued me from. Even in a room full of people, he knew no shame. It is most fortunate for him that we were not near a balcony."

A twinkle replaced the aggression from a moment ago, "Maybe the next time I will let you take care of it in your own way. Besides, it might be nice to see you throw someone else into something for a change. Heaven knows, I could use a little diversion tonight."

As they both looked around the room, Sarah felt an expectation of danger. She shivered uncontrollably.

"Are you cold? We could go upstairs for your wrap." Since they were already heading for the library, Sarah wished for no more delays. Something was troubling her handsome husband and it wasn't the ball. There were frown lines gathering between his dark brows and a purposeful gait to his walk. Even now strong hands crushed her own. Yet she didn't cry out. What she really wished for, was to be held in his arms for a moment. Their last fight still haunted her.

"Sarah?"

"I am sorry, Warrior. My mind is dwelling on the past. But to answer your question, no, I do not wish for covering. Only that this evening was over, and the evil one I fear exposed."

They passed several people on the way to the library, but no one bothered to so much as nod. They simply looked away. Sarah assumed they were uncomfortable with seeing a man drag his wife in public. The one thing Sarah had learned since arriving back home was that the English had rules for everything. Apparently dragging people was definitely against one of them, although flirting was not. It was all most confusing.

Reaching the huge double doors leading into the library, Sarah hesitated. What if Simon wished to tell her that he wanted to be free? That if she could not trust him, there was no marriage. Perhaps the man of law would be waiting with another paper for her to sign.

Simon looked questioningly down on her. Then, as if shrugging off her hesitation, shoved open the doors. His arm muscles bulged beneath the strain. He was a handsome man, her husband, strong and powerful.

Almost as an after-thought, he pulled her inside, and then headed straight for the bookshelf. By the way he pulled out books, without even looking at them, she knew he was searching for something.

"Peter pulled me aside a moment ago. He wants to meet sometime before midnight on the bridge. He says he knows who is behind the smuggling."

Confusion marred her beautiful features. "Then why are we in the library?"

"There is a hidden lever somewhere along this shelf. It opens up the bookcase. Behind it lies a secret passageway, leading out to the back of the house. I don't want anyone to know I've left." His fingers slid books in and out, searching. "When I was a child I found it accidentally. Apparently, the previous owners were not the trusting sort. But it turns out to be a good thing for us. The way I see it, we can slip out undetected and slip back in, sometime after the unveiling."

She forgot to breathe, "We?"

Turning around he smiled, "Yes. You do want to go with me, don't you?"

"But I thought you didn't want me following you?"

"I've been thinking about what you said in our bedroom today. About trusting you. You're right. I keep saying the words, but doing little to show it. Come with me, China. I need you."

Heart pounding Sarah ached to believe him. "Really?"

His grin widened, his words like a soft caress, "Really. I could use a good back up."

Suddenly she remembered John. Wasn't he was supposed to be his back up? What had changed so completely that now he wanted her to come with him? Maybe John was right. After all, he warned her to refuse, if Simon offered to take her with him. Maybe her husband was not who he claimed to be. Maybe...her smile faded.

"Will Hilary be there?"

She noticed the stiffening of posture before he gave her an intense look that spoke volumes. When he did speak, it was without apology. "I don't know. Does it matter?"

She knew what lay between them. The unspoken insinuation that this so called meeting had been planned to rid him of his much tiresome China bride. That, not only didn't he trust her. She didn't trust him. After all, who would even know they had gone. As far as the rest of the party would be concerned, they never left. What better cover up for murder, than at least a hundred guests giving you an alibi? Still, the question remained. What did it profit him to end her life? It all made no sense. Especially since Grandfather was so certain he was not the evil one of her nightmares.

He waited. Green eyes, dark with emotion.

Dropping her own to the floor, she shrugged. "I suppose it doesn't. Jealousy guides my words."

His soft laughter made her head jerk up in surprise. "You find my flaw humorous?"

"No. Your honesty."

Reaching out, his hand caressed her face. The lamplight casting a soft glow to his features, softening the look in his eyes. Once more the warrior was gone, and the gentle man who came to her in the night surfaced. "You really have no idea how beautiful you are, or you would know there could never be another that even compared. Especially Hilary."

The gold of her jacket complimented the dusky red of her blush. "I think you are most handsome, as well."

Now it was his turn to blush. "Now if there is nothing else, perhaps you could help me look."

If they were to be completely honest with each other, then she needed to confide in him about her own enemy.

"Well, there is one thing."

"Can't this wait?"

"I don't think so." And she didn't.

Heaving a huge sigh, he crossed his arms and leaned back against volumes of Keats and Shakespeare. "All right. But remember, the longer it takes to get away, the more chance there is of being discovered."

"Do you know of an evil doer who is called by a name not his own?"

A raised eyebrow and slight grin was her answer. "Do you mean a nickname? I swear, China, you can complicate the simplest things."

Exasperated, she blew a stray curl out of her face and stated firmly. "A man with the title, 'Twister'?"

Now she had his interest. He pushed off the shelf and asked...no demanded, in a voice use to being obeyed. "Where did you hear that name?"

"It came to my mind yesterday. A memory. I believe it belongs to the one who took my destiny. Do you know of such a man?"

Hostility rose from somewhere inside her husband, forming an aura of danger. Unconsciously, Sarah took a step back, to separate from it. He hardly seemed to notice. And even though he made no effort to follow, this very same energy backed her further into the center of the room.  If a name alone could cause this kind of reaction in him, she dreaded to think what the man himself would evoke.

It took a moment, but Sarah noticed him forcing himself to regain some sort of control before speaking again.  "I know of only one man that goes by the name Twister – and he is the traitor I have been chasing for the last two years.  Are you sure he killed your parents?  Although, it wouldn't surprise me."

In wonder, Sarah watched him walk over and check the lock on the library door.  How strange life was, full of connections.  The same destiny that had taken her away to America had brought her back into this house.  Grandfather said that such things prove the God of all things must exist.  How else could such things happen?  There was a sense out of chaos.  Shock made her legs weak.  Automatically, she sank down onto a chair before answering.  "I saw the markings on his arm.  It was a snake twisted around a moneybag.  The title 'twister' was underneath."

"It's a nickname."  Simon poured himself a drink and took a long swallow of the brandy he had made for himself.  "Do you want anything?  You look as pale as a ghost."

When she simply shook her head, he continued, "There are a group of street thugs who go by the name of 'Knockers'.  They are notorious for knocking on establishments, and if no one answers, helping themselves to the belongings inside.  Apparently the man we are searching for belongs to them.  Or, at least he did when he was younger.  I have had several men searching the back streets of London these past months, and as of yet there doesn't seem to be any sign of him.  Or, of anyone who knows him."

He tried to reach out, to comfort her, but she only shook her head before asking, "So what does the name mean?"

"It's his talent.  He was a con man of sorts.  Either talking others out of their money, or simply creating a diversion so his partners could pickpocket from the unsuspecting victim.  At any rate, apparently he was very good at it.  Or at least talented enough to bribe guards, because his real name never appeared in the books at Newgate."

"It seems he is still good at the art of deception."

They both fell silent. Each lost in their own thoughts. Slowly the sounds from the party outside the library drifted in to intrude on talks of criminals and secret meetings. They didn't have much time. The brush of silk, as Sarah rose to begin searching for the mysterious opening, caused Simon to study his wife closely before saying, "Maybe it would be best if you stayed behind, after all."

She opened her mouth to argue, but the sound of his glass being placed firmly back down, the drink hardly touched, caused her to pause in confusion. Once more he was the warrior.

"It would be too dangerous, especially if he is the same one who attacked your parents. For all I know, this meeting could be a trap. Peter, one of his cohorts. There is a very good chance, that if my father recognized how much you look like your mother, he will as well. I can't take that chance."

"I was a child. What good would it do to kill me now?"

"You mean besides that you are the only witness to what happened eight years ago?"

"But I don't remember anything that happened that night."

Worry made him sound harsher than he intended, but he did not want her in that kind of danger. He had thought to keep her with him tonight. At least then he would know where she was. He had long since given up any hope that she wouldn't find some loophole in being forced to stay behind, and follow him. Besides, he could use her calm logic tonight, her intuition, and even her odd skills. She was one of the best fighters he had ever seen.

But more than any of those things, she was a treasure, his treasure. That came before everything else. Yes, since knowing her, he had watched how she handled; addled servants, eccentric relatives, and even an attempt on her life. Why just now, she had calmly informed him of the attacker's name without so much as a tear. But taking her with him tonight, would be foolhardy.

His heart clenched in response to the sweet stubbornness, he saw in the lift of a chin. Somehow, his tawny haired lioness had found a way into his heart. And from the soft curls framing her face to the long slender hands that could kill a man if she wished, he loved her. He would always love her. Yet, whether she knew it or not, she needed him in a way no one else ever had either. She needed him to protect her, from herself. Yes, even if from an insane sense of loyalty to some Chinese custom. She drove him crazy sometimes.

"I am not afraid, Warrior."

"I didn't say you were. But, I am." His voice choked slightly as he tried to explain. "Don't you understand sweetheart? I could lose you."

Her shoulders relaxed a little, her smile softening the harshness of her words, "If it is my time to leave this earth, even so great a warrior as you could not stop it."

Her words humbled him. He could tell by the confident way she stated his strength, that she trusted him more than he deserved to be trusted.

"Sarah, you said yourself, Hilary could be there tonight. She won't talk if you're there glaring at her. I was not thinking clearly when I asked you to come."

The love shining from her eyes clouded over with familiar jealousy. He nearly smiled, but stopped himself. What was that old saying? Something about not telling your enemy your weaknesses? There was a reason for that one.

"So it is not that I am in danger, but rather that my being there will stop you from gathering information?" Her lips pressed firmly together, she muttered, "Then I will stay hidden in the shadows."

"And what if I need to...use other methods than talking to gather information from Hilary?"

Fury made her eyes the color of deep roasted coffee. He was glad there was distance between them. He had experienced her temper before. Unbelievably, she took in a deep fortifying inhalation of air and answered calmly, "I will not interfere."

"So you say. But I have no desire to dive into the Thames after my witness when you are through-not interfering."

Her hands clenched and unclenched within the sleeves of her jacket.

"Your words have no bearing on what I must do. I will follow, whether you know of it, or not."

"Then you are taking a chance I will never catch the man who murdered your parents."

His words tore into her gut. Wrenching a knife around in places kept safe from exposure for so long. For just a moment, she thought she saw a look of regret cross his face. As if he hated hurting her. Then he seemed to steel himself for what he must do. She too, knew what she must do. He was right. Past experience had shown she had no control over her emotions where Simon was concerned. She would be a liability.

At last making up her mind, she closed her eyes and promised. "I will stay."

She never heard him approach, but simply was aware of his nearness a moment before he gathered her into his arms. She wanted to cry. Instead she placed a hand to his chest, feeling the life beat within it. With that one gesture, she was stopping him from coming any closer, while at the same time gaining comfort from the solid form beneath her palms.

His hand tilted her chin up as he placed a soft kiss to her lips. A tear slipped from her eye and trailed down her cheek. Silent testimony of how hard this was for her. Twice in one night he had been forced to break her heart.

The regret in his voice was obvious, no longer a hidden thing. "This is for the best China, and if it makes you feel any better, you can stay here and help me find the opening. Even wait for me, if you want. Then, if anything goes wrong, you can send the lieutenant after me."

Her head snapped up, angry that he had dared to say the words.

He nearly smiled then, thinking about his wife and her bad Karma. One thing was certain she would never bore him. He began again. Carefully rephrasing his words, "If I am late coming back, then you know where to start looking for me."

She simply nodded. Then unable to resist any longer, sank against him, drawing strength from his nearness. She breathed in the scent of him, as if it were life giving.

Letting go of her, he stepped away. "I have to go."

Forcing a smile, Sarah spoke with conviction, "I know, you are a warrior, after all. So, let's find your latch."

Together they found it. With them both looking, it took only a manner of minutes to discover. However, it took much longer to force the rusted door open, after sliding the bookcase out of the way. Soon a dark tunnel yawned dangerously before them. The cavernous hole was full of spider webs and crumbling moldy walls. The sight of which, caused Sarah to shiver in response. It was not a good omen.

Retrieving a lamp from the desk, she reluctantly gave it to him. All traces of fear now gone. Although she did worry her bottom lip a little as she gave a slight smile of encouragement. "If you are one minute past twelve o'clock, I will come looking for you Warrior. It is my way."

"Sarah…"

"This is not negotiable."

His slight nod showed he knew when to surrender. Then with a quick kiss to her cheek, he entered the tunnel and was swallowed up by darkness. A single point of light was the only evidence he still existed in the inky blackness. Ever so slowly, Sarah pushed the old swollen door closed and swung the shelf back into place. She then looked at the clock. It was five after ten. The warrior had less than two hours to return. And if he didn't? A million possibilities crossed through her mind, but only one surfaced as the truth. She would mourn his loss for the rest of her days. For her warrior had won his China bride's heart.

The click of a door being unlocked spun Sarah back around. Her instincts warned that this was not simply some harmless lost guest. They would have knocked first. And they would not possess a key. Her eye fixated on the skeleton key still hanging from the keyhole. It soon began a strange dance, wobbling back and forth, before finally falling noisily to the oak floor. This was not good.

She barely managed to step back into a corner, before hearing flirtatious giggling, as a young couple entered the library and slid the heavy doors back in place. At first, they didn't seem to notice her standing there in shadow of the bookcase. That is until the young man, dressed in jet black with a glorious royal blue cape, swooped in and spun his lady around for a kiss. Sarah gasped.

It was Kate.

Sarah wished she could disappear back through the bookcase, but knowing it to be impossible, she decided it was a better idea to interrupt them now. Yes, much better than an embarrassing time later. Besides, Kate was most unwise to be kissing the masked stranger. Sarah had experienced firsthand what sort of evil the English could do hiding behind a mask. No, it was never a good idea to flirt with the darkness within a man.

She cleared her throat and stepped into the lamplight.

The masked Don Juan saw her first. For just a moment she could have sworn he had a look of shocked confusion. Then, as if more a gut reaction than anything else, he reached beneath his cape and drew out a pistol. However, before she had time to react, Sarah saw him stick it against Kate's ribs, pressing so hard that she cried out in surprise.

"Keep quiet, or the girl dies. I need only one of you."

Shock held her immobile. She recognized the voice at once. He was the head of the Sympathizers. Banister. A chill went up her spine as a cold sweat broke out all over her body. Whatever he was doing here, didn't bode well for her or Kate. And now that he had been discovered? Well, there was little reason to keep either one of them alive. No, their only protection lay in the fact he probably didn't want to shoot them in a house full of witnesses.

Fighting down anger at seeing how terrified Kate was, Sarah concentrated on what her options were. Uncertain, she decided to stoll for time. "What do you want Banister?"

A self-depreciating laugh slipped out from underneath the mask. "I had planned to kidnap you Lady Conway. Unfortunately, it appears I have been pursuing the wrong woman."

Kate's face grew even whiter at his words. Sarah knew, very much more of this and the innocent girl would faint. But there was no time for theatrics. So instead of giving sympathy, Sarah tried to communicate, through her actions, the importance of remaining calm. Not bothering to even look Kate's direction, she walked over to the desk and casually leaned against it. Glancing down, she took in the location of Simon's silver letter opener, only a scant six inches away. She just needed a distraction.

"And now what will you do? You can hardly take us struggling out the front door."

"I need only one of you," he repeated yet again, more a question than stating a fact.

Sarah studied him for a long moment. She found it strange, that for some reason he seemed hesitant about killing them. Which surprised her. But also, gave her the opening she needed.

"What if you simply tied Kate up and took me with you? I give you my word not to try and kill you, at least until we have left my husband's home."

"Kill him?" The words were little more than a croak coming from Kate's throat. This time her fearful gaze shot to Sarah, horror written all over her face.

Sarah ignored the question. Right now there were more important issues at hand. What Kate thought of her right now, didn't matter. What mattered more was saving their lives. Leaning over on one hand, the weapon now touched her fingertips. "What do you choose English traitor?"

"I hold the gun. I make the deals."

He shook Kate like a rag doll for emphasis. His punishing grip was the only thing now holding the poor girl up. However, with Kate slightly slumped over Sarah now had a clear shot. The only problem being that if she took it, she would miss the one opportunity she had to have some questions of her own answered. Sliding back up to an upright position, she crossed her arms serenely, before commenting conversationally.

"It is as you say. But I do not understand why you choose this course at all. My husband has already voted against the Sympathizers. Your kidnapping of me changes nothing."

"Except maybe in sending a message."

Her look showed she doubted his words. "Then why not kill me instead?"

"Sarah!" gasped a barely conscious Kate.

"Who says I won't." He shrugged and pulled Kate over to the open window, glancing out of it. "Except perhaps, that I don't normally kill women. After all, even we criminals possess some sort of morality. It so happens, that is not a line I wish to cross. Unless I am forced to, of course. Why even this kidnapping is not my idea. No, I deal more in coercion and manipulation. Most things can be solved, so I have found, with a little gentle persuasion on the part of the imbeciles who work for me. No, this my dear, is a favor for someone else."

"I assume you mean Twister?"

Surprised admiration stopped him in his tracks. The window now shoved out of the way, he shrugged, "He was of the impression you didn't know who he was. I am surprised you did not call the authorities, while you had the chance."

Adrenalin was flowing through her body. Her body growing hot, her breathing coming faster and shallower. She was so close now. It was not the time to let emotions rule her head. "I needed proof first. The word of an American is not enough. They would think I have an agenda."

"That makes sense considering who he is. Why, I would even doubt good English stock like Kate here, without proof." He motioned to the window. "You go first girl."

Kate was whimpering now. Biting her lip to keep from all out sobs.

Sarah's eyes narrowed, turning her golden brown eyes to dark chocolate. She knew his intention without him saying it. He would take them outside and then let one of his cronies kill Kate. They both knew it. After all, he could no longer allow either one of them to live. Her, she knew, he would take to the evil one and let him kill her at his leisure. For although the one called Twister did not really know her, the hate between them was longstanding. Her death would not be quick.

How ironic it was that Simon went in search of the evil one and the whole time all he had to do was stay with her to find him. Life was full of ironies. To think, Simon actually left her behind to keep her safe. Yet she believed every moment of life was perfectly coordinated. Yes, evil must run its course, but in the end good always triumphed. That is, provided one was willing to take advantage of an opportunity. Being here to save Kate was one of them. She would not allow evil to win.

"Duck Kate," Sarah yelled as she swiftly snatched up the letter opener and threw, in one fluid movement.

Thank goodness that for once in her life Kate did not argue with her.

Her aim was true.

As the makeshift knife hit his right shoulder between two main muscles, Banister automatically let go of the gun. Unfortunately, with him no longer holding her up, Kate dropped toward the ground–or, so Sarah thought. However, instead of fainting, suddenly Kate twisted around, putting a shoulder into Banister's middle, before smoothly flipping the large man out the window. She performed it perfectly. Just as Sarah had taught her earlier.

Sarah could only stare, as the young girl slammed the window shut behind Banister with such smooth coordination, it would have impressed even Grandfather. Latching it closed, Kate turned around and gave a shaky smile of pride. That is, right before she swooned. Sarah watched as Kate slowly slid down the very window, she had so bravely thrown Banister through a scant moment before.

Sarah smiled. At least the girl had waited until after throwing him out the window, before fainting. Perhaps some of the English were not so worthless after all. A shout from outside the window drew her attention.

Unfortunately, they had little time for fainting. Simon was in danger. Even now, no doubt Banister was finding his horse to warn the evil one. Without wasting another moment, Sarah walked over to the slumped body of her sister in law. A glass of cool water held carefully in her hands. Once reaching her, Sarah bent down, smiled reassuringly and – threw the contents into the passed out girl's face.

It was highly effective. Kate woke with a start...sputtering and fighting mad. But the important thing was, she was awake.

"Are you completely insane?" Kate shouted furiously at the beautiful serene woman standing over her. "Look at the mess you've made." She pointed down, as water dripped off her hair and onto her clothes leaving behind a dark trail of evidence. Unconsciously, rubbing at it, she rose on unsteady feet. "I can't believe you just did that, after I saved you."

Sarah ignored her, walked over to the bookcase and found the latch almost immediately.

"I am talking to you Sarah."

"I needed to awaken you."

"We have smelling salts, you know."

"I was unaware. If you're over your faint now, perhaps you could help me. We have to find Simon and warn him. He might be walking into a trap and I don't think he knows about Banister working with the evil one."

"What are you talking about? What trap? And who is this 'evil' one? Can't we just go find Father and..."

Sarah released the latch and started pulling at the bookshelf. The adrenalin of earlier was wearing off and her muscles trembled beneath the strain. Noticing Kate, still standing in the middle of the room, dripping all over the wood floor, Sarah ordered over one shoulder. "You are wasting time. Come help me move this bookcase."

Enough was enough. Kate had had all of Sarah's oddities for one day. Did she not even notice how close they had come to being killed for Pete's sake? And now she expected her to help rearrange the library in order to save Simon.

"Absolutely, not. This has to stop now." Sarah yanked harder on the bookcase. "I mean it, Sarah. I know you're in shock, not thinking properly, but what we need to do is find Father, not move some bookcase. It is the only way we can possibly..."

Her eyes widened in surprise as the bookcase slid out of the way, revealing a weathered, oak door.

"How did that get there?"

"Simon said the previous owner carried the spirit of fear within him."

"Simon did not say that."

Sarah sighed, wiping off her aching hands. Then, pulling hard at the rusted handle, she felt it give way. "He said the man feared being stolen from, so he built this secret passageway. It was a way to hide his valuables and a means to escape thieves if they ever did break in."

Kate peered into its dark interior. A shiver of dread went down her spine. "But where does it go? It doesn't look safe at all. And besides, wouldn't it be a lot simpler to sneak out the window? I mean, that's what you usually do, isn't it?"

"And risk meeting up with Banister and his men?"

"Oh. I had forgotten about him."

"Besides," Sarah grabbed a cold lantern from the inside of the buffet, quickly pumping the kerosene up into the wick before lighting it. "This is the way Simon went. Grandfather says a wise man walks in another's steps in order to understand their journey."

Kate just stared. "What?"

Sarah sighed. She really didn't have time for this. "There are signs. I believe this is called 'tracking'."

"You can do that?"

Memories of Sarah throwing the letter opener expertly at her target caused Kate to reply with a resigned shrug. "Never mind. Of course you can do that. I am just surprised you don't build a boat and sail us there."

Sarah paused a moment in confusion, "It would serve no purpose to build a boat, we are far from water."

"It's a joke, Sarah."

"Oh, English humor. I will never understand it. Now we have to go, there is not much time if we are to reach Simon before Banister warns the evil one."

Amazing to Kate, Sarah did not even hesitate before plunging into the dark passageway. Her hand held lantern the only light in the passage's pitch black interior. However, it was more than lack of courage, or the mere unseen that caused Kate's hesitation. No, what frightened her most was what she did know.

For one thing, they could die if they followed Simon tonight.

Yet, in spite of everything that had happened, another part of her understood that this might be the only chance she ever had of doing something really exciting in her dull superficial life. Her heart raced in anticipation, a cold sweat breaking out on her forehead. Could she do it?

"If you are afraid, then you must stay. You will be a hindrance to me. For this night requires facing what you fear the most."

Sarah's words brought rebellion to her young soul. She was not a coward. She was an adventurer. Sarah herself had said so. What else had she said? Something about not having to be unafraid. No, it was more the act of pushing past the fear. That was true bravery. Right?

"Are you coming?"

"Just a minute. I have to think."

"There is no time."

It was now or never, the lantern had begun to move. Kate looked once behind her, then, with a hoarse shout to wait, she took a step into the darkness towards the light. Her adventure had begun.

# Chapter 22

The passage led to the back of the house and only a few feet from the carriage house itself. Sarah was impressed that a man filled with such fear had the good sense to plan his getaway so completely. For fear often clouds judgment. A whiff of cold air caused her to start shaking uncontrollably. She should have brought an outer garment. If emotion had not driven her forward, she would have remembered. The damp air was chilling her to the bone through the beautiful, if not, impractical silk clothing covering her body. Simon was right about one thing, the clothing of her ancestors was not the proper attire for the bone chilling English cold.

"I'm freezing. Maybe we could get Harrison to drive us."

Apparently Kate had very little understanding of how the art of spying was accomplished.

"We cannot. However, Simon did go to the carriage house. Perhaps we can find outer garments there."

"Are you absolutely certain? I mean...he could have gone anywhere from here."

Sarah sighed.

Kate grimaced, as understanding dawned, "Oh, yes, I quite forgot. The tracking thing. Sorry."

Ignoring her sister in law's apology, Sarah ran for the shelter and warmth of the carriage house. Already she was regretting bringing the young girl along. If Kate was this apprehensive at the beginning of their journey, how would she manage when confronted with much worse obstacles than cold?

Still, to leave her behind would be taking a chance that Banister would somehow find a way to harm the girl. Kate knew too much now. No, better that she was with Sarah.

The lantern lit up the inside of the carriage house. And for just a moment, Sarah allowed herself the luxury of remembering the last time she and Simon had been here. The thought warmed her and gave her added courage.

"What's wrong? Why have you stopped, and why do you have that secret smile on your face?"

Embarrassed, Sarah changed the subject by yanking two wool cloaks from a peg along the wall. They were mud encrusted and badly in need of repair, but they would provide warmth. "Put this on."

"But it's so, well, rather disgusting don't your think? Could we possibly go back and fetch our own cloaks at least? Surely a few more minutes would hardly-"

"There is no time."

"Oh. Fine then, I'll look like a beggar, if it pleases you. I only hope I don't die wearing this thing, or I will never live it down."

The irony of such a statement seemed lost on the young girl as she cautiously slipped the object over her head.

"I need you to stay focused. Are you a good rider?"

Kate watched in fascination as Sarah saddled Thunder in record time. He was the fastest of the four horses left. Simon must have taken Chancellor. "Yes. But I have never ridden...without a side saddle." Sarah continued to cinch up the man's saddle, unperturbed by Kate's shocked reluctance.

"It is easier. And we will have to ride hard."

Kate's biting of a lower lip was the only sign she had her doubts. Still, Sarah was impressed that once Kate knew there was no other choice, the young girl adapted. It was a good sign.

Automatically coming out of her stupor, Kate went to the farthest stall, bringing out a white-footed thoroughbred named Ellie. The whole while Sarah heard her talking softly, whether to herself or the horse, Sarah couldn't be sure.

"If I am to ride that scandalous way, I'll ride my own horse. That would be wiser. Yes, then I won't slow you down too much. Or kill myself," she muttered under her breath.

"A most wise decision my husband's sister."

"Don't you think that considering we might very well die tonight, that you could at least call me Kate? I know it hardly makes sense given the nature of our business, but hearing my name comforts me somewhat. Lends a bit of normalcy, if you will."

A slight smile turned up a corner of Sarah's mouth, exposing a small dimple in her right cheek, "As you wish my...Kate."

As Kate fumbled with putting on her saddle, Sarah took the lantern out into the yard looking for signs of Simon's departure. It took only seconds to find his direction. He was heading for the docks and no doubt the burned-out warehouse. She wondered why, but decided most likely he went to fetch something from there before his meeting on the bridge. What? She had no idea.

By the time she came back into the carriage house, Kate was struggling with the cinch underneath her horse. Every time she pulled it tight, the horse would expel his pent up breath and it would fall slack once more. "Ohhh! Ellie if you do not stop behaving in this impolite manner I shall sell you to the regiment. Believe me, they shall ship you off to India, where you will only dream of good green English grass."

Laughter eased the knot in Sarah's stomach. "I do not think the horse knows of this India, for she is doing it again."

Sure enough Ellie's stomach was bloated with air.

Exasperated Kate threw the cinch and hands up into the air. "I give up. Sarah, you will just have to leave without me. I shall hide in the cold wet hay and hopefully, come morning, we all will have survived the night."

Obviously her sister in law leaned towards the dramatic. Calmly, Sarah walked over and pulled the belt tight, then waited a few moments. The minute Ellie expelled her breath; she was ready, cinching it even tighter, before securing it. Then walking the horse over to a well-placed stool, she motioned for Kate to mount.

"Is there anything you can't do?" Asked a very impressed Kate.

"Dance. I can't dance."

And to that both girls laughed. Not in true humor, but as a way to break the tension suffocating them. It was in that moment of laughter that

Sarah briefly allowed herself a twinge of self-pity, once more regretting the death of her parents. If they had lived, her life would have been much simpler. She would have been, very much like Kate. Carefree. Safe. She shook off the melancholy filling her soul. But her life was not simple and Simon needed her.

However, as she double-checked that her weapon was still safely strapped her ankle, she swore to herself that if the God of all things ever granted her a normal existence? She would never complain of boredom again. Or wish for an adventure.

No, she would create new memories instead. For the only memories she held now were filled with images of danger and surviving. Sarah shook off such thoughts. She was not one to dwell too long on things that could never be. Like having a family of her own, sewing by a crackling fire, or even cooking for a husband. No, there was no sense in feeling sorry for herself. That would never be her destiny. Even if, her husband wasn't Simon, the spy, and he already had a cook.

Shaking off such thoughts, she looked around her. Here she stood, holding a horse for a frightened English girl, dressed in stable boy rags. Her own body was alert and ready to do battle if necessary.

No, her life was far from Kate's normal one.

"Are you secure?"

"Yes, at least I suppose so." Then with teeth chattering, Kate asked seriously, "I suppose there is still no chance we could go to father with all this?"

"If you wish to stay behind, I will understand."

Her shaking hands clutched the dirty cloak closer, her chin coming up a notch. "No. If you're not afraid, then I shan't be either. Besides, who knows, you might actually need my help tonight."

The ridiculousness of that statement widened Sarah's brown eyes. But rather than trample the young girl's feelings, she climbed up on her own mount and acknowledged truthfully, "It has been known to be true. After all, many a valuable treasure is found nestled inside the most odd of packages."

"Thanks." Kate's braid swung over one shoulder as she looked suspiciously at the serene face of her sister in law. "I think."

Sarah smiled reassuringly, "It grows late. Remember we must no longer speak. Follow closely and don't hesitate if I ask anything of you. Your brother's life may well depend on it. Understand?"

"I understand."

The girls traveled in silence, the sound of their horses' hooves on slick cobbled streets, sounding near deafening, in the quiet night. The few carriages and lone cloak covered pedestrian hardly gave them a glance as they traveled down dark alleyways and streets toward the docks. But the sound of the great clock tower striking eleven caused Sarah to urge her horse on. They were running out of time and soon they would be missed.

Once reaching the burned out shell of the warehouse, Sarah skidded to a stop and jumped from her horse throwing her reins up at Kate. "I'll be right back. Watch for evildoers."

Kate's mumbling of ,"and then what?", hardly slowed Sarah down. She had no patience left to reassure the girl again. Within seconds she had made it to the make shift office just the other side of the burnt building. The shiny new lock reflected in the pale light coming from a street lamp several feet away. Impatiently she ran a hand along the door ledge. No key. In frustration she jerked on the lock, hard, but it held fast.

She debated with herself the wisdom of breaking down the door. But unfortunately there was little time for niceties. Rummaging through the pile of discarded material along side the new office building, she found a brick. And after several swift licks, the lock gave way. Pushing the door open, she hurried inside.

The dark interior made it almost impossible to make out much of anything. Groping around for a lamp and aggravated she did not think to bring one with her, at last her hands slid against smooth glass. She tried not to think about the attempt on her life last time she was alone in one of Simon's offices, focusing instead on lighting the lamp.

Outside she could now hear the soft fall of rain, as it echoed off the windowpane. She groaned. Now Simon's tracks would become even harder to make out. She must hurry.

Looking around, she spotted the safe instantly. It lay nestled underneath a file cabinet. Only there was a problem. It was standing wide open. Its dark empty interior did not bode well. Automatically, she sank to her knees on the dust-covered floor and began to search the safe. Shock made her sit back on her haunches. Everything was gone, even the plans for Simon's ship. Why would Simon need ship plans to meet with Peter?

Unless, he wasn't meeting him.

Blood rushed from her face, leaving her pale and trembling.

No, there could be only one reason Simon would empty the safe of everything. Most importantly, his ship plans. He planned to leave the country. With Hilary. Perhaps that is why he refused to take her with him.

Yet, in spite of what logic told her, her mind frantically searched for any evidence to disprove her theory. She didn't want to believe Simon a traitor. Or, most important of all, that he would leave her. Because then everything else he said was a lie as well. Including that he loved her. And she refused to accept that.

It was then that she remembered something that gave her hope. It was Banister's presence at the ball. Didn't that alone prove her husband's innocence? Or did it? Once more, internal conflict warred between her heart and her head.

After all, how had Banister slipped in undetected? And why would anyone want to kidnap her? Her family's fortune was long gone. Except for what now belonged to her husband, according to English law, she possessed nothing of worth. A husband, she reminded herself, that she knew less about than her own past. None of this night made any sense.

Even though she knew it was useless, she ran a hand one more time along the inside of the safe. Nothing except in the far back corner was a key. Not certain why, Sarah slipped it into the small pocket at her waist.

From outside, a muffled scream reached Sarah's ears.

Kate.

Without a moment's notice, to the cold downpour that saturated her clothing as she left the building, Sarah ran for the horses. Rounding the corner, she stopped suddenly in indecision. Drawing in great gulps of air, her heart sank at what she saw, or didn't see that is. She was too late. The horses were gone along with Kate. The only evidence that they had ever been there were the puddles forming in their tracks. Pushing back dripping hair out of her eyes, she peered closer at the tracks before they had a chance to disappear all together. From what she could make out, there were at least two other horses.

Anger filled her soul. The men must have followed them from the carriage house. She should have been more careful, but she had let her fear for Simon's safety make her careless. She searched the dark stormy night. It was her fault Kate was now in their hands. If only she had come alone, then perhaps Kate would be safe. But even that assumption left more questions than answers.

If that were true, why did they take Kate and leave her? None of this night made any sense. Stepping back against the wall of the office for the bit of shelter it offered from the wind picking up from the north, Sarah tried to think what to do next. Did she still go to Simon? Or find Kate? She couldn't do both.

It was then that John's promise came to her like a beacon of light on this terrible stormy night.

He would also be on the bridge tonight, watching. If she could just find him. Perhaps together they could rescue Kate and find a way to save Simon from doing something foolish. A crack of thunder made her heart pound in reaction. The hopelessness of the situation becoming even clearer, as lightening ripped through the sky overhead. She would never reach Simon in time to warn him. Not on foot.

As if on cue, the sound of a horse thundering towards her, brought her head up in shocked defiance. So, the evildoers had made a mistake after all. They were coming back for her. Good. If she were wise as a fox, she would not only escape, but have a horse as well. Slipping the small knife from the inside of her pants leg, she palmed it and placed her feet shoulder width apart for balance. She did not have long to wait.

A dark figure rode out of the blackness, as if in a nightmare. His cape billowing in the now fierce wind, his hat pulled low over his forehead to avoid the weather's relentless attack. Sarah stood her ground. How she wished she were not alone in this fight, for the man seemed well built and taller than her own five foot two by at least a foot. But it was not his size that worried her most. No, it was the aurora of power and determination in the horse's stride and his own, upon its back. A shiver went down her spine.

What if this was the one called Twister? Coming back to finish the job Grandfather had interfered with eight years before. Childhood fears and flashes of memory left her breathless and afraid. She had escaped death once at this man's hands, could she again? No enemy made her feel as weak as he did. No other invaded her dreams.

A dull pain made her look down almost in wonder at her hand. Water mixed with blood ran down from her palm, disappearing inside one silk sleeve. Automatically, she loosened her grip on the knife and forced herself to relax. If any enemy would defeat her this storm covered night, it would not be fear. So with cool logic, she focused rather, on what she would do once the dark one reached her.

She could tell the man saw her in one of the flashes of light coming from the turmoil in the heavens, for he turned his horse her direction. The time had come then.

The huge dark beast slid to stop in front of her, sides heaving. Pupils dilated. To see the man himself was impossible from this angle, so she stepped to one side and turned to face him. If destiny decreed she was to die by his hand, she would at least know her enemy's name.

"Sarah?"

She nearly burst into tears, her relief was so great. "Simon. I thought you were at the bridge."

"I just left there. Thank goodness you're all right. Peter said there would be an attempt on your life tonight. That Banister…" His green eyes narrowed under the brim of a rain spattered hat. "What are you doing here? I thought I told you to stay put." He waved away her attempt to explain. "Never mind, get up here. We have to get back to the house before we are missed."

Now anger, a welcome relief from all the tension of the past few minutes, filled her. She ignored his hand and replaced her knife. "Banister has Kate."

"He what?!"

"There is no need to shout at me as if I gave her to them."

There was no mistaking the quiet fury surrounding him now. Sarah took a step back and answered calmly, trying her best not to be intimidated. Her husband was a dangerous man and would not respect a show of fear. "I left her with the horses while I went into your office. When I came out, she was gone. I believe the tracks lead east. With Chancellor there is a good chance we can catch up with them."

The horse pranced around in agitated impatience.

Simon's voice was low and dangerous. "I think I know where they are going. I want you to stay here until I get back. You'll be safe here."

"No."

"Sarah, I don't have time to argue with you."

"You're not going without me."

His eyes were hard upon her. She raised her head a notch and glared right back, ignoring both the stinging rain and bitter cold slashing at her face. No matter what she had told Simon, she knew that Kate being nearly killed, and now kidnapped was her fault. If they had not dressed alike, none of this would be happening right now. Besides, Simon was not being completely truthful with her. He had emptied his safe and even now knew more than he was divulging. Most importantly, he had the only horse for miles around. She would not be left behind again.

Something in her eyes must have convinced him.

"All right. But it is a long ride and this storm will probably not let up."

She took his hand and let him pull her up behind him. "I will not complain." With that said she scooted up against his warm wet back and hung on. She felt him squeeze her hand in encouragement, then kick the horse into a run. The sound of the storm and deafening clashes of thunder made any further talk impossible.

Ten minutes of stinging rain and chilling wind made her grateful that Simon was buffeting most of the assault with his own body. Yet still they rode on, past the ships and towards the edge of London. The small bridge where Sarah received her first kiss from Simon flew past. They were now following the river's edge hugging it too closely for Sarah. Perhaps Simon was having trouble seeing in the blinding rain, for that could be the only explanation she could come up with to take such a chance. Still she wished he would not ride so close to its swollen churned up mass. Even the best of swimmers would not be able to defeat such a foe.

What seemed like hours, but probably only half an hour later, Simon turned south. Slowing down only once, he soon reached a small outcrop of trees gracing a long driveway that led up to a modest estate. The rain was easing up finally, yet Sarah somehow felt colder inside. Numb. As if the rain had sucked all the warmth from her body and emptied it out into the black English soil. Although she tried to force her body otherwise, she began shaking, her cold hands gripping Simon's body closer for warmth.

He stopped at last in front of a small thatched roof house on the left, and slid off the horse. Reaching up, he pulled her down beside him. "This is the gatekeeper's cottage...or it was. It should be dry inside. I'll take care of the horses. Why don't you see if you can start a fire."

"We must not stop. Kate needs us."

Simon bent down and kissed the mutinous words off her lips.

"It won't help Kate if we are caught. Believe me, they are not going anywhere for a while and this is a safe enough place as any to watch from. I need time to plan what to do."

He was right of course. Yet, it was so hard to wait. Kate had to be terrified.

Patiently, he waited. Rain ran off his coat and pooled on top of the already saturated ground. No doubt he was afraid to leave without her promise she wouldn't run off again. For the first time she smiled, if just a tad self-depreciatingly.

"I cannot leave, if I don't know where I am."

Her answer seemed to satisfy him. With a curt nod he turned on his heel and headed for the small lean to, that at one time must have served as a barn.

It felt strange when she entered the cottage. Drops of rain plopped to the floor through the badly in need of repair roof, and yet there was a feeling of welcome inside. As if this little gatekeeper's house, had known only happiness once before. The previous family had made it their home. This one had known love. She could tell. Houses were like echoes of their previous owners. Embedded in their walls were a signature of sorts. A feeling.

Looking around, she noticed there were still many objects left behind from the last residents. Blankets, and even discarded clothing lay hidden in an old dusty trunk. Along the walls, jars of fruit and vegetables lay scattered on broken shelves. Whatever, or whoever had caused the family to leave, must have happened suddenly. There had been little time for packing. Sarah only hoped it was for a better life and not a tragedy that caused such haste.

Perhaps they had left for America and a chance to live out their dreams. She hoped so, for every item left behind was obviously made with love and carefully tended, despite the years of neglect since their leaving.

She couldn't stop shaking.

Her anger no longer keeping her warm, she realized Simon was right. They had to first get warm and then form a rescue plan. She just trusted Simon was also right about Banister not harming Kate. The thoughts of her friend suffering were too difficult to bear, so instead Sarah concentrated on the simple task of removing her clothing. After wrapping a dusty, but dry brown and yellow quilt around her body for warmth, she dug through the old trunk trying to find dry clothing for Simon and herself. The sound of the front door banging open made her jump.

A little self-consciously she gripped the blanket closer together and gave a wan smile. "I was searching for something to wear."

His eyes drifted down to one exposed leg, "I like what's underneath that blanket better."

She blushed at the compliment. Pushing at the drying curls of hair that were falling into her eyes, she changed the subject, "I haven't started a fire yet, but the house is very welcoming. There are blankets, clothing and food, as if some weary traveler might want to stop and rest."

Shaking off the rain from his outer garments, he hung them on a peg by the door and commented dryly, "A house is not a living thing, China. Fortunately for us, apparently its owners had to leave in a hurry. Sometimes another's misfortune is simply your good luck."

A frown marred her beautiful features, as she snorted her disapproval. "You are entirely too jaded Warrior. Sometimes a gift from heaven is just that...a gift."

Strangely enough he didn't argue with her. His green eyes softened and a sexy half smile made her stomach tighten with anticipation. "And if I understand your grandfather's teaching, since you saved my life, that makes me your gift."

He had her there. Huffing with displeasure, Sarah started rummaging through the trunk once more determined to ignore him.

"If you keep mumbling about your husband in those unflattering terms sweetheart, I will begin to think you don't appreciate your gift."

She spun around and flung a dry pair of pants his direction. "Don't you have a fire to start?"

His laughter followed her to the bedroom, where she slammed the door shut to the mocking words, "I don't know, it looks like I already started one."

Coming out a few minutes later to a cozy fire burning in the hearth and Simon staring into its flames, Sarah wondered how such a terrible night could still contain moments of contentment. Simon was safe. And they were together. It comforted her, and made her feel guilty at the same time. Quietly, she went over and laid a comforting hand to his shoulder.

Their clothing and shoes were laid out neatly before the fire, a small fog of steam rising from some of the objects nearest the flames. In the quietness of the room, the task before them seemed impossible. How easy it would be to just stay here. But as Grandfather said, integrity and honor were better bedmates than a man's regrets.

Sitting down beside him, she placed a hand to his cheek. Their eyes met and held. When he smiled, it was touched with sadness. "This is all my fault, you know. I thought by handling things myself, I could somehow keep you and the rest of my family out of this mess. Now, instead I've put you all in danger. I was such a fool."

"You did what you thought was best. Besides, the destroyer of lives created this trouble, not you."

Catching her hand up in his, he kissed the inside of her palm, and moved away. The time of regrets was over and once more he was the warrior. He went to retrieve his saddlebag from beside the door. Dropping it onto the table in the center of the room. The table tilted precariously towards him, as he rummaged through the bag, one of its legs slightly shorter than the others.

"If I am right, they have Kate holed up in the main house. Probably the wine cellar. There is an old room down there that they use to keep locked."

"How do you know of this place?"

He looked away and stared harder into the flames. "That hardly matters. What does, is that this man wants me, and I plan to give him what he came for."

"I do not see how this will help free Kate."

The calmness of her tone was deceptive, inside she was shaking with fury. The one called Twister would not steal her family from her again. No matter what he decided, she would not allow Simon to sacrifice himself. Traitor or not, he was hers. With a quietness she did not feel, she asked matter of fact, "What is your plan?"

He stepped away from the fireplace and over to the table. "Come here and I will show you." Pulling out a sheet of paper and a quill from the bag, he dipped it in ink and began drawing. "This is a layout of the house." His hands did not hesitate once. With quick clear marks, the house plans took shape. Sarah felt uneasy.

What was this place that both her husband and the evil one knew of it?

449

"I will go in the front and allow myself to be taken. During the distraction, you will climb in this window here, which leads to the kitchen and sneak downstairs to the wine cellar. If I'm right, Kate will be there." He pointed to a section of the wall filled with wine racks.

"And if you're not?"

For once, he grew serious, "I have to be right." Then continuing on, added, "You may have to take out a guard or two. I don't know how many are guarding her. Of course, I plan on putting up enough of a fight, that it will take most, if not all of the available men to subdue me. The only advantage we have is that they have no idea you are with me. I wish there were another way, but you're all I've got China. Can you do this?"

"I am not afraid."

The look on his handsome face was bittersweet, "I know you're not. You are the bravest soul I know. That is not what I meant. What I am asking from you is this, under no circumstances do I want you to try and save me. I can take care of myself. What I really need from you, is to harness that stubborn temper of yours and do as I say. If you can't, then I swear, I will tie you up myself and leave you here."

"But..."

The quill slammed down, blotting the paper. "If you want to do something to help, get Kate out of there and find John. He will know what to do. He went back to the party after my meeting with Peter." Simon noted Sarah was silently watching him, unperturbed by his show of temper. He sighed heavily. "Believe it or not, he was supposed to look out for you. I had no idea you weren't at the house, until I saw you standing there at the warehouse."

"Why did you empty the safe?"

"There will be time to explain everything later. For now, what I want-"

"I need to know."

"Another test, Sarah?"

The fire crackled a warning, the rain falling softly against the windowpanes reminding her to tread lightly. Her doubts stood between them. Again. They both knew it, whether she admitted it aloud or not.

"Simon, I no longer care if you are a smuggler. The confederacy government itself is smuggling cotton across the Gulf. I just need to know what I am walking into, how best to protect you because... well, I can't seem to stop myself from loving you."

The last words seem torn from her very heart. For once he had to understand and trust her.

It seemed he did. She saw him physically relax, his eyes soften. Gently, his strong hand cupped her face. The eyes looking deeply into her own, held all the love in the world. Shaking his head in wonder, he asked, "When did all this happen, China?"

Pride could not keep the tears from her throat. "I believe it was when heaven gave you to me that day in the hotel room." She shrugged at his growing smile. "Apparently, given all the times I have thrown you into things, I am not very good at receiving gifts either."

"Oh, I don't know. I think some gifts are little harder to accept than others."

"So, will you trust me with the truth?"

The fire still crackled, the rain still fell, but what lay between them had changed. He nodded. "I told you the truth. I'm not a smuggler. Though sometimes, I wonder why I bother to stay honorable. It hardly makes me rich and because of my foolish honor, I may lose everything I love, including you, if things doesn't go as planned today."

"If you're not leaving me, then why empty the safe?"

Turning away, he ran a hand through drying hair. "I don't know what I think I am protecting you from. For some uncanny reason you seem to know people's true nature, despite my best efforts to shield you. The truth is...you are partly right." He watched as she steeled herself, "I thought I might have to leave in a hurry tonight. See, I have been acting on my own for over two weeks now. After what happened on the beach, I was told that Peter was the man behind all the smuggling and ordered to stop investigating."

"But you didn't."

"No. I knew it was someone else. And I also knew he was still out there. I could feel it. John tried to reason with me. Even helped me at

451

times, when it might have meant losing his reputation. The very one he had worked so hard to achieve, despite my uncle's failures. But then even he doubted if I was a man looking for an enemy, or obsessed with one."

"John said he was supposed to watch you."

"Sad, but true. My superiors warned me repeatedly I was overstepping my bounds. When I actually shipped illegal cotton? Well, let's just say, if I don't prove my theory soon? I will have to leave England on my own. That, or else, spend the rest of my life on a penal colony in Australia."

"But you won't leave."

He kissed her forehead, running a thumb under golden eyes, and promised, "No. I won't leave. At least not without you."

"Then we will have to not only save Kate, but unmask the evil one as well. If not, well then I get my wish to take you to my America."

"Does it never occur to you that I might be lying?"

Clear eyes met his. "No."

His deep laugh shook the rafters, "That is exactly why I fell in love with you, you know. The reason, I try to protect you from my true nature. Because regardless of how jaded I am, you still hope I will choose the way of honor. The funny thing is, I find myself wanting to be near you and that world embracing optimism of yours. While deep down, I am worried that given the facts of human nature, you will lose the trust I see in those beautiful brown eyes. If you lost those things all the good in the world would disappear. Because sweetheart, I may be your gift, but you're my salvation."

She was crying now.

Laughing, her pulled her onto his lap and admonished, "Warriors don't cry sweetheart, or have you forgotten?"

Wiping her nose on the worn cotton shirt now warming her body, she sniffled, "I do not have to be a warrior until later."

He looked out at the night. Already the darkness was easing the way for dawn. "Not much later, I'm afraid. We don't have time to go into all of it, but I will tell you this much. I gave some cash to Peter. Which, seeing as he is under investigation, makes me look pretty guilty. Even John doesn't know I gave it to him."

Shock made Sarah say, a little unsteadily, "Why did you?"

"I believed him. Not at first, but I took another look into his affairs when you seemed so certain about him. It seems Hilary has signed many a document using his name. Apparently she is in league with a governor in Mexico, shipping over illegal cotton. She's been using her brother's name to do it. In exchange for the cash I gave him, Peter turned over all the documents he had. I guess, the only thing Peter is guilty of is being a fool."

"Then it's over."

Simon shook his head, replacing his silky white shirt with a borrowed one from the trunk. She moved slightly out of the way, yet remained on his lap. "Hardly. True, Hilary has escaped to Mexico. However, because of her, the Sympathizers losing the vote in the House of commons, and even his own ignorance. Peter now has to leave the country, or suffer the hangman's noose. The only proof I have of any of this, are those documents. I think I mentioned, that they were given to me by a suspected traitor. It is hardly over sweetheart."

Placing her off his lap, he pulled on his damp Hessians continuing, "Peter also wanted to warn me that there was a plot to kidnap you last night. He overheard a conversation Hilary had with Banister. Oddly enough, he seemed genuinely worried about you." Simon buttoned up the borrowed shirt of coarse wool, as he lovingly studied her reaction to that bit of news, "You have that effect on others, you know."

"What?"

"Making people fall madly in love with you."

Her heart warmed at his words. Her shoes already dry, she slipped them on easily before replacing her knife. Their voices continued exchanging bits of information, the whole time ignoring the fact they were dressing for battle. "I am glad Peter is not as terrible as you thought. I truly liked him."

The rain had stopped. Sarah worried her bottom lip. She was glad for warmth's sake, but from a battle standpoint, disappointed. The noise would have covered much.

"He did give me a name however. It was a man in Texas. Pat Milno. He might be connected somehow. It seems he is an Irish storekeeper in San Antonio, Texas. Peter heard Banister arguing rather loudly with someone at his gaming house. Something about the storekeeper contracting a man named Roy Bean to freight cotton. Apparently Bean is a known renegade, and Banister was worried the man might steal part of the cotton and sell it off before it ever reached Mexico. I have always found it odd that thieves have such a low tolerance of each other. Nevertheless, what I found interesting was that Milno has a brother who is son in law of the governor of Coahuila Mexico."

Sarah gasped, "Do you think he might know who was behind the Mexican smugglers?"

His face hardened. "It's a strong possibility. However, from the looks of things, I may be proving my innocence while on the run."

"Regardless, I will go with you."

It was not a request. He gave a resigned sigh. "I know."

They both knew none of this would matter if Twister succeeded tonight. There would be no one to prove anything. Peter would forever be an exile and Hilary would become a very rich American. Meanwhile, Twister would continue to destroy lives. Evil would win. Sarah braided her hair, tucking it inside her shirt. It could be used as a weapon otherwise.

Both had finished dressing now and neither one of them could think of anything more to say. Out loud. Given the chance Sarah would have begged him not to sacrifice himself to the evildoers. With a lump in her throat, Sarah watched him check his gun and powder one last time before getting his cloak. Rather than put it around his own shoulders, he wrapped it around hers.

"Simon, I do not need it." It would only hamper her ability to fight.

He seemed to understand, but firmly replaced the cloak anyway saying, "Just until we reach the house. Hide it outside the kitchen window if you like. Kate might have need of it."

She had forgotten Kate might need something dry and warm once she had been rescued.

"Do we go on foot then?" She was rambling, anything to put off this heart-wrenching moment.

"Yes. I've left Chancellor saddled up in the lean to. I want you to ride him back to the house. If you can't find John, then Father will know what to do. That reminds me. Sarah, if anything happens to me in there."

"It won't."

He laughed at the fierceness in her voice. "Well, just in case, I want you to get those documents to John. Do I have your word?"

She stubbornly refused to answer, her hand on the door handle.

He reached down and covered it with his own. When he spoke it was to gentle her. "Sarah, I assure you, I don't intend to die. But, I do need your promise."

Her sigh was loud enough to wake the dead. "You'll be delivering your own messages husband, so I suggest you don't die on me."

With that said she yanked the door open and pushed past Simon and out into the early dawn. Admiration made his heart swell with pride and wonder. Leave it to his China wife to think that by willing it so, she could change destiny.

He shut the door, and watched the tiny figure swallowed up by his frock coat, set off for the house. His stomach clenched at the beauty of her courage. One promise he would dare make to himself was that, if they ever lived through this, all in the world he wanted was to settle down with his China wife and raise beautiful strong babies. Yes, his only request was that God would allow him the peace of knowing she was safe. A man in love could ask for no more than that.

Daybreak filled the woods surrounding the house. Sarah would have been slightly awed by the God of heaven's display of shadowy color on the wild roses and green lawn stretching before them if she hadn't been so nervous. Truth be told, the house was lovely. It was a simple two story, with both an upper and lower porch. Orange light now bounced off the beveled windows, giving them a look of multifaceted diamonds rather than simple glass. And although the garden was a bit neglected and the outside of brick and wood, covered in ivy, needed a whitewash...Sarah felt a connection.

Which made her wonder, yet again, how Simon knew of its existence. And why she felt as if she had been here before.

The touch of his hand on her arm startled her. When she looked back it was not Simon her husband, but Simon the warrior standing just back of her right shoulder. His face was hard as flint. The muscles of his powerful arms and chest straining against the slightly too small shirt. He leaned down to whisper-no order, her back around to the kitchen. She was not upset by his abrupt tone or attitude. It was the way of a warrior in battle.

Obediently she nodded and ran low across the lawn to the thick shrubbery along the side wall of the house. Once there, her chest tightened and her blood ran cold. It was not that she was frightened for herself, only for Simon. An uneasy feeling made her instinctively pray that he would be kept safe. It was all she would allow herself. Otherwise, she would not be able to keep her promise to him. To let him be taken.

Closing her eyes to wipe out all thoughts but the rescue of Kate, Sarah once again gained control. She breathed in the crisp morning air and continued on around to the back of the house. Taking off Simon's coat, she hid it in the bushes and waited. Simon made it to the front door a few minutes after she had found her position. And unless the ones who guarded were asleep or deaf, they would notice his smashing of a front window.

She did.

Soon the sounds of a house waking up in chaos issued. There were shouts, feet running up and down stairs, and then there was fighting. She could hear the fight from where she stood. Not allowing herself to think too much about what Simon was up against, she began trying windows. It took only three tries to find an open one. Thank goodness the kidnappers were careless, as well as easily fooled. Climbing through, Sarah gave herself a moment for her eyes to adjust to the semi darkness inside. It would only make matters worse if she stumbled over something and was captured.

After a short time, she could just make out the rough wooden table in the middle of the kitchen, as well as pots and pans that hung from a cobweb covered ceiling. It was nearly daylight and the hazy light sifting in from outside was quickly illuminating everything in the room. She had to hurry. There was a door to right, if Simon's drawing was correct, she would begin there. She must prepare her mind. For surely, at least one guard remained to secure the door with Kate inside.

After careful consideration, she shrugged, remembering Grandfather's advice about choices. The simpler ones were always best. So, taking that into account, she curled up a fist and...knocked.

The rough looking man who answered was rubbing sleep from his eyes when Sarah's front snap kick knocked him back down the stairs and onto the wine cellar floor. How he had remained asleep with all the commotion coming from the front was beyond her. She was just thankful for his laziness. He was moaning loudly and barely conscious by the time she slipped down the stairs, knocking him out the rest of the way, with a light tap to his temple.

Checking around and finding no other threat, she tied him up with a piece of rope from the cottage. She had tied it around her waist, just in case. Tearing off a piece of her shirt, she stuffed the rag into his mouth. She was running out of time, no one, even Simon would be able to hold a house full of evildoers much longer.

"Kate!" The time for quietness had passed. If they didn't get out of there fast, it would be too late.

"In here!" The voice coming from inside a room along the back wall sounded hoarse with barely restrained tears. "It's locked. You have to get out of here before they come back."

It was dark as night. The pale light finding its way to the cellar was not strong enough for hunting a key. And she had already searched the man's pockets laid out at her feet. It couldn't be helped, she would have to chance that Simon was still creating a diversion. "Move away from the door."

That said, she felt along the wall until her hand touched a shovel. Raring back she slammed it several times against the handle to the door to no avail. She dropped the shovel and ran a hand through disheveled hair. The door was too thick to kick open. Now what?

Kate's face rose up against the bar filled window at the top of the door. "Get out of here Sarah."

Ignoring her pleas, Sarah started to feel along her waist pockets for any object she might use to pick the lock. It was then she felt the forgotten key, taken from the warehouse's safe. It was worth a try.

How easily it slipped into place, a soft clicking sound giving Sarah hope. With one simple turn of the key, the heavy oak door was opened. Kate ran into her arms sobbing. "I thought they would kill me. How did you ever manage to find me?"

"Not now. We have to get out of here before they bring Simon down."

Her face cleared instantly, "Simon is here?"

Sarah was pulling her towards the stairs, ever watchful for signs of activity in the kitchen above. "He has allowed himself to be captured, so I could free you. After I take you to Chancellor, you are to ride like the wind and find John."

Now at the top of the stairs, she could just see the open window. It was so close Sarah could almost touch it. Morning light flooded the kitchen making her feel more exposed than ever. Shoving Kate towards the window, Sarah ordered, "Now."

They barely had time to dive out the window, before Sarah heard voices coming into the kitchen. Motioning for Kate to crawl until they were out of line of sight, she quietly eased up and pushed the window closed. It was then she recognized a voice in the sea of angry shouts.

Trembling, she slid back down to her hiding place, her mind racing with indecision. Kate's own eyes were wide with shock, as she scooted over and tried to peek into the window. No doubt needing as Sarah did, to see for herself. Sarah jerked her back down and placed a warning finger to her lips. Kate nodded, but a disappointed sadness filled her dark hazel eyes. Tears gathered and threatened to fall, but Sarah was grateful Kate kept them in check.

It had been a night of disillusionment. But life was like that sometimes, and it must not prevent you from moving ahead. From doing what had to be done. But, before she could do anything else, she had to get Kate out of there. From the weary, heartbroken look in her red rimmed eyes, her sister in law could not take much more. Grabbing up the frightened girl's cold hand, and the discarded coat with her other, Sarah bolted towards the opposite corner of the house rather than the woods.

Once out of earshot, she quickly threw the heavy coat over Kate's shoulders, quickly explaining, "Did you notice the gatekeeper's cottage when they brought you here?"

"Yes, vaguely, why?"

"You will have to go through the woods. It will take a bit longer, but with all of them in the kitchen, there is less a chance of getting caught. Once reaching the cottage, you will find Chancellor saddled and waiting for you."

Kate looked indecisive, chewing on a chapped lower lip. "But what about you?"

"I'm going back for Simon."

A horrified gasp escaped Kate's throat, "Alone? But you'll be killed. Sarah I heard them talking, saying something about getting rid of a few loose ends. If you go back there, they will have both you and Simon."

"Then I suggest you ride as if Satan himself were after you." When the young shivering girl opened her mouth to argue yet again, Sarah cut her off impatiently. "If I do not go back, Simon will die. You and I both know that now."

And she did. Sadly, Kate nodded her head. "But why would...what will you do once you go in there?"

"Grandfather says, some moments have to unfold before another is revealed."

Huddling in the coat, Kate admonished with a wobbly smile, "If you don't have a plan Sarah, just say so."

Sarah brushed the long wavy braid back off her shoulder and tucked it back into her shirt, before grinning, "I saved you without a plan, didn't I?"

Brightening, Kate reached over and gave Sarah's hand a squeeze, "Yes, you did. You will be careful?"

"Always."

Kate hated to leave, but Sarah kept looking back worriedly towards the kitchen. "I have to go."

Wondering if this would be the last time she saw the small, slender girl with endearing, if not odd ways, Kate gave her one last hug. "I'll send help."

Both girls knew it would be too late.

"Good."

Then because Sarah wished it, Kate took off running.

After watching, to make sure she safely reached the woods, Sarah turned and headed back towards the kitchen. She had a husband to save.

Men were now emptying out the doors. It had begun. They were searching for her and Kate. Giving one quick glance inside to make sure the kitchen was empty, Sarah pushed open the same window she had exited a moment ago. Without a sound, she slipped back inside. There were muffled voices coming from the front room. Unfortunately, she couldn't tell how many. The door leading to the cellar lay wide open, its gaping darkness sending a chill up her spine. At least they had not taken Simon down there.

Truth be told, she did not want to go back there. She hated to admit a weakness, but tiny dark rooms were hers. In them, lay little room for error and only one way out. No, open rooms were best, if you had to fight your way out.

She shook her head at the endless talk inside herself. Who was she kidding? The odds were insurmountable, no matter which room they had taken Simon to. Kate was right. Very likely, they would both end their lives here. But she could not leave Simon.

A shadow walking past the kitchen window caused her to duck down beside the pie safe, her chest heaving with fear. She blinked her eyes, willing herself to stay in the present. Her emotions were out of control and not only because of Simon. Her memories were choosing this inconvenient time to start trying to resurface. They kept interchanging with the present, like a disappearing ball and cup game.

How she wished Grandfather was here right now. Kate was right. She had no plan. And last time she checked, one woman against an army was not enough. She closed her eyes to even her breathing. It was then she heard a gentle voice from her past whisper, 'Do what comes next darling'. She flinched to the very core of her being. It was her mother's beautiful voice. It had come back to her. At this most inopportune time. And not only her voice, but past memories were flooding back as well. Flashing uncontrollably, as if filling up the empty folders of her mind. Now was not a good time. She had to be able to concentrate.

She felt close to tears, while at the same time, filled with unspeakable joy. There didn't seem to be any way to stop the onslaught once it had begun. Why now? This place?

Suddenly she remembered being lifted on her father's strong shoulders. Even remembered the made up stories her mother told using Sarah as the heroine, and…her parent's laughter. She put a fist to her stomach, and one to her mouth to keep from crying out. So much emotion assaulted her senses, that it was nearly overload. Every memory of past happiness was enough to nearly knock her to her knees. For some insane reason, her other life had come back to her, here at this moment. In this house.

Dizziness and shock made her reach out and grab hold of the pie safe. Speaking of which…she remembered it too. Spinning around to stare at the kitchen around her, she gasped. She remembered this house, growing up here. This was her house. A new wave of emotion sent her head reeling. Pressing an open palm to her throbbing head, she tried to force the memories back to where they had laid dormant for so many years. She had to gain some sort of control. Simon needed her. She didn't have time for this. She had to breathe, to gain control, to…she covered the sobs emptying out of her mouth.

It was then she looked up.

Light green eyes, devoid of sympathy, looked back into hers with cold calculating curiosity. She would have screamed if she could have breathed. For standing before her, in flesh and blood, was the man of her nightmares.

John.

A familiar coldness swept over her. Still, lost in the clutches of the past, she sounded more horrified than angry, "How could you have killed them?"

"Ah, so you remember. That is really too bad Sarah. By the way, you look awfully pale, perhaps you should sit down. Then you can save me a lot of trouble, by telling me where exactly Kate is."

Everything suddenly became so surreal. Here stood the man who claimed to be her friend, who had rescued her twice, no three times. Yet in his eyes, dwelt the other man. The one who had methodically killed her parents, chased her down through the dark streets of London, and then fought Grandfather for her life. How had she not seen it? How had she not recognized him?

Her grandfather's words came back to her. About how not knowing would keep her safe. She stared down at the revolver in John's hand now pointing straight at her heart. The time of secrets had past.

"Why do any of this?" Was her tortured response.

Unbelievably, she thought she saw a passing glimmer of regret, his lean body relaxing, as his grip on the gun loosened a little. But, of course, she was mistaken. How could he feel anything as noble as regret? No, men like him, felt nothing. He only pretended such things as regret.

"Do you really think it matters at this point? Ah, Sarah, I so wanted to keep you alive, at least for a little while longer. I have to admit, I have rather enjoyed our little game. But now you have spoiled everything by your stubborn nature. If only you wouldn't have insisted on following Simon. I did try to warn you, if you recall. Now I am forced into this. And although I am tempted to see what you taste like, before having to kill such perfection, it is inconvenient timing."

Licking her lips, Sarah fought the dizzy fear assaulting her senses. She would be sick if he touched her. And she did have a choice. She was not ten any longer. And she was not alone. Simon was somewhere in the house. If she could keep John talking, there was a chance her husband would find a way to free himself. Surely if the Chinese were taught the art of escape, British spies were as well.

She forced her eyes away from the gun aimed at her heart and spoke softly, "You must have been only a boy when you chased me that night."

"Seventeen, to be exact. But living on the streets of London makes one grow up rather fast. Do you realize, you are the only one that ever got away from me? I believe that must be the reason why even now, when I know there is no other way...well, it will be rather bittersweet for me when our relationship comes to an end. The chase has been interesting to say the least."

"You could have killed me anytime. Why wait until now?"

He threw his head back in laughter, and Sarah felt the bile rise in her throat. Only the insane, or someone without a soul, would find any part of this humorous. But then again, what had she expected.

Not this. Not from the man she thought he was, pretended to be. Was none of it real?

Flashes of John's hurt expression; when he was unwelcome during dance lessons, of him pledging his love for her and then the times he saved her, saved Simon. It made her doubt everything and everyone, worst of all, her own judgment.

After his laughter died down to a slight chuckle, he admitted with a shrug, "I did try to kill you dear heart. Twice to be exact, but as I have said earlier, you have eluded me beautifully."

When she simply looked confused, he placed a hip on the rough wooden table in the middle of the room and explained, "You can imagine my shock when I laid eyes on you that first evening. You're as beautiful as your mother was. Killing such a beauty as she, bothered me a little, but it couldn't be helped. However, if your father had lived, dear Uncle Henry would have gone to prison. I couldn't allow it. You see, my mother and I would have been kicked out on the streets, once again. My father,

463

certainly wouldn't have lifted his head out of a drunken haze long enough to stop it from happening, that's for sure."

He gallantly shoved a chair her direction, "Do sit down Sarah, before you fall down." When she refused his offer, he shrugged and continued, "As you wish. Anyway, one night I replaced the account books with a very good copy of my own, implicating your father in a gambling ring. That bit of genius was perhaps the only decent idea my mother ever had, in her short pathetic life. Then, the night my uncle was too foxed to pick up your family at the theater, I convinced him to send me instead."

Suddenly, it all became clear why Henry felt so terribly guilty. He had to suspect that John knew more than he was saying. But why cover up for him? Sarah heard a slight shuffling sound coming from the other room. When John grew quiet, she immediately drew his attention back to her. "So Uncle Henry suspects you killed my parents for him? Is that why he is still protecting you?"

Anger saturated his voice until it quivered. Apparently she had struck a nerve. It was the first time, since entering the room, he had shown any real emotion whatsoever. "Oh, he owes me. But not for that. No, my dear, you see my uncle was devastated to learn that I had loaned the coach to his brother."

"But it was you, not your father who –"

"You and I know that dear Sarah, but believe me, unlike you I am a very good liar. My poor uncle believed me, in fact still believes his brother responsible for the crime. This is why he went to jail without hardly a whimper, when he was accused of it. Oh, and then there was that other secret, of course."

A chill ran through her veins as she asked quietly, "What was so terrible a secret that it would condone murder?"

The heavy wooden mallet lying in the sink was within arms reach. All she needed was for him to let his guard down for even half a second, then she could put an end to this sickening confession. The click of a hammer being pulled back, stopped her instantly.

"Let's not be foolish, shall we. Unless you really don't intend to try and change my mind about killing you."

Easing away from the mallet, her golden eyes shot fire, "To be able to do so, I would have to assume you had a conscious."

He threw back his handsome blond head in laughter at her insult. It took several seconds to get a hold of himself before admitting regretfully, "We would have been so good together. I never wanted it to end this way. If you recall, I saved your life in the warehouse that night Hilary shot at you. Fortunately for you, she never was a very good shot. No, what I really wanted, was you alive. It could have been perfect. With your intelligence and my cunning, the world would have been ours for the taking. In fact, I really believe I am half in love with you still."

The only thing keeping her from scoffing out loud at that ridiculous statement, was the gun aimed straight at her heart. Looking past his shoulder, she noticed a bloody and bruised Simon fighting off a wave of nausea against the hallway wall. The shadowy hall hiding him from the men crossing the window behind her. She had to buy him a little more time. Together they might have a chance.

"What you wanted was impossible, I belong to Simon."

"Oh, yes...there is that. It seems as if my dear cousin possesses quite a lot of things that were really meant to be mine. You. My father. The inheritance."

Shock momentarily made Sarah forget all else, except his outrageous statement. "You believe Uncle Henry to be your father? But, that's impossible."

"Is it? Or, a very convenient lie, wouldn't you say? My mother, God rest her soul (which is not very likely), confessed the truth to me that night when I went to pick up Uncle Henry at the gaming halls. How she had been a young maid in the house, when Henry and his no account brother ruined her life and mine. All about how dear old Henry came to her cottage one night drunk and heartbroken. Seems he did not take kindly to being forced into marriage, with a woman he barely knew. So, he decided to rebel by drinking too much and having a fling with the downstairs maid. Only the fling resulted in a son. Yours truly."

Sarah almost felt sorry for the unwanted bitter boy he must have become. "How did you end up on the streets?"

His voice sounded weary now, resigned. "When my mother went to Uncle Henry with the news she was pregnant, his father overheard and dismissed her on the spot. Uncle Henry, by this time, was happily married and denied everything. He did, however, press a few guilty pounds into her palm before kicking her out onto the streets. Mighty decent of him don't you think?"

He shrugged. "After a few months, with no family to turn to, she had little choice but to earn her way using the only asset she had left. Her looks. Unfortunately, those lasted only long enough to buy us a few lean years. It was during this time, that I found my own sort of talent, shortly after joining a group of street kids."

"The Knockers."

He raised an eyebrow, "I'm very impressed, Sarah. What else did you learn about me?"

Simon was signaling for her to move towards the right. Casually she rolled up her right sleeve, as she moved in closer and to the right. John smiled when she looked down at his own right arm with a faint showing of a marking on his forearm. "Ahh…my tattoo."

"I remembered seeing it that night. A snake wrapped around a moneybag. Reminds me of another evil one who lived long ago. Grandfather's bible tells of him. Perhaps you too, know of this story."

His hand shook with emotion, although his face remained calmly serene, "Now you are just trying to make me angry. I am hardly a Judas."

"Aren't you? He, too, was a money hungry coward who betrayed someone he loved."

Cold green eyes narrowed in on her, and she felt terribly alone. Even with Simon motioning for her to wait for his signal. She knew this stranger in John's body meant to kill her. And a part of her believed, that though she had defeated destiny once, she would not do so again. She took a calming breath and went over in her mind the path she would take to destroy her enemy before she died.

"Goodbye Sarah. I find I have tired of you, after all."

A furious roar filled the room as Simon lunged forward, knocking John to the ground. The deafening sound of a gun going off sent Sarah to her knees. Trying to cover her ears, a searing shot of pain ripped through her left arm. Dazed, she stared down in morbid fascination at the blood spreading through the cotton garment covering her upper arm.

"Sarah the gun!"

The sound of men running drew her attention for a moment. She was going to pass out. Once more, she was back at the hotel where she and Simon had met. Him, fighting for his life. She, simply an observer.

"Can you hear me, China?"

The urgency in Simon's voice drew her back to the present. She forced back the pain back, and immediately began searching the floor. Men's shouts were everywhere. Hope died in her breast. They could not win this battle. Yet still she groped the floor in a vain attempt to find the weapon. Her mind settled on only one thing. To save Simon. After several more precious seconds, she realized the weapon was nowhere to be found.

Just as that thought took shape, her father's death swam before her tear filled eyes. The weapon would not save them, just as it had not been able to save her father. She shook off the traitorous thought. Forcing back the memory, and feeling of defeat it evoked. Suddenly she knew what she must do.

Sending a prayer heavenwards, she stood facing the two men in a struggle to the death. Her mind was clear, and her heart rate slowing. 'One can defeat only one enemy at a time Little One', her grandfather's voice called out to her, 'do not become your own.'

Without paralyzing fear holding her hostage any longer, Sarah was able to react. Quickly she ran to John and placed a well-aimed fist to his left kidney. Instantly he crumpled in agonizing pain. Then with pain filled rage, he threw Simon off him and against the table. Spinning around, he lunged at Sarah. In one smooth movement, he wrapped an arm around her throat, choking her into submission.

Panic made her clutch at his arm, digging into the flesh until blood trickled down his arm and onto her sleeve. But, they both knew she was fading fast. Her blows were becoming weaker, the room swirling through pain dulled eyes. Soon she would no longer be able to defend herself, for it took all her life energy just to stay alive.

Simon was on his feet once more. Vaguely, she noted he too was bleeding from wounds he must have sustained during his interrogation. His beautiful face battered beyond recognition. She wanted to call out to him...to warn him away. If he did not escape, her sacrifice would be for nothing. Twice she had saved him. And twice he had stayed anyway. She had to stay conscious, to make him understand. A sound she did not recognize came from her own throat, part whimper, and part fury.

"Hold still, sweetheart", the blurry figure of her husband ordered from some place outside of herself.

Then there was a thundering roar. Right before the world went dark and Sarah slipped blissfully into the abyss of unconsciousness. Her last thought and prayer being that of Simon. That he lived.

# Epilogue
*Seven Months Later*

What she really wanted at the moment was to push her terribly arrogant husband into the fountain behind him.

"Sarah, it is perfectly natural to feel sick. It is your first dinner party and a lot is at stake. I know you have you sights on the Howards. But, as I told you before, those twins are nothing but trouble. Even tied up and gagged, they would still find a way to ruin tonight. They are not servant material, China."

She reluctantly took the glass of cool water her husband offered, a worried frown marring the perfection he still saw in her face. "Well, if not servants, then what would they be good at?"

"You did hide the silver before leaving them alone in the kitchen, right?"

"Simon, that is not funny."

"It wasn't meant to be."

A commotion was coming from the open French doors that led into the parlor. Sarah grew even paler than before. Concern for her health made Simon ground out irritably. "What is going on in there?"

When she started for the door, he pushed her back down on the stone bench. "I'll see to it. You stay here."

"They are my orphans, Warrior."

His wife's stubborn pride drew a long sigh from him. "Then why am I reaping all the benefits?" He asked sarcastically.

The noise coming from inside the house was escalating. Sarah felt another wave of nausea come over her. She gripped the weathered oak next to her. An action not lost on her husband. "Sarah, are you all right?"

Oddly enough his voice of concern brought tears to her eyes. This night was not going at all like she planned. She felt weepy and irritable. To top it off, now those awful boys were ruining their only chance at a better life. They ought to be horse whipped.

"I was just remembering one of Grandfather's sayings."

Her handsome husband quirked one eyebrow, "And that is?"

"No matter how you wish it, you can't make a silk purse out of a sows ear."

Simon gave her one of his, 'I told you so' grins, which only served to anger her further. He was most arrogant, her husband.

"Does that mean you're finally listening to reason and giving up on those boys? I happen to know that the warehouse-"

She straightened her spine as if preparing for battle, "No, it just means my plans for them have changed a bit."

It absolutely amazed him sometimes how beautiful she was. That she never even realized it, even more so. Yes, even pale and out of sorts, she was a force to be reckoned with. And he would always owe heaven greatly for giving her back to him that day, seven months ago.

For two horrible days, he had thought he had lost her. Just remembering how close he had actually come, scared him to death. He had promised himself then, as she lay unconscious, that if God allowed her to live, he would never complain again about her orphans. Or, for that matter, her grandfather's inane sayings. He would just love her.

"By the way, I happen to be crazy about you, Sweetheart."

Cocking a tawny head at him, all traces of the valiant defender momentarily gone, she gave him one of the sweetest smiles on earth. "You know why, don't you?"

Two dark figures where barreling down on top of them. Arms flaying about, voices raised in argument. It was most distracting.

"No. Why don't you tell me."

He had such sexy ways. Even with half the party now in the rose garden and the two offending black haired boys squirming at the end of Albert's arms, she still had to hold herself back from touching him. For right at that moment, she would have liked nothing better than to be kissed senseless by her warrior husband.

He had given up so much for her the last few months. His government spying, allowing her to turn Rose Hall into an orphanage and even refusing to sail without her on his business ventures. It was nearly as if, he too never wanted to spend one day apart. To ever take one moment together, for granted. Yes, her heart swelled with love each and every time she looked at him. He was her gift.

"I'll tell you later. It seems we have company."

Maggie started apologizing almost instantly. "Miss, I had no idea them hoodlums would stoop to thieving. Well, actually I did, just not this sort of thieving, if you know what I mean."

Sarah didn't.

"My granddaughter they have taken my work, destroyed it and placed it in little cookies. I have lost much face with this."

"What are you talking about?"

"Its them boys Miss Sarah –"

"It wasn't my fault" the cook chimed in, "They told me it was you that ordered his sayings cut up into little bitty pieces, and stuffed in cookies."

The boys looked awfully pleased with themselves. In fact, too pleased to not be guilty of something. Sarah raised a hand to silence the crowd and narrowed in on the twins. "What did you do?"

Both boys immediately looked up innocently. It was almost convincing too, if Sarah hadn't known them better, but unfortunately she did.

Simon, the traitor, was fighting a grin. Sarah ignored her husband and the feeling of nausea coming in waves and asked once more. "I asked you both a question."

Finally Christian, the cockier of the two, shook free of Albert and answered her. "Nothing really. We found a couple of pages of that old man's writings and gave them to Cook."

"Took them you mean. In China, you would forfeit a hand for this."

"Grandfather! I mean, most honored teacher, you are scaring them."

"Hah!"

Grandfather was right. The boy looked more defiant than ever. "We were helping you out, China man."

471

By now most of the guests had found their way into the garden, more curious than anything else. After all, the Conways were known for their odd ways. And lately the town's gossip had been a little on the dull side.

Sarah groaned. The Howards. Of course, they would be near the front of the crowd. Those boys would never get a home, or an occupation at this rate.

Tears of frustration clogged her throat, "Christian how could you?"

Suddenly the defiant eleven year old crumpled, his eyes shifting to his brother in panic, "You said it would help Miss Sarah feel better. Now she is crying again."

"I said it would help her feel better if it worked. It didn't."

Curious now himself, Simon walked over and lifted the boy's chin, so he could look him in the eye. "If what worked young man?"

Now uneasy with the whole plan, Christian sighed before answering, "We found Miss Sarah all upset the other day. When we asked her why, she said it was because her grandfather was leaving to find his fortune."

"I said destiny." Sarah pointed out.

He looked confused a moment, then shrugged, "Oh, well, I guess we could change the name of the cookie."

"You were saying?" Simon silenced his wife with a look.

"Well, me and William, we wanted to help. So we came up with a plan to make the China man rich, so he could find his fortune right here. Don't you see? Then Miss Sarah wouldn't be sad any longer."

"Christian I never meant for you to…"

"Sarah let the boy speak."

"Anyway William had this idea. We heard about fancy cooks coming up with recipes and making a fortune. So we thought maybe we could help Cook and the China man come up with something."

Simon's lip twitched. "Weren't you supposed to let them in on it?"

The young boy kicked at a stray rock before admitting, "I suppose. But we rather figured they wouldn't listen to the two of us. They haven't listened to much, since the incident with the cream."

Exasperated, Cook threw up her hands in defeat, "Incident? You ruined near a whole gallon of cream using that contraption you built."

"It just needs a little tweaking that's all."

Sarah reached over and ran a hand tenderly over William's head to calm him. "It's all right. Maybe your next invention will be better."

"Sarah", Simon drew her attention over to the matter at hand, "I don't think they need to be encouraged in that regard."

Blushing, she nodded.

Christian gave her a grateful smile and continued, "We thought since the China man wanted to make his fortune we would call them fortune cookies. Pretty clever, huh?"

"Continue."

"Yes Sir."

"Anyway, we had Cook cut up those sayings of his and told her to make cookies with them inside. For the guests. Rather a good idea if you ask me."

"I didn't."

"Right."

One of the dinner guests cleared his throat. Sarah turned to find Lord Howard thoughtfully puffing away on his pipe. Then, as if it took great effort, he finally mused out loud, "I think the boys may be on to something."

"I beg your pardon?" It was his wife's look of horror that nearly made Sarah smile. She was not overly fond of orphans, especially these two.

Simon nodded and stepped up. "I happen to agree. Maybe we could all discuss it tomorrow at my office."

"Excellent idea."

The two young men in question had a look of confusion on their faces.

But, as usual, it was Christian who spoke up. "Does this mean we won't be getting our hands cut off?"

A horrified gasp came from the cultured ladies. Sarah smiled. Simon raised an eyebrow in censure, before answering, "That depends on Mister Lee."

"Oh blast, I suppose that means we have to go and apologize for borrowing -"

"It's called stealing." Sarah admonished gently. "And no deed, no matter how honorable its intention, is worth a man's good name."

"But we don't have a good name, we're orphans."

"Never mind," Sarah interrupted just in time. "Why don't you go back to the kitchen for now? We will deal with this later."

Would the boys never learn to stop while they were ahead? She really was going to be sick. Simon noticed her distress and insisted everyone go back inside. And not a moment too soon either.

Handing her a handkerchief, Simon studied her closely.

"Do you think you could be carrying?"

"Carrying what?"

Leading her over to the bench, he looked deeply into his wife's innocent brown eyes and stated a little plainer. "A baby, Sweetheart."

Wonder filled her face as she slowly sank down on the bench. "I never thought of it, Warrior. I suppose it is possible."

"I would say, knowing how much I can't seem to keep my hands off of you, it's more than possible."

Looking up into his face, Sarah felt unspeakable joy. "Oh, Simon. A baby." Suddenly her smile disappeared, as her grandfather's voice could be heard chastising the two boys in Chinese, as Maggie slammed the door shut on poor Lord Howard. She sighed. "But I wonder, how will we ever explain this odd little family to him? Or why his father, an Earl, married a poor orphan girl from America."

"That one's easy, sweetheart."

His voice held such tenderness it caused her heart to swell. How she loved this man. Then with a twinkle in his eye, he explained, "We will simply tell him the truth."

"And what is that Warrior?"

"That when I needed her most…she came and saved me."

# About the Author

**Tammy Watson**

Tammy lives on a state park in the deserts of Texas with the love of her life of over thirty years, and two crazy weimaraners. Writing has always been her passion, but she also has a bit of a dramatic flair and studied theatre in college. Tammy has written numerous plays, novels, skits, and a bi-weekly humorous column in a local newspaper.

As a couple, they love traveling and adventure. They are always on the trail hiking, biking, rock-climbing, and camping. Her love for history and mystery has found its way into her novels, as well, and she spends years researching for each of her books.

www.ingramcontent.com/pod-product-compliance
Lightning Source LLC
Chambersburg PA
CBHW020628020726
47494CB00001B/103

*9 7 8 0 9 8 4 2 2 8 7 5 1 *